FBI Agent Pe   at do you know about Z

"Blond, tv   last night from this ca   les on his face."

The FBI   d you get this description?"

"I saw him. Around five forty, five forty-five yesterday evening." She described the encounter.

"And you didn't take him back to his parents?"

She winced. "He took off on his own, down the path that led back to the campground. His father waved at me."

"So you know Mr. Fischer?"

The agent's direct gaze made her squirm. "No. I mean, I didn't then. I met him this morning."

"You're certain that Mr. Fischer was the man who waved at you?"

In her mind's eye, she saw again the man's silhouette. The sharp profile, the bulge at the back of the neck. Fred Fischer? "It was very dark," she finally murmured.

Perez stepped closer. "Are you certain that Zack reached this man?"

She relived the brambles snagging her, the flash of Zack's sweatshirt as he disappeared into the shadows on the path near the river. How could she have let a two-year-old run off like that?

"Did you see Zachary with the man?" Perez pressed.

"No!" The word came out too loud. She swallowed, lowered her voice. "The last I saw of Zack, he was running away from me, down the path, toward the man who waved." The fingers of her left hand clenched into a fist as she remembered the boy's tiny fingers slipping from her grasp. *I am guilty of letting him go.*

ENDANGERED

PAMELA BEASON

BERKLEY PRIME CRIME, NEW YORK

THE BERKLEY PUBLISHING GROUP
Published by the Penguin Group
Penguin Group (USA) Inc.
375 Hudson Street, New York, New York 10014, USA
Penguin Group (Canada), 90 Eglinton Avenue East, Suite 700, Toronto, Ontario M4P 2Y3, Canada
(a division of Pearson Penguin Canada Inc.)
Penguin Books Ltd., 80 Strand, London WC2R 0RL, England
Penguin Group Ireland, 25 St. Stephen's Green, Dublin 2, Ireland (a division of Penguin Books Ltd.)
Penguin Group (Australia), 250 Camberwell Road, Camberwell, Victoria 3124, Australia
(a division of Pearson Australia Group Pty. Ltd.)
Penguin Books India Pvt. Ltd., 11 Community Centre, Panchsheel Park, New Delhi—110 017, India
Penguin Group (NZ), 67 Apollo Drive, Rosedale, Auckland 0632, New Zealand
(a division of Pearson New Zealand Ltd.)
Penguin Books (South Africa) (Pty.) Ltd., 24 Sturdee Avenue, Rosebank, Johannesburg 2196,
South Africa

Penguin Books Ltd., Registered Offices: 80 Strand, London WC2R 0RL, England

This is a work of fiction. Names, characters, places, and incidents either are the product of the author's imagination or are used fictitiously, and any resemblance to actual persons, living or dead, business establishments, events, or locales is entirely coincidental. The publisher does not have any control over and does not assume any responsibility for author or third-party websites or their content.

ENDANGERED

A Berkley Prime Crime Book / published by arrangement with the author

PRINTING HISTORY
Berkley Prime Crime mass-market edition / December 2011

ISBN: 978-0-425-24498-2

BERKLEY® PRIME CRIME
Berkley Prime Crime Books are published by The Berkley Publishing Group,
a division of Penguin Group (USA) Inc.,
375 Hudson Street, New York, New York 10014.
BERKLEY® PRIME CRIME and the PRIME CRIME logo are trademarks of Penguin Group
(USA) Inc.

PRINTED IN THE UNITED STATES OF AMERICA

10 9 8 7 6 5 4 3 2 1

To my father, who always believed in me.

ACKNOWLEDGMENTS

I'd like to thank my agent, Curtis Russell, who has been a tireless advocate for my writing. I'm grateful to my editorial team at Berkley Prime Crime, Tom Colgan and Amanda Ng, for shepherding this book through the publication process and answering my sometimes-naïve questions. Special thanks go to my critique buddies who read this manuscript and helped me improve it: Pat Gragg, Jo Adamson, Norma Roth, Royce Roberts, Susan Chory, Karen Brown, Pat Read, and Brian Roesch.

1

IT was almost time.

This was the man's favorite hour. Dark enough that shadows obscured details, light enough that the campers had not yet gathered all their possessions. Food and utensils and toys and clothes and children were scattered everywhere. People were so careless. He wrapped his arms around his knees and drew himself into a tight ball. In a few moments, the sun would be completely obscured by the western escarpment. Down here in the valley, there was no gentle dimming into peaceful dusk. Instead, a wave of darkness slithered across the canyon, changing light to dark as if someone had closed a door. Campers would crowd into tight knots around their campfires or withdraw into their tents and RVs, fleeing the night as if it were dangerous. Then he'd be free to do what he'd come here for.

He perched in a U-shaped seat formed by two cottonwoods that had grown together. Nobody would notice him under the overhang of golden-leaved branches. Not here in the shadow of the cliffs. He listened to the noise from the campers in the valley, all too audible over the gurgle of the river.

Even from this distance he could hear the drone of RV generators, the crackle of campfires, and even the occasional blare of a television or radio. To his right, he recognized the crunch of gravel as a car pulled into a parking lot. Behind and to his distant left, footsteps rasped rhythmically in the dirt as a jogger slowly approached on the road shoulder. Just across the road, on the signboard at the campground pay station, a warning poster about cougars flapped with each gust of the rising breeze.

At the first campsite beyond the pay station, a small boy, little older than a baby, crawled across an expanse of wind-smoothed rock, his lips pursed as he pushed a toy truck along the miniature sandstone hills and troughs.

Exhaling softly, the man splayed his fingers across his thighs. Under the baseball cap, the toddler's hair was the color of the buttercups that bloomed after the spring rains. He knew that kind of little-boy hair; he knew how silky it would feel under his fingertips. The memory made his throat constrict.

A few yards beyond the boy, the child's dark-haired mother tinkered with a sputtering camp stove. From the thick woods encircling the campsite came the rustle of downed leaves, the firecracker pops of dry twigs shattering underfoot.

The rustling concluded with a sharp crack followed by a dull thump, as if a heavy object had fallen to the ground. A flock of crows rocketed up from a ponderosa's twisted branches, cawing their displeasure at being displaced from their nightly roost. The boy stood up and watched the dark cloud of birds pass overhead toward the river.

His mother took a few steps in the direction the noise had come from. She faced the trees, peering into the growing darkness. "Fred? You sound like a moose out there. That is you, isn't it, Fred?"

The blond boy, one hand outstretched as if to catch the last straggling crows flapping over his head, toddled through the grass toward the road and the river beyond. As the boy came closer, his head tilted skyward, and the sight of that rapt little face under the bill of the cap made the man's heart race. He loved that expression, that mixture of wonder and curiosity that small children reserved for other creatures. But small children should never be left to wander alone. Terrible things could happen to little boys.

The boy's mother left the woods and returned to the picnic table, turning toward the rock ledge where the boy had been playing.

"Zack, it's getting too dark to play on the rock now." Her voice rose. "Zack?"

"WHERE are the cougars?" Sam Westin held her cell phone to her ear as she lifted one foot to a picnic bench and stretched her cramped leg muscles.

"Hello to you, too, Sam," Ranger Kent Bergstrom chided her. "Weren't you supposed to be here yesterday?"

"Don't remind me," she said. "Did you know there's a bullet hole in the signboard at Goodman Trailhead? A heart shot to the cougar." She lifted her chin to gaze again at the startling beam of sunlight skewering the plywood and Plexiglas. It pissed her off just to look at it.

"Yeah, they nailed that one two days ago. Let's go grab a beer; I'll fill you in."

A frosty mug of anything sounded like heaven right now. Sam squelched a moan of self-pity. "I wish. But SWF is only funding me for four days to do this story, and as you've so tactfully noted, I'm running late. Can you give me a hint where I might find Leto and the cubs?"

"Check Sunset Canyon. I found prints around the river, not more than fifty yards from where you are, just this morning. They were big prints; I'm pretty sure it was Apollo. I followed them up the creek. He was headed for Sunset."

"Is our favorite camp unoccupied?" She referred to a secret box canyon she and Kent had discovered while conducting a wildlife survey two years ago.

"Far as I know. You're going up there now?"

"Yep." She couldn't wait to get into the backcountry.

"It's five forty. The sun's setting."

"Really?" she responded sarcastically. In the time she'd stood there, the sun had sunk halfway behind the escarpment, casting a third of the valley into darkness. In another fifteen minutes, the shadow would cover the parking lot and the skewer of sunlight would disappear from the signboard.

"I just meant that you'd better get a move on."

"I'll jog all the way." While it was still daylight on the plateau above, she had nearly six and a half miles to hike up a steep trail through a sandstone canyon that would already be in purple shadows.

She pressed the End button, then punched in a Seattle number. As she listened to the repeated rings at the other end, she pulled a digital camera from her backpack with her free hand.

In the campground across the road, she heard the faint shouts of a woman. "Zack! Come here right now! Right now! I mean it!"

Probably one of those dog owners who constantly threatened their pets but never bothered to train them. While the woman continued to call out and the phone repeated its high-pitched rings in her ear, Sam snapped a one-handed photo of the light passing through the vandalized board, then stuck the camera into a pocket of her hiking vest.

"Save the Wilderness Fund," a breathless voice finally responded over the airwaves. "Lauren Stark."

"It's Sam. I'm in Utah. I just reached the park."

"Finally!"

"Hey, I'm sorry, I can't help it if this yahoo plowed into my Civic in Idaho. It took forever to get the fender pulled out, and the trunk—" Sam made a chopping motion in the air. "Never mind. You're right, I'm late and we don't have time to discuss why. Are we ready to go?" She paced back to the picnic table and checked the zippers on her backpack.

"The new page is up with the usual information about the fund and your first article of backstory on the cougars. But—oh God—we're running so late, I'm hyperventilating just thinking about it. Adam wants something impressive to show on the news, something you know, like wowee—"

Adam? How had Adam Steele gotten into the mix? Sam had a sudden sick feeling that she'd landed this job only because of some backroom negotiation by the television reporter. A puff of breeze sent golden leaves spiraling down around her. She turned her head to study the shadow creeping across the canyon floor. "Lauren, I promised you a new article today, and I *will* deliver. I'm going to look for the cats right now. I'll send you something by nine o'clock your time."

"We'll be here. And don't forget the chat session tomorrow night."

Sam groaned and pulled a leaf from her hair. "Didn't I have two days in the backcountry before that?"

"That was before you showed up a day late. We've been posting an ad for the chat session for five days; we can't change the schedule now."

"Of course you can't." She'd have to hike back down tomorrow for a dependable electrical connection. Maybe this combo of wilderness and Internet was not going to be so great, after all. She was already exhausted and she hadn't even started this job.

"Tomorrow, eight P.M. Utah time," Lauren reminded her.

"I'll be there." Snapping the phone shut, she stashed it inside another vest pocket, trying to ignore the enticing aroma of grilling hamburgers from the nearby campground. Crackers and cheese would have to suffice for dinner tonight. After hefting the backpack upright on the picnic table, she balanced it with one hand and turned to push her arm through the shoulder strap.

Her hip bumped against a warm body. A small figure stumbled away and banged into the signboard with an audible crack. Sam gasped and let go of the pack, which fell back onto the picnic table with a dust-raising thump. A toddler blinked at her, his blue eyes huge under the bill of a red baseball cap. His lips trembled as he raised a plump hand to his forehead, dislodging the cap. It tumbled to the ground at his feet.

"I'm sorry, honey." She knelt next to him, patted the shoulder of his Pooh Bear sweatshirt. "You scared me."

The urchin jammed his thumb into his mouth and regarded her silently from above a small fist. He couldn't be more than three years old.

"Are you okay? Did you hit your head?"

At the reminder, his blue eyes filled with tears.

"You won't cry, will you?" she murmured hopefully, plucking a pine needle from his honey blond bangs. "Where's your mommy?"

The child jerked the thumb out of his mouth, whirled around and slapped a chubby hand against the Plexiglas-covered notice. "Kitty!" he chortled.

"Big kitty," Sam agreed. "That's a picture of a cougar."

He poked a stubby finger toward the bullet hole above his head. "Hoe."

"Hole," she couldn't help correcting. "Bullet hole. Bad hole. There shouldn't be a hole in the cougar." She sounded like a dolt. Jeez, she didn't have time for idiotic conversations with toddlers. She should be a half mile up the trail to Sunset Canyon by now. Where were the boy's parents? She quickly surveyed the parking lot. Only a ground squirrel scampered through the dusty gravel between the vehicles.

The child turned toward Sam and softly patted her left breast where her T-shirt bore the emblem of a mountain lion on a rock. "Cougie!"

She captured the tiny fingers, slippery with saliva. "That's another cougar," she told him. "And it's also sexual harassment, as you'll find out in a few years."

Gently, she brushed back his fine hair, so soft she could barely feel it against her weather-roughened fingertips. A crisscrossing of scratches marred the toddler's pink cheeks, probably from the blackberry vines bordering the parking lot. She found no lump on his scalp, so he couldn't have hit the board very hard. Recovering his baseball cap from the ground, she slapped off the dust and tugged it back onto the boy's head. The parking area was now completely in shadow. She was running out of time.

The woman still shouted from the campground. Her

cries now sounded more distant. "Zachary! Where are you, Zack? Zacharryyy!"

The child ducked his head under the arch of a black-berry bramble and peered down a narrow trail that forked left to the river, right to the road. "Mommy?"

So Zack was not a recalcitrant dog, after all. No wonder the woman sounded so insistent.

"You came down that path, didn't you, Zack?" Sam stood up, moved back to the table, and pulled her pack upright. The boy followed her.

She thrust her arms beneath the backpack's straps and hefted it onto her shoulders. "Go back to Mommy now."

"Zachary! Come here right this instant!" The shouts were faint now.

Sam cupped her hands and shouted toward the camp-ground. "He's over here." Could the woman hear her over the rustle of leaves in the breeze and the babble of the river?

"Mommy mad." The boy's whisper was barely audible.

Sam patted his small shoulder. "She's just worried. She'll be so happy to see you, Zack."

He pulled a circle of black plastic from his sweatshirt pocket and thrust it in her direction. "Twuck!"

The plastic piece was imprinted with a tiny tread pat-tern and had a center hole for a diminutive axle. "Looks more like a wheel," she said, pushing it back into his hands. "I bet Mommy would help you find your truck and put this wheel back on it."

"Zack!" A man's tone this time, deeper and closer. It sounded like he was only a short distance through the trees, standing on the edge of the road where it overlooked the river's bend.

The child stared uncertainly in the direction of the voice.

"Now your daddy's calling you, too, Zack."

The toddler thrust his thumb back into his mouth. Sam winced, remembering all the places that thumb had been in the last few minutes. She cinched the waist strap on her pack and huffed out an impatient breath. "Okay, we'll go together. But we've got to make it fast."

Taking his hand, she pushed her way through the gap in the blackberries. A thorny branch snagged the netting at the side of her vest, bringing her to an abrupt halt. She let go of the little hand to free herself, and the boy darted into the shadowy cut between the brambles.

"Wait, Zack! Take my hand!"

The toddler disappeared amid the dark foliage. After several seconds of wrestling with the thorny branches, she tore herself free. Sucking on a bleeding knuckle, she took a step down the overgrown trail, squinting into the gloom. She was anxious to be on her way while she could still see the ground under her feet.

His head and shoulders backlit by the glow from a kerosene lantern across the road, a man blocked the other end of the tree-lined path. Zack's daddy.

"Got him?" she shouted.

The rush of the river drowned the man's response, but he raised a hand in thanks. Sam waved back, then hurriedly retraced her steps to the trailhead lot. The hubbub of RV generators, crackling campfires, and excited squeals of children faded as she jogged over the bridge and up the rocky trail to the canyon rim above.

2

SAM followed the waning light to Sunset Canyon, where the sun rested squarely on Rainbow Bridge. The camera lens framed the burning orb, which appeared to have settled on top of the natural rock arch. The lineup of setting sun and arch was an autumn phenomenon the rangers kept to themselves, not wanting to encourage visitors on the steep trail at dusk. She carefully positioned herself and snapped a couple of photos. Even with the polarizer, the image would include sundogs—circles of light floating in space. But sometimes those imperfections made a photo more interesting. But nothing she saw through the lens was remarkable. *Wowee,* she reminded herself. She needed wowee.

She freed herself from her pack and sat on a low rock, the camera in her lap. The best hope of spotting wildlife was to become one with the surroundings. A magpie flitted to the skeleton of a piñon snag ahead. Focusing a bright eye on her, it squawked a harsh note, no doubt after a handful of trail mix or some other such easy meal.

Go away, she willed the bird. It abandoned the branch and hopped closer.

Her stomach growled, the noise loud in the quiet canyon. She'd already eaten the cheese and crackers. Apricots in an hour, she promised herself, picturing the dried fruit she'd packed. As if reading her thoughts, a chipmunk skittered from beneath a nearby rock and approached her backpack with spasmodic movements. Leaning down slowly, she picked up a pebble for defensive ammunition. As she straightened, she saw a flash of movement near Rainbow Bridge.

She let the pebble drop from her fingers and had her camera zoomed in when the big cat strolled out onto the rock arch, a black silhouette against the fiery orange sky. *Oh, yes. Thank you, God.* On her feet now, she snapped the photo, one eye on the rough path and the other on the cougar in the distance as she stealthily moved toward the rock bridge. If she stuck to the shadows, she might be able to get close without alarming Leto. It *was* Leto—even in the dim light, she could see a divot of fur missing from the female cougar's left flank, the scar left from her bullet wound.

Pricking her ears, Leto turned her head. Sam froze and held her breath. A second, smaller cougar emerged from the shadows onto the bridge. Judging by the size, it was Artemis, Leto's female cub. Sam pressed the button and prayed the cats' ears wouldn't pick up the tiny ping of the shutter. The cub, now nearly as large as the adult cat, crouched low, hesitated a second, then pounced on her mother's tail. Leto hissed and cuffed Artemis.

Sam used the distraction to trot a few steps closer. She needed to put the sun behind her. As she passed beneath the bridge, the two mountain lions suddenly rose, their muscles rigid, their glowing eyes focused in Sam's direction. Her heart skipped a beat; she was easily within their leaping range. She kept her gaze locked on them as she slowly walked backward up the canyon floor.

On the other side of the bridge, with the sun at the proper angle, she paused and focused. The cats watched her silently, their amber eyes merely curious, not telegraphing the concentrated focus of hunters, at least not right now. Their calm was a little creepy. Was it possible they remembered her? Or were they so accustomed to people that they were unafraid? That didn't bode well for human or beast.

The white markings on the cats' muzzles gleamed in the growing darkness. She snapped several more photos. The cougars tracked each movement she made. The intensity of the moment was almost painful. Awesome, in the true meaning of the word.

The digital camera beeped to signal the memory card was filled. The cougars flinched at the noise but held their ground.

The bottom pocket of her vest held two more memory cards. Moving slowly, she slid her hand down and pinched the zipper pull between her fingers. The hiss of the nylon teeth was barely audible. Then the zipper stuck. She glanced down at it, just for a second. When she looked up, the lions were gone.

A quick perusal of the surrounding hillsides revealed no sign of the cats. Without a sound, they had vanished into the brush and rocks. It was a great magic trick, one she'd witnessed all too often. She let out her breath and, holding the camera in front of her, trudged back to her pack, checking the images on the camera's tiny screen as she went.

In the last picture she'd taken, everything was colored the same golden hue; the lions were nearly indistinguishable from the rock bridge. She sighed and pressed the Delete button. The next image was not much better.

The third photo brought her to a dead stop. The shot captured the cougars just as they'd turned to look at her. Two pairs of mountain-lion eyes burned brightly, staring directly at the photographer. The burnished amber of the cats' fur glowed against the cobalt of the darkening sky beyond.

"Wowee! Yes!" She raised a fist in victory as she continued down the rocky wash.

Twilight made the desert rodents bold. A kangaroo rat leapt across her path. As she hauled her pack up by a shoulder strap, a chipmunk burst from beneath the top flap, streaked up her arm and flung itself onto a nearby boulder.

"Great." Now she'd have to look for chew holes in her

food packets, not to mention those disgusting black-rice droppings the little varmints always left behind.

Before reshouldering her backpack, she dug out her halogen flashlight and moved the beam over the bridge and surrounding cliffs. Only the leathery flutter of a couple of bats moved within the circle of light.

Twenty minutes later, she found the entrance to the tiny box canyon. Lowering herself to the first available rock, she unbuckled her pack. With camera and laptop computer inside, her load was at least eight pounds more than someone five foot one and 115 pounds should carry. After pulling a packet of ibuprofen from her pocket and a plastic bottle of Merlot from her provisions, she took a sip of wine to wash down the pills.

She glanced at her watch. A few minutes after nine, Utah time; an hour earlier in Seattle. She'd have to hustle to make the nine o'clock deadline for SWF. She unpacked her laptop and, sitting cross-legged in front of it, powered it up. The screen readout told her that the laptop's two batteries were strong. So far, so good. She switched off the flashlight. Using moonlight and the illumination from the computer screen, she opened the file containing the rough draft she'd begun earlier.

Before leaving her office in Washington State, she'd written about Leto's history, about how the female cougar had been found fourteen months earlier just inside the park boundary. She'd been crippled by a hunter's bullet, her eight-week-old cubs trailing behind her, a feline trio nearly starved to death. Sam, Kent, and other volunteers had nursed the three cougars back to health. And although her seasonal ranger contract had been up, Sam had returned to Heritage in the autumn to release the cats. This was the backstory currently featured on SWF's new website.

She double-checked the article she'd started last night in the Idaho hotel, a story about coming to Heritage to search for the cougars. Her fingers flew over the keys as she added details of the sunset sighting, along with an emotional paragraph about how uplifting it was to see the lions now, when they were back in prime condition. She stuck in a couple of sentences about how cougars often cross paths with humans without being seen, using Kent's information about Apollo's prints on the riverbank as a prime example. Finally, she closed with the image of the bats circling in the dark over the bridge, emphasizing her feelings of loneliness and loss after the lions had vanished.

Fifteen minutes to deadline. She downloaded three photos of cougars and the sunset from the camera to the computer. They looked even better on the larger screen.

At first, the cell phone delivered nothing but static. She extended the antenna, dialed the satellite, and entered her access code. After connecting computer to phone, she dialed the SWF modem number and transmitted the text and photos. Long after the file names disappeared, she sat watching the message area in the corner of the screen. Finally, a popup appeared: *1 txt, 3 jpgs recd. Thanks, Sam!*

She turned off the phone and computer. She'd actually pulled it off. A day late, but if she'd come yesterday she might have missed Leto and Artemis and would have had to substitute God knows what, maybe a paw print or something lame like that. Looked like luck was on her side for once. She'd pulled off wowee.

Which reminded her. She checked her watch; it was in between news broadcasts in Seattle. She disconnected the phone from the computer and dialed a familiar Seattle number.

He answered his cell phone on the fourth ring. "Adam Steele."

"Greetings from the Utah wilderness," she said.

"Guess what? Tom broke his leg; I'm the anchor tomorrow: noon, six, *and* eleven."

"What a stroke of luck," she said. "Except for Tom, of course."

"Yep, I'm on my way."

"Congratulations," she said. "Did you by any chance

promise SWF to put something about my cougar series on the news?"

"I might have. We can always find space for interesting animal stories. But you had the job, anyway, babe. SWF was impressed by your pitch."

She wondered about that. Which was more persuasive, an "I can do it" from an Internet writer or a promise to get that Internet story on television?

"You'll knock their socks off," he said.

"I've already started." She told him about the cougar photo.

"All right! I knew you could do it. We're a terrific team, Sam."

She wasn't so sure about that, either, but it sounded good when he said it. "Good luck tomorrow, Adam. I know you'll knock their socks off, too."

"Yes, I will. Dinner at DiAngelo's when you get back."

He would pick the only restaurant in the whole Pacific Northwest with a dress code. "How about Hot Sauce John's instead? Blake could come, too."

"No third wheels, babe; I want you all to myself. And who are you going to see in a barbecue joint? You want to reinvent yourself, you've got to meet the right people."

She suspected that DiAngelo's would harbor more people who were "right" for him than for her, but who knew, his luck might rub off a little. And she loved the looks of the other women when she walked in on the arm of Adam Steele. "Good point," she said. "DiAngelo's it is. Now I've got to go. The raccoons are lining up for my autograph."

He laughed. "Good night, wild woman. Be careful out there."

"Good night, Mr. News Anchor." She hung up and sat rubbing her forehead for a while. She wasn't trying to reinvent herself, was she? Since graduating from college with her wildlife biology degree, she'd been a zookeeper, an environmental consultant, a seasonal ranger with the National Park Service, and a freelance writer. This technoid wilderness writer Sam Westin was simply an amalgamation of all the preceding Sam Westins.

She breathed in the blessed quiet of pure wilderness. Reclining against a boulder, she sipped from the plastic bottle, swirling the wine in her mouth. Instead of a pleasant cherry undertone, the bouquet of her Merlot held a hint of formaldehyde. That's what you got when you stored alcohol in plastic bottles.

Mediocre food and drink were irrelevant in the larger scheme of things. Whether she owed this job to Adam or not, it was great to be back outdoors. If she'd spent one more day writing another insipid travel article in her office at home, she'd have been homicidal.

This new cyber-reporting thing might pay off. It seemed like a crazy mix, computers and outdoor adventure, but if that's what it took to get people interested in nature these days, she'd pack a laptop along with her granola.

The Merlot tasted better with each sip. The stars overhead were brilliant, even brighter than she remembered from the Kansas fields of her youth. A canopy of diamonds twinkling against black velvet. Galaxies, foreign worlds. Beautiful. So incredibly beautiful.

Then the phone buzzed. She stared at it in annoyance for a second, then picked it up. Her home number was on the screen. "Blake?"

"Hey, roomie, where are you?"

"The middle of nowhere. It's wonderful."

Blake's sigh rasped against her ear. "Are you in some podunk town where every man has three wives?"

She laughed. Blake's vision of Utah hadn't progressed into the twentieth century, let alone the twenty-first.

"I'm on top of a plateau in Heritage National Monument. You should see the stars; they're unbelievable. And I saw the cougars, Blake! Almost close enough to touch." She told him about the tremendous photo.

"Fantastic. Your series is going to blow them away. Contributions will roll in so fast that SWF will pay you twice what they do now."

Blake fretted about her bank account nearly as much as she did. The guy made little more than minimum wage working in a greenhouse. The cabin they shared was hers; she cut him a deal on rent in exchange for his help with chores. He probably worried every day about the possibility of a rent raise, and truth be told, she'd been seriously considering one lately.

"What's up in Bellingham?" she asked.

The rural area she'd settled in, just outside of a small college town eighty miles north of Seattle, was growing by leaps and bounds. The conflicts between the longtime residents and newcomers made for a volatile mix.

"It's raining, of course. And the Minestrones cut down another big alder."

Sam grimaced. "The Minesteros."

"You call 'em what you want. I told 'em they were ruining their property values. He just gave me one of those Ronald Reagan looks."

She chuckled. "I won't even try to imagine what you mean by that. Any evening grosbeaks yet?" The migration of the black and yellow finches was an eagerly anticipated event each autumn.

"Not even one. The Minestrones probably scared them off."

She hoped that wasn't true. "Blake, I'm on battery power here . . ."

"Oh yeah. I just wanted to tell you that Reverend Westin phoned. I told him you'd trooped off to Utah to save wild beasts from gun-toting good ol' boys."

"What'd he say?"

Blake's voice slipped from his usual tenor to an imitation of her father's baritone. "Good heavens! What has my Summer gotten herself into now?"

A groan escaped her lips. "Did he want anything in particular?"

"I don't think so. We chatted. He asked if you were still dating Adam the Magnificent and if I thought you two would have any announcements soon. He—of course—mentioned yet again he wished you had a husband and children like normal women do. You know, a normal life. Then he remembered who he was talking to."

"Oops. Did you get the lecture?"

"Not this time. Actually, he was quite restrained, considering I'm a pimple on God's face."

"That isn't right," she said. "I think you're an abomination against humanity—"

"You do?" He sounded hurt.

She snorted. "Of course not, Blake. I'm quoting Dad, or trying to quote him—"

"I know, I know. He believes you'll find your way back eventually."

She made a scoffing sound. "He would."

"Hey, he even has hopes for me."

"How kind of him." She could hear her father now, cheerfully sharing with Blake what he thought were words of comfort.

"Simon's here beside me. Say hi, Si." A startled meow filled the airwaves.

"You twisted his tail!" Sam accused when Blake came back on the phone.

"Did not. Anyhow, we're baking cookies. Maple nut bars, to be specific."

Her mouth watered. "Save me some."

"I don't know if they'll last that long. Eric's coming over tomorrow. Just for coffee, he says. But my maple nut bars will soften his heart, if anything can."

"Save me *one!*"

"We'll see." A buzzer sounded in the background. "That's the oven! Gotta go!" He hung up.

"Bye," she murmured to the dial tone. She turned off the phone and took another swig of wine to wash down the excess saliva in her mouth. Maple nut bars, indeed.

A gentle breeze stirred, blowing a whisper of rapidly cooling air against her face. An owl hooted somewhere not far away.

As she snapped together the short aluminum poles of

the tent frame, a chorus of faint yips erupted in the distance. They started slowly, then transitioned into sharp barks, faster and faster. Sam clipped the yellow nylon tent to the frame and sat back on her heels, listening.

Coyotes. The cries of a hunting pack always unnerved her, even though she knew it was natural group communication. It only sounded like cruel laughter to human ears. The mad cackles grew fewer, then stopped. Sam took another sip of Merlot, screwed the cap back on the bottle, pulled her sleeping bag out of its stuff sack and spread it on the floor of the tent.

The howling began seconds later, a thin keening. Much better. A sound that seemed to fit with darkness. Other coyotes added ghostly voices to the mix, harmonizing. Then a lower-pitched wail joined in. *Ah-rooooooooooo.*

The hairs stood up on the back of her neck. Sam crawled out of the tent. There it was again. *Yip, yip, ah-ah-rooooooooooo.* That was no coyote. The pitch was wrong. A Mexican lobo? A few pairs of the endangered desert wolves had been released in the Southwest, but the papers kept reporting the discovery of yet another lobo's body, riddled with bullets. Had any survived?

She pressed a button to illuminate her watch. Not quite ten o'clock.

For Kent, that was early. Pulling out her notepad, she looked up his cell number. Even if he was a ranger in a park with dilapidated equipment, her friend was part of the connected generation. He'd have his C-phone in a pocket.

"Yeah?"

"It's Sam."

"Sam? I thought you were up on the plateau."

"I am."

"How come *my* cell phone doesn't work worth a damn up there?"

"I'm using SWF's satellite phone. Say, are there lobos around here now? I heard this incredible howling."

"To your east, on Horsehip Mesa?"

"Yeah." She looked in that direction, then felt foolish

when her gaze met only the sandstone boulders surrounding her campsite.

"It's Coyote Charlie."

She'd forgotten about the park's phantom. "Is that nutcase still wandering around here? It's been—what, two years?"

"Little over three. He's persistent."

"Does he do this just at the full moon or—"

He cut her off. "Can't talk now, Sam. We're looking for a missing kid. Could be pretty serious, because it's only a two-year-old. Well, a two-and-a-half-year-old. Zachary Fischer."

Her stomach lurched. "Zack? It couldn't be."

"You know him?"

"I saw him. In Goodman Trail parking lot. This afternoon . . . evening, whatever—right after I talked to you." She pictured the man at the end of the path. "He ran back to his father."

Silence stretched between them for a long moment.

Kent finally said, "His mother and father told us he just disappeared."

Her chest constricted as though squeezed inside a giant fist. "I'm coming down."

"No way. We're covered; the whole crew's here. And in case you haven't noticed, it's dark."

"You're understaffed. And there's moonlight." She held out a hand, examined the shadow it cast onto the rock beneath it.

"It's not a full moon yet; not bright enough to hike through Sunset Canyon. You know how narrow that trail is along the cliff."

"Exactly. I *know*."

"We'll probably find him before you could even get here. Don't do it, Sam. Please. That summer you were a ranger, how many times did you tell visitors not to hike at night?"

He had her there. After a day of driving and hiking, not to mention multiple swigs of Merlot, the idea *was* a little crazy.

"If Zack turns up during the night, call me and leave voice mail, okay? Otherwise, I'll be down first thing in the morning." She gave him the number.

She turned the phone off, unzipped her vest, and massaged her stomach with her free hand, trying to smooth away the knot of anxiety that had settled there.

3

THE wine helped her get to sleep, but it didn't keep her there. A little before 4 A.M., a scratching sound outside her tent woke her. She sat up, peered through the mosquito netting. At first she saw nothing, then she noticed a blur of furry movement near the pack she'd left propped against a rock. She cursed herself for not stringing up her food or hauling it into the tent.

The creature was bigger than a chipmunk. She squinted. The moon was low in the west now, its light not much help in the canyon shadows. She could barely make out a pointed nose, a bushy tail. If it was a raccoon, it was a small, pathetically skinny one. The marauder stood up, placed its tiny paws on the pack. Striped tail, large rounded ears. A ringtail! She'd never seen one before. Prints, droppings, even captive ringtails in zoos, but never the actual creature in the wild.

Where was the camera? She ran her hands over her vest beside the sleeping bag, identified her cell phone, two memory cards, a roll of antacid tablets, a wadded-up kerchief. Well, shit. She pressed her face close to the netting.

The camera was out there, along with the computer, strewn across the canyon floor. Some professional she was.

The ringtail stuck a paw into the space at the end of a zipper, widened the gap, pushed its nose into the pocket. As Sam leaned forward, her sleeping bag hissed against the foam pad beneath. The shy mammal jerked its head toward her. Its huge slanted eyes, outlined in white, gleamed in the moonlight for a fraction of a second. Then, with a flick of its tail, the ringtail was gone.

Like the cougars. Here one minute, gone the next. *Vanished.*

A toddler's face suddenly flashed into her thoughts. Was Zack still missing? Unzipping the mesh flap, she crawled out of the tent, taking the phone with her. She dialed the satellite and punched in her voice mail code.

"You have two new messages," the mechanical voice told her. One, left that afternoon, was from Key Corporation, wanting to know if she would write a piece about birdwatching in the Columbia Gorge for their e-zine. The other was from Lauren, exclaiming over her story on the website, how fantastic it looked, how the director, Steve Harding, was so glad she and Adam Steele had talked them into doing the field reports. "Dynamite!" Lauren concluded.

Sam exited voice mail and dialed Kent's cell number. A message told her his phone was currently out of service. It probably had a dead battery by now.

"Shoot," she said softly. Then she remembered. Top left outside pocket of the backpack. She padded over, pulled out the two-way radio she'd bought just for this purpose, and tuned it to the park communications channel.

A blast of static ripped the quiet darkness. The signal was probably blocked by the rocks around her tent. She switched it off, tucked it into the back of her panties for lack of a better place, and scrambled to the top of the highest boulder, keeping a hopeful eye out for the ringtail. She settled her backside on the cool sandstone and tried the radio again.

"Sector nine-three. No sign here." A weary female voice. "Starting sector nine-four."

Damn. The rangers were still searching. No happy ending yet. She chewed a knuckle.

"Sector eight-two clear. Moving on to eight-three." Sounded like Kent.

She rubbed her bare feet with her hands. October nights were too cold to go without shoes. Zack had been wearing sneakers, a sweatshirt, sweatpants, and a baseball cap when she'd seen him. He was dressed warmly enough to survive the night, assuming he still wore the same clothing.

Where could he be? Was it too cold now in the valley for rattlesnakes to prowl after dark? She tried to remember if there were any old mineshafts near the campground; she knew there were abandoned claims in the park. The river was low, but the current was still too strong for a two-year-old. God, there were so many horrible possibilities. Why hadn't Zack's parents kept better track of him?

Why hadn't *she* taken him back to his parents? The scene replayed itself in her imagination. The man waving. Zack couldn't have been more than a couple of yards from him at the time. Surely it had been Zack's father. Her memory looped back, started again. Zack scampering away down the path. Black shadows over the trail where it dipped between the brambles. The background gush of the river.

The eastern horizon revealed only a faint edge of gray under the stars. Still too dark to hike down. She pulled her clothes from the tent and dressed, then sat down before the laptop. SWF would fire her for sure if they knew she hadn't even zipped their equipment back into the protective cases. Thank God it hadn't rained, that it was too dry for dew, that rodents hadn't chewed the cords.

She powered up the system and clicked the shortcut icon to SWF's website. There was her photo, in all its glory—Leto and Artemis, looking as if they were about to leap onto the viewer's head. A headline, "Cougar Celebration," appeared in large red type above her article.

Instead of Summer Westin or even Sam Westin, the byline said "Wilderness Westin." What the heck? She clicked the name.

A popup appeared with a bio of Summer "Wilderness" Westin and a photo. She blinked in surprise. Instead of using the photo she'd supplied, which featured her in outdoor gear with camera and notepad in hand, they'd used an old one from the SWF fund-raiser where she'd met Adam. The event had been held after hours at Seattle's Woodland Park Zoo, and the keepers had trotted out a few of the tamer animals for show.

The boa constrictor draped around her shoulders was a better accessory than any fashion designer could have conjured. The red bark of the madrone behind her and the burgundy mottle of the snake's skin framed her pale skin and platinum blond hair. Bright trumpets of tropical blossoms dangled from a vine near her right temple. She raised an eyebrow. She didn't remember those flowers: they seemed unlikely in Seattle, even in summer.

"Darn you, Max," she muttered. Maximilian Garay, a young digital artist at SWF, was an expert at manipulating photos on the computer.

She'd worn a tank top on the day the picture was taken. Now the spaghetti straps were gone, and he'd cropped the photo to emphasize the snake and her bare shoulders. The perpetual frown lines on her forehead had been erased. Her gray eyes were now decidedly green.

It was a slick job, she had to admit. She looked downright sexy and about twenty-six years old. A flaxen-haired Eve eager to commit the first sin offered. *Fine*, to use Max's term of ultimate praise. A little too fine. At thirty-seven, her real self could only be a disappointment.

The bio information they'd included for Wilderness Westin was basically Sam Westin's history but worded in such a way to make it sound as if this Wilderness character routinely forded raging rivers and scaled vertical cliffs in pursuit of wildlife. She returned to the home page.

"Eee-ha!" the computer speaker yelped, startling her. Accompanied by a thunder of clopping hooves, a miniature deer darted from the left side of the page, with a cougar in hot pursuit, followed by a tiny human figure with a camera, who stopped to take a photo, then ran to catch the animals. The trio galloped off the right side of the window.

Sam couldn't help grinning. They didn't call him Mad Max for nothing. The guy spent hours of his own time creating video sprites like these.

At last, a sliver of pink lightened the sky behind the mountains to the east. She packed only the electronic gear, food, and a few clothes, leaving her camping supplies zipped inside the tent. The tiny box canyon was a secret place. The only intruders she expected in the next twenty-four hours were of the furry variety. She'd help find Zack, get a good meal and a hot shower, do her chat session and recharge batteries at the hotel tonight, and then hike back up tomorrow.

AT 8 A.M., she crossed over the bridge at Goodman Trailhead and dumped her backpack into the trunk of her car. Feeling as light as helium, she strolled into Red Rock Campground and spotted Rangers Bergstrom and Castillo slumped on a picnic bench. More gray-green uniforms were grouped nearby.

"Hey, Kent." She slid onto the bench beside her friend. His expression remained unfocused for a few seconds, as if he couldn't remember who she was. But then, he'd been on duty for at least twenty-four hours.

"Sam!" He brushed a strand of sandy hair from his forehead. His gaze flicked up to the ridge before traveling back to her face. "When did you start down?"

"First light." Up and down the same trail in little more than twelve hours, with a heavy pack. Almost thirteen miles round-trip. When she leaned over to tug her sagging wool socks up out of her boots, she felt a little stab between her shoulder blades.

"You remember Rafael, don't you?" Kent pointed to his colleague, Rafael Castillo. As one of the park's two law enforcement rangers, the chunky black-haired man wore a holstered .38 on his right hip.

She sat up and nodded in his general direction. "*Hola, Rafael. ¿Qué pasa?*"

His dark eyes lit up. "You speak Spanish now?" He rattled off a few unintelligible words.

"*Hola, Rafael. ¿Qué pasa?*" she responded.

He laughed and slapped his knee, his gold wedding ring flashing in the sun. "I forgot you're a joker."

"Most people say *smart-ass*," Kent said.

Rafael smoothed his grimy uniform pants across his thighs. "We could use a little humor right now."

How she missed this, the camaraderie of working with others, being part of a team. Living with Blake and dating Adam kept her from being a total recluse, but she spent the better part of her time in solitary confinement these days.

"No trace of Zack?" she asked.

"No." Kent raised a hand to scratch his stubbly jaw.

Rafael lowered his chin into dirt-stained hands. "The boy . . . it's terrible." He shook his head. "I've got a three-year-old and a two-year-old at home. They're babies."

"I saw him yesterday," Sam said.

Rafael's eyebrows shot up. "You saw Zachary Fischer?"

"Kent didn't tell you? I saw him in the Goodman Trail lot." She turned to Kent. "Right after we spoke on the phone."

Kent said, "We hung up at five forty. I checked my watch right before I left the station."

Rafael straightened. "The parents called headquarters at six thirty. You were probably the last person—"

She hurriedly cut him off. "No, he ran back to his father. It was dark, and I got caught in the brambles, but then I saw his father at the end of the path. I yelled and asked if he got Zack, and he waved back."

Rafael glanced across the campsite, where a wretched couple sat on a weathered outcropping of stone, the woman cradled in the man's lap. The law enforcement ranger indicated the man with a jerk of his chin. "Him?"

"Those are the parents?" Sam asked.

Kent nodded. "The Fischers. Fred and—"

"Jenny," Rafael supplied.

Fred Fischer stroked his wife's arm slowly, a stony expression on his face. Jenny laid her head wearily against her husband's shoulder. The couple wore matching bulky navy blue sweatshirts and jeans, matching loops in their earlobes.

Had the man at the end of the path worn an earring? All she could remember was a silhouette. It had been too dark to see details.

Fred Fischer's shoulder-length brown hair hung in strings. Flowing tresses on fair-haired males always conjured up Jesus in Sam's imagination, which made her feel simultaneously ridiculous and sacrilegious. She'd spent too much time studying stained-glass windows in her youth as she waited for the minister to hang up his robes and emerge as her father.

"You saw Zack run to Fischer?" Rafael asked again.

"I only saw the man's profile—the light was behind him. Did Fischer have his hair in a ponytail last night?" She raised her hand to the back of her neck. "I remember a bulge here, maybe a flash of blue material as he waved." She shook her head in frustration. "He was at least ten yards away, and it was pretty dark by then."

Rafael stood up, adjusted the holster on his belt. "Come get a close look."

As they approached, the Fischers glanced up. When the woman raised her head from her husband's chest, Sam saw that a large red birthmark covered the jawline on the right side of her face and descended down her neck. Jenny twitched her long hair forward to cover it.

Rafael nodded at Sam. She squatted to be on eye level with the couple. "Mr. Fischer?"

Weary hazel eyes swiveled to meet hers.

"Remember me?"

Nothing.

"From the path, last night, over by the trailhead. Five fifty or so? Zack ran from me to you?"

Fred Fischer's eyebrows came together in a V. "What?"

Jenny's hand shot out, and her broken nails clutched at Sam's jeans. "You saw my baby? You saw Zack?"

Sam focused on Fred's face. "Mr. Fischer, remember how you waved to me? I waved back?"

Jenny examined her husband's perplexed expression.

Fred shook his head. "I don't remember that."

Sam swallowed around a sudden constriction in her throat.

Jenny's hand still hung on to the baggy denim at Sam's knee. "I don't understand. You saw Zack last night?"

"I think so. He never told me his name. Was he wearing a Winnie-the-Pooh sweatshirt?"

Jenny let go of Sam's jeans and pressed her hand over her own cracked lips. A tear rolled down her cheek.

"There were scratches on his face." Sam indicated cross-hatching with a finger raised to her own cheek.

"He didn't have those before," Jenny sobbed. She clutched at the collar of her sweatshirt, wadding the material in her fists.

"Mr. Fischer," Rafael asked, "did you have your hair in a ponytail yesterday evening?"

"What?" The father raised a dirty hand to the oily strings that hung loose around his shoulders. "I don't know."

Jenny said, "Yes, you did. I remember it was all coming out when you got here, when I called—" Her voice skipped like a needle on an old scratched record. "I called and called. Oh, my baby!" Twisting her neck, she buried her face in her husband's shirtfront.

Fred Fischer wrapped his arms around his wife, but his eyes were fixed on Sam. Tired, cold eyes. "Zack wandered off just as it got dark." His tone was mechanical, as if he were repeating the information for the hundredth time. "And we never saw him again."

It sounded so final. Feeling like she'd been kicked in the stomach, Sam returned to the picnic bench.

Rafael followed. "You said it was dark," he theorized. "Maybe Fischer didn't see you. Maybe you just thought he was waving. But you definitely saw Zack with this man?"

The boy disappearing down the narrow path, the brambles snagging her vest, holding her back. "Zack ran away from me, toward him. There was shrubbery between us. I just assumed . . ." Letting her words trail off, Sam lowered her head into her hands.

If Fischer hadn't waved at her, then whom had he been signaling? Could Zack have darted down the left fork, to the river? If the silhouetted man wasn't Fischer, then who—?

"You're back?" a gravelly voice barked in Sam's ear.

Kent and Rafael Castillo stiffened. Sam felt her own muscles clench, too. The speaker was an older woman with a severe iron gray bob and a rumpled National Park Service uniform. Meg Tanner, assistant superintendent.

Sam held out her hand. "Hi, Meg. I'm here writing some articles about how the cougars are doing. How are you?"

Tanner ignored Sam's outstretched hand. "Been better." She leveled a gnarled index finger at Rafael. "Castillo, I need you to take a report from Site 21."

His square face brightened. "They see something?"

Tanner shook her head. "Another theft."

"Why can't these people lock up their stuff at night?" With a groan, Rafael pushed himself up from the picnic bench. He stalked away, muttering to himself.

"At least it's not a gun this time," Tanner said to his retreating back. She returned her gaze to Sam. "I thought you were up on the plateau. Didn't we give you a special permit?"

"I was. And yes, you did." Sam wondered for the fiftieth time if she'd done something during her summer employment here to piss Tanner off. "When I heard about the missing boy, I came down to see if I could help."

"Good. We can use another experienced tracker."

That was the closest thing to praise she'd ever received from the assistant superintendent.

"Just don't try to be a hero," Tanner added. "I know how you tend to go off on tangents."

Tangents? Sam's temper flared. Then she remembered that she was on a tangent of sorts right now. Save the Wilderness Fund was paying her to produce wildlife stories, and here she was, volunteering to search for a missing kid. "Yes, ma'am," she replied.

"Stick around. Rescue 504—the Explorer Scouts—will be here any second; we'll organize the second wave then." Tanner walked a few steps, then turned back. "Coffee's over there on the stove." Her thumb jerked toward a picnic table close to the Fischers. "Help yourself."

Tanner joined an overweight man in park service uniform. Sam recognized the bulky profile of Superintendent Jerry Thompson.

"I'm taking her up on that coffee." Sam strode toward the table.

Kent followed. "You've obviously forgotten the Tanner touch."

He was right. She had blanked out Tanner's talent for producing sludge. The stuff tasted like asphalt.

Kent rubbed the back of his neck, pills of sweat-dampened dirt rolling up like mealy bugs under his fingertips. "Once I thought for sure I had Zack. I saw something moving on the river path. But it was only a raccoon."

That reminded her. "I saw a ringtail last night." A fellow wildlife biologist like Kent would appreciate the wonder of it.

"Cool. Wish it had been me."

They walked back to the bench and sat down again. A muscle in Sam's thigh started twitching. Aggravating. A reminder that she was getting old and out of shape. She'd spent way too much time behind a desk recently. She dug her knuckles into the offending area. "Did you find any evidence that Zack's still in the park?" she asked in a low voice.

"We didn't find any evidence that he's not." He looked at her sideways. "You think someone took him?"

"There *was* a man, I swear. And his father didn't remember me."

"Maybe he will later. None of us are processing too well at the moment. It's been a long, long, long night." Pressing his index fingers to his eyelids, he rubbed in circles.

Sam closed her own eyes, tried to relax the tension in her neck muscles. When she opened her eyes, she nearly jumped off her seat. Jenny Fischer stood less than a foot away, staring at her.

"Will you find him?" The woman's blue eyes burned with pain. She held out a hand in supplication. "You know what my baby looks like."

Sam took the woman's cold fingers in her own warmer ones. She and Kent, lounging on a picnic bench, drinking coffee, must appear totally uncaring to this desperate mother.

Kent stood, put a hand on the woman's shoulder. "Everyone's looking for Zachary, Mrs. Fischer. Fresh volunteers like Sam here are coming to take over for those of us who have searched all night. And we'll all be back this afternoon after we've gotten some sleep."

Jenny withdrew her hand from Sam's and twisted her fingers together, staring at some point in the middle distance.

"I was trying to light the stove." Jenny's voice was hoarse. "I didn't have my eyes off Zack for more than a minute." She pulled a small orange toy from the pocket of her sweatshirt.

Jenny held a tiny plastic truck with only three wheels. Sam blanched. Zack's *twuck*. The little boy's mother pressed a fingertip onto the empty metal axle. A drop of blood oozed out of her pale skin. Jenny didn't seem to notice. "This was Zack's favorite toy. I was always worried that he'd pull off a wheel and choke on it." Her voice cracked.

Her gaze returned to the same distant point. "How was I to know that something even more terrible could happen to my baby? Fred said that—" Jenny's hand rose to her mouth. A tear slid down her reddened cheeks. "Oh God, did a mountain lion eat my baby?"

Sam realized that Jenny's eyes were fixed on the signboard near the pay station. It held a poster identical to the one Zack had noticed at Goodman Trailhead, the standard National Park Service flyer: WHAT TO DO IF YOU SEE A COUGAR.

"No, Mrs. Fischer," Sam said. "A cougar wouldn't take a child." Out of the corner of her eye, she saw Kent's jaw clench.

"Kids wander off all the time," she continued. "Sometimes they go farther than you can imagine."

Kent recovered. "Sam's right. Last May a five-year-old chased a squirrel away from the picnic grounds. It took us twenty hours to find him huddled under a bush three-quarters of a mile away. He was hungry and thirsty, but he was fine."

The young mother's eyes met Sam's. "He was fine," Jenny repeated.

"I'm sure Zack will be fine, too." Sam regretted the words as soon as they came out of her mouth. Who was she to be giving this mother trite assurances?

"Zack will be fine," Jenny echoed. She stumbled away as if under the influence of some mind-numbing drug, back to her husband's arms.

"God." Kent shook his head. "If I ever have kids, I hope I never go through anything like this." He stared at the ground and rubbed his fingers over his lips, hesitated a moment before asking, "Sam, you said you saw Leto and Artemis yesterday?"

"Yeah. I got a great photo." She tried to summon back the magic she'd felt standing beneath the rock bridge with the cougars looking down on her.

"But not Apollo?"

"Just the females. The photo's on the SWF website."

"I told you about the tracks by the river. Apollo's tracks."

He couldn't think . . . No. "They're just tracks, Kent."

"You said Zack went down the path by the parking lot. The search dog got really excited there, then lost the scent down by the river."

Had Zack turned down the path to the river? She would have sworn he ran toward the man.

"Since it's so dry now up on the mesas, most of the deer are in the valley." Kent paused for a moment, then added, "So the cats are coming down, too."

"It's only natural that the cougars come down for water," she whispered. "That'll change when the rains begin."

Her friend's blue eyes were intense. "I think Apollo killed a poodle a week ago."

"A poodle?" She picked up her mug and took a sip. The tar didn't taste any better lukewarm.

He leaned closer. "According to the owner, it was a tea-cup poodle, one of those itty-bitty furballs. A hawk or a coyote could have picked it off. But it might have been a cougar. There wasn't enough left to provide many clues."

She screwed up her face. "You found it?" A gruesome vision of scattered doggy curls and bloody jeweled collar rose up in Sam's thoughts. Someone's beloved pet, gone forever.

Kent dipped his chin and said in an even lower voice, "Nobody else knows."

"A poodle, maybe. But a cougar taking a kid?" she said. "It's not likely."

"Not likely," he agreed. "We'd have found remains by now."

Sam shuddered at the thought. Her mind switched to another track. "Zack might not even be in the park now. If the man at the end of the path wasn't Fred Fischer . . ." She couldn't bear to finish the sentence.

"There's only one exit from the valley, and we had that gate closed ten minutes after the parents called. The gate-keeper said that nobody had driven out for forty-five min-utes, and we've checked every car since then." Kent set his cup on the picnic table and yawned. "So, until there's evi-dence to the contrary, we've got to look for Zack in the park.

"There's a little kid lost out here somewhere." He yawned again. "He's probably cold and terrified, and all I can think about is breakfast. A Denver omelet. Ham and cheese." He shook his head and then tilted it back, covering his eyes with dirt-encrusted hands. "I'm bad."

She put a hand on his arm. "Real bad."

A van pulled into the gravel parking space alongside the campsite, followed by a station wagon. Teenagers, adults, and dogs piled out in a frenzy of shouting and barking. The humans wore blue T-shirts with an Explorer Scout insignia on the front and SEARCH AND RESCUE printed on the back. The dogs sported the same designs on their blue packs.

A sharp whistle interrupted the commotion. Thompson positioned himself beside the troop leader. The superintendent's gray hair was matted at the crown from wearing a park service helmet all night. Beside Sam, Kent reached up to feel his own hair.

"Yours is okay," Sam murmured. "And I don't want to hear a word about mine."

"There are around twenty volunteers coming in from Las Rojas, too. They should be here any minute," Kent said. He stood up. "I'm taking off."

"Find that omelet."

"Find that kid." He retreated with a trio of uniforms to a park-issue vehicle and drove away.

A stack of posters lay on the table under a flashlight. She helped herself to one. The chubby-cheeked laughing toddler stared out at her from the yellow paper. MISSING. In the grainy photo, dark blurs of clothing surrounded the child. A woman's hand lay protectively on Zack's shoulder. A hasty enlarge-and-crop job.

Sam studied the cherubic face. The little boy looked so happy in the photo.

"Please be okay," she whispered.

4

SAM'S search assignment was the valley campgrounds and trailhead parking lots.

"But those places have already been searched," she pointed out.

"Humor me," Tanner told her. "The Explorers can beat the bushes. We need adults talking to campers, assessing the possibilities down here." The woman looked around to make sure nobody was listening to the exchange, then lowered her voice a notch. "I heard about your encounter with Zack in the parking lot, about the unidentified man. Worse things happen to kids these days than getting lost."

Sam was unsure of how to respond. "I'll keep my eyes and mind open."

"You do that." Tanner gave her a slap on the shoulder that sent her staggering from the campsite.

The scouts from Rescue 504 fanned out onto the hillsides. Their singsong calls chimed across the valley as they worked through their assigned sectors. From the western rise, a female voice yelled "Zachary!" A male voice echoed from the east: "Zack!"

She started her own search with the trail where she'd last seen Zack. Taking the left fork, she walked to the river, across from where Kent had sighted Apollo's prints. The muddy soil was crisscrossed by hundreds of prints from boots and dog feet. There was no way to tell where little boys or cougars had walked. She studied the rippling river for a long while, pacing its banks, looking for anything out of place caught in the rocks at the bottom of the shallow water.

Around her neck she wore a yellow Explorer Scout bandanna, and her right arm was encircled by an armband with the troop's insignia and the words SEARCH PARTY. In spite of the official paraphernalia, she received a lot of dirty looks as she peered into cars and tents. The scowls softened when she handed posters to the park visitors, asking them if they'd seen a blond two-year-old in a Winnie-the-Pooh sweatshirt and red pants. Even a Mexican woman who spoke little English quickly understood the gist of the poster.

"Ay, Madre de Dios," she sighed, crossing herself.

Sam had swapped her heavy backpack for the smaller knapsack she used for day trips. In it, she carried notepad and digital camera just in case she ran across something worth capturing. The two-way radio was zipped into the outside pocket, the volume tuned to its lowest setting. She heard the scoutmaster report in now and then, as well as the rangers talking. A fender-bender backed up traffic at the north gate. Another theft had been reported at Miller Bend Campground. Normal park activity didn't stop just because a little boy was missing.

During her stint as a seasonal ranger, Sam had participated in two wilderness searches. She was not accustomed to inspecting places where hundreds of people tramped every day. Tracks were impossible to sort out. She scrutinized cars, peeked into each stall in the restrooms, including the men's, much to the surprise of one gentleman who hadn't answered when she knocked on the door. She lifted the lid on each garbage can, climbed into two Dumpsters, examined and collected litter from beneath cars, picnic tables, and ditches beside the road.

By noon, she'd decided that people were pigs. No, she corrected herself. That was an insult to porkers everywhere. No pig left a wake of debris like your average *Homo sapiens*.

Children were everywhere in the campgrounds. A good percentage of them appeared to be less than four years old, and at least half of those were blond. They ran up the paths, rode tricycles on the loop road: how could an observer tell which child belonged to which parents? She'd certainly never questioned whether the man at the end of the path was Zack's father.

"Miz Ranger." A middle-aged camper motioned her over. He gestured at his picnic table. "I had everything right here last night."

"What?"

"Someone stole my grapes. And a half wheel of Camembert and a fresh loaf of French bread." Folding his arms, he glared at her. "Now what am I supposed to do for food?" His foot tapped impatiently on the ground.

A kid was missing and this loser wanted to know what he was going to eat for lunch? It was no wonder she hadn't made the cut for a permanent job in the park service. She didn't have the patience for this.

"Keep an eye out for this missing boy." She slapped a poster down on his picnic table. "And I'm not a ranger."

Another visitor quizzed her about howling noises. Just coyotes, she told him; no wolves in this part of the country. No point in mentioning Coyote Charlie: tourists might not think he was the comic-book figure the rangers did. Odds were that nobody in the valley campground could hear him up on the plateau, anyway.

She was on her hands and knees peering beneath a big RV when the door suddenly swung open. The sharp aluminum corner gouged her back before clanking to a stop against her knapsack. A big man hastily jumped down onto the cement block that served as a step. He grabbed the door, swung it shut. "Sorry," he said breathlessly. "The dang closer thing's broken."

By the time she stood up, his tone had changed from

apologetic to irritated. He thrust his belly forward, distorting the image of Mickey Mouse on his tight blue T-shirt. "What the heck you doin' down there, anyway?"

She rubbed her back. Scraped but not bleeding. "I'm looking for a missing kid." Peeling a crumpled poster from the roll, she held it out to him. "He disappeared last night."

An odd expression lingered in the man's eyes as he examined the photo. The hair on the top of his head was a thick and unvarying brown, but the thinning sides showed multiple threads of gray. Didn't the guy know how silly a cheap toupee looked?

His fingers moved on the edges of the page, caressing the paper. His tongue flicked out, swiped wetly over thick lips. A warning prickle crawled across the back of Sam's neck.

"Have you seen Zachary?" she asked.

"That his name?"

Clearly printed at the bottom, she thought with annoyance, taking a step closer to point it out. Something crunched under her foot. A blue plastic block. Two red ones and a yellow lurked nearby. She scooped them up. "These yours?"

He stared at them for a long moment. "LEGOs," he finally said.

He took the colored cubes from her, his fingers clammy against her palm. Holding the blocks to his chest, he gave her a tentative smile. "For the grandkids."

Did that also explain the Mickey Mouse T-shirt? "Where are they?"

"Who?" He looked around him.

"The grandkids?"

"They're not with me today." He turned to go back into the camper. "But thanks for asking."

A very strange man. She placed her hand on the door beneath his. "Could I trouble you for some water, sir?"

He turned, one foot on the camper threshold, one on the makeshift step. "What?"

She smiled. "A glass of water? It's a long way to a drinking fountain. You do have water inside your camper, don't you?"

"Inside?" The man's pale eyes darted nervously to her face and then down to his own hand on the door handle. "Well, I mean, it's just that it's really messy."

"No problem." She pulled the door out of his hand. "I'm not the housekeeping police. I'd really appreciate it, Mr.—?"

The man stepped up and turned toward her. "Wilson, the name's Wilson." He gestured for her to enter.

It was no easy task to squeeze past Wilson. The fleshy roll of his belly brushed against her back like a soft warm pillow. Was he actually leaning *into* her? She stifled an urge to flinch.

In the kitchen, freshly washed pans and a couple of plates were set out to dry on a kitchen towel. Wilson opened a cabinet door and reached for a glass. Sam spotted familiar yellow and blue boxes on the upper shelf.

"Ah, animal crackers," she said.

A rush of color flooded the man's face. "For the grandkids," he mumbled. He filled the plastic tumbler with water from the tap and handed it to her, swiped with a dish towel at the few drops that had splashed onto the counter. "But the kids aren't here.

"I'm all by my lonesome this trip." That tentative smile again. His large hands fiddled with the dish towel, wringing it into a twisted rope.

Sam sipped her water slowly as she surveyed the camper. More LEGOs were spilled across a Formica tabletop. Toys. Animal crackers. Mickey Mouse. But no kids in sight.

Near the door, a blue jogging suit—nylon-knit pants and hooded jacket—hung from a hook. Dried dirt darkened the elastic cuffs of the pants, and another patch of the crusty material speckled a sleeve. River mud? She suddenly found it difficult to swallow. She felt Wilson's gaze on her, but when she raised her eyes, his quickly flitted away.

A calendar adorned the wall over the table. *Miranda, 5:00, VFW* was scribbled into the square for today's date. At the rear of the camper was a double bed, neatly made, its cotton cover tight with corners tucked under, institution-style. Hardly messy.

Wilson pulled open the undersink cabinet, stretched out the dish towel, and hung it on a peg to dry. From another peg hung a small red baseball cap.

Sam felt as if the air had been sucked out of the room. "That cap. Is it yours?"

Wilson studied it as if unsure of how it had gotten there. "No," he finally said. "I found it down by the river, when I went for a walk this morning. Why?"

"The missing child was wearing a red baseball cap." Could the search parties have missed Zack's cap down by the river? She doubted it. She tried to breathe normally. Wilson, in his blue jogging suit, could easily be the man she'd seen at the end of the path. The bulge she'd noticed in silhouette could have been the hood pushed down behind his neck.

"A hat like this one? Really? Oh my." He wrung his hands.

"Can I have it? I'll take it to the rangers."

He reached for it reluctantly. "Well, sure, of course, if you think it might help."

She took it from him. The red fabric was damp.

"I washed it. It was dirty, and I thought, you know, maybe one of my grandkids would like it, so I rinsed it off."

Again the grandkids.

His gaze fell on the glass in her hands. "Well, if you're done—"

She handed him the empty tumbler. "Thank you, Mr. Wilson. If you see Zachary Fischer, please tell a ranger."

After he closed the door behind her, she tucked the baseball cap into her knapsack, then walked to the rear of the RV. A blue Volkswagen Beetle was attached to a tow bar behind the rig. She wrote down the license on the car's back plate along with the RV's number. As she walked away, she caught a flicker of movement as the curtain at the kitchen window dropped back into place.

She stopped outside the campground and used her cell phone to call the ranger station about Wilson. The woman who answered didn't seem too excited. "Yes, ma'am," she responded in a honey-coated Southern drawl. "Thank you for the tip."

"Look," Sam urged, "Ranger—"

"This is Ranger Gates, ma'am."

"Ranger Gates, did you really get what I told you? The toys, the animal crackers, the mud, the *red baseball cap*? I'm holding that cap right now; do you want me to bring it in?"

"I'm sure later will be fine, Miss Westin. Please continue to search until your area is complete."

Sam gritted her teeth. "Can you forward me to Ranger Castillo?"

"Ranger Castillo is in the field and can't be reached at present, ma'am."

"You will treat this as important, right?" Sam asked, exasperated. "You will have a law enforcement ranger check out Wilson?"

"You saw no trace of Zachary Fischer in Mr. Wilson's camper?"

"Well, not of him specifically. Just the cap."

"And Mr. Wilson stated he'd found that by the river this morning."

"Yes."

"Is there a name on the cap?"

She pulled it out to check. "No."

"And Mr. Wilson said that he had not seen the child?"

"That's right, but Zack could be hidden in that camper."

"And no one in the vicinity has actually seen the child?"

The phrase *circumstantial evidence* came to mind. "That's correct," Sam responded dismally.

"I'll pass your information along. A ranger will speak to Mr. Wilson as soon as possible. We will not allow him to leave the park before then. Please complete your search area."

Sam hung up, feeling as though she'd failed to impress a robot. She started to call Kent, then remembered that he was sleeping. Stuffing phone and baseball cap back into her knapsack, she cursed Ranger Gates and continued her search.

The last parking lot on Sam's map was at the base of a cliff called Red Wall. A dozen rock climbers rappelled down the sheer surface. The climbers were mostly teenage boys and girls in identical turquoise T-shirts and khaki shorts.

A dark-skinned boy stood backward on the edge of the cliff above, glancing over his shoulder to the canyon floor a hundred feet below.

"Sheeeyiiit," he screeched, clutching the ropes fastened at the waist of his harness.

From above, a male voice answered. "We've got you. This is all about trust, man."

Sam recognized the efforts of Outward Bound, an organization that used outdoor activities to turn around the lives of juvenile delinquents. They'd used the park for a decade or more.

A handful of teens had reached the bottom and were removing their harnesses under the watchful eyes of adult supervisors. A week ago the kids had probably belonged to six different gangs hell-bent on shooting each other.

The new climber stepped over the edge and braced his legs against the rock wall, testing the rope. He made the mistake of glancing down again. "Oh shit!"

Even from the base of the cliff, Sam could see that the kid's knees were shaking.

The counselor's voice from above was calm. "Keep going."

The boy pushed off from the wall and let out the rope. He swung back in a few feet lower. "Hey, it works!" He pushed off again, this time with more confidence. *"Eee-haaa!"*

The yell reminded Sam of Max Garay and his rampaging sprites. She dug the camera out of her knapsack, switched it to video mode, and focused as a red-headed girl stepped over the edge.

"Cowabunga!" the girl bellowed, pushing off without hesitation and sliding down the rope in one reckless motion.

The dark-skinned boy reached the bottom of the cliff

and landed on the hard-packed ground with a thud, only seconds before the fearless redhead. He high-fived her. "Yo, Cameron."

"Awesome, huh, DeWitt?" the girl answered.

Sam smiled, remembering the first time she'd rappelled. It was fun, assuming you had faith in your teammates and your equipment. She stowed the camera and went back to work.

A few minutes later, she waded into the last garbage bin in her sector, stirring the smelly refuse with a long stick, making sure a two-year-old wasn't among the debris.

What a horrible, sad way to spend a day. She scrambled down from the bin, staggering a little as she landed off balance. A horn blared behind her, and she jumped out of the way of a white van with a large folded antenna on the roof. KUTV NEWS 9 was painted in large letters on the vehicle's side. As the van passed, she recognized the man sitting behind the driver. Silver hair, neatly clipped matching mustache. Buck Ferguson's pale blue eyes were tracking her, too. If he had been carrying one of his state-of-the-art rifles, a tiny red laser dot would be centered on her forehead.

Every ranger in the park had butted heads with Buck Ferguson at one time or another. They had voted him Most Likely to Have Shot Leto.

The van parked in front of the signboard. A female reporter climbed out of the front passenger's seat, followed by the driver, a youth in jeans and T-shirt who now shouldered a TV camera. Ferguson followed. The back of his windbreaker sported the logo of his company, Eagle Tours.

Since she'd been dating Adam, Sam had longed to watch a television news crew in action. But she had a bad feeling about this one. The cameraman positioned the reporter and Ferguson on either side of a WHAT TO DO IF YOU SEE A COUGAR poster. The reporter spoke for a few seconds, then pushed the mike under Ferguson's nose. Brows knitted into an earnest expression, he spoke at length to the camera.

Damn. This couldn't be happening. Not so soon. Sam joined the knot of onlookers that had gathered, arriving just as Ferguson delivered his punch line. "How many more kids like Zachary Fischer will have to die before the liberal elitists realize that it's people who need protecting, not cougars?"

The gray-haired woman standing next to Sam gasped. "Oh my God. A cougar!"

Sam said loudly, "There's no evidence that Zack has been killed by a cougar."

The cameraman turned, focused his lens on her. Staring straight at the glass eye, she said, "There's no evidence that Zack is dead."

A look of disgust crossed the reporter's perfectly made-up face. She thrust her hand in front of the lens. "Al, turn that thing off. We're done here." She stalked to the van, her high heels clicking on the asphalt.

"Well, well. The little pretend ranger is back." Ferguson touched a finger to his nose and sniffed loudly. "Pee-yew. Something around here really stinks. Or is it some*one*?"

A bystander laughed nervously, and another moved farther away from Sam. Ferguson was right. After crawling through bushes and restrooms and garbage bins, she desperately needed a shower and clean clothes.

She walked closer to the van. "We're still searching for Zack Fischer! Report on the search!"

Ferguson climbed in. The doors slammed shut. The reporter stared straight ahead as they drove away, but the gaze of the cameraman briefly connected with Sam's. Buck Ferguson waggled fingers at her in jarring similarity to the mystery man at the end of the path. She felt like screaming.

Three o'clock now. Zack had been missing since sundown yesterday. More than twenty hours had passed, and the local TV news was manufacturing answers where there were none. A red-hot wave of frustration washed over her. She walked to the nearest restroom and splashed her face with cold water.

Her sector was finished. She called in her search results to park headquarters. Probably to head off another harangue,

Ranger Gates wearily stated that although Wilson had not yet been interviewed, he was on the list.

How many people were on this list? Were there any solid clues? Gates couldn't or wouldn't tell her. Sam hung up before she said something she'd regret. There had to be something, somewhere, that would point them toward Zack's location. If only she could think. Food might help; she'd had nothing since dawn but Tanner's sludge. Deciding to start again at the beginning, she returned to her car and moved it to Site 44, where the Fischers had stayed for two days.

The campsite was abandoned: the coordination effort had moved to park headquarters. She pulled off her search party bandanna and armband and sat on the picnic table, chewing stale crackers and cheese and studying the area.

Along the gravel road, bright sunlight filtered through autumn leaves, spangling the area with golden light. Birds twittered in the trees. It seemed unfair that such a terrible thing could take place on such a beautiful day. But she knew all too well that fairness had nothing to do with it. On the morning her mother died, the summer air had smelled of wild roses and she'd seen her first golden eagle. She had been nine years old.

She slid off the table, walked to the rock ledge where Jenny and Fred Fischer had been sitting this morning. This was where Zack was last seen by his mother. She crouched and tried to envision the world through a little boy's eyes.

Birds everywhere. A chipmunk in the bushes. And although she couldn't see the river, she could hear its constant murmur across the road. Kids were attracted to water. That's no doubt why Zack had shown up in the parking lot yesterday evening.

Through the trees, she could see the front of Wilson's RV. Which meant he might have seen Zack playing here. Wilson, with his LEGOs and animal cookies.

A small blur of orange at the base of a nearby bush caught her attention. Sam leaned over and grabbed it. The plastic truck that Jenny had been fingering. Would she

want it back? It would be a good opportunity to speak to
Zack's parents again.

The feeling of being observed suddenly prickled up her
spine. She turned her head toward the woods. Leaning
against a large ponderosa was a tall, lean man, his gray suit
and burgundy tie distinctly out of place amid the trampled
grass and gnarled trees. His arms were folded authorita-
tively across his chest. His dark eyes regarded her with suspicion.

"Who are you?" he demanded.

5

SAM stood up. "*You're* the one who scared *me* to death. *I* get to ask the questions. Who are *you*?"

Something glinted in his eyes. Annoyance? Amusement? He reached into his breast pocket and extracted a leather wallet. Stepping toward her, he flicked it open. "FBI."

A gold-toned badge on top. Photo ID on the bottom. She grasped the wallet and compared the photograph with the man. Good-looking picture, although a trifle severe. Better-looking man. Raven hair, a square jaw with the blue-black sheen of whiskers lurking under just the bronze skin. Deep brown eyes, not the dense hue of chocolate, but a dark clear brown. Like a potent tea, or maybe an expensive brandy.

"Special Agent Chase J. Perez," she read aloud.

He pulled the wallet from her grasp and snapped it closed. "Okay, now we both know who I am. Who are *you*?"

"Summer Westin."

He returned the wallet to his breast pocket, traded it for a pen, and pulled a small notepad from a rear pants pocket. "How do you spell that?"

"Summer?"

His lips twitched, but he kept his gaze focused on the pen point he had pressed to the page. She had to give him credit for poise. "The whole thing."

She spelled it.

"Middle name?"

It took her a second to come up with it. "Alicia."

He looked up from the notepad.

"I never use it," she explained.

His expression was skeptical. "ID?"

"You're kidding, right?"

"No. But first"—he dug into a pocket inside his suit coat, brought out a plastic zipper-lock bag, and held it open—"the toy."

Feeling like a shoplifter caught in the act, she dropped it into the bag.

"Now," he said, zipping the bag, "the ID."

Disgusted, she exhaled loudly. "It's in the car." She stomped the fifty yards across grass and gravel to the vehicle, slid into the front seat, dug through her knapsack for her billfold. Through the windshield she observed Perez watching her. His right hand had disappeared under his suit coat. Probably resting on a pistol in a belt holster, just in case she emerged with a weapon.

She took him her Washington State driver's license. He jotted down her license number and birth date, flipped the laminated card over and back again, then scrutinized the photo, compared it with her face.

"You shaking down everyone in the park?" she asked.

Again, the hint of a smile. He pressed his lips together briefly before responding. "Only women from Bellingham, Washington, who are making off with certain toy trucks." He handed back the license.

"I was not 'making off' with it. I was going to return it."

"This is a crime scene. You shouldn't be touching anything."

"Really? You should have gotten here earlier to tell that to the other hundred people who tramped through here today, Special Agent Perez."

The scowl that darkened the FBI man's face made her regret her sarcasm. Kent was right, she *was* a wiseass.

The crunch of gravel distracted them both. A park-issue truck pulled up behind her car, and a familiar lanky form emerged. Kent strode over, distinctly cleaner than earlier in the day. Shaking hands with Perez, he said, "Ranger Kent Bergstrom. Sorry it took me so long." He scrunched up his nose and flapped a hand in her direction. "Whew, Sam, is that you?"

Her face flushed at the reminder of her aroma. "Dumpster diving," she explained. She glanced at Perez, whose expression remained impassive. Either the agent was naturally stoic or he lacked a sense of smell. Lest he think she routinely waded through garbage, she added, "I was looking for Zack."

Perez's chin lifted a fraction of an inch. "That's very . . . astute of you."

It sounded vaguely insulting. "Thanks," she said. "I think."

"Most civilians would never . . ." he started, then abruptly switched tack "Why did you think he might have crawled into a Dumpster?"

"Two-year-olds can get into all kinds of places, can't they? Besides, he might not have crawled in on his own," she said.

Agent Perez, his eyes still fixed on her, nodded briefly.

"My God." Kent's eyes were wide with horror. "I never thought of that." He rubbed his eyes briefly as if to erase an ugly image that had formed there, then turned back to Perez. "Anyway, sorry. I had to finish a theft report, and then I had to give some illegal campers the boot."

Sam frowned. "Not the mother and the two little girls? Down in that flat spot by the river?"

Kent nodded. "Yeah. Mexican migrants, I think. Barely understood English."

She sighed. "They probably don't have money for the campground fee."

"I sent her to the national forest. At least I hope she understood; I showed it to her on the map." He glanced at Perez. "We have a real problem with the homeless."

The FBI agent made an impatient gesture. "They're everywhere."

"Got that right. We see too many illegal Mexicans here." Apparently Kent had a sudden thought about Agent Perez's probable ancestry, because he hastily added, "And other homeless, too. Sometimes we chase them around for weeks, even months. About three years ago—I was a summer hire then—we had this one guy, about my age, and his teenage girlfriend. They kept popping up all over the park. The girl had the most beautiful eyes, big and brown, like a whitetail deer. She was only about Sam's size but a lot younger."

Sam suddenly felt like an elderly dwarf. She corrected the slouch of her back and tried to relax the frown line etched into her forehead.

Kent continued. "Sixteen, maybe seventeen years old. And she was out to here, at least eight months pregnant." He held his hand out in front of his abdomen, measuring an imaginary belly.

The gesture looked strange on a man. Evidently Perez thought so, too: his gaze remained fixed on the outstretched hand until Kent dropped it back to his side.

Perez abruptly changed the topic. "So, you two know each other?"

"Oh yeah," Kent said. "I've known Sam for years."

Perez turned to her. "I thought your name was Summer."

"Sam's my nickname," she said. "Better than Sum, don't you think?" Then, hearing the double-entendre, she added, "S-U-M, I mean, not S-O-M-E."

"Got it the first time." Perez's gaze shifted to Kent. "What's the connection between you two?"

Kent explained her seasonal employment in the park a year ago, that they were fellow wildlife biologists, Sam's follow-up article about the cougars. Perez took in the information without a change in expression. He looked back to Sam. "You're a biologist, a writer, and a photographer?"

"She's Wonder Woman," Kent said. "Odiferous Wonder Woman."

Sam jabbed him with an elbow.

Perez touched the tip of the pen to the notepad again. "So you're a journalist." His tone made the word sound like an epithet.

"I'm not the press," she told the agent. Although it felt slightly disloyal to Adam to say it, the last thing she wanted was to be lumped in with the media team she'd just seen in action. "I'm a freelance writer and photographer. And I only do wildlife and outdoor stories." She mentioned the Save the Wilderness Fund. Perez wrote it down.

"And now she's doing online stuff, you know, on the Internet?" Kent contributed.

The FBI agent scribbled some more. "So you're a blogger." The way he said it made her think that he didn't have a lot of respect for the medium.

Oh, jeez. Just what she needed: to be categorized with all those unpaid bloggers out there sharing recipes or dog training tips. "I am paid to write online *articles*," she stressed.

"I see." Perez lifted his gaze toward her. "What do you know about Zachary?"

"Blond, two and a half years old. Disappeared last night from this campsite. Cute little guy, with scratches on his face."

The FBI agent was attentive now. "Where did you get this description?"

"I saw him. Around five forty, five forty-five yesterday evening." She described the encounter.

"And you didn't take him back to his parents?"

She winced. "He took off on his own, down the path that led back to the campground. His father waved at me."

"So you know Mr. Fischer?"

The agent's direct gaze made her squirm. "No. I mean, I didn't then. I met him this morning."

"You're certain that Mr. Fischer was the man who waved at you?"

In her mind's eye, she saw again the man's silhouette. The sharp profile, the bulge at the back of the neck. Fred Fischer? "It was very dark," she finally murmured.

Perez stepped closer. "Are you certain that Zack reached this man?"

She relived the brambles snagging her, the flash of
Zack's sweatshirt as he disappeared into the shadows on
the path near the river. How could she have let a two-year-
old run off like that?

"Did you see Zachary with the man?" Perez pressed.

"No!" The word came out too loud. She swallowed,
lowered her voice. "The last I saw of Zack, he was running
away from me, down the path, toward the man who waved."
The fingers of her left hand clenched into a fist as she
remembered the boy's tiny fingers slipping from her grasp.
I am guilty of letting him go.

"Where are you staying?" Perez asked, his pen poised
over his notepad. "I may want to talk to you again."

"Tonight, the Wagon Wheel Motel in Las Rojas. Tomorrow, I'm not sure. If I can help in the search for Zack, I will.
Although he may not be in the park."

The FBI agent studied her for a moment. How did he
part his hair with such knife-edge precision? "What makes
you say that?"

She ticked off the reasons on her fingers. "A, we haven't
found any sign of him; B, a two-year-old can't walk far;
C, the man at the end of the path."

A helicopter thundered overhead, flying slowly and low
to the ground. Sam held her hands over her ears.

When it had passed, Kent said, "Civil Air Patrol." Search
volunteers.

Perez nodded, turned, and strolled through the campsite, hands clasped behind his back, slowly scrutinizing the
scenery. Kent trailed the FBI agent to the rock ledge.

"This was where his mother last saw him." Kent pointed.

Perez nodded, paced around the smooth rock outcropping, studying it from all angles. Then he stopped and squatted next to a thicket of twigs, staring at something on the
ground. He raised his head. "Could it have been a cougar?"

Sam approached, peered over his shoulder at a large
four-toed print. "That's a dog print. See the toenails? Cougars retract their claws."

"Canine," Kent concurred.

Exasperation was written on Perez's features. "I know that's a dog print. A big shepherd, maybe a Lab. But this one?" His index finger indicated an equally large, but rounder impression to the side of the dog print.

"Too smudged to tell," Kent said.

Perez straightened, jotted down a note. "So it could have been a cougar."

"No." Sam's voice was firm.

Using his pen, Perez pointed to the sign on the signboard that bordered the campsite. WHAT TO DO IF YOU SEE A COUGAR. Addressing Kent, he asked, "Why do you have those posted?"

Kent hooked his thumbs in his belt. "The park service requires them in every park with a cougar population."

Sam explained further. "The cougars in this park stay mostly in the high country, away from people."

The agent's eyebrows lifted. "Mostly?"

Kent swallowed before responding. "They sometimes follow the deer down or come down for water in dry season. But there's never been a cougar attack in this park. And only one in this state, as far as I know, and that was way back in 1997."

Perez's expression was skeptical. "Less than a year ago, a woman was killed by a mountain lion in a California park."

Sam scoffed. "Well, of course in *California!* People there go jogging through wild areas like they're running down Hollywood Boulevard."

When the FBI agent regarded her curiously, she realized her words had been too vehement. Even Kent was frowning. But then, they didn't live next to L.A. transplants who had just chain-sawed three acres of mature forest to plant a lawn.

Perez wasn't ready to give up. "There have been a number of cougar attacks in the West. They're on the increase."

Sam waited a second for Kent to respond. When he didn't, she jumped in. "They only happen in areas where the people are destroying the lions' habitat. How would you react if your home was wilderness one year and subdivisions the next?"

Perez's steady gaze told her he was not impressed. "Several people have been attacked across the western U.S. and British Columbia. Some were killed."

Sam grimaced. Each incident was a blow for wildlife recovery organizations. Many reports were unconfirmed, but she could see it would do no good to argue that with Mr. FBI.

Kent finally spoke up. "Those incidents are unusual. Cougars don't normally behave like that."

Perez shrugged. "You're the wildlife expert in the park?"

Kent nodded. "The cougars here have plenty of open territory, and plenty of prey—mule deer and jackrabbits and bighorn sheep. They have no reason to seek out humans."

Someone had to say the unthinkable, just as Kent had this morning. "Look," Sam told Perez, "if a cougar *had* killed Zack, we'd have found his body by now. Or at least . . . parts of it." Even saying the words made her feel a little queasy.

"Unless the cat dragged him off. I understand they can carry prey a long distance." Perez tugged at the knot of his tie. "Do you know where their lair is?" he asked Kent.

Sam snorted. "Cougars don't have *lairs*. Mother cats might use the same cave or thicket for a few weeks while their cubs are too small to travel, but aside from that they roam around throughout their territory."

The FBI agent's face took on a deeper hue. Sam continued, enjoying the man's embarrassment. "Adult cats have a range of forty to sixty square miles. But they're rarely seen. They're elusive creatures."

Perez turned to Kent. "I may need to check it out for myself. If so, I'll want you to take me to them."

Right, she thought. *Just knock on the door of a cougar lair: "Cougars, meet the FBI—he's got a few questions for you."* Addressing Perez, she said, "It would make it easy for you, wouldn't it, to blame a cougar?"

He raised an ebony eyebrow.

"Then it wouldn't be an FBI problem, would it?" she pressed.

"Our judicial system does make it difficult to arrest wildlife, no matter how strong the evidence." His expression remained solemn, but there was a sparkle in his dark eyes.

Was he making fun of her? She retorted, "Then you could go back to your coffee and doughnuts."

"Cappuccino and biscotti," he corrected.

Sam was grateful when his jacket chirped, covering for her lack of a snappy comeback. He plucked a cell phone from an inner pocket and flipped it open. "Perez."

With a glance over his shoulder, the FBI agent moved away from them into the woods until his voice was too low to be heard.

"Could you stand about a half mile away from me from now on?" Kent said to her. "Maybe he'll forget we know each other."

She felt a twinge of regret. "Sorry. It's just getting to me, all this emphasis on the cougars. If everyone assumes that a cougar ate Zack, they're going to stop looking for him. He's out there, somewhere, waiting for help. And they're going to go after the cougars. With guns."

"Sam, believe me, I know what's at stake here. But we have to find a way to get everyone to help, not just alienate them right off the bat." He fanned the air in her direction again. "Don't you need to be somewhere? Somewhere downwind?"

She gave him a half smile. Kent couldn't stay mad at her for long. "I do need to get going, but first I want to give you something."

She returned to her Civic, pulled out her search notes and the baseball cap, then trotted back to Kent. Perez joined them just as she was ripping out the page onto which she'd copied Wilson's license number and noted the toys and cookies.

"I told Ranger Gaines—"

"We don't have a Gaines," Kent said.

"Female, Southern accent?"

"Gates," Kent corrected. "Archaeologist. She's new. Georgia Gates."

"Gates, then. I told her all this on the phone, but be sure it gets checked out." She held the scrap of paper out toward Kent.

"May I see that?" Perez pulled the page from her hand and studied the text. She told him her impressions of Wilson. The FBI agent listened impassively.

"He's weird," she concluded. "And there was mud on his clothes, like he'd been down by the river. If the man I saw wasn't Fischer, it could have been Wilson."

"No law against being weird," Perez responded. "And anyone could have gone to the river. But we'll check him out."

"Here," she said, holding out the cap. "I think this is Zack's cap. Wilson had it in his camper. He said he found it down by the river this morning."

"Which makes sense, since that was close to the last place you saw Zack last night."

"The last place I saw him was halfway down the path between the road and the Goodman Trailhead parking lot. There's a lot of riverbank between there and the RV area. If I were you, I'd get Wilson to show you exactly where he found the cap."

Perez locked eyes with her for a long moment. His clear brown gaze didn't tell her whether she'd just scored a point with him or lost ten. She'd always pictured a typical FBI agent as an overweight older fellow with a crew cut, not as a tall, handsome bronze specimen who looked several years younger and in better shape than she was.

He held out his hand for the cap. When she placed it on his palm, he gave her a curious look.

"Wilson washed it."

Frowning, Perez folded her page of notes into a neat square and pushed it into the breast pocket of his jacket, then extracted another plastic bag from his pocket and slid the cap into that.

Turning his back to her, he said to Kent, "Something's come up. We've got to get back to park headquarters."

Sam checked her watch as she walked with them to the parking area.

"Where are you going?" Perez asked.

She yawned and stretched her arms over her head. "I've got a couple of hours before I need to do this chat thing for Save the Wilderness Fund. I thought I'd see if the search party needs more help."

Kent grabbed her sleeve. "Sam, you're dead on your feet. And take my word for it, you need soap like a fish needs water."

"But you were up all night, and you're—"

"This is *my* job. You go do yours."

He was right. She was on day two of her assignment for SWF, and what had she done for them? "I'll be back at park headquarters tomorrow at first light."

"I hope this will all be wrapped up by tomorrow." He looked at Perez, who had preceded him to the truck and now stood impatiently beside the passenger's door. Kent turned his back on the agent and rolled his eyes. "They always travel in pairs, you know," he whispered. "If you think this one knows nothing about the great outdoors, you should see the other one. She's wearing high heels." He raised his voice. "Get some rest. I'll see you tomorrow."

Sam climbed into her car and headed for the tiny town of Las Rojas.

6

SAM took a long, hot luxurious shower before she walked to the adjoining Appletree Café and ordered takeout: the cook's specialty, chicken and dumplings. She added apple pie for good measure. The dining room was filled. The scene felt familiar, reminiscent of the small town she'd grown up in. Cowboy boots and jeans marked the locals, most of whom were drifting out now. Rural folks ate early. The second wave, the tourists, were just now starting to filter in.

While she waited for her order, Buck Ferguson emerged from the men's room. Sam pulled herself up on a counter stool and tried to blend into the wallpaper as she watched him work the room. Several of the townspeople hailed Ferguson as he passed. He clasped hands like a politician running for office, switching the toothpick in his mouth from side to side as he exchanged greetings. Then he saw her. Even as he moved toward the exit, his eyes remained fixed on her as if daring her to look away first.

The bell on the door clanged. Sam looked toward the sound, breaking away from the glaring contest. Fred Fischer entered. His clothes were different and his freshly washed hair was gathered into a bushy ponytail, but the shadows under his eyes were, if anything, deeper than they had been this morning. His mouth had a grim set to it.

It made sense, she guessed, that the Fischers would be here. The Wagon Wheel was the closest motel to the park. Fischer turned toward the counter, his hazel eyes glittering with anxiety or sorrow or anger or maybe all three. His lips were pressed into a thin line but still quivered a bit at the corners.

Buck Ferguson smacked Fischer lightly on the arm with a fist. "Stay strong," he told the younger man before he strode out through the door.

It seemed an odd thing to say to a stranger, but then it was Buck Ferguson saying it. Fred Fischer turned toward the counter, his face inscrutable. Again, she pictured the silhouetted form slowly turning from the light, compared the memory with the man before her. The dark baggy clothes, the bulge at the back of the neck. Yes. Fred Fischer could definitely have been the man she'd seen. But so could Wilson. Probably any number of men.

Fischer's eyes narrowed, and Sam had no difficulty reading the expression in them now. It was anger. His hands balled into fists. He covered the distance between them with three steps. Leaning close to her ear, he growled, "Leave me alone."

A chill prickled down her back. "I'm sorry if I was staring," she said, "It's just that—"

A waitress appeared at his elbow with a tray. "On the house," she murmured in a hushed tone.

Fred Fischer took the tray and backed through the door, his shoulders hunched over the covered dishes. Sam wondered if Jenny was sobbing in their room.

Why had Fischer gone after her like that? What reason did he have to be hostile? Unless, of course, he blamed her for losing Zack. No. *Leave me alone* meant he thought she was attacking him in some way. Because she'd accused him of being the man on the path? Or because he had been there but didn't want anyone to know?

When the bell above the door sounded again, Sam was surprised to see Agent Perez enter. He was accompanied by a woman whose chestnut hair was secured in a French twist with a gold-toned clasp. The partner Kent had hinted about. Her burgundy lipstick was glossy; her green linen suit and white blouse were spotless and wrinkle-free. Sam suddenly felt as if she'd been dragged behind a truck all day.

The FBI agents slid into the corner booth by the window, Perez taking the bench that faced the cash register. When he spotted Sam at the counter, he frowned.

Now *that* was annoying: she'd been nothing but cooperative to him. Except for that little smart-ass remark about spelling *Summer*. And perhaps the comment about coffee and doughnuts. And maybe the one about the length of the riverbank.

She slid off her stool, determined to make a better impression. Her blue jeans and coral turtleneck were clean; her hair was brushed into shining waves across her shoulders, and her scent was now Irish Spring instead of Eau de Garbage. She even had on beaded earrings and a trace of lipstick.

She approached the table. "Evening, Agent Perez."

The green-suited woman raised an immaculate eyebrow.

"Summer Alicia Westin, nicknamed Sam," Perez informed his partner. "Reporter," he added. The chestnut-haired woman nodded at the warning, silently shook out her cloth napkin, and spread it across her lap.

"Freelance writer," Sam corrected. "Nature articles."

Perez completed the introductions with a wave of his hand. "Special Agent Boudreaux."

"Any news?" Sam asked.

"None that we can share." His partner didn't even raise her head from the menu.

"Miss?" Sam was hailed by the counter waitress, who stood with a steaming tray in hand.

Back in her room, she opened the California Chardonnay she'd purchased at the liquor store across the street. She sat down on the bed with her tray, used the remote to switch on the television.

". . . cougars prowling our national parks. Is your family in danger? Stay tuned for our exclusive report on KUTV News 9, right after this short break."

"Crap!" Sam hissed. She punched the Mute button on the remote but kept her eyes on the screen throughout an ad for toothpaste and then another for mouthwash.

When the reporter's face appeared again, she clicked the sound back on. Carolyn Perry, whose name appeared at the bottom of the screen, was presenting the lead story tonight. Sam recognized her as the woman who'd been videotaping with Ferguson earlier.

"Cougar. Panther. Puma. Painter. Mountain lion." Each name, dramatically pronounced by the reporter, accompanied a different still shot of one or more big cats. The varied quality of the photos told Sam that the footage had been hastily pasted together. "Early pioneers feared this animal, calling it the cat of the mountain, or 'catamount.' "

A map appeared briefly on the screen. "The American lion once roamed all over the United States."

Roamed all over the Americas, Sam corrected mentally. *From Nova Scotia to Patagonia.*

"Although they were brought to the brink of extinction by farmers and ranchers in the early 1900s, mountain lions are now protected in many areas. They're on the increase in our national parks and forests.

"And as the population of mountain lions increases, so do mountain-lion attacks." The map was replaced by a still of a man confronting a snarling cougar with a long, stout pole in his upraised hand. To Sam, it looked more like the man was attacking the cougar than the other way around.

A swift cut led to a video of an earnest zookeeper talking to the camera as he closed the door of a cage. "An adult cougar can weigh up to two hundred pounds. They can leap twenty feet in any direction. Their usual prey is deer, but they will kill other animals if deer are not available."

"Such as rabbits, porcupines, and bighorn sheep," Sam said, filling in the sound gap as the focus moved to a still photo of a newspaper article.

"Only seven months ago, Betsy Lumas was attacked and killed by a cougar as she jogged through Rocky Heights Park in Southern California."

That was the first incident Perez had referred to. There had been no doubt that a mountain lion had killed the young woman. But all the evidence indicated that the attack had been defensive. The woman had clearly not been taken as prey. Her body was untouched except for the killing bite to the neck and claw marks on her shoulders. Lumas must have surprised a cougar at its kill, interrupted the cat's stalking of prey, or maybe stumbled between a mother and her cubs.

A familiar clip appeared. Sam remembered the video from when the story had broken. Betsy Lumas's husband tried to maintain his composure in front of the camera lens. "Betsy loved nature; that's why she jogged in the park. For a mountain lion to kill her . . . that's the worst possible thing I can think of . . . What a horrible way to die, with a mountain lion at your throat."

Simultaneously, the voice and picture changed. "In Oregon, these recreational bikers reported a close encounter with a big cat." Two teenagers holding the handlebars of mountain bikes recounted a near collision with a cougar on a backcountry trail.

Sam frowned. Hardly a deadly situation. The story moved on to the Colorado incidents. No relevant photos available, apparently. The audio track accompanied a generic shot of a cougar on a ledge.

To Sam's astonishment, SWF's home page appeared on the screen, along with her article "Cougar Celebration" and her photo of Leto and Artemis on the rock bridge.

"This appeared today on the website of Save the Wilderness Fund, a nonprofit environmental organization. This story highlights the increasing cougar population in our own state. It even states that a male cougar has been prowling close to Red Rock Campground in Heritage National Monument."

Carolyn's voice dropped in pitch. The newscaster clasped her hands in front of her and solemnly regarded the TV audience. "Yesterday evening, two-year-old Zachary Fischer disappeared from that very campground."

The camera zoomed in on the smiling chubby face from the posters, then cut to the tearful Fischers, seated side by side in what looked like the TV studio.

"He was there one minute, and he was gone the next." Jenny sobbed into the camera. "There were signs everywhere about cougars, but we didn't really pay attention." The camera cut to the warning sign. The familiar signpost— WHAT TO DO IF YOU SEE A COUGAR—filled the screen as Jenny's tearful voice announced in the background, "We didn't know our baby was in such danger."

Next up was a familiar chiseled face. Caroline's voice said, "Buck Ferguson is the owner of Eagle Tours, a company specializing in ecotourism and hunting expeditions." Amazing how the anchor could mention the two specialties together without even a hint of irony.

On the wall behind Ferguson's leather chair was a deer head with an impressive rack. And what was that form on top of the bookcase—a stuffed bobcat? Maybe the editor thought that Ferguson's "liberal elitist" comment in the park was too inflammatory to air; this footage seemed to have been shot in Ferguson's own den.

"People shouldn't have to put up with this. There are too many cougars in that park." Ferguson's mouth curved into a self-satisfied expression. "The ecosystem just can't support them. It was only a matter of time before something like this happened."

A quick dissolve went back to the carefully groomed newscaster, now positioned in front of a blown-up photo of Zack. "How could this have happened to little Zachary Fischer? Are other campers in danger? Join Martha McAdams, author of *American Lion*, Superintendent John Quarrel of the U.S. Forest Service, and Buck Ferguson, local wildlife expert, here at ten thirty P.M. on Special Report. This is KUTV News 9, your source for all the latest news."

Sam punched the Power button on the remote and the screen went blank. She sat cross-legged on the chenille bedspread, stunned, staring at a photo of a mule deer on the wall. The timing on the shot had been perfect—the shutter had snapped at the exact moment the buck had raised his head, liquid eyes focused on the camera, ears pricked, a light frosting of snow outlining his antlers.

Her cell phone trilled, jolting her out of her bewildered state. She rushed to dig out the instrument from her knapsack. "Westin," she finally breathed into it.

"Sam!"

"Lauren, have you heard about this missing kid down here? Jeez, they showed the website and implied—"

"Sam! It's past seven. The chat session! Get online!" A click, followed by a dial tone.

"Ooops." Sam threw the phone onto the bed, quickly connected the laptop to electricity and phone line, clicked the shortcut icon to jump onto the Internet. Three minutes after eight. She massaged her temples as she waited for the website to fill the screen. Finally the log-on window appeared. She typed in her user name and password, and then the system took its sweet time logging her in, filling in the little timing strip one agonizing square at a time to denote its glacial progress. It would be a hell of a note if SWF's first chat session began without the host.

The chat screen finally appeared. Lauren had been covering for her. *Wilderness Westin is online*, she'd typed. *Let's talk about wildlife.*

Let's talk about cougars killing kids, someone called Levin468 had responded. *I saw the news. Did Leto eat that baby?*

Was Levin468 local? Hopefully the story had aired only in Utah. Sam took another sip from her wineglass before typing *There's no evidence that a cougar took Zachary Fischer.*

A question from MZigor sprawled across the screen. *How about those killings in Mesa Verde, CA, and B.C.?*

How about them? she responded.

MarcGem joined the conversation. *Ur 1 a those treehuggers, Rnt U, Wild? If Ur kid was hungry n there was only 1 dodo bird left 2 eat, youd kill the kid instead a the bird.*

Jeez, the venom was unbelievable. *Wrong, MarcGem. Eat the bird.*

I can't believe U said that! ElizWong9211 typed.

Sam's fingers flew. *Think about it.* She added, *You idiots,* but only in her head. *If there's only one bird left, the species is already extinct.*

No one applauded her wisdom. The best she got was a comeback from MZigor that read *Ur a smart babe. How bout swinging thru my jungle? I gotta real thick vine U can hang on2.*☺

Creep. *The topic is wildlife, MZigor.* Hint, hint. Where was the monitor? Was anybody up there in Seattle listening?

Im wild. U got 2 b hurtin 4 it af

Suddenly the letters stopped and MZigor's name disappeared from the list of those tuned in.

She had to get this thing back on track. She typed *In Heritage National Monument, the cougars prey almost exclusively on mule deer.*

Then why did they kill Zack? CapJaneway asked.

Evrybdy's tweeting "lion eats baby," a new visitor chimed in. *Follow me on Twitter.*

She wasn't following anyone into the mapless minefield of Twitter. Were numskulls tweeting this crazy rumor around the world? Sam repeated her keystrokes. *There's no evidence that a cougar killed Zack Fischer. We don't even know that he's dead.* Was nobody listening?

Another message from MarcGem appeared. *Kill all cougars.*

Shit! The muscles in her shoulders clenched into knots as she waged battle with keystrokes for the rest of the hour. One minute before nine, Sam ended the thread, reminding the readers that cougars deserved protection, that Zachary Fischer was officially still missing, that the search for the little boy continued.

She sat back, took a deep breath, ate a few mouthfuls of cold dumplings and congealed gravy. The e-mail icon blinked at her. She had no doubt what sort of messages she would find if she opened her Inbox.

"Don't you think that went well?" she asked the deer on the wall. It stared back, eyes huge with surprise.

Footsteps and muffled voices sounded in the hall. There was the metallic jangle of a key in a nearby door. The Wagon Wheel Motel wasn't up to electronic cardkeys.

A muffled voice said, "Later, Nicole."

Perez? Next door? She trotted to the bathroom, grabbed the water glass from the countertop. Placing it against the bedroom wall, she pressed her ear against the glass bottom and listened intently. More footsteps, a couple of muffled thumps. Kicking off his shoes? The footsteps, lighter now, neared her position. A clunk close to her ear. Assuming his room was a mirror image of hers, the noise was probably his gun thumping down on the bureau.

Thank God for small towns. Her room was next to the FBI agent investigating Zack's disappearance, in the same motel with the distraught parents. If anything of consequence happened, she'd know about it.

Her cell phone rang, startling her. She ran to the bed and picked it up, half expecting to hear Perez's voice.

"Sam," Lauren groaned. "How could it all go so wrong?"

She swallowed. "I saw the story on the news."

"I can't believe Adam Steele did that to us."

"Adam? I was watching Utah news."

"Adam promised to get us some attention, and he certainly delivered. Check out the story on the KSEA website. What can we say about a big donor who just knifed us in the back? Uh-oh. I have to put you on hold for a sec." The connection went to a soothing New Age piece playing in her ear.

Sam moved back to the computer and pulled up the television station's site. "Missing Child Taken by Cougar?" was first in the list of links under Feature Stories. Clicking it launched a video that showed Adam at the KSEA desk. He looked blond-god handsome and serious. Seriously handsome. He dipped his chin, looked straight at the camera, and intoned, "Yesterday evening two-year-old Zachary Fischer disappeared from a campground in Heritage National Monument. Is little Zack lost or is the answer something far worse? The park is known for its rebounding cougar population." The SWF website appeared behind him on a screen—her article "Cougar Celebration" and its accompanying photo. "This story, newly launched on Save the Wilderness Fund's website, points out that cougar tracks were found close to the campground from which little Zachary disappeared." The video stopped. Four seconds from "Dynamite!" to disaster. Adam had precipitated the media avalanche?

Lauren was back. "Harding just dropped by to thank me for all this free publicity for SWF." Her tone was acidic. "We look like idiots. He's thinking about killing your assignment."

"No! That would play right into their hands."

"Whose hands?"

Good question. The media? The anti-cougar faction? "I'm sure this is only a temporary firestorm, Lauren. They'll find the kid and everything will be okay. You've got to let me report on the search." That reminded her. "What's up with this Wilderness Westin stuff, anyway?"

"Adam suggested that, too. Said it would give you a persona people can remember, like the Crocodile Hunter on TV." She huffed, then said bitterly, "Like we need to be remembered right now . . ."

Adam would think about names and image; five years ago he had changed his last name from Steeke to Steele, and it had made a world of difference in his career.

"The suits here loved the idea, even talked about giving all our writers and scientists nicknames. At least they did yesterday." Lauren exhaled loudly into the receiver. "This series of online reports were supposed to bring SWF *positive* attention, not sink us like a torpedo!"

"A cougar did *not* take that child." Sam kept her voice low. If she could hear through the walls, so could Perez. "I'll prove that. Stay tuned."

"Do I have any other choice?" Lauren retorted. "Speaking of which, I need your article for today. We can't leave up what we've got there now."

"I thought the chat session—"

"The deal was for a new article every day, right?"

"Right," she said wearily. "I'm on it. I'll send you my article within the hour."

Sam hung up and sat staring at the flying stars of the screen saver on her laptop. If only she were flying through space right now. She pressed her eyes closed and gathered her thoughts for a minute, then brought up the word processing program and threw together some notes about the events of the day. She couldn't exonerate the cougars, but she enumerated all the other possibilities and hit hard on the anti-cougar sentiment growing in the area. For visuals, she had only the bullet-riddled cougar sign from yesterday. Pulling a yellow MISSING poster from her pack, she snapped a photo of that and uploaded it as well. She couldn't think of any way to tie the rappelling video of the Outward Bound group in with her search story, but she sent it, labeling it FOR MAX. At least she'd make him happy today.

Had she helped keep the focus on the missing boy at all? Blake's prediction of future work from SWF was a ridiculous fantasy. Would they even let her continue? And if Zack was found dead or never found, this whole trek would be one big nightmare.

With transmission complete, she turned off the laptop and collapsed onto the bed. Damn the television news. Rolling over, she snatched up her cell phone and stabbed in Adam's number.

He sounded breathless when he answered. "Hey, babe, what a rush, huh?"

"I can't believe you used the SWF website in your breaking news story."

"Wasn't that great? Everyone had the missing kid—and I can't believe you didn't give me that, by the way—but thanks to you, I was the first to throw the cougars into the mix."

And throw me off the cliff, she thought bitterly.

"The manager's blown away. I couldn't have done it without you. Thank you, thank you, thank you for your fabulous story and photo! Hey, I've only got a minute—is there anything new?"

"Adam! The TV coverage makes it sound like a cougar took Zack."

He finally paused for a breath. "We never said that. We only posed the question."

"SWF is threatening to kill my assignment."

"What? That'd be crazy. I'll give them a call. Don't they know controversy is everything?"

To you, she thought, *not to a nonprofit organization.* "A cougar did not take Zachary Fischer."

"Man, that would be great, if I were the first to break that news. Can you prove that?"

"I will."

"Then you go, girl! Keep in touch with each development, and keep up the good work. Are we a fantastic team? I owe you two dinners when you get back. Love ya." He ended the call.

She tossed the cell phone onto the bed and stared at it as if it were a coiled snake. Had it only been last night that she'd been rejoicing at this assignment? *Fantastic team?* Had Adam actually said that? She felt like she'd been mown down by a semi. The buck stared at her from its snowy isolation.

"Oh, shut up," she told it. She lay back, closed her eyes, and tried to think about what to do next.

RANGER Rafael Castillo pulled up in the driveway of his house. His mind was on three things: dinner, a hot shower, and sleep, in that order. A blue VW Beetle was parked by the curb out front. The car looked familiar: he was pretty sure he'd seen it in the park. He fervently hoped that the driver was visiting one of his neighbors. It was ten o'clock, and after being on his feet for most of the last forty hours, he was not in the mood for socializing.

He hung his hat and jacket on the pegs in the hallway.

Canned laughter from the television rumbled in from the living room. Bad sign. Anita usually turned it off as soon as the kids were in bed. He stalked into the living room, prepared to get the bedtime process under way immediately. It was a school night, those kids should be asleep.

A strange man sat with his back to Rafael on the worn couch, balancing two-year-old Katie on his knees. He was one of those aging men who couldn't admit that his hair was going; the brown thatch on his crown was clearly a rug. A shrill giggle came from the toddler's lips as she leaned back, clutching the man's thick fingers in her tiny fists.

Katie's giggles turned to excited shrieks as the man pulled her toward him. He bent over, pressed his lips against her bare stomach, made a rude noise with his mouth. She battered his thighs with a flurry of bare-footed kicks. He pulled her toward him again and nuzzled her neck. Over the stranger's shoulder, the little girl caught a glimpse of her father standing behind the couch.

Her amber eyes widened. "Papi!" she shrieked happily.

The man straightened and pushed Katie away, settling her on the couch beside him. Pressing a hand over his toupee, he turned toward Rafael.

Miranda came down the stairs, clutching a pink stuffed bunny in her bejeweled hands. "Rafael!" she said, as if surprised to find him in his own house. "I didn't hear you come in."

"Evening, Miranda." Rafael shifted his gaze meaningfully from his mother-in-law toward the man on the couch.

She held out her slender hand to the stranger. He enfolded it in his own large paw. "This is my good friend Russ Wilson. We met at the VFW a couple of days ago." She wore brighter lipstick than usual, and her best gold earrings dangled from her ears. On the prowl again.

The man rose to shake Rafael's hand. Wilson was half a head taller, and at least fifty pounds heavier. His handshake was soft and clammy.

"Wilson," Rafael repeated. There was something important about that name. "Didn't I see your car in the park?"

"Probably. I go there often, especially this time of year. The leaves are so pretty and—"

Now Rafael knew why Wilson was ringing alarm bells in his weary brain. Russell Wilson was the name of the "suspicious camper" that Sam Westin had called in. But Bill Taylor, the park's other law enforcement ranger, had interviewed Wilson this afternoon and reported that although the guy seemed a tad nervous everything appeared to be in order. He was a doting grandpa who hoped his grandkids would stop by again soon.

"Are you in Site 62?" Rafael asked him now, although he already knew the answer. "The brown and tan RV? We knocked last night, but nobody answered. That was around midnight."

Wilson held up his hands in mock surrender. "Hey, I was inside, in bed. But there was so much shouting last night, what with the missing kid, that I couldn't sleep. So I took a sleeping pill. It would have taken an explosion to wake me up."

Rafael was a pretty heavy sleeper himself. At least Anita was always telling him so. "Mind if I check your ID?"

"Rafael!" Miranda chided. "How rude!"

"No problem," Wilson responded. He withdrew a worn wallet from his back pocket. "I already talked to several people today, a blond search party girl this morning and then a ranger this afternoon, but if there's anything I can do to help, I'm your man." After thumbing through a few plastic cards, he extracted a driver's license and extended it toward Rafael.

Taylor would already have this information, but it never hurt to double-check. Taking his notepad from his shirt pocket, Rafael jotted down the information. Orrin R. Wilson.

He looked up. "Orrin?"

Wilson grimaced. "If your first name was Orrin, wouldn't you go by your middle name?"

The photo was definitely the same guy, bad rug and all. The address was Rock Creek, about forty-five miles away. The plastic laminate was shiny. He checked the expiration date. Thirteen months away. "This looks new."

Wilson shrugged. "It's a replacement. I lost the first one a couple of weeks ago. I had it in my pocket when I was out jogging, and it must have slipped out somewhere."

Jogging? The man didn't really look the type. "Going back to the park tonight?"

Wilson nodded. "I'm paid in advance for the rest of the week."

Rafael knew that already; he'd checked the campground receipts himself.

"Papi!" Katie interrupted, frustrated at being ignored.

Oh hell, anything more could surely wait until tomorrow. He handed Wilson the license and swept his daughter up from the couch. "Time you were in bed, *mi hija*." Smoothing back her curly hair, he kissed her forehead. She rewarded him with an angelic smile. God, he was glad his kids weren't lost out there. Zack's folks must be in hell.

"I was just coming to get Katie." Miranda took the toddler from his arms. "MacLean called Anita around five thirty; she's out cooking somewhere."

Anita had recently gotten into the banquet trade. The pay was good and heaven knows they could use the money, but the MacLean fellow seemed a little too slick: Rafael wasn't at all sure that the man didn't admire Anita herself even more than her terrific cooking.

"Susie Reilly was babysitting, but you know her mother won't let her stay out past nine on school nights. So Nita called down at the VFW. And Russ and I were just getting ready to dance—"

"*Sí, comprendo.*" He cut off his mother-in-law's prattling; he didn't need to hear every picayune detail. "Sorry about your date," he said to Wilson.

The man smiled. "That's okay. I don't mind helping out; I love kids." His expression darkened. "Any sign of the missing boy?"

Rafael shook his head.

Miranda clucked sympathetically. "The other kids are all asleep, but Katie wouldn't quiet down." She gave the toddler a stern look. "Russ will drive me home. But first I'll finish putting this little one to bed."

"Thanks, Miranda. I'm on my way there, too. I can barely stand up." Rafael stumbled toward the master bedroom. Maybe his wife's new catering business wasn't going to be so great, after all.

7

SAM'S eyes slowly focused on a strange metal growth that gleamed dimly above her. Another second and she had her bearings. Wagon Wheel Motel, Las Rojas, Utah. The brass stalactite was a fire sprinkler. The light over the bureau was still on, the rest of the room in shadows. Her laptop loomed open on the table. She was still in jeans and turtleneck, on top of the covers. Eleven o'clock. Darn it! She'd slept right through Special Report, missed Buck Ferguson and KUTV's panel of "mountain-lion experts." She was afraid to guess what Adam was going to do on the eleven o'clock news in Seattle.

Footsteps whispered across the hall carpet outside her room. The thump that awakened her had probably been a door closing. The outside door at the end of the hall whined softly on its hinges.

She rushed to the window, pushed the curtain aside just a fraction. Across the parking lot, Agents Perez and Boudreaux opened the doors of a Ford Taurus. Both were clad entirely in black, Perez looking like an exceptionally fit burglar in a sweatshirt and jeans, Boudreaux more like an elegant Catwoman in stretch pants and turtleneck sweater. It was a sure bet that these two weren't out to track down a rogue mountain lion.

Her hiking boots were within reach; she tugged them on as she watched the Taurus pull out and turn west. Then she was out of the room, camera slung around her neck, car keys clenched in her teeth as she pushed her arms into her dark green windbreaker.

She turned the Civic west on Elm. Devoid of moving vehicles. Damn. She cruised slowly, passed Main. There! A blur of movement. The Taurus turned right behind a two-story building.

Sam drove to the next street over: First Avenue, where she'd lived in a rooming house the summer she'd worked here. She parked, pulled the jacket's hood over her hair, and jogged down a stretch of gravel that bisected the block. The moon was nearly full tonight, showering enough heavenly light to render the streetlights nearly useless.

LAS ROJAS COMMUNITY CENTER, a wooden sign labeled the cement-block two-story across the street. A security light illuminated a basketball court and play area to the side. A dilapidated swing swayed in the slight breeze, as if a child had just leapt out of the seat.

Cradling the camera, Sam sat down cross-legged in the shadow of a woodpile, praying that all scorpions and other crawly things would stay tucked inside the stacked logs.

She used the zoom feature on the camera to inspect the community center, but the viewfinder revealed little. The windows were black.

She yawned. Absolutely nothing happened for forty minutes. Maybe she'd lost the agents, after all. Maybe she was just sitting in someone's yard for no apparent purpose. Maybe she really wasn't cut out to be an investigative reporter.

A soft mew sounded at her elbow. A tabby cat curiously peered at her, mewed again, then rubbed against her. "Go away," she murmured in a low voice. He rubbed harder, leaning his weight against her.

"Go home. Get!" He purred, sounding like a jet engine in

the quiet evening. He crawled into her lap, curled up in the pocket of her crossed legs. She sighed and rubbed his ears.

A rusting Suzuki Sidekick pulled up to the curb in front of the community center. Then Fred Fischer emerged from the driver's side, and the interior light revealed Jenny's profile for an instant: her head was lowered, her lips pressed against clasped hands. Praying? The door clicked shut, killing the light on the sad tableau.

Fred carried a large padded envelope to the basketball court. At the edge of the lighted area, he pulled the lid from a metal garbage can, shoved the envelope inside, and replaced the lid. He trotted back to the car. The Sidekick drove away, the only moving vehicle on Main.

What the heck was that about? She scanned the area through the zoom lens. Nothing happening over there. With a curled paw, the cat snagged the dangling loop of her camera strap. Sam pulled the strap away. He grabbed for it, digging well-honed claws into her blue-jeaned thigh. She gave up and let him chew on it for a minute.

Ten more minutes passed. Her legs ached and her butt was getting cold. Her shoulder muscles were cramping. She made herself wait, tried to sit still. Surely the Fischers hadn't stopped by just to drop off garbage.

Something moved in the shadows on the other side of the basketball court. She raised her camera and zoomed in again.

A flash of motion caught Perez's eye. "Over there," he murmured. "Behind the bleachers."

Nicole focused her binoculars on the location below. "Two of 'em."

"You want to go, or me?" It felt strange to have only the two of them there. Normally there'd be at least a half-dozen FBI agents crawling over the place, but there hadn't been enough time to get a team from Salt Lake into place.

On such short notice, the only available assistance was the county sheriff. Rural areas like this were always under-

manned, but at least a third of city and county law enforcement was in the National Guard and serving somewhere
overseas these days. The sheriff's name was Wolman,
Wafford—something like that: no, Wolford, that was it.
Perez didn't expect much from him; the man was carrying
at least sixty pounds more than he should be. He'd probably
never dealt with anything more serious than a burglary.

The sheriff unsnapped the holster flap that secured his
revolver. "I'm going," he wheezed.

Nicole pulled her nine-millimeter from the holster at
the small of her back. She told Wolford, "You stay behind
me until I give you the word. Got that?"

The sheriff frowned, annoyed.

"Chase, you're the photographer."

He turned back to the window, camera in hand. He
itched to be in on the action, but fair was fair. He'd spent
the afternoon prowling the park while she'd interviewed
the parents and visitors and park service personnel.

The two figures approached the garbage can. "Better
hustle," he warned.

Nicole and Wolford dashed out of the room.

The camera whirred briefly as he caught the action on
film. One hunched figure stepped hesitantly into the light,
revealing a maroon windbreaker, faded jeans, high-top
tennis shoes, dark hair cut into a flattop. The other remained in the shadows, gestured to his partner, pale hands
fluttering in the moonlight. Hurry up.

Flattop pulled off the lid of the garbage can and reached
in. The streetlight illuminated his sharp chin and heavy
eyebrows. The photos might even prove good enough for
court. Flattop pulled out the bulky envelope. Perez clicked
the shutter. That one would make a great enlargement, the
smile on the face, the hands clutching the bag.

"Hands over your head! FBI!" Nicole's voice.

The figure holding the envelope clutched it to his chest.
The one in the shadows turned toward the voice.

"Stop!" Nicole bellowed. "I'm pointing a gun right at you.
Hands up! Now!"

Flattop reluctantly placed the envelope on top of the garbage can. Both figures slowly raised their arms above their heads. Perez waited for Nicole and Wolford to appear. Then a loud crash pierced the darkness.

"Shit! Get out of my way!" Nicole's tone left no doubt about who was at fault.

Flattop recovered the envelope. Both figures took off, quickly disappearing into the darkness. Pressing the camera to his chest, Perez galloped down the dark stairs.

He rushed out of the building, catching a glimpse of Nicole's figure for just a second before she disappeared around the far corner. To the side of the basketball court, the sheriff was scrambling up from his hands and knees, a toppled picnic bench beside him. Perez jogged off after Nicole, leaping over a teeter-totter to take a shortcut.

He rounded the corner and nearly plowed into her. She stood, hands on her hips, watching a yellow pickup pull away from the curb a half block away. The body of the vehicle floated just inches from the pavement. The truck streaked off down the vacant street.

"Lowrider," Nicole puffed. "They won't get far." The two of them reversed direction, jogging through the playground to the parking lot. Nicole slid into the driver's seat of the Taurus parked in the shadow behind the Dumpster. As she gunned the engine to life, Perez slipped into the passenger's seat and pulled his seat belt across his chest in one smooth move. The sheriff piled into the back, landing with a grunt.

"Seat belt, Sheriff!" Nicole spat out the words.

The Taurus tore out of the lot with a spray of gravel. Perez reached for a black metal receiver on the dashboard and adjusted the knobs.

"Got 'em?" Nicole glanced at him out of the corner of her eye.

A light flashed on the receiver's panel, accompanied by a small ping. "Got 'em."

Wolford shifted his weight in the backseat. "Sorry," he grumbled. "That bench is usually on the other side of the basketball court."

Nicole muscled the car around another corner, and the yellow pickup appeared ahead, just beyond the reach of the Taurus's headlights. The truck bounced over a pothole, its tailpipe leaving a comet tail of sparks as it dragged across the pavement.

She closed the gap. "I'll try to swing around and cut them off after we pass those parked cars up there."

Ahead, several vehicles lined both sides of the street in front of a dilapidated apartment building. A grizzled dog strolled out onto the pavement from between parked cars. Its eyes glowed orange in the pickup's headlights as it stopped, transfixed at the sight of the truck barreling down. Perez found himself stomping an invisible brake into the passenger's-side mat.

"Shit! Not Tom's dog!" Wolford moaned in anticipation.

The taillights ahead of them flashed red, and the rear end of the truck skewed to the right side of the road. Nicole slammed on the brakes, throwing everyone against the seat belts, nearly standing the car on its nose. The yellow truck slid across the pavement and slammed sideways into a vintage Pontiac. A hubcap popped off a pickup wheel and rolled down the street.

Lights snapped on in the apartment building as Perez and Nicole leapt out of the Taurus, their guns drawn. The hubcap clanged off a curb somewhere ahead.

Nicole approached the lowrider, standing near the back fender, her gun pointed at the driver's door. Perez positioned himself behind the truck, aimed at the back window. Two heads inside, not much movement. "FBI. Show us your hands."

Two sets of hands came up.

"Out of the car. Now!" he bellowed.

The driver's door cracked open. A figure stumbled out. Flattop. The dog trotted in the driver's direction, its tongue lolling in a friendly canine grin.

"Hands on your head!" Nicole yelled. Her pistol was fixed on the driver. "Passenger, out of the car, now! Hands on your head!"

She strode closer to Flattop. "Interlace your fingers," she instructed. "Step away from the vehicle."

Flattop thought about the instruction for a minute, then wove his fingers together with elaborate care, frowning fiercely at the hound standing beside him. Behind him, a sneakered foot pushed open the driver's door with a creak. The passenger slid out, one hand clutched to his forehead. The dog stuck its nose into his crotch, wagging its tail.

"We shoulda just run you down," the passenger complained.

"Hands on your head!" shouted Perez. "Interlace your fingers! Step away from the vehicle."

Nicole and Sheriff Wolford rushed to handcuff the two.

Flattop's jacket was purple, not maroon. A high school letter jacket. The other kid also had close-cut hair, but his was blond instead of dark. Both stank of sour beer.

SAM arrived in time to witness Agent Boudreaux jerk the dark boy's arm up behind his back. She stood in the midst of a growing knot of onlookers, camera dangling from her neck, trying not to pant noticeably. She'd followed the chase on foot, cutting through backyards and driveways, tracking the vehicles by sound.

Boudreaux clicked the cuffs on her suspect. "Where's Zack?"

"Huh?"

The agent spun him around. "The kid you grabbed. Zack."

A ransom job, then. It was the only thing that made sense. With luck, Zack would be recovered tonight and she could get back to writing about wildlife tomorrow.

"It wasn't us!" the other boy yelped.

The sheriff laughed. "I don't see anyone else here, Pat."

"You know these boys?" Boudreaux tucked a loose strand of hair neatly behind an ear. Sam remembered that she hadn't even looked in the mirror before bolting from the hotel room. She combed her fingers through her tangles, didn't find anything that remotely resembled a part on the top of her head.

"Yeah, I know 'em. That's Patrick Wiley." The sheriff thrust out his chin to indicate the dark-haired youth. "And this is Billy Joseph. They go to school with my kids." He shook his head. "I'm having a hard time believing you two would do a thing like this."

"We didn't kidnap him. We never seen him." Patrick danced in place.

"Honest." This came from Billy.

Boudreaux chuckled. "That's a funny word for you to pick, kiddo." She pressed his head against the cab. "Spread your legs. Any needles in your pockets?"

"Your father is going to be mortified." The sheriff pressed Billy Joseph's face down onto the pickup's hood.

Sam snapped off a quick photo. The flash was bright in the night.

"Hey, can I get a copy of that?" a man in pajamas asked her.

"Fuck!" The loud response came from the man standing at her right. "That was my grandma's car. Fuck!"

"Watch your language, Robert!" a shocked female voice behind them warned. "There are ladies present."

Perez holstered his pistol and walked toward the by-standers, his hands out in front of him. "Whoever took that photo had best keep it to himself."

Sam dropped back behind Robert, glad for once to be short and easily lost in a crowd.

"Mind your own business, folks. Go back to bed."

None of the onlookers moved an inch. She peered between the bodies in front of her, watched the dog trot to Perez. She was gratified to see that even FBI agents attracted unwanted fauna at times. Perez nudged the hound away and walked toward his partner. The dog followed.

The sheriff droned the rights statement as he and Boudreaux patted down the suspects. No weapons. Sam stepped out, hazarded another quick photo of the scene, stepped back before the flash had died away.

"We were just supposed to pick up the money," Billy said. "He was gonna give us a thousand. He said—"

"Do you understand your rights?" Boudreaux interrupted.

"Yeah, sure," Billy muttered. "I guess so."

"I'm gonna go get the patrol car." The sheriff trotted off into the darkness, puffing heavily.

Perez, the dog by his side, took charge of Patrick. "Who promised you the money?"

"Don't know his name," the kid mumbled. "He had long brown hair, kinda straggly."

"Yeah," added Billy, "And an earring." He sounded more enthusiastic by the minute. "And a beard."

Perez exchanged skeptical glances with Boudreaux. Shaggy-haired stranger. Even Sam knew that it was the most common description invented on the spot.

"Where were you supposed to deliver the money?" Perez asked.

The youths stared at each other for a long moment.

Perez snorted impatiently. "Give it up, boys. Where's Zack?"

"We don't have that kid. The Burger House on Fifth— that's where we're supposed to take the money. He said we could take a thousand out—exactly a thousand or he was gonna kill us—and then we're 'sposed to put the rest in the trash bin outside by one A.M."

The patrol car rolled up. The sheriff emerged, a swagger to his step now. "Everyone go on back to bed," he instructed the crowd. "Show's over."

The sheriff had no more influence on the group than Perez had. Sam knew from living here for a summer that this was the biggest late-night show to hit Las Rojas for quite some time.

"Anyone I see on the street in fifteen minutes gets a ticket for interfering with a police operation."

That finally did it. The crowd began to disperse, and Sam walked away with them.

* * *

JENNY Fischer would never have believed that time could pass so slowly. The cheap plastic clock on the bedside table made actual ticking noises as the luminous hands moved from minute to minute. Although she lay on the motel bed and her gaze was fixed on the clock, she could feel Fred hunched in the chair in front of the window. "See anything?" she asked.

"A whole lot of dark."

That pretty much described what she saw when she looked within her soul as well as outside the window. A whole lot of dark. They'd delivered the ransom as promised, then retreated to the motel room as instructed. Would they ever be able to pay back the fifty thousand to her parents? If it brought Zack back, she didn't care. She bit her lip. It was a terrible thing to be praying that your child had been kidnapped instead of eaten by a wild animal. The clock ticked off two minutes more. She rolled over so she wouldn't have to watch it.

"I can't believe they brought in the feebs so fast," Fred muttered half under his breath.

"I'm glad they did," Jenny said. "The FBI knows how to handle these things."

"You should get some rest," Fred told her in a low voice. "Sweetheart," he added, as if it were an afterthought. "I'll go out in a little while and see what's happening. Go to sleep."

How she'd welcome the nothingness of sleep! If only the blackness would roll in and erase the images that looped through her mind. Over and over, she replayed last night at the campsite.

The shadow creeping across the valley, cutting short the October day. Fussing with that nasty old camp stove. Fred off gathering firewood. Zack playing on the rock ledge. That horrible cougar warning poster fluttering in the breeze. A mosquito's whine. The cawing of crows against the background static of the river across the road.

And then the bare rock ledge, an orange toy truck the only sign that her baby had ever been there. She running, shouting Zack's name from campsite to campsite, alone with her horror. Why had it taken Fred so long to come?

She turned her head and cried softly into the pillow. "Zack!"

THE FBI agents cruised the last block to the Burger House without benefit of headlights. Nicole eased the car into the shadow of a massive oak tree a half block away from the fast-food outlet. She turned off the ignition.

Perez pulled a pair of binoculars from the glove compartment, scanned the hotel. Nicole kept her gaze on the garbage can outside the front door of the Burger House. She twirled a strand of hair impatiently around her index finger. "See anything?"

The neon VACANCY sign and a yellow bulb over the office door were the only lights visible at the Wagon Wheel Motel. "Half the rooms have the curtains parted," he said. "Including yours. And mine." He shifted the binoculars. "At least ten different parties could be keeping an eye on the Burger House. I can't see anyone."

Nicole straightened. "Shit, is that a rat?"

A rounded shape scuttled toward the garbage can, climbed the ribbed sides of the metal container, and nosed its way inside through the swinging flap. "Yep," he confirmed as a long tail snaked through the crack. "Think it's looking for the ransom?"

A second furball crept out of the shadows toward the garbage can. "There's another one." She clapped a hand over her mouth as if she might gag.

Perez stifled a smile. His partner preferred animals stuffed and mounted in museums. He suspected that Westin woman he'd met this afternoon would say the same about people. Especially Californians.

He scanned the hotel again. The Fischers' Sidekick was back in place in front of their room; all was dark. The only movement was a large moth, intent on battering itself to death against the light outside the hotel office.

Wearing latex gloves, Nicole peeled back the flap of the manila envelope they'd recovered from the boys' pickup, slid the sheaves of money out, and carefully placed the envelope into a large plastic evidence bag. She fanned the bills in her lap with her fingers.

"All there?"

"Looks like it," she said. As she reached the middle of the stack of bills, she gasped, then picked up another and divided it in the middle. "The idiots didn't do the sandwich like I told them; they put in the whole fifty thousand!"

He shrugged. "Parents do strange things when their kids are involved."

She slid the money into another plastic bag and zipped it closed. "I'm putting this in the hotel safe; we'll get it back to Jenny's parents tomorrow."

"Speaking of tomorrow." Perez checked his watch. "It's a quarter till two." He yawned. "Looks like we're not going to see any more action tonight. Either the boys pulled this off themselves or the guy that hired them knows about their arrest."

"Damn. I hate small towns." She sighed. "Still, for one night we haven't done too badly. I love busting dumb punks."

KENT Bergstrom stood at the rim of Jade Pool, the last unexplored area in his search quadrant. Moon and stars shimmered in the still, dark water. In summer, the rangers had a hard time keeping swimmers out of the pocket of crystal liquid. Now, at the end of the dry season, the water was not so clear or so high, but it was still deep enough to conceal a two-year-old. It was a long shot, more than five miles up the trail, but they'd decided to extend the search to six miles out tonight. They'd examine every mesquite bush until they found that kid. Or determined that Zack wasn't in the park at all, which was Kent's growing suspicion. Something was up in town; the FBI agents and Superintendent Thompson had been closeted for a half hour, waving around some fax that they didn't share with lowly wildlife rangers.

He stripped off his service belt and radio, then peeled off his boots and socks. No sense in soaking them as well. He sighed, took a deep breath, and waded in. Damnation! The water was just as cold as he'd thought it would be. The drop-off was steep; he gasped as he stepped off into a deep spot. Searching for lost kids was not how he'd envisioned his career. But jobs for wildlife biologists were few: you either worked for the government or for a zoo. Except in rare cases like Sam, who seemed to be doing all right with her wildlife photos and stories.

Well, he couldn't write or even spell worth a damn, so this ranger job had better work out for him. He shuffled to the center of the pool, where the water was up to his waist, sliding his bare feet carefully over the moss-slick bottom, moving his hands under the water's surface.

"Zack?" he asked the ripples around him. *Fool.* If Zack were in here, he wouldn't be capable of answering. Something slid across his toes, floated away. He bent and felt the bottom with his hands. A newt, maybe? Frog? No fish inhabited Jade Pool. His fingers closed around a long slick, gloppy piece of—? He pulled it up. Thank God. No smell of decay, no waterlogged skin or limp flesh. Only a sock, once white, now green with moss. And big enough to fit on his own foot. After taking a final turn around the pool, he waded out, put the sock in his trash bag before starting the long hike down the mountain. If he was lucky, he could catch a couple hours' sleep in his truck before he had to begin his next shift.

The calls of volunteers grew louder as he descended. "Zack! Zachary!" Sort of mesmerizing, those voices echoing back and forth in the cool blackness. Pack horses had been known to fall asleep on familiar trails, and he felt as if he might likewise nod off at any minute. However, he doubted that his feet would continue to plod along like those horses'. More likely, he'd fall right off over the edge, land on those two girls from Rescue 504 down there just off the trail. As he passed, the chunky one raised a whistle to her lips and puffed out an ear-shattering blast.

Wide awake now, Kent stepped off the trail and slid down to their position. More footsteps and panting noises signaled the approach of other searchers, human and animal.

"Look!" The heavyset girl held her flashlight perpendicular to the ground. Highlighted in the beam was a tiny dust-covered sneaker. Kent's breath caught in his throat.

"Wasn't Zachary wearing sneakers?" she asked.

"Yeah." Kent stared at the tiny shoe. "Red ones, just like this."

SAM was taking her second shower in twenty-four hours when she heard the toilet flush in the bathroom next door. She felt it as well: a surge of scalding water suddenly lashed her from the showerhead. Jamming a hand over her mouth to stifle a yelp, she turned off the tap and stepped out of the tub.

If Perez was back, then everything was under control. For now. She hadn't heard anything from the Fischers' room. Surely there'd be celebrations if Zack was back. Oh God, did that mean he was dead? First light, she'd be out there finding out exactly what had happened.

A second later the shower started on the other side of the wall. Was that the squeak of a bare foot stepping into the bathtub? She waited another second, then flushed her toilet.

"Aaargh!" The thump against the wall was probably Perez's elbow or knee. She smiled.

Her father's voice surged into her thoughts. *You should be ashamed of yourself, Summer.* As penance, she tried hard not to envision what Agent Chase J. Perez looked like without clothes. Yawning, she slipped into bed.

At four thirty A.M., the shrill bleat of the phone next door woke her. She rose, pressed the drinking glass to the wall.

"You're sure it's his." Perez's voice was now a weary octave deeper. A rustle: he was taking notes. "Powell Trail—where's that?" Several um-hums, then he said, "First thing after daylight." A slight hesitation, then, "No, second thing. It'll be midmorning. Bag that shoe." The click of the receiver in its cradle, a word grumbled in Spanish, then the creak of springs again.

Sounded like the searchers had found a shoe on Powell Trail in the park. Zack's shoe? She rubbed her forehead. Did that mean the ransomers were holding Zack in the park? She was too tired to think. Tomorrow would be soon enough to find out. Heck, it *was* tomorrow. But dawn was still a couple of hours away, and if the FBI was going back to bed, then she was, too. She crawled back between the sheets.

8

IT was nearly eight thirty when Sam awoke. The room next door was silent; Perez was gone. She couldn't believe she had snored through his exit. Why hadn't she set the alarm?

She quickly checked the TV morning shows. Every station was still hinting that Zack was killed by a cougar. The telephone line at park HQ was busy. She worked up the courage to go back online. First the SWF site. They'd wisely chosen to lead with a video clip from KUTV News 9 in which Assistant Superintendent Meg Tanner stated, "The entire valley has been searched twice, and we've found no evidence of a cougar attack on Zachary Fischer." The two-second segment must have aired on the news before she'd tuned in; she didn't remember it.

Her story about the continuing search for Zack seemed tepid in comparison to the inflammatory stories on other sites, particularly one named Sane World, which featured a video clip from KUTV News 9, with Jenny Fischer on the screen. "We didn't know that our baby was in such danger," she sobbed. The video was set up to loop: the voice and image played over and over. "We didn't know our baby was in such danger . . . We didn't know our baby was in such danger . . ." Sam clicked the Stop button to end the wrenching repetition. The video was labeled as having come from YouTube. *Great.*

Sane World's website included a photo of the MISSING poster with Zack's face, and an article that made her hyperventilate after the first paragraph.

SWF Aware of Cougar Danger at Campground

Wilderness Westin, star reporter for the Save the Wilderness Fund, proudly stated on the group's new website that a large male cougar was known to frequent the area in which two-year-old Zachary Fischer disappeared less than forty-eight hours ago.

The SWF organization has consistently put the lives of wild animals above those of people. This—

Her cell phone bleeped. "Anything new, babe?" Adam asked.

She gritted her teeth. But maybe by giving him something, she could refocus the television coverage. "There's a rumor of a ransom attempt for Zack," she said. Maybe that would get Adam and the rest of the news hounds off the cougar track.

"Not much I can do with a rumor."

"Seems like you ran with the rumor about cougars, Adam."

"That's different; there were the warning posters and the quote from the mom."

"All I can say is that the local police and the FBI were chasing a couple of kids last night and it had something to do with Zack Fischer."

"Really? I'll check it out. Guess what? They've extended my anchor gig, I'm on again today from noon to midnight."

"I'm thrilled for you."

He failed to notice her sarcasm. "Thanks," he said. "What are you going to do today?"

She snorted. "Damage control. And oh yeah, I think I might help look for the missing kid."

"Be careful out there. Keep in touch. The second you find out anything new, let me have it, okay? Bye, babe."

She called Lauren, got her voice mail, left a message to keep the faith, that she would find a way to fix this. She checked the park phone line again. Still busy. Kent's cell phone went straight to voice mail, so she wasn't going to get any news from him.

Hurriedly packing her gear, she checked out and picked up a cup of coffee to go at the café, feeling the eyes of the locals burning into her back as she waited at the counter. She hoped that was paranoia: how many of them knew she was Wilderness Westin, star reporter for SWF?

A handful of people, five adults and a couple of kids, blocked the south gate into the park. A woman held a sign that read PROTECT CHILDREN, NOT COUGERS. One of the children carried another—SAVE A CHILD, SHOOT A MOUNTAIN LION. The other kid wore double cowboy-style holsters with weapons that Sam prayed were plastic.

She honked. The group didn't budge.

In her rearview mirror Sam saw the KUTV News 9 van angle onto the shoulder behind her. Carolyn Perry, microphone already in hand, stepped out of the vehicle, the driver-cameraman hard on her heels.

The arrival of the press emboldened the protesters. The placard-carrying woman bounced her sign up and down, glaring at Sam's Civic like a shepherd threatening a recalcitrant sheep. *Why me?* Sam thought. Then it came to her: the SWF sticker on the windshield.

The reporter hurried in her direction. Sam pressed the gas pedal; the Civic lurched forward a couple of feet. The protesters bleated and scattered. She couldn't resist speaking to the placard-carrying woman. "Get a dictionary, lady, and learn how to spell."

As she drove away, she heard a loud thump. She checked

the rearview mirror and saw the woman raise her mangled sign from the back of the Civic.

At park headquarters, Zack's poster was taped onto the front door. So they hadn't found him.

"Hang in there, Zack," she whispered. *Wherever you are.*

A table in the lobby was laden with a large coffee urn, homemade sweet breads, a plate of sandwiches, and several boxes of cookies. The work of church ladies. The same food miracle occurred during every crisis in the small town where she'd been raised.

The reception desk was empty. Sam helped herself to a hunk of pumpkin bread. Zack watched from a poster across the room. A map on the wall was partially cross-hatched, and she walked closer to study it. Like Tanner had said in that news clip, search crews had double-checked all areas close to Red Rock Campground. In the section she had searched yesterday, red backslashes crisscrossed the black lines, and red initials, RC, appeared in the lower corner next to SW, which someone had scrawled in black marker on her behalf. RC had to mean that Rafael Castillo had either preceded or followed her in the same sector. Good. The law enforcement officer wasn't likely to miss much. She hoped he'd interviewed Wilson.

An *X* and the word *Shoe* marked a location about four miles up Powell Trail. She frowned. It was a steep, rocky climb. Impossible for a two-year-old to walk there by himself. And the Powell Trailhead was at least three-quarters of a mile from Goodman Trail parking lot, where she'd last seen Zack.

Sam ventured into the hallway, heard the faint voices of the FBI agents, with a man and woman responding. Perez and Boudreaux were questioning the Fischers. She pressed herself to the wall beside the threshold. Although the door was closed, the conversation was audible. Not exactly eavesdropping, she told herself.

Agent Boudreaux expressed sympathy that the ransom note and subsequent arrests hadn't solved the case. "We're still looking, but so far there's no evidence that these boys ever saw Zack."

"Why would somebody *do* something like that?" Jenny wailed.

A man cleared his throat, then said, "For the money." Fred Fischer.

"That money," Jenny said, "Where is it?"

"It's safe. We'll return it to your parents, Mrs. Fischer," Perez said.

"*We* were the ones who asked for it," Fred said. "We should be the ones to return it. They'll be expecting that."

"This is standard FBI procedure, Mr. Fischer." Boudreaux's smooth tone again.

"But . . ." Jenny's voice broke, forcing her to pause before she continued, "If the kidnapper doesn't get the money, won't he . . . In that note, he said . . . Oh, no, won't he . . ."

"The money would not have kept Zachary safe," Boudreaux told her. "We don't believe that your child was kidnapped for ransom."

"But," Jenny began again, "if not for money, then what? Oh, God—" Her words stopped and a wretched sobbing began.

"We suspect the ransom note was sent by someone who saw the story on the news and wanted to take advantage of your situation. We're still hoping that Zack is merely lost, Mrs. Fischer," Perez said. "But it's our job to consider all the possibilities."

For a moment, Sam heard only Jenny's stifled sobs. Then Perez asked, "What made you come to this park, Mr. Fischer?"

Again, the throat clearing first, then, "I wanted to get away from the city. I wanted to show Jenny and Zachary this place."

"So you know the park?"

"Sure. My family used to come here all the time when I was a kid. We lived in Orem until I was eighteen."

"I see." Sam pictured Perez thumbing through notepad pages.

Boudreaux took the offensive. "We've come across some disturbing information."

"About . . . about Zack?" Jenny's voice quivered with pain. Sam hoped Fred had his arm around her.

"No, ma'am. This is in regard to Mr. Fischer's record."

Fred immediately blurted, "That's completely irrelevant!"

A rustle of paper, then Perez's voice. "You were arrested six years back for striking your previous wife?"

"That was a lifetime ago." Fred stumbled on the words. "I drank then. Now I'm sober; now I'm in AA."

Perez pressed on. "At the time of your arrest, hadn't you also kicked your four-year-old stepdaughter?"

A sob from Jenny. "Fred would never do that!"

Fred's voice, a controlled snarl. "Beverly said that. It wasn't true."

More shuffling of papers. In a flat tone, Boudreaux read, "An examination of Elizabeth Snow, four years of age, revealed bruises on buttocks and rib cage. When questioned about her injuries, the girl said, 'Daddy kicked me.'"

Tense silence followed. Sam imagined Fred Fischer squirming in his chair before he answered. "I tripped over her on the stairs. Like I said, I'd been drinking. It was an accident." A swish of clothing, a squeak of leather indicating a shift of position. "I loved that little girl like she was my own."

"And where is Elizabeth now?"

"How the hell would I know? *Step*daughter, remember? I don't have any rights."

"That's right, she wasn't your child." The briefest of pauses, a crinkle that could have been the turning of a page. "And Zachary's not your child, either. Isn't he adopted?"

"Yes." Fred again. "Jen can't have children, so we adopted Zack. What's the big deal?"

Perez said, "Maybe you're regretting the thirty thousand dollars you spent on the adoption?"

A chair leg scraped the floor. "How the hell—? You have no goddamn right!" Fred had definitely lost his temper.

"Zack's still young enough that many couples would be willing to adopt him. And they'd probably pay more than thirty thousand," Perez said, his voice calm.

Thirty thousand dollars? With their ancient rusting Suzuki and their cheap clothes, the Fischers didn't look like they had two cents to rub together. But maybe the original adoption fee came from Jenny's parents, too.

"Frankly," Perez added, "I'm surprised you qualified to be adoptive parents. Especially you, Mr. Fischer. Not only is there your previous record, but I see here that you don't work regularly. You've been a house painter, worked at a lumber mill. And now you're driving a truck?"

"I've been a truck driver for five years. I drive all over the West."

"But you've changed employers three times in five years?"

Fischer interrupted. "I'm independent. I've got my own rig: I work for whoever gives me the contracts. That's the way the trucking business works. Got it?"

Neither agent responded. Fischer continued, "I work all the time. Ask Jen, she's always whining about me being on the road! Not everyone can go to some pansy college, you know. Some of us have to do *real* work for a living."

Another muffled sob from Jenny.

"Don't try to make something out of this that it's not." Fischer angrily bit off his words. "I'm a good worker. And a good father. I loved Lizzie then, and I love Zack now."

"Aren't there times when you'd like to strike your adopted son?"

"No!" Jenny cried. "Fred would never hit Zack!"

"Where was Fred when Zachary first disappeared, Mrs. Fischer?" Agent Boudreaux's voice.

Tense silence.

"Gathering wood," supplied Fred.

"Yes, he was off in the trees, gathering wood for the fire," Jenny echoed. "I was making our supper. Fred was crashing around, sounding like a moose—"

"For chrissake, Jen, they don't need to hear every damned detail."

"Zack had already eaten, he was—" Her words were drowned by another sob.

"Mrs. Fischer, how long after you noticed Zachary was missing did your husband show up?"

"What *is* this?" Fred's tone rose in pitch. "I came as soon as I heard Jenny shouting."

What were they getting at? Sam remembered hearing the man's voice, shouting for Zack, only minutes after hearing the woman's. The man had been close to the Goodman Trail parking lot. Maybe Fred had seen the little boy go down the trail and gone after him, unbeknownst to Jenny? And then what?

"How long, Mrs. Fischer?" Boudreaux pressed.

"I don't know," sniffed Jenny. "It seemed like a long time."

"It was only a few minutes!" Fred interjected. "Then I started searching for him, too. I was the one who called the ranger station at six thirty."

"We have a report of Zachary in the Goodman Trailhead lot around five forty-five."

"Where's that?" Jenny asked.

A paper rustled, no doubt a map. "Here," Boudreaux said.

"There?" Fred asked. "By the river? Wasn't there something on the news about a cougar by that river? And wasn't that where that guy found Zack's baseball cap? Did he say he saw Zack there?"

"No, it was a woman." Perez's voice again. "She reported that Zack ran back down the path back toward the campground. Toward you, Mr. Fischer. And that you waved to her."

"I remember that woman now. But not from any parking lot. That never happened. I don't know anything about any parking lot." Fred's voice held not a shred of doubt. "We looked all over, then we called the ranger station at what, six fifteen?"

"Six twenty-nine," Perez verified.

"The first time I saw that woman was yesterday morning, at the campground. And she was at the café last night, too. Like she was following us. Silver-blond hair. And she's real short."

Sam bristled. She preferred the word *petite*.

Jenny chimed in. "She said that Zack would be fine. Like she *knew*." Her voice sounded simultaneously hopeful and suspicious.

Fred's tone grew louder. "Maybe *she's* got Zack! You should be checking *her* out."

"We're checking everyone," Boudreaux assured them.

The pumpkin bread turned to heavy clay in Sam's stomach. *She* was a suspect?

Perez asked, "Were you two together all night after Zachary disappeared?"

"No," Fred explained. "We split up. So we could search faster."

"Where did you search, Mrs. Fischer?" Boudreaux's tone was softer now.

"I didn't really . . . I stayed at the campsite, thinking maybe Zack would—"

"And you, Mr. Fischer?"

"I took the Suzuki, around eleven or so. I drove around the campground, calling him."

"Just around the campground? Do you mean the ring road?"

"When I didn't find Zack there, I drove the road by the river, too. All the way to the end of the valley, then back."

"What time did you return?"

"Christ, I don't know. Three A.M., maybe? You can ask the rangers: they were all out there, too."

"Mr. Fischer, did you make your son disappear the night before last?" Perez's tone was cold, clinical.

Gasps from Jenny. "Oh God, no!"

Fred's voice cracked. "Hell no, of course not! What's wrong with you people? We're not the criminals here, we're the victims! Zack's the victim!"

"And we're working on finding him," Perez said. "Did you go straight to the hotel from the park yesterday afternoon?"

"I took Jenny to the hotel and then I went to the police station."

Another rustle of paper. "Our records show you checked

in at twelve forty-five P.M. but you didn't show up at the
police station until almost two thirty."

"I took a walk—is that against the law now?" Fred's
anger was unmistakable.

"Not at all," Agent Boudreaux said soothingly. "Do you
remember the route you took?"

"Hell no. I don't know this dump of a town. Some sort
of circle, I guess. My mind was occupied with Zack."

"Of course. Thank you for your cooperation, Mr. and
Mrs. Fischer," Nicole Boudreaux's tone was smooth, cor-
dial. "I have one more question—have either of you had
contact with Zachary's birth parents?"

Silence hung heavily for a few seconds before Jenny
responded, her voice wavering as she struggled to control
her emotions. "No . . ." She sounded perplexed. "Our lawyer arranged the whole thing. We don't even know who
they are. Why?"

Agent Boudreaux ignored the question. "Mr. Fischer?"

"Don't know 'em."

A notepad slapped shut. "Then that about sums it up for
now. There's just one more thing. We'll need pictures of
both of you."

"What the hell for?" barked Fred.

Perez answered. "Standard procedure. We can take a
couple now."

"I have one of Fred and me and Zack in my billfold,"
Jenny volunteered. "Would that work?" A creak followed
by rustling noises proved that she was pulling it out. "They
used it for the . . . for the poster."

"This is fine," Boudreaux assured her. "You wait at the
hotel. We'll let you know as soon as we discover anything
more."

"But what about the shoe?" Jenny asked, her voice trem-
bling. "The rangers said they found Zack's shoe. What
does that mean?"

"We'll let you know as soon as we discover anything
more," Boudreaux said again.

Scuffling sounds indicated that all parties were rising to

leave. Sam quickly strode down the hallway and ducked into a big locker room.

A young woman in National Park Service uniform sat on a bench before an open locker. She blinked at Sam in surprise. Shiny black blunt-cut hair, delicate Asian features. Vietnamese, or maybe Korean.

"Can I help you?" The accent was Southern Bible Belt, a startling contrast with the woman's features. The voice on the phone. Ranger Gates. Sam had envisioned a buxom Southern belle with poufy tresses.

"I'm looking for Kent Bergstrom," Sam said hopefully. Poor Kent; she used their friendship to explain her bumbling all over the park.

Georgia pointed at a doorway off the locker room.

Kent knelt on the floor of the equipment room, pushing packets of freeze-dried meals into the pockets of a well-worn nylon park service backpack. A chocolate-chip cookie protruded from between his lips. A stuffed sleeping bag lay on the floor beside his knees as well as several quart-sized water bottles.

"Hitting the trail?"

He removed the cookie. "Mesa Camp, here I come! Am I ever ready."

He had shadows under his eyes. "You look tired," she said.

"That would be because I've been up all night. But this will revive me."

"Heading up Powell Trail?"

"Nope," he said. "Been there, done that, last night. They're sending me up the East Ridge Trail and over the top. Backcountry patrol. Blue skies, birds, clear air."

"They can spare you from the search party? I'd think they'd be even more focused now that there's some real evidence that Zack's in the park."

"They're still searching around the shoe site. Hey, if Thompson wants to give me a break, I'm taking it."

Soul mate, Sam thought. Trouble had always sent her running for the woods, too, even as a young child.

A cloud passed over his face. "I hope they find him. But it's going on two days now."

"He could still be alive, Kent."

He shrugged. "You think a two-year-old could walk up Powell Trail?"

"Not by himself. Maybe someone carried him." Which, she dared to think, meant Zack was most likely still alive.

He yawned, scratched at the stubble on his cheeks. "Thompson's getting out more helicopters today. Maybe they'll spot something from the air." He looked up. "Georgia Gates told me about Buck Ferguson on Special Report last night. That damn jerk! But I hear that some asshole in Seattle sabotaged you first."

What would Kent think if he knew she'd been dating the asshole who started the whole cougar hysteria? She hoped nobody in the park would discover *that* association. "I saw Ferguson on the news earlier," she said. "The stuffed heads behind him were a nice touch."

Kent jammed a package of freeze-dried food a little harder than necessary into his pack. "I'd like to stuff *his* head! We've seen him carrying rifles in the park three times just this year."

"Well, you be careful. There will be more nutcases out there with weapons. Speaking of weapons," she said, "where's yours?"

"I hate guns, you know that." He zipped up a pocket. "Thompson's been wanting to send me to law enforcement training, and so far I've said no. But now that the yahoos in Washington gave their blessing for the whole world to carry guns around the park, I'm beginning to think that it might not be a bad idea to carry a pistol. For the people, not the animals."

"Just bury them deep, at least a hundred yards away from trails and water sources."

They both laughed; it was the standard instruction for handling human waste. "I'm on my way up Powell," she said.

"Good. Maybe *you* can prove that Apollo didn't carry the

kid up there." He stood up, hefted the backpack, snapped shut the buckle of his waist strap.

"Hey, Kent, did you hear the forecast?"

"Cold front rolling in slowly from the west. Scattered showers predicted late Saturday night or early Sunday morning."

She tried to visualize the calendar.

"This is Thursday," he added helpfully.

"And you call *me* a smart-ass. Keep an eye out," she said. "You don't want to be caught on the mesa in a thunderstorm."

"Don't worry, Mom." Kent raised both arms, flexed to make his biceps bulge. "I'm Superman."

"Don't forget your radio, man of steel." She held it out.

He clipped it to his belt, beside a large canister of pepper spray. Liquids inside his pack sloshed as he turned. "I'm outta here."

"Just remember—"

"Bury 'em deep!" he shouted as he slipped out the back door.

"Be careful, you fool," she murmured.

She exited the crew room. As she scooted past the park superintendent's office, she caught a quick glimpse of Thompson, Tanner, and the FBI agents gathered around the desk inside. The Fischers were gone.

In the reception area, Ranger Gates was on the phone. Assistant Superintendent Tanner came into the room, spotted Sam. Her brow instantly bunched up into a frown. Sam pulled the Rescue 504 kerchief and armband out of her pocket and pressed them into the woman's hands. "Just wanted to return these, Meg."

The woman's expression softened. "Thanks for helping out."

Sam opened the door to the whock-whock-whock of a helicopter passing by. As she slid into her Civic, a familiar white van pulled in next to her space. KUTV News 9. Carolyn Perry climbed out of the front passenger's seat. Did that woman never rest? Several other people with a variety of equipment spilled out of the back, including Buck Ferguson, who was dressed today all in khaki, except for a VFW flag on his collar and a black Eagle Tours baseball cap. He held a hunting rifle casually in one hand. The crew immediately set up for a shoot, taking no notice of Sam sitting in her car.

"Get Superintendent Thompson out here," Perry commanded a woman holding a clipboard. The minion disappeared into the building.

The reporter positioned Ferguson next to her, then signaled for the camera to roll.

"Two-year-old Zack Fischer has been missing for two nights and a day now. We're here in front of Heritage National Monument Headquarters to find out what's happening. With me is Buck Ferguson, local wildlife expert. Mr. Ferguson, why do you think the search is taking so long?"

Ferguson made a big show of engaging the safety on his rifle before parking it under his elbow and focusing on the camera. "The FBI is spending all of its time persecuting the kid's parents instead of focusing on the real culprits."

The reporter edged her face closer to his. "You believe that cougars are the real culprits?"

Sam admired the woman's technique. Carolyn Perry was always careful not to state a personal opinion of her own.

"That's right. That's why they're not going to find him: no little kid could survive a cougar attack." Ferguson looked at the reporter for the first time. "Since the government outlawed hunting here, the mountain lions have multiplied like rabbits. They're a menace to society."

Thompson burst from the ranger station, right into Carolyn's ambush. "Superintendent Thompson!" She shoved the microphone under his nose. "Some have made allegations that you have killer cougars in your park. Do you plan to do anything about these animals?"

He swallowed and turned toward the camera. "I've just been on the phone with the USDA's Wildlife Services branch."

Sam's jaw dropped.

"If we find evidence of a cougar attack on the missing child, hunters will be dispatched to take care of the problem."

The reporter, surprised, was speechless for once. Buck Ferguson nodded, looking pleased with himself.

"Official hunters," Thompson hastened to add. "Government-sanctioned hunters."

The smile disappeared from Ferguson's face. "And how long will we have to wait for that?" he spat in the direction of the microphone.

Ignoring him, Thompson reiterated, "And only if we find sufficient evidence of a cougar attack."

A blue van with the logo of an NBC affiliate from Las Vegas rolled into the space on the other side of Sam's Civic, people pouring out of its doors even before the engine had stopped. Thompson, eyeing this arrival with panic, quickly turned and strode back toward the ranger station. Perry smiled gleefully at her competitors as they rushed past in hot pursuit of the park superintendent.

Sam rolled up her window and backed out of her spot. Strange how the reporter hadn't mentioned the arrest of the two teens last night. She could think of three possibilities: one, the TV crew didn't know about the event, which seemed unlikely in such a slow news area; two, another reporter was covering that angle of the story; or three, they didn't want to divert attention from the killer-cougar theory. She hoped for scenario number two.

The meadow across from the Powell Trail parking lot held a small red and white helicopter. A man sat in the pilot's seat, clipboard in hand.

She quickly stowed her laptop and food packets in her backpack, hoping she'd be well up the trail before the mechanical beast started up. While it was wonderful to have air support in the search for Zack, she knew how the machines terrified the animals in the park. She'd once seen a buck leap off a cliff when a helicopter buzzed him. Wildlife and helicopters did not mix.

The MISSING poster had been taped over the trailhead

signpost: she had to lift it out of the way to grab a registration card from the stack beneath. The poster also obscured
one of the park service postings about cougars in the area.
Someone had spray-painted a red *X* over the cougar notice.
Blood-colored rivulets dripped down from the *X*. Damn.
She touched a finger to one of the thin streaks. It came
away wet. She lowered the poster to cover the disturbing
image, noting with horror that she'd left a smudge of scarlet
across Zachary's cheek.

She was penciling her license number and destination
on the registration card when Agent Perez bounded up, a
gray-green park service knapsack over one shoulder.

"Wilderness Westin, I presume. Blogger extraordinaire.
And television star."

Sam snorted. "I am not a blogger! And the television
coverage," she said, "was not *my* idea."

This morning Perez's FBI badge hung from the pocket
of a dark blue flannel shirt, which was tucked into a leather
belt with an Indian design. In less than twenty-four hours,
she'd seen him in a suit and wingtips, a black sweatshirt
and jeans, and now he sported khakis and leather boots
with deep lug soles. Did FBI agents carry an outfit for
every occasion?

"Do I pass?" He plucked off his badge, flipped the wallet closed, tucked it into a back pocket of his trousers.

She turned her gaze back to the card. "Depends on what
you're up to."

He shrugged. "Hiking." Over her shoulder, he read her
scribbled destination. "OT near Sunset Canyon. OT?"

"Off trail." She pointed at the orange tag that dangled
from her shoulder strap. "I have a special permit to travel
cross-country."

"Trails not interesting enough for you?"

"Like I told you, I write about wildlife. There's more
wildlife off the trails."

"Why did you choose this particular route this morning?" He shrugged off the borrowed knapsack, knelt, and

rummaged through the pockets. He wore a pistol holstered on his right hip.

"I heard at the ranger station that Zack's shoe was found on this trail."

"And what do you intend to do with that information?" He extracted a gray-brown felt wad from his knapsack, slapped it on his leg, then crammed the crushed fedora onto his head. A raven-haired Indiana Jones.

She pressed her lips together to keep from laughing. When her voice was under control, she said, "I just want to have a look around, see if there's any evidence of cougars."

"We're running an investigation up there. We don't need amateurs mucking up the scene."

She smiled. "I happen to know that dozens of volunteers have already mucked up your scene."

His expression darkened.

"I'll stay out of your way," she promised. "Did you check out those tips I gave you yesterday?"

"We check everything."

"The weird camper—Wilson?"

"No criminal history; no warrants on vehicle or owner."

Darn. "How about the baseball cap?"

"Mrs. Fischer confirmed that Zack had one like it; Mr. Wilson confirmed that he found it down by the river and that he washed it." Perez's clear brown eyes bored into hers. "You're taking an awfully personal interest in this case, Ms. Westin."

"Remember, I saw Zack the night he disappeared. I was not mistaken about the man I saw—there was definitely a man at the end of the path, Agent Perez. And he definitely waved. But I still don't know if it was Fred Fischer or Weird Wilson or someone else."

She shoved her permit card into the box. "And now I know that someone carried Zachary Fischer up this trail."

"Or some*thing*."

"You didn't sound like you suspected a cougar when you were grilling the parents at park headquarters this morning."

Lifting one black eyebrow, he assessed her coolly for a long moment. If Special Agent Chase J. Perez were an animal, she thought, he'd be an owl. Or maybe a hawk. A sharp-eyed creature that knew how to bide its time. Finally he said, "That door was closed."

She shrugged. "Flimsy government construction. I have exceptional hearing. And I know an interrogation when I hear one."

"We call them interviews."

"Sounded like you were interviewing those poor parents pretty hard."

"Standard procedure. A lot of supposed kidnappings are murders or fatal accidents covered up by relatives."

She remembered Fred's growl at the restaurant: *Leave me alone*. The man had been downright hostile. "Fischer could have lied about seeing me on the path because he didn't want anyone to know that he'd taken Zack." She thought for a minute about the timing. "There wasn't enough time for him to carry Zack up the trail before going back to the campsite and reporting him missing, but he could have handed him off to someone else."

Perez shrugged. "Or hidden the corpse and then carried it up the trail later during the night."

Sam winced. "Why would anyone carry a body so far? He could have driven it anywhere."

Perez shook his head. "Rangers at the gates were checking cars. And we're not necessarily looking for rational behavior here. People do weird things with corpses."

She wasn't ready to visualize Zack as a corpse yet. "On the other hand, if Fischer didn't take him, those boys last night could really have kidnapped him."

Perez looked startled. Behind them, the helicopter's engine whined, beginning its warm-up.

"It's a small town, Perez; you can't keep anything secret. Everybody knows about the arrests," she said over the racket. She added hopefully, "If it's a kidnapping, that would mean that someone has Zack, that he's still alive."

"Unlikely. The boys were rank amateurs, and there's been no further word from the supposed kidnapper. Right now, it looks like a couple of local teenagers decided to cash in on Zachary's disappearance. But we're keeping our minds open to all possibilities. Which, by the way, I would suggest you do as well."

"Meaning?"

"Meaning that the ransom-without-kidnapping scenario would work just as well if a cougar dragged the boy off."

She hitched up her pack. The din of helicopter blades whock-whocketed through the atmosphere. Turning, she glared at the infernal noisemaker and noted that the blue van had pulled up near it. A reporter with a battery-powered microphone and a female camera operator waited just clear of the helicopter, expectantly looking their way.

Perez spotted them. "Drat."

Sam smiled and shouted over the racket, "Have a nice day, Agent Perez."

He leaned close, wafting a whiff of a citruslike fragrance her way. Lime aftershave? "Stay out of trouble," he said into her ear. Retrieving his knapsack, he trotted toward the chopper, studiously ignoring the reporter and camera.

As the helicopter rose, Sam plugged her ears with her fingers. It quickly disappeared through the trees overhead. Perez would be at the shoe site within minutes. With a groan of self-pity, she started up the trail.

The two-way radio rasped static from her pack's side pocket. Tanner, informing park personnel that a suspicious vehicle had entered through the north gate. Two men, two dogs in a pickup with an empty rifle rack. "Everyone keep a lookout for these guys, just in case they have those guns with them. Utah license, TYG 898."

So it begins. Why weren't these macho types volunteering to search for the child instead of picking up their weapons? Zack could be huddled under a bush somewhere up above, dehydrated, hungry, alone. Not nearly enough people were looking for him. It hadn't even been two whole

days, and people were ready to believe that the little boy
had been eaten by a cougar. Even Perez.

And Thompson was already buckling under pressure,
promising to call in USDAWS. How would the government
hunters decide which mountain lion was the perpetrator?

She'd shown everyone the cougars, up close and personal.
She'd identified the rock bridge in the photo. And then Adam
had broadcast it to the world. They'd wait for the cats in Sunset Canyon. She'd even told the world that Apollo had been
to the river, so close to the campground. They'd be after the
male cub. But they'd shoot any cougar they could find. And
probably more than one. And none of the bloodshed would
help Zachary Fischer. She blamed herself for being so specific. And damned Adam for using it against her.

NEARLY two hours later, she spotted Perez's lanky silhouette at Dripping Rock. The place was a welcome oasis,
where the air was cool, damp, and soft to the skin, re-
freshing after miles of intense sun. A hanging garden of
chartreuse lichen and maidenhair ferns spilled down the
limestone wall, dripping beads of moisture into the fine
sand below.

Perez blocked the trail, one foot up on the rock ledge
that bordered the drop-off. The crease in his trousers was
still sharp, she noted with irritation. Hers were streaked
with red dust. Sweat stained the armpits of her turquoise
T-shirt. Strands of hair had glued themselves to her sticky
forehead; she wiped them out of her face.

"This where Zack's shoe was found?" she asked.

He jerked a thumb toward a location up the trail. "Up
there."

Uncapping her water bottle, she sipped the lukewarm
liquid and surveyed the terrain. The cottonwoods and willows lining the valley floor were at the height of their brief
color show. They'd be brown in two weeks, and then leaf-
less within a month. The river was a shining ribbon, green
against the red rocks that rose beside the water. October

was her favorite month in the high desert: crisp mornings, sunny afternoons, golden leaves of cottonwoods and aspens glowing among the evergreens.

"Nice scenery." Perez's voice was wistful. Turning, he motioned her to follow him up the trail. "Come on. I've got something I need a wildlife expert to look at."

9

SAM and Perez rounded one of many switchbacks that zigzagged up the cliffside. Above them, high-pitched voices
called Zack's name. Rescue 504, still hard at work.

The rocky slope dropped off steeply from the trail,
broken here and there by cactus and mesquite and an occasional courageous juniper that had taken root in a crack.
Perez stopped twenty feet above a yucca that bore a flag of
orange tape. He stepped over the stones that marked the
trail's edge and slid down the slope, motioning her to
follow.

She discarded her pack, then sidestepped down to join
him beside the yucca.

"Is this cougar poop?" He pointed toward a patch of
dark material on the ground.

"Scat. It's called scat."

"That's the official name for animal poop?" His face
was impassive, but his eyes had that glint again.

She had to fight to keep a smile from her face. "Yes."

Kneeling, she examined the droppings. Reddish pulp,
interspersed with tiny seeds. "This is probably from a ring-

tail. They're mostly fruit eaters. Cougar scat would contain fur, maybe bone fragments. No self-respecting cougar eats berries."

He frowned, his eyes still fixed on the droppings.

"Sorry to disappoint you," she said.

The ledge out of which the yucca grew was crisscrossed with dozens of shoe prints. "I see you've kept your evidence scene pristine."

He rolled his eyes.

"What kind of shoes was Fred Fischer wearing?" Sam asked.

"Nike cross-trainers. Way too common." He pointed to several smudged imprints in the dust that appeared to be Nike swooshes. "Half the volunteers are wearing them."

She thought about the Mickey Mouse camper. "What kind of shoes does Weird Wilson wear?"

"I don't think that man could hike uphill for four miles," he said. "But I'll check." He sighed heavily. "Criminals should be required to wear custom-made boots with their initials cut into the tread."

Sam raised an eyebrow. "Maybe they could issue them on release from prison."

"It would be a good start," Perez said, again with a perfectly straight face. Either the man had a wry sense of humor or none at all. "This is cougar territory, right?"

She studied the surrounding area. A cougar could easily traverse the rocky terrain: they could run up nearly vertical slopes. "Could be. But why would a cougar drag Zack up here? It's much more likely that the shoe fell down from the trail." She pointed toward it. "Especially if an adult was carrying Zack. He might not even notice a shoe falling off." Where would the mystery man take Zack?

Perez seemed to read her mind. "Where does this trail go?"

"Up past Jade Pool, through a canyon, past some ruins, on up and over the plateau. Tons of places for a person—not a cougar—to hide a kid. Speaking of which, I've got to go."

After gaining the trail, she took out the digital camera and snapped a couple of shots of Perez kneeling below, jotting notes on his pad. He glanced up, a frown darkening his handsome face. She waved and turned away.

Public place, she thought as she hiked on. *No expectation of privacy, no risk of lawsuit.* Farther up the trail, the Rescue 504 scouts sprawled across rocks on either side of the trail, wolfing an early lunch from paper bags. All the teenagers were scratched and dirty from crawling over the hillside.

A thin freckle-faced girl spoke in anger to another scout. "People deserve to get killed, the way they've treated animals. So what if a cougar eats a baby or two? There're a lot more people than cougars."

"No animal is as good as a person," a boy retorted. "Any mountain lion that comes near anyone I know is as good as dead. Right, Wanda?"

The olive-skinned girl to his right nodded. The freckle-faced girl gave the boy the finger.

The boy's hand moved to his waist. His fingers wrapped around the hilt of a large hunting knife sheathed on his belt. The scoutmaster was nowhere in sight. Sam waded into their midst. "Hey, we've got to stick together and do our jobs, okay? For Zack."

She explained that nobody had found evidence of a cougar attack. Perez approached as she added, "It's a crime to harm any animal in a national park."

Wanda was dubious. "So they're just going to let twenty mountain lions roam around wherever they want?"

"Twenty?" Sam squeaked. "There can't be more than five, tops."

The girl swiveled toward her boyfriend. "That Buck guy on the TV last night said that since they weren't allowed to hunt here anymore, there were probably twenty mountain lions in the park."

A throb started deep inside Sam's skull. "Buck Ferguson," she said, carefully enunciating each syllable of the blockhead's name, "doesn't have a clue what he's talking about."

"But he—"

"I'm a wildlife biologist. I would know, wouldn't I?"

Sam addressed a question to the whole group. "Can you guess which animal in the U.S. attacks and kills the most people?"

"That's easy!" one boy scoffed. "Grizzly bears."

Sam shook her head. "Not even close."

"Dogs," the freckled girl volunteered.

"Right on." Sam touched her index finger to the tip of her nose. She continued up the trail, hoping she'd given them something to think about. Perez rushed to catch her.

"Did I hear that girl say that hunting was once allowed here?" he asked.

"Sure," Sam said, stopping. "It used to be national forest land. It's only been a national monument and a wildlife preserve for less than a decade. What does that have to do with anything?"

"I don't know that it does." It was annoying, the way the man could talk in circles. "Do you know this Ferguson well?" he asked next.

She wrinkled her nose. "I know him better than I want to. I met him when I worked here as a seasonal. He runs an outfit called Eagle Tours, passes himself off as a 'wildlife expert' and a tour guide." She snorted. "Before Heritage was protected, Eagle Tours regularly took wealthy clients through here on hunting trips." She pictured Leto when she'd first seen the mother cougar, barely able to crawl, ribs outlined through blood-spattered fur.

Perez was thoughtful. "On the news this morning, he did seem knowledgeable about the area's wildlife."

"Did he happen to mention that hunters pay him a thousand bucks a head to shoot cougars?"

Perez's clear brown eyes said no.

"I thought not. He usually leaves that out of his wildlife lectures." Anger knotted the muscles between Sam's shoulder blades. "Buck the Bison," she muttered.

"What?"

She'd actually said it aloud? "Uh," she stuttered, embarrassed, "I like to match people with animals. Ferguson's bullheaded, a big square guy, so I think of him as Buck the Bison."

Perez's face remained solemn, but his eyes crinkled slightly at the corners.

"Believe me, he's a buffalo in temperament. You should have seen him in action yesterday, first at the park with a news crew and then later at the Appletree Café, just before you came in. He ran into Fred Fischer there."

"Sorry I missed that."

"It was curious. Ferguson smacked Fischer on the arm and told him to 'Stay strong.'"

Perez perked up. "Did you get the impression they knew each other?"

"Maybe. Or Ferguson was just playing to the crowd as usual."

"Hmmm." He whipped out his ever-present notepad and scribbled something.

Across to the west, a line of blue-shirted backpackers zigzagging up a trail caught Sam's eye. After he'd pocketed the notepad, Perez's gaze fell on them as well.

"Outward Bound," Sam explained.

"Ah." Perez nodded. "Strange concept, reforming wayward youth by making them swim raging rivers and trek through jungles."

"Actually, they teach them to climb here. They're off to the Curtain."

"The Curtain?"

She smiled. "The Curtain is an unusual slot canyon—sort of a deep crevice in the mesa, formed by a creek that runs mostly underground. It has five chambers that descend down through the mountain."

Enthusiasm warmed her tone as she tried to describe the geological feature. The scenery defied words. "Millions of years of geology—limestone and sandstone and shale lit up by shafts of sunlight that filter down to gleaming pools and waterslides below. You have to rappel down from the top to get in. The colors and shapes of the rock walls are incredible, like a rainbow curtain rippling down. The Curtain is always done last on Outward Bound's itinerary. It's an experience that the kids'll remember the rest of their lives."

"Sounds interesting."

"Interesting doesn't begin to describe it. Kent—Ranger Bergstrom—and I explored it when I worked here." She looked up the trail. "As a matter of fact, this trail eventually connects with the one that goes to the Curtain."

"So the Curtain is popular."

She shook her head. "The trail's not on the maps, and most of the underground area's off limits. Kent and I were probably the last people to go all the way through. The middle chamber's been closed for nearly two years: the overhang's crumbling." Hmmm. Had anyone searched the Curtain yet? She'd call the ranger station tonight and ask, head up there tomorrow if they hadn't already assigned it to someone else. Why was she still standing here chatting? She shifted her backpack. "Gotta go, Perez. See you."

She'd walked for only a minute or two before she heard his shout. "Westin!"

Down the trail, Perez and a black-haired girl stood side by side just a few feet off the path. The girl repeatedly jabbed her finger in the direction of the ground. Perez gestured for Sam to return. She frowned in frustration but walked back.

The patch of loose dirt that Perez indicated held two large depressions of rounded pads and toes.

"A cougar, right?" The girl's face was eager for approval.

They *were* cougar tracks. Sam pointed. "This one is a right forepaw; this one a right hind paw print. This"—she indicated a gouge in the lichen covering a bordering rock—"is probably a left forepaw."

The teenager's face shone. "I'll look for more."

Perez jotted a note on his pad. "Can you tell if the cougar was carrying anything?"

Sam rolled her eyes. "You've been watching too many Daniel Boone movies. This is an eighth of an inch of dust on top of solid rock—you're lucky to get a print at all."

The agent removed a small digital camera from his pack, took several shots of the prints.

"It doesn't mean anything other than that a cougar has

been in this area," she told him. "These prints might have been here for weeks; there's been no precipitation recently. And Zack's shoe could easily have fallen down from the trail. The creature that brought it here is most likely human."

Perez gave her a dark look.

"If there's nothing more . . ." she said.

There wasn't. She picked up the pace, breathing hard now. *Damnation.* Now Perez would report the cougar tracks near the shoe site, adding to the kill-the-lions fury. She had to find Zack.

The trail was steep, the altitude high. Why would someone carry Zachary up a trail into the backcountry? Only one reason made any sense: to hide him, dead or alive. She worked on her mental list of suspects.

Fred Fischer. He said he knew the park, his whereabouts during the early hours of the search were unknown.

Jenny Fischer? No. Remembering the scene at the campground when Jenny showed them the toy truck, Sam dismissed Zack's mother from the suspect list. It was hard to believe any woman could fake pain that convincingly.

A pedophile? Her mind immediately supplied Wilson. But even if the creep was a child molester, why would he bother to carry a child into the backcountry? The man might trot around in jogging suits, but he didn't look like he could climb a steep trail. Why not just stuff Zack into his camper and take off with him? And the rangers had already discounted him as a suspect.

An unknown kidnapper, someone who wanted a child? But why take the child up to the plateau instead of just driving away? Maybe they'd seen the guards on the gate, as Perez had reminded her. The park was long and narrow, only eleven miles across at its narrowest point, an easy distance for a strong walker. She thought about Kent's tales of homeless people in the park. Maybe a lonely hiker had taken advantage of finding an unsupervised toddler?

Buck Ferguson? Nobody had been keeping tabs on him the night that Zack disappeared. Ferguson knew the park, too. And he also had a lot of loyal followers who would be willing to help him out. He'd certainly been poised to take advantage of the situation and accuse the cougars.

She ascended the trail with renewed energy. Proving Buck Ferguson guilty of a crime would definitely make her day. But everything came back to the missing child. She had to find Zachary Fischer.

Jade Pool was her lunch stop. Water trickled over the edge of the cliff above into the small pond below. The brilliant green moss that bordered the rocks around the pool gave the place its name. She allowed herself five minutes to wolf down a bagel smeared with peanut butter, a few swallows of tepid water. Then she moved on, looking for any sign of a small child.

The cliffs that fell away from the trail were open, steep, and lacking in vegetation, for the most part—no chance of concealing a child there. But Sam was familiar with several clefts and crevices in the area. Unfortunately, they were well off the trail and time-consuming to search, but she made herself trek to every one. She found nothing more revealing than a cellophane bag that had once contained potato chips.

10

THE lizard froze, its long slender toes tensely gripping the lichen-covered rock. Shiny black eyes swiveled back and forth in their sockets.

Leopard spots on the reptile's head spilled down to a pair of black tiger stripes that ringed its neck. White flecks dappled the smooth sea green scales that shimmered over its body and long tapered tail.

Kent remained immobile, one foot in front of the other, positioned as he had been when he first spotted the animal. *Crotaphytus collaris*, "collared lizard," commonly called a mountain boomer. They were spooky, usually flitting away before they could be identified.

It was a miracle that he had seen one today. A helicopter had flown overhead no less than five times in as many hours. Every living creature in its right mind was hiding in crevices, cowering beneath overhangs. Kent felt his own urge to flee every time one of the mechanical monsters thundered past. He hoped the mountain lions were as invisible as the rest of the park's fauna.

The lizard pushed itself up on scaly forelegs, its front

claws scratching against the rock. It raised a pointed snout into the breeze and bobbed its head at the sound of faint voices and footsteps. Hikers, still out of sight behind a tall fin of sandstone, were approaching on the trail.

He took a step toward the reptile and flung his arms in the air. The startled lizard sprang from its basking rock to the ground, sprinted away on its hind legs. Running upright, its claws digging into the dirt, its tail streaked out behind as it disappeared down the path. A twelve-inch-long dinosaur. He couldn't wait to tell Sam. She was the only one who would appreciate the significance of *Crotaphytus collaris*.

The voices were closer now. Was that stink a cigar? Kent heaved a sigh, put on what he hoped was an authoritative expression, and trudged forward to greet the hikers.

They met where the trail rounded the tallest hoodoo in the fin, the formation known as the Hawk. It was a spire of lumpy red rock topped with a hooked protrusion that, he supposed, with an overactive imagination or a good dose of LSD, could look like a raptor's beak.

The expression of surprise on the lead hiker's face was quickly replaced by wary distrust as he took in Kent's uniform and badge. In his hand, he held a silver flask, which he quickly capped and slid back into his hip pocket. His camouflage fatigues were so recently purchased that they still showed creases from packaging. As Kent neared, the man slid his rifle down to his side, moving it out of sight behind his leg.

As if I wouldn't notice, Kent thought sourly. The two men that followed were dressed in similar hunting garb and also carried rifles. Another flask peeked from the breast pocket of the third man's vest. A pair of liver and white hounds gazed at him curiously. One woofed softly but fell silent when its owner jerked sharply on the leash. At the sight of the dogs, Kent's anxiety level rose. The cougars stood a good chance of remaining invisible to two-legged killers, but a hound's nose was a weapon they couldn't beat.

Kent folded his arms across his chest. "Howdy, boys. What kind of a hike are you on?"

The leader pushed his black baseball cap back from his

forehead, revealing steel gray eyes wrapped in heavy wrinkles. Kent blocked the trail, waiting. The man pulled the cigar from beneath his mustache and spat on the ground, narrowly missing the toe of Kent's boot. Asshole.

The leader explained, "We're volunteers, here to find Zachary."

The two men standing behind him nodded vigorously. More assholes. The eyes of the hounds were glued to their owners' faces, waiting for a cue.

Kent focused on the leader. "We appreciate you helping us search." He smiled for emphasis. "But what's with the firearms?"

Under the bill of the black cap, the leader's gaze remained steely. "We got the right to carry," he said.

"True enough," Kent said. *Thank you, Congress.* "But you don't have the right to shoot weapons in the park."

"But the cougar hunt . . ." the last one in line began, then let his words trail off.

"There is no cougar hunt." Kent unfolded his arms, rested a hand on his service belt, wishing for once that the metal flashlight under his fingers was a pistol. "Anyone caught injuring wildlife here can be charged with a federal offense."

The two dog handlers exchanged looks of confusion. The leader pulled his cap down. "First we've heard of it," he growled.

"Now you know," Kent said. "It's also illegal to even carry a weapon if you've been drinking. If you leave the park immediately, return home, and lock up those guns, I'll let you go. Otherwise, I'll have to write you a citation."

The three stared at him. Pushing aside the strap of his backpack, he unbuttoned the flap of his shirt pocket and reached for the citation pad inside. "It won't be cheap," he warned.

"We're on our way out," the leader mumbled, already turning his back to Kent. The second in line incongruously murmured "Thanks" before the whole troop wheeled around and started down the trail.

Kent trailed the three men for a half mile, making sure

they were headed back toward the park's north entrance. He called in the incident and asked for a ranger to meet the men at the trailhead and make sure they left the park. Then he turned off on the trail toward Navajo Leap. He still had six miles to cover and God knew how many jerks to lecture before reaching Mesa Camp. The last time he'd been on this route for backcountry patrol, he'd seen a spotted skunk, a white-breasted Swainson's hawk, and a coach-whip chasing down a pocket mouse. While he realized that such biodiversity was probably too much to hope for on this trip, he hoped that at least the animals would outnumber the assholes.

BY late afternoon Sam had gained the plateau, where the air, while still warm and heavy from the relentless sun, seemed somehow more breathable. A helicopter reverberated overhead. Looking up, she spotted a pair of legs and a rifle muzzle hanging from an open side door. Who was riding shotgun? And why? Had Thompson already lost what little spine he had left?

She had to give SWF something to use on their website, some sort of defense against the television news, against websites like Sane World and its ilk. Did she dare write about Fischer's record or Zack's adoptive status? She couldn't identify sources. But enough people had heard about the ransom note and the shoe on the trail for those to be called public knowledge. The phone and laptop had been biting into her back all day; it was time to head back to her camp and fire off the only ammunition she had: words.

At the top of the rise where line-of-sight communications would be most clear, she turned on the radio and caught Kent reporting an encounter with hunters near the Hawk. The thought of her friend, armed only with pepper spray, facing down three rifles made her nauseous. But he'd sounded upbeat when he said he was on his way to Mesa Camp for the night. The guy had balls.

As she rounded a pile of boulders, she nearly collided

with a tall figure walking in her direction. She stopped in her tracks, startled, then catching her breath, murmured, "Hello."

The jerkiness of the man's movements told her that he'd been startled, too. His hair, a dull reddish brown, was cut in ragged chunks, as if he'd trimmed it himself without benefit of a mirror. Compared to the tanned skin around his eyes, his cheeks were pale, as if he'd shaved off a heavy beard recently. His jean shorts drooped on his thin frame and his dirty tennis shoes had holes in the toes. Around his waist was tied a brown shirt. In his hand he held a cluster of half-eaten red grapes.

As if deciding she was not an enemy, he beamed a smile at her. "Hi." He thrust the fruit toward her. "Grapes?"

The small red globes smelled heavenly. Did he mean her to take one or two, or the whole bunch?

"Don't worry, I have more." He thrust them closer.

"Thanks," Sam said, taking the cluster from him. "You know you're off the trail."

He gave her a quizzical look. "As are you."

Touché. Since he didn't have a pack, she asked, "Just out for the day?"

He winked. "For the rest of my life. How about you?"

Pulling off a grape, she popped it into her mouth, unsure how to continue this strange conversation. She didn't want to go on her way and run the risk of revealing her camp, which was only a short distance away. Feeling a prickle of unease, she wondered if he'd already discovered her tent and her cache of equipment. She checked his eyes for evidence of drugs, but his blue-eyed gaze was serene, even friendly. And if he had stumbled upon her camp, he'd clearly taken nothing. He was not even carrying a knapsack or a bottle of water.

She slowly chewed another grape. Finally, to cover her awkwardness, she mumbled, "It's a beautiful day for a hike."

"Indeed. A gift from the Creator."

Ah. She understood now. He was one of those religious

types who chose to believe that nothing bad ever happened in the world without a good reason; that everything in life proceeded according to some mysterious plan. He wasn't smoking pot or dropping acid; his drug of choice was God.

But all was not right with the world. "Have you heard about the little boy lost down in the valley?" she asked.

"He's not lost." The man took a step downhill.

"Wait!" Sam put out her hand. "Why do you say he's not lost?"

He tilted his head a little, studying her as if she were an unusual bug. "None of us is lost. He'll be taken care of. The Creator will provide for him." Taking a step closer, he raised his hand and briefly stroked a knuckle down the length of the silver-blond braid that hung over Sam's shoulder. "Your hair is the color of moonlight."

It was a little creepy, but Sam made herself stand still and wait to see what he'd do next.

He turned and walked away.

She called after his retreating form, "If you see Zack, could you tell a ranger?"

He gave no sign that he heard. "Thanks for the grapes," she yelled.

She watched until he had disappeared from sight. Strange fellow, a little otherworldly. And his platitudes were annoying. *Have faith. God will provide.*

Sam had never seen evidence that passive faith did anyone much good. There was only one religious saying that she liked: "God helps those who help themselves." And it didn't even come from the Bible. Not to mention, it was an easy way out for God. Was she the only person who noticed that the Supreme Being seemed to have no responsibilities?

But platitudes aside, it was kind of nice to meet someone so mellow in the midst of all this furor. She liked the idea of having hair the color of moonlight. And his grapes were crisp and delicious.

Back in her private canyon, which thankfully showed no sign of intrusion, she fixed a quick dinner, mixing soup from an envelope into steaming water, then set up the computer and uplinked to the satellite. Under the headline "No Proof of Cougar Attack," SWF had run the article she had written yesterday with few changes, accompanied by the photos of the MISSING poster and the bullet-ridden signboard.

Sam ground her teeth. Not exactly the beautiful story of nature's magic that she had envisioned. There was a second page, however, in which the SWF crew had inserted standard text about geologic features and climbing opportunities at Heritage National Monument, along with a grainy photo of teenagers rappelling down a cliff that came from the video clip she'd sent. She leaned closer. Why hadn't they used a film sequence instead of making a frame into a still image?

Suddenly a tiny figure slid down over the entire page like a spider on a silk thread. "Cowabunga!" Cameron's voice yelped from the speakers, startling Sam. Cameron stopped at the bottom of the page to high-five with another sprite, which ran over from the left margin. Then they both dissolved into the text behind them.

Sam sat back, laughing. Mad Max strikes again. At least someone was getting some enjoyment from this expedition. Cowabunga, indeed. Sam wished she were a wild teenager named Cameron right now instead of a worn-out writer named Wilderness Westin.

Steeling herself for the inevitable, she pulled up several news sites. Sane World's page ran largely unchanged. The organization had added only an ad that offered T-shirts for the "unbelievable price of $7.99!" Gleaming cougar eyes stared out from the black fabric. THEY'RE OUT THERE was scrawled in burning red letters beneath the eyes.

On KSEA's website, there was no mention of the FBI or any ransom attempt. But there was a sidebar in which the secretary of agriculture was quoted as saying, "I have authorized the dispatch of game control officers to Heritage National Monument. The government will do everything necessary to protect visitors."

"Oh no, no, no." She groaned and buried her face in her hands, wanting to cry. Or scream. *Please God, let Zack have been taken by a human and not a cougar.* She brought the thought up short: what was *wrong* with her? *Please,* she amended, *let Zack have just wandered off, let him be safe and sound.*

Maybe, just maybe, Zack had been found while she was hiking? She disconnected laptop from phone and then called park headquarters. The news was not promising. The Explorer Scouts had gone home. Rangers would check the backcountry. The unfamiliar voice sounded surprised when she asked if the ruins and the Curtain had been searched.

"I'd have to check that," he said. "I'm sure every place that should be searched has been."

This guy had a lot more faith in the park administration than she did. Right now, Thompson and Tanner seemed more interested in controlling political damage than in searching the backcountry.

She'd just set her phone down when it buzzed.

Adam. "Why didn't you use the ransom tip I gave you this morning?" she asked on answering.

"It didn't go with the other elements," he explained. "You have to focus to create a good story."

She felt like banging the phone against a rock. "You're focusing in the wrong direction." She told him about the shoe.

"You made my day! What a team! So we can say a cougar carried—"

"No!" she yelped. "We don't know how the shoe got up there."

"Okay, I got it, no need to get agitated; we're all a little stressed out right now. I'll find some way to run with it. Thanks, Sam." And then he was gone.

We're all a little stressed out right now? His tone of voice told her that Adam felt like a hero. She felt like a salmon swimming upstream, hoping against all odds that the result would be worth the journey.

The blades of a helicopter sounded a distant drumbeat somewhere to the south. The annoying vibration drifted away, back toward the valley. She was glad to be out of the madness down there, glad that Kent was, too. Mesa Camp was a beautiful spot on a high open plateau; he'd have a spectacular view of the sunset. She wished she were there with him instead of stuck in front of a computer.

In growing darkness, she wrote the latest about the search for Zack. She created a paragraph about the ransom delivery and car chase, then another about the shoe on Powell Trail. Sam frowned, tried to come up with a connection or at least a decent transition. After a couple of false starts, she gave up the idea of linkage and decided to emphasize the confusion of events. She stressed that no sign of cougar attack had been found—all the clues pointed to as yet unidentified humans. Zack was still out there, and he could yet be alive.

She uploaded the photo of Perez inspecting the site where the shoe had been found. His knees were bent, one hand stretched out toward the ground, his eyes fixed on something there. He'd be glad that the photo was only a three-quarter view and his face was tilted downward; he was unrecognizable.

She sat with her chin on her knees, staring at the screen. SWF had hired her to write about the cougars, and here she was sending them reports about ransom notes and recovered shoes and photos of FBI agents. How could everything go so wrong in two days?

"Oh, Zack!" She knotted her fingers into her braid and pulled until her scalp hurt. "Where are you? Please be somewhere warm and safe. And please, please, please, give me a clue where that is."

A faint scratching noise drew her attention. Pebbles against rock, something big moving in the area just beyond the canyon mouth. The oddball with the chopped-off hair, coming back? A chill prickled down her spine.

The last glow of sunset was gone. The sky was black and empty now: the moon had not yet risen. Leaping to her feet, she blinked several times, trying to adjust her eyes to the darkness after staring at the computer screen.

She ran her hands over the dozen pockets of her vest.

Where was her pepper spray? She scrambled quickly to the top of the van-sized boulders that surrounded her tent.

She scrutinized the charcoal-colored shapes of the surrounding rock, surprised at how fast her heart was beating. Solitude and wilderness had always represented security, even serenity to her. But that was before she'd learned that a kidnapper, maybe even a murderer, was skulking around the plateau.

11

SAM didn't need moonlight to pinpoint Agent Perez's location; his flashlight did that for her. He trudged up the hillside, moving the light around him onto the surrounding rock formations as he walked. At one point he did a little sideways leap, tripped over the bristly skeleton of a desiccated cactus. The hiss of a Spanish curse drifted up to her.

She grinned. The beam of his flashlight had probably picked up some small movement, a night-hunting lizard or mouse or snake.

At the narrow entrance to her campsite, he turned off the flashlight and stood for a few seconds, listening for movement inside the pocket of boulders.

Her interactions with Perez were starting to feel like some sort of weird tag-team game. She held her breath, waited on top of her boulder until he reappeared next to her tent, the glow from the computer screen highlighting the toes of his boots.

Damn! The laptop was running down the battery. Worse yet, she'd left the photo of Perez on the screen. She slid down the boulder on her backside and landed with a thump beside him.

Perez tripped backward over a tent pole, barely recovered his footing, struggled to slide his right hand around the strap of the large backpack he now carried. Going for his gun.

"You don't intend to shoot me, do you, Agent Perez?" She stepped closer. "How'd you know I was here?"

He straightened, took a deep breath. "OT near Sunset Canyon."

Her permit notation wasn't nearly enough information to find the hidden canyon. She'd bet that the FBI agent had a marked map and a GPS device in his pocket. And that the helicopter she'd heard a half hour earlier had dropped him off. Perez wasn't even sweating, and he'd somehow traded a small knapsack for a fully loaded backpack since this afternoon.

"What are you doing here?" she asked.

"Visiting." He eyed the satellite phone, camera, and laptop scattered across the canyon floor.

Stepping in front of him, she flipped the laptop screen down. "I'm working," she said.

"Obviously." He unbuckled his waist strap and shrugged out of the shoulder straps, letting his backpack slide to the ground. "Don't let me stop you."

He sat down cross-legged, facing her. His steady gaze was disconcerting.

"I'm almost done." She turned the laptop around so he couldn't see the screen before flipping it open again. She sat down, closed the photo file, spell-checked the text file, sent it to Seattle, and then waited for the response. The modem's beep at the end of transmission seemed loud in the quiet evening. She punched the End button on the phone and shut down the laptop.

"Very high tech." Perez indicated the equipment with a wave of his hand.

"Have batteries, will travel," she quipped. "Is this an official interrogation, or were you just hoping for a cup of tea?"

He sucked in a breath, then said, "I thought you should know that the superintendent has scheduled the Wildlife Services hunters."

"What? He said he'd wait for evidence! Damn it!" She glared at him. "It was because of those prints, wasn't it? Just because they were within a hundred yards of the damn shoe, you—"

He held up his hands. "It wasn't me. The volunteers reported their find, and Superintendent Thompson made his decision."

"They really called off the search for Zack?"

"The search on foot has halted. They'll continue helicopter flyovers tomorrow."

"Kid killed by cougar, case solved. So why aren't you on your way back to Salt Lake?"

"I'm not that easy to get rid of, Miss Westin." His brown eyes bored into hers. "Agent Boudreaux and I made the decision to keep going until we find more evidence, or at least until the day after tomorrow."

She swallowed around the constriction in her throat. "Is that when the hunters arrive?"

He nodded. "They'll want everyone out of the park then."

She wrapped her arms around her knees, her mind racing with images of hunters marching shoulder to shoulder. They'd have dogs, of course, to flush out the cougars, and they'd use the damn helicopters to spot them from the air. Maybe they'd even shoot the lions from the helicopters. They'd slaughter every mountain lion they came across. Leto, Artemis, Apollo. Others she had never seen, that no one had ever seen before.

What could she possibly do to stop the massacre? Maybe if she wrote about how many taxpayer dollars were spent every year to slaughter wildlife? Most Americans were unaware that their government paid to have thousands of animals killed every year.

Would they care?

A howl drifted out over the mesa, a mournful sound. It was answered by a series of excited yips that built up to a long drawn-out wail.

Perez lifted his chin and gazed the direction of the sound. "Wolves?"

She shook her head. "No wolves in this part of the country. Those are coyotes. You hear them almost every night up here."

The yipping increased in volume and speed until it resembled hyenas surrounding their prey. Then, the evening air was shattered by a shrieking lament that no canine was likely to produce.

Perez tensed. "What the hell?"

"It's Coyote Charlie." She stood up, retrieved her binoculars from her pack. "Didn't Ranger Bergstrom mention him to you?" She walked to the narrow mouth of the small canyon.

He was right behind her. "Coyote Charlie?"

"A local nutcase," she said. "He's been here for years. I caught a glimpse of him summer before last, near the ruins. And Kent swears he appears every full moon to howl with the coyotes. He even saw Charlie buck naked once."

"What did the rangers do with him?"

The question surprised her. "Nothing. He's not doing anything illegal, except maybe camping without a permit." She paused. Where would a naked Coyote Charlie attach a permit tag?

Perez pulled his notepad out of his shirt pocket. "What does he look like?"

She rubbed her forehead, trying to remember. "He was a long way off, and I was using binoculars. And it was more than a year ago. When I saw him, he was wearing clothes—pants and a long-sleeved shirt. He had a long scruffy beard, long hair. Medium colored, light brown or maybe dark gray—it's hard to tell at night. Tall, skinny. Scruffy."

"Got it—heavy on the scruffy." His pen scratched across the page. "What else do you know about him?"

"Virtually nothing. Backcountry campers catch sight of him now and then, or hear him howling."

He shook his head. "That's disturbing."

"Why do you say that? I think Charlie's great."

His head jerked back and his expression was contemp-
tuous. "You're kidding. What's to admire?"

"The freedom. He's completely uninhibited. He wants
to run naked under the full moon, he does it." She could
almost feel it herself; soft, fresh air on exposed skin, gliding barefoot over smooth sandstone through a landscape lit
with lunar magic. Like a wild animal, surrounded only by
nature. But this was probably not an image an uptight FBI
agent could appreciate. She glanced sideways at Perez to
check.

The guy was clearly distressed. As he stared at her with
frank concern, he ran his fingers through his hair, making
it stand on end. "Do you have any idea how many schizo-
phrenics are out there, listening to the voice of the devil,
receiving orders from angels or dogs? This guy may think
he's getting mental transmissions from those coyotes or
even from the moon."

He looked up for a moment as if beseeching the heavens
for sanity. When he lowered his head, his straight hair fell
back into place, except for one ebony strand that slipped
onto his forehead. "Do you know his real name?" he asked.

She shook her head.

"Why do they call him Coyote Charlie?"

"Well, the Coyote part is pretty obvious, but I don't
know about the Charlie part. Maybe it just sounded good.
He's kind of a legend with the park staff. It would ruin the
mystery, wouldn't it, to know everything about him?"

They were outside her tiny canyon now, sitting on the
sloping plane of the plateau. Sprawled straight-legged on
the wind-scrubbed rock beside her, Perez gazed silently at
the full moon, at the pinpoints of light strewn across the
heavens like crystal beads on black velvet. Moonlight now
brightened the open space, lending a blue sheen to Perez's
raven hair, a chiseled-stone appearance to the planes of his
face. His jawline was dark with whiskers. Sam was pleased
to see that at least he had to work at some aspect of personal grooming.

The canine chorus started again. The unearthly shriek

joined in, closer than the other howls. Sam stood and raised her binoculars to her eyes, scanned the surrounding hillsides and plateau. Nothing but moonlight on rocks.

Perez rose to his feet. "How far away do you think he is?"

She cocked her head, listening to the howls. "Sounds like it's coming from Horsehip Mesa. That's his usual haunt, just above the ruins. It's about three miles, at least an hour and a half away. In daylight." Her feet hurt just thinking about it.

"Damn. The chopper pilot told me they won't fly over the park after dark. Something about squirrelly winds over the canyons."

She nodded. "That's right. Updrafts, downdrafts, thermals."

"This Coyote guy may know something about Zachary Fischer."

The child's face welled up in her memory, along with the feel of those damp little fingers. She shook her head. "I doubt it. The rangers have never considered him a troublemaker."

"Forget your romantic ideas about galloping naked in the moonlight," Perez told her. "Consider the evidence. Zack's shoe was found on Powell Trail, and Powell Trail leads up here. This wacko might have seen the kidnapper."

As far as she knew, Coyote Charlie had never been reported in the valley. And there was the shadow figure at the end of the path, the man that she had abandoned Zack to.

"He might *be* the kidnapper."

Her mind's eye supplied a vision of Charlie squatting on top of crumbling adobe, howling at the night sky, crouched over a small body like a coyote over a rabbit. Damn her overactive imagination! There was the rock bridge; it'd shave more than a mile and a half off the journey. But it'd be dark and dangerous . . .

She stood up, extracted her penlight from her vest pocket. "Let's go."

Perez hesitantly retrieved his own flashlight from the ground. "Three miles in the dark? Isn't that a little crazy?"

"We have moonlight." She impatiently tapped the pen-light against her thigh. "And I know a shortcut."

He aimed his flashlight at his chin and snapped it on, adding devilish shadows to his grinning face. "Coyote Charlie, here we come."

Maybe the man wasn't so uptight, after all.

A blood-curdling howl beckoned them.

RANGER Rafael Castillo sat in his truck, watching the campground. Someone had to have seen something on the night that Zack had disappeared; more than half of these vehicles had been here at the time.

Things didn't look good for that little boy; a ten-mile radius from the campground had been searched, and nobody had discovered any trace of Zachary Fischer. When the ransom demand had been faxed to park head-quarters, Rafael suspected the kid had been snatched and spirited out of the park, no matter what the gatekeeper said. But now that the child's shoe had been found on a trail that led to the interior, he didn't know what to think.

The lights were on inside Russ Wilson's camper, but he didn't see anyone moving around. Maybe Wilson was reading. Or maybe he was watching TV: an electric cord anchored the RV to the outlet that bordered the parking pad. The FBI agents had run a check on the vehicle, as they had on several others in the campground. It had come back clean, registered to Orrin R. Wilson in Rock Creek.

But he still had a funny feeling about the guy. He'd had Zack's cap in his camper—what were the odds of that? Tomorrow, he'd get the Utah DMV to pull Orrin R. Wilson's driving record. Sometimes even parking tickets could say a lot about a man. Where would he find a couple of hours to do that? These double shifts were killing him.

The rhythmic ticking of soles on pavement caught his attention. A man jogged along the asphalt road on the far side of the loop. In and out of the pools of light spilling from RV windows and kerosene lanterns, Wilson ran slowly, tonight dressed in black sweatpants and burgundy hooded sweatshirt, bright white athletic shoes. So he hadn't been lying about the jogging, anyway. He came to a stop at the drinking fountain next to the restrooms.

Tonight Wilson wore no toupee, and Rafael could see that although graying hair clung to the sides and back of his head, his crown was hairless, just as Rafael had suspected.

The sweat on Wilson's face and bald spot gleamed in the bright light over the restroom entrance. As he wiped a drip from his chin on the back of his sleeve, a little boy came out of the restroom and walked up to the fountain. Wilson held the child up to the spout, clasping the small body tightly between his legs and the metal drinking fixture. A smile crept onto Wilson's face as he gazed down at the boy, and it stayed there when he set the child down on the ground. Rafael felt relief when a woman exited the women's side of the building and took the child away with her.

So Wilson was still here. And he did like kids. Maybe he was just fondly remembering his grandkids, but maybe he was the kind of creep that liked kids too much. After making sure that mother and son and Wilson returned to their respective campsites, Rafael drove away.

His mother-in-law sure knew how to pick them. Her first husband, Anita's father, had drunk himself into an early grave. He gripped the steering wheel hard, trying to sort out his thoughts. Did his uneasiness about Russell Wilson come from his experiences as Miranda's son-in-law, as a father, or as a law enforcement officer?

THE rock floor fell away into blackness below. Sixty feet beyond the yawning space, the flat white plane of the mesa continued.

"You said you knew a shortcut," Perez growled. "I can't fly."

"You won't have to." Stepping down onto a narrow ledge a foot below the rim, Sam directed the flashlight onto the rock at her feet. "Stay close to me, and watch your step."

He climbed gingerly down beside her and peered over the canyon lip. "Must be at least forty feet down there."

"Closer to sixty in the middle," she said in a soft voice.

"How are we—" He stopped in midsentence as Sam's flashlight beam revealed the narrow strip of limestone that spanned the canyon. She stepped out onto Rainbow Bridge.

Perez sucked in his breath, hesitated a second before asking, "Have you done this before?"

"Of course." But only once, and that had been in daylight. She tried to sound confident even as she fought the urge to hold out her arms like a tightrope walker.

When she was about ten feet onto the span, she noticed that Perez remained on the lip of the canyon.

"Hey, FBI, you coming or not?" She squatted, placed a hand on the stone. The grainy surface was warmer than the air, having absorbed the sun's heat all day. Making a fist, she thumped it against the wind-worn rock. "It's solid."

He switched on his flashlight and sidestepped out beside her, sweeping the beam nervously back and forth over the bridge surface and into the yawning space below.

The smooth surface of the rock arch gleamed in the moonlight. Sam cautiously advanced, preceding her steps with the penlight's beam. The circle of light slipped off the lip of limestone to her right, revealing a drop-off into inky space only inches away.

"Just keep the rock in front of your feet. And don't look down." The warning was as much a reminder to herself as it was encouragement to Perez.

She held her breath all the way, thankful that her flashlight highlighted not a single serpent. The warm, smooth rock of the arch was everything a desert snake could desire on a crisp fall night. She thought about how the cougars had sprawled across the wind-worn surface.

Where were Leto and her cubs now? Waiting silently in the shadows nearby, watching these two foolish humans risking their lives in the moonlight? No, they were probably prowling the canyons, hoping to surprise a sleeping deer. Or crouched under an overhang somewhere, still traumatized by all the flyovers today.

After reaching the other side of the canyon, Perez ignored Sam's outstretched hand and stepped down carefully beside her. He exhaled heavily, and she felt his breath, warm on her shoulder and neck.

The howling began again a few seconds later.

"He's not far away now. Keep your voice down. Sound really carries out here at night." She dowsed her light and climbed up to the top of the mesa, Perez right on her heels.

"There." Sam pointed. The apparition stood with his back to them, bare feet spread, arms outstretched. Coyote Charlie wasn't naked tonight. Splotched fatigue pants hung loosely from his narrow hips, and a T-shirt clung to his lean chest. He wore a kerchief over his hair. As the series of coyote yips increased in volume from the other side of the canyon, the man clenched his fists, threw back his head, and belted out a haunting howl.

Perez drew the pistol from his belt, held it with both hands as he walked toward the ghostly figure. As the mournful note wavered and faded away, Perez's footsteps became audible on the hard rock surface. Coyote Charlie swiveled to face the FBI agent.

"Hands in the air!" bellowed Perez. He halted, his feet shoulder distance apart. "FBI!"

Charlie was motionless for a moment, hands held stiffly out to his sides. Then he bent at the waist and, with a scrabbling of hands and feet, abruptly disappeared from the horizon, leaving only a star-spangled sky where he had stood.

Perez sprinted forward. Sam ran after him, catching up as he slammed to a stop at the edge of the mesa. Their flashlights revealed a series of narrow ledges jutting out from the sheer cliff face at their feet. The ultra-high-pitched squeaks of bats were shrill in the night air. A shower of pebbles rattled somewhere below.

She couldn't resist needling Perez. "That worked out well."

He sputtered what she suspected were Spanish exple-
tives.

"Give it up, FBI. We're not going to catch him tonight.
He knows this area like the back of his hand."

"Damn." He sighed. "What's down there?"

"The ruins."

He peered more intently into the blackness below.

"You can't see them from this angle. This cliff is a crescent-
shaped overhang, what they call a blind arch. Beneath it are
some Anasazi ruins. Below that, a waterfall that comes out of
the Curtain. And there's Goodman Trail, which leads up
through Sunset Canyon; it comes out about a half mile from
here, behind those hoodoos." She indicated a row of rock sen-
tinels to the west. Normally a brilliant red in daylight, they
were dark gray and sinister-looking in the moonlight.

"I want to go down there."

She groaned. "We've already got nearly an hour hike
back to my camp."

"I don't want to go down there tonight," he clarified.
"But first thing tomorrow. Okay?"

"Since when does the FBI need my permission to go
anywhere?"

He turned and faced her. "Since this FBI agent needs a
guide. Can you take me to those ruins tomorrow?"

Sam considered. "If we can stop off a few places along
the way, looking for Zack."

He nodded. "Even better."

"You'll have to keep up."

He stiffened. "Haven't I so far?"

"And only if you'll share information."

"We'll have to see about that." He slid the pistol into the
holster at the side of his belt and visibly relaxed. "It's a fine
night for a moonlit stroll."

He was right. The Temple Cap sandstone gleamed like
new-fallen snow in the bright moonlight, the whiteness
broken occasionally by spiky bursts of yucca and stark
skeletons of dwarf junipers. The air was reasonably warm,
too, somewhere around sixty degrees right now. If Zack

was out here somewhere, as long as he was sheltered from the wind—

"That child might make it through a night like this," he said, startling her.

She resolved to block embarrassing thoughts from her brain when Perez was in the vicinity.

For a long moment he stood in silence, head thrown back, examining the sky.

"You know," he finally said, his words so soft that she had to strain to hear them, "I'd forgotten the stars." He shook his head. "How could anyone forget the stars?"

Over an hour later, they returned to the hidden canyon. Sam shoved her gear into her tent and immediately sat down to untie her laces. Perez picked up his pack. "There's not enough space for another tent here. I'm going to camp outside."

"Suit yourself." She yawned and kicked off her boots and sat rubbing her neck.

"Whiplash?"

"Huh?" The man had a knack for startling her with his perception.

"I noticed the back of your car. You got rear-ended recently?"

"Three days ago." She yawned again. Perez might have zipped around in a helicopter today, but she'd hiked more than a dozen miles, and that on almost no sleep from the night before. "My neck's just a little stiff."

He set down his backpack. Then he slid his hands under the collar of her shirt. The motion made her shiver. He rubbed his palms over her neck and upper shoulders for a moment, creating a warm friction, and then his long fingers began to knead the muscles along her backbone. "How's that?"

"Mmmmm." Sam was pretty sure she shouldn't be enjoying the massage as much as she was. She needed to stay alert, stay on the job. For Save the Wilderness Fund. For Zack. For the cougars. But his long fingers felt heavenly as they expertly manipulated her sore muscles. She leaned back into his hands.

"Feels good," she murmured, her voice embarrassingly husky. What a cliché. He'd think she was deprived of sensual contact. Which, actually, she was. Fans imagined that the gorgeous Adam Steele had a hot sex life, but in truth he was so busy that their intimate encounters had been few and brief. And he wasn't a toucher, except for laying his arm across her shoulders now and then. And she didn't want to think about Adam in any way right now.

Warmth flooded downward from Perez's fingers. In another minute, she'd be making little mewing sounds. "Were you a masseur in your former life?"

"CPA," he said.

"An accountant?"

"Lots of agents come from accounting backgrounds." He pulled his hands out from beneath her collar and moved them lower down, pinpointing the V between her shoulder blades. His thumbs started little curlicue movements. Along with a not wholly pleasant burn in her injured muscles, tingling sensations crept through her body. In a minute he'd know she wasn't merely deprived. Depraved would be a more accurate description. There was Zack, she reminded herself. Her job. She couldn't become a puddle of warm ooze.

She swallowed, sat up straighter. "Much better," she said briskly. "Thanks."

He rubbed for a couple of seconds more, then stood up. "You're welcome." He shouldered his pack again. "Good night."

She crawled into her tent and zipped the flap shut.

He paused outside. "I still want to question Coyote Charlie."

You would, she thought. "Good night, Special Agent Chase J. Perez."

His footsteps slapped softly against the limestone of the canyon floor, then faded away.

She closed her eyes but couldn't drift off. Her neck still tingled where Perez had rubbed it. She checked her watch: to her surprise, it was not quite eleven o'clock. Sliding out of her sleeping bag, she found the portable radio in her pile of gear, crawled out of the tent, and carried the radio to the top of the biggest boulder. Perez was nowhere in sight, but she could see shadows moving just beyond a row of upthrust rocks; that had to be him. She raised the radio to her lips, pressed the button. "Three-three-nine, come in, three-three-nine."

After two more tries, Kent answered, breathless. "Three-three-nine." She guessed that he hadn't had his radio on his belt but had to scramble for it.

"Hey, Kent, it's Sam."

"Sam? I wondered who'd be in range up here at this hour. You have a radio?"

"Of course not."

There was a short silence, and then he said, "Smart-ass."

"You gave me that one." She laughed. "How's it going there?"

"Aren't the stars incredible? I saw a collared lizard today. He ran away on his hind feet, just like one of those nature films on TV."

"Whoa, I'm jealous. I've never seen that."

"The G-D helicopters scared everything else away. Everything except good ol' boys. Castillo wrote five citations for menacing with firearms today; Taylor's up to three. Hope we're not becoming another Yosemite."

She knew what he meant: rangers on constant patrol with pistols and nightsticks.

Kent continued. "I had to read the riot act to three hunters packing rifles. They weren't exactly polite, but they left peaceably enough. I've got Mesa Camp all to myself. Your turn."

"Enjoy the peace and quiet, Kent. Anything new about Zack?"

"Nope. And damn, that can't be good . . . They'll be asking me to hunt down Apollo next."

He obviously hadn't heard about Wildlife Services being

called in. Sam chose not to enlighten him. Let him be happy
for one last evening.

"Oh, wow! Just saw a shooting star! Or maybe a UFO—
I'll have to ask FBI Man if he knows anything about that."

Sam considered telling him that FBI Man was spending
the night in her camp but decided against it. "Kent, I saw
Coyote Charlie tonight."

"Naked?"

She snorted. "Not this time. I only saw him from a distance, and he, uh, vanished pretty quickly. Does he ever
come down to the valley? Does he live nearby—maybe in
Las Rojas or Floral?"

"Hmmm. I've never heard about him except up in the
high country. But he's got to live somewhere not too far
away, right?" For a few seconds she heard only breathing.
"Wouldn't it be weird if he turned out to be the high school
English teacher or something?"

Somehow she'd never thought about Charlie talking, let
alone holding down a job. Perez was right: her concept of the
park phantom was too romantic. Charlie was, after all, human.
"Do you know how he got the name Coyote Charlie?"

"I'm trying to remember." His breath rasped across the
airwaves. "Scotty—that's where I first heard it."

"As in 'Beam me up, Scotty'?"

"As in Scotty McElroy—he heads up the local branch of
the Sierra Club. He was hiking this area twenty years
before it became Heritage National Monument. Scotty's
the one who first called him Coyote Charlie."

Sam made a mental note to tell Perez.

"Are you looking for Coyote Charlie?"

"He might have seen something that would help find
Zack. I just want to ask him a few questions."

"Don't we all!" He laughed. "You'll wear out the soles
of your boots before you catch Charlie."

"Thanks for the vote of confidence. Good night, three-
three-nine. Over."

"Night, Sam. Three-three-nine, clear."

* * *

PEREZ rested his head on his rolled-up pants and listened to the quiet murmur of Summer Westin's voice. He could tell by the rhythm that she was using a two-way radio, but he couldn't hear the actual words. Briefly he considered walking closer to her camp, but in this bright moonlight, she was sure to spot him.

What a beautiful night. He hadn't camped more than once or twice since he was a kid. Summer Alicia Westin was a paradoxical combination of wilderness savvy and the edginess that he'd noticed in people with high-stress, high-tech jobs: like they had too many wires feeding into too few circuits.

He remembered an old Lakota legend about a wizard whose beautiful wife was repeatedly stolen away by supernatural animals—magic buffalo and thunderbirds. No animal would need to carry off Summer Westin; she'd follow any of them willingly.

The two kidnappings he'd worked on so far had ended in shallow graves in the woods. But then again, this might not be a kidnapping; the evidence didn't add up. Fischer's uncorroborated story of his whereabouts the night of his son's disappearance, and then again during his walk about town the next day. The ransom note. The shoe on the trail. Paw prints near the campground, near the shoe.

Westin was right, it would make his life and Nicole's easier if it turned out that a big cat had grabbed the kid—then it would be a case for the animal experts, not the FBI.

What a jumble of disconnected events and people: they needed more than just two agents on this. The local cops weren't good for much of anything.

There had to be a pattern in there somewhere; there always was. He closed his eyes to review what he'd learned so far.

SAM ran her fingers over a worn cross-stitched rose on the ancient pillowcase she always traveled with. It had been her first embroidery project at the age of nine. The feel of the thick cotton thread always brought back thoughts of the Kansas countryside where she grew up. And as always, a trickle of guilt intertwined with the memories of her family. According to their expectations, she should be a well-settled matron by now. Not Wilderness Westin, cyber-reporter in the midst of a major disaster story splashed across the television news by a man she previously thought of as a romantic interest.

What would tomorrow bring? At least by accompanying Agent Perez, she'd learn of any new developments about Zack. Poor little kid. This would be his third night alone. If he *was* alone. And if he was still alive.

He could be facedown in a creek. In the trunk of a car, gagged and bound. With some toddler-loving pedophile. And because he was still missing, trigger-happy good ol' boys were going to murder any cougar that showed up in their gun sights.

Quit it. She closed her eyes, concentrated on seeing cougars free and healthy. She envisioned Zack safe and warm, playing with his toys, laughing with his mother.

Imagining Jenny Fischer conjured up Fred as well. Could he have intentionally injured his son?

Could Coyote Charlie be a villain? She'd always envisioned him as a vagabond who identified more with wild things than with his own species. A lost sixties type on a spiritual quest, sort of like the odd hiker she'd met this afternoon, but one who prowled around at night with other nocturnal animals.

Perez had hinted that Coyote Charlie might be psychotic. She'd read stories of Vietnam vets going berserk, murdering their families while reliving Viet Cong attacks in the middle of the night. What did the world look like from Coyote Charlie's eyes in the wee hours? Did he relive some mad past? Was he a gentle creature rambling in the moonlight, like the mule deer, or a predator who took advantage of the darkness to stalk his prey? Did he prey on children?

Predators of children. Wilson. LEGOs and animal crackers. Zack's red cap. There was something slimy about that man. He was a cave-dwelling salamander, pale and soft, afraid of the sunlight. But Perez had said that Wilson's record had checked out. And he didn't fit in easily with the shoe. She remembered the feel of Wilson's soft belly as she'd brushed up against him in his RV. Could he hike four miles without having a heart attack?

She pulled the sleeping bag up to her neck. The howling started up again. It sounded a mile or more away. Just coyotes this time. Natural predators, hunting natural prey.

Humans are so out of sync with nature, she thought. They hunt for sport, not for food.

Dread of the upcoming slaughter sat on her chest like a stone. Her mind continued relentlessly down the same depressing track. People as predators. Hunting animals. Hunting each other.

The last thought kept her awake for a long time.

12

DAWN was heralded by the rumble of yet another helicopter passing low overhead. Sam peeled away the warmth of her sleeping bag. She wove her hair into her usual loose French braid, then crawled out of the tent. To her surprise, Perez was seated cross-legged a few yards away. He'd used her stove and pot to make coffee.

His self-sufficiency earned him major points on her mental score sheet. She added another point to his total when he held a steaming cup out to her. A man who spontaneously gave neck rubs and made coffee was definitely a rarity.

"So we're off to the ruins this morning," he said. "And, depending on what we find there, I may want to see the Curtain, too."

He was certainly a bossy type first thing out of bed. She subtracted five points from his score.

"Let me rephrase." He passed a hand over his face, changing his look of chagrin to a charming smile. "Good morning, Miss Westin. Could you please take me to the ruins this morning? And maybe later we could see the Curtain, too. At your convenience, of course."

At least he was observant. And adaptable.

"You're in luck," she told him. "I just happen to be going that way. After I check my e-mail." Perez's coffee was a little weak for Sam's taste, but a big improvement over Tanner's sludge.

He held out an apple and a banana. "Fruit?"

She took the banana, sat down, and peeled it in silence. Although it was lovely to have a hot cup of coffee handed to her first thing, this was way too much conversation for this hour.

Hoo-hoo-hoooo. Hoo! Hoo! As the call faded, Perez raised a questioning eyebrow.

"Great horned owl," she told him.

She chafed her hands against her upper arms. The air was chilly, a reminder that winter was coming on. Zack had been missing for more than sixty hours now. If he were up here exposed to the elements, the chances for his survival were slim. It would be best if someone *did* have him. Someone who wanted a little boy to love as their own. The vision of the man at the end of the path played in her mind like a videotape in slow motion: he turned from the campground toward her, raised one hand to salute her. If only she could see his face.

The pink light of dawn unveiled dull skies and a cool breeze. Clouds drifted over the plateau, building up against the escarpment to the west. Sam hoped the storms would hold off for a couple of days, as predicted. Late tomorrow evening or early Sunday, Kent had said. The area was desperate for rain, but if Zack was huddled under a bush somewhere barely clinging to life, a cold drenching would end his chances for sure. The only consolation was that if a real gully washer developed, the planned parade of USDAWS killers might be postponed for a while.

Perez's phone chirped and he answered it. "Any progress?"

She turned on her laptop and satellite phone, checked her e-mail and the latest reports. Two news sites carried stories on cougar sightings near schools and playgrounds.

"What does Wilderness Westin have to say about this?" challenged one site.

She brought up KSEA's page. Yep, Zachary Fischer was still listed under Feature Stories and the article included a video of last night's broadcast. Adam again, now looking more comfortable at the news desk, in front of a photo of SWF's home page with her article and a photo on it. *Her* photo, of Agent Perez bending over—a red shoe? What in the hell? "Today," Adam said to the camera, "as this latest article on the Save the Wilderness website explains, a shoe was found on a trail in Heritage National Park. Is this all that remains of Zachary Fischer?"

"Damn it!"

"Something interesting?" Perez had ended his call and now sat watching her.

"Never mind. They find any trace of Zack down below?"

He shook his head.

She clicked over to SWF's website. They'd run the story she'd sent last night and used the photo of Perez inspecting the ground. Max had pumped up the colors: now the rocks were a deeper maroon and the vegetation was greener. And sure enough, a new element had been added: a small red sneaker now was the focus of Perez's gaze.

Mad Max was altering reality again. She clicked the photo credit. It reported "composite image" and listed her as photographer along with someone named Doug Grafton, who no doubt owned a photo of a toddler's red sneaker. Legal but definitely a little sneaky.

She wrote a quick update about USDA Wildlife Services being dispatched despite the lack of evidence of a cougar attack, about how taxpayer dollars would pay for the slaughter. In e-mail, she begged Lauren to add this information to the website ASAP.

When she clicked Wilderness Westin's e-mail icon, a message box popped up to tell her that the e-mail folder had exceeded its limit of eight hundred messages and that the surplus notes were stored in another file in the system. With some trepidation, she opened the e-mail folder. Judging by the headers, most of the messages were rants against nut-cases that protected wild animals instead of people. Crap.

Kim, the SWF office manager, reported that the FBI had called to check Sam's employment status. She glanced up at Perez.

"What?" His expression was innocent.

"Never mind," she said again, and turned her gaze back to the list. The capital letters of one header leapt out. I HAVE ZACHARY. She gasped.

She clicked the header. The message opened.

I Have Zachary.

It had been sent by someone logged in as 102236. How helpful. She turned the laptop around. Perez read it, then reached for his pad and pen. "Who's 102236?"

"I'm a writer, not a tech-head. I don't know how to do a trace."

"We'll check it out," he said.

"Should be easy. You already have SWF's number."

He raised an eyebrow quizzically. After a second, his expression relaxed. "It wasn't me," he said. "We had the Seattle office check out this Wilderness Westin character."

She turned the laptop back around, studied 102236's message again. "Think I should respond?" she asked.

"Couldn't hurt. String him along; maybe he'll come back with something more."

Give me proof, she typed to 102236. Her hands hesitated above the keyboard as she suddenly envisioned a severed finger, a small ear arriving via FedEx. After adding *Tell me something about Zachary that you couldn't learn from the news,* she clicked Send.

Moving to an online phone directory, she requested a number for Scott McElroy, the Sierra Club hiker Kent had mentioned. He was not in Las Rojas, as she'd originally guessed but lived in Floral, the small town on the opposite side of the park. She copied the number into her pocket notepad.

Perez buckled on his pack and Sam loaded her knapsack for the day, taking her minimum load of equipment: satellite phone, radio, camera, notepad, first-aid kit, snacks, jacket, water. She zipped the computer and the rest of the camping gear into the tent.

As she was crawling out, Perez said, "Is there any way . . ." He hesitated. "I'd rather not go across that rock bridge again. If we don't have to."

His reluctance was charming. "Okay. We'll go via Zig-Zag Passage instead." She didn't tell him that there was no way she would have taken him over Rainbow Bridge, anyway. Crossing the rock arch was expressly forbidden by park regulations; she couldn't risk being caught in daylight.

As they hiked, Perez quizzed her about the park's topography. "If there's a bona fide trail down to the ruins, why would Charlie travel up and down the cliff walls?"

"Maybe he does it for thrills, maybe just to prove to us that he can do it. Or maybe it's a shortcut, like Rainbow Bridge. Who knows? Why does he run around with coyotes?"

"Good question. And what does he do when he's not up here howling?"

"Anybody's guess, FBI."

"Could you stop calling me that?"

"All right. Perez."

"Chase," he said.

"Does this new familiarity mean that you've decided I'm not a suspect?"

"I'm ninety percent sure." He gave her one of his deadpan looks.

She laughed. "I don't know if I can call you Chase. What kind of a name is that, anyway? Chase Manhattan? Short for Charles?"

He leaned his head back and focused on the sky above, scratching the underside of his chin as he considered whether or not to enlighten her. Finally, he said, "In this case, it's short for, uh . . . Starchaser." He checked for her reaction.

She willed her lips not to smile. "Starchaser?"

"My mother's full-blood Lakota—you'd probably say

Sioux. *And* I have a sister named Raven. And a brother named Wolf." His eyes dared her to laugh.

Uh-oh. She would never have suspected that he was one of those extra-sensitive Native American types. "That's interesting," she said carefully.

His gaze lingered on her hair, her face. "I'll call you Summer. With your coloring, that name suits you. Do you have a sister named Spring or Autumn, or a brother named Winter?"

"My mother was diagnosed with ALS at the time I was born. So, no sisters; no brothers, either."

His face registered his discomfort. "Sorry," he said gruffly.

She shook her head. "I don't know why I mentioned it." Her father and grandparents always mentioned the timing in the same breath, as if it were part of the explanation. *When Summer was born, the doctors discovered that Susan had Lou Gehrig's disease.* So the two events were inextricably linked in her memory, and she could never think of her own birth without the pain of guilt for her mother's fatal illness.

She needed to change the subject. "In Lakota culture, is a starchaser a good thing to be?"

"According to legend, the stars are spirits. They carry messages from the Creator to people on earth. So I suppose that a starchaser could be someone reaching for the heavens, trying to be powerful. Or maybe seeking a message." He shrugged. "It's a made-up name; my mother thought it sounded romantic."

"With a name like Summer, I can identify," she told him. "People usually ask me if my folks were hippies."

"I don't think many hippies become Methodist ministers."

So he had checked her family background as well as her employment record. She let his words hang in the air, hoping it would make him feel guilty.

"Just doing my job," he said.

At times Sam made a point of diverting from the trail to check out a side canyon or the shadow under an overhang. No sign of Zack. In fact, she didn't see any signs of any other humans along the way, except for footprints in the dust and a scrap of cellophane, which she pocketed. At another time, she would have celebrated the lack of people in the backcountry. With Zack still missing, it just added to her frustration.

At nine A.M., they stood in a bowl-shaped canyon, a sheltered oasis filled with spindly willow trees.

"Nice," Perez observed.

"It's nice most of the time." A thin sheen of water on the hard rock floor reflected the sunlight. Sam pointed. "That's Curtain Creek."

She waved her hand at a series of potholes scoured into the smooth surface. The largest was nearly three feet deep. "When enough rain falls on the high mesas, the water roars through there. It's what carved out the Curtain."

She slapped her open hand on a vertical wall of sandstone next to a crude arrow etched into the rock. "And this is where Curtain Creek comes from. ZigZag Passage."

The V of the arrow pointed toward a narrow crevice. At ground level, only eighteen inches of sandy floor separated the opposing cliff faces. The walls undulated up, opening out gradually toward the top.

Perez stiffened. "*This* is your other shortcut?"

Sam slid her arms out of her daypack. Clutching the shoulder straps, she held the pack on one hip as she sidestepped into the narrow space. She glanced back to make sure Perez was following.

He stood at the opening, scanning the close walls. "You've got to be kidding. This is only a crack. A claustrophobic crack."

"That's one reason it's not an approved trail." She raised a finger toward the sunlight above. "Blue sky overhead; look at that if you find it claustrophobic. Take off your pack, hold it next to you, and come on."

He peered over her head, scrutinizing the passage beyond. "Haven't there been earthquakes around here? We could be squashed like cockroaches under a shoe." A solid rock wall loomed a short distance away. "It doesn't look like it goes anywhere."

"It zigs. It zags. Then it opens up again. Don't worry— it's a short passage."

His rugged face was fixed in a frown.

"Well, get out your map, Starchaser. Take the long trail to the ruins, and I'll see you there in a couple of hours." She started down the passageway.

By the time she reached the bend in the path, Perez was thumping and muttering behind her. She glanced back. He shuffled sideways, his nose only inches from the rock wall.

The sunlight sifted down from above in narrow shafts, illuminating the layers of rock. The hues were those a master artist would have chosen, blending subtly from one into another. Dove gray. Celadon. Mauve. Bronze. Cream. Buttercup yellow. Each shade represented hundreds of years of geological processes at work.

"Aren't the colors incredible?" she murmured.

"Lovely."

His sardonic tone made her smile. "This is called a slot canyon, for obvious reasons," she told him. "ZigZag Passage is just a tiny preview of the Curtain."

"The famous Curtain is another crack in the ground?" He reached the bend in the path where the walls were farther apart, set the pack down and turned to face her, his shoulders brushing the rock on either side. "I can hardly wait." His inflection implied just the opposite. "I was never one for the sideways-shuffle type of line dances. We Indians like to move forward."

"I thought 'Native American' was the politically correct term."

"No tribe called this place America, so why should we call ourselves Americans? We Lakota called ourselves the People."

She scoffed. "Dozens of tribes called themselves the People."

He shrugged. "I didn't say it was a perfect system. But

according to my great-grandmother, it worked fine until you White Eyes started herding us around."

"Uh-huh." She completed the short distance to the sun-lit opening ahead.

Perez emerged behind her, breathing a sigh of relief and stretching his arms wide.

"You said that you dance?" she asked. "Do you go to the local powwows here in Utah?"

"I'm Lakota." Perez intoned flatly. "Well, half Mexican, half Lakota. Not Navajo, not Hopi, not Zuni."

Obviously a sensitive point. "I didn't mean to imply that all tribes were the same," she backpedaled. "I know you're stationed in Salt Lake, so I thought you might be interested in local activities."

The rocky path, although bounded by huge slabs that had sheared away from the cliffs above, felt remarkably open after ZigZag. One of the bright yellow MISSING posters was taped next to the vertical slash from which they'd just exited, adjoining a crude arrow identical to the marking they'd found on the other side.

At first the poster startled her, as if it might be a clue left by the kidnapper pointing to Zack's location. Then the probable explanation occurred to her. "Outward Bound must have left this. They went through ZigZag yesterday, on their way to the Curtain." Which reminded her how fast time was passing. She tried to pick up the pace but soon lost Perez and had to backtrack to find him. He was not far behind but hidden behind a petroglyph-covered spire of sandstone that he'd stopped to investigate. Cream-colored figures danced across a shiny vermilion background. Fat deer ran before three stick figures with enlarged heads. Jagged rays zigzagged down from above the stick figures; the point of origin two curious ovals covered with spots.

"Aliens attacking earth?" he guessed.

"Wouldn't the FBI know all about that?"

He rubbed his knuckles across the dark stubble on his chin. "That's an intergalactic problem; CIA jurisdiction."

His face was stoic; only a spark of light in his dark eyes revealed that he was anything but serious.

He compared his own hand with an etching of a hand on the rock. His was nearly twice the size of the painted one. "Fremont?"

She shook her head. "I don't think so. The hand signature was a favorite of the Anasazi. The new park archaeologist, Georgia Gates, could tell you more." She heaved a sigh. "Kent tells me the staff's working on a plan to develop the archaeological sites here."

"You sound like you disapprove."

"I'm not keen on focusing on attractions like that, at least not in this park. People should come here to see nature, not man-made features. Have you been to Mesa Verde?"

He nodded.

"Then you know that it's wall-to-wall people there. No wonder the cougars attack them."

He gave her a curious look and she knew her joke had not come off. "Okay," she said, "Mesa Verde was made into a park to protect the archaeological sites. But Heritage was set aside to protect the beauty of the backcountry. More people will wreak havoc on the ecosystem."

"Aha." He sounded pleased with himself. "They'll scare away prey animals, leaving the predators hungry."

Hungry enough to eat two-year-old boys? Was that what he was hinting at? "I didn't say that. The truth is, too many visitors scare away both prey and predators. If the park administration focuses on ruins, that means less money for natural resource protection, aka flora and fauna." Kent would be a wildlife biologist with no funding for recovery or protection programs. "Pretty soon, all that'll be left is asphalt and rocks and picnic tables."

His chin came up. "And Native American history."

She sighed. "C'mon, Perez, we're wasting time. Let's hike while we argue. We need to hustle if—"

A trill of notes sounded from Perez's chest pocket. He extracted the cellular phone and turned his back to her.

She resigned herself to a break, took out her water bottle and phone, and punched in the number she'd found for Scott McElroy. It felt strange to be making phone calls in the middle of the wilderness, her butt parked on one boulder and her back against another as she watched a golden eagle riding a thermal way up in the sky.

"McElroy here." He pronounced it Mackelroy. She identified herself and mentioned Kent.

The elderly man was more than willing to talk about Coyote Charlie. "He told me himself that was his name. Well, the Charlie part of it, anyway. I may have added the Coyote."

"You talked to him?" She was still having a hard time picturing Coyote Charlie as a normal, talking human. She took a swig of water.

"Uh-huh. A couple of us were up on Table Mesa—now there's a stupid name for you—"

"Means the same thing, table and mesa."

"You're a sharp one!" She heard him take a sip of something, and then he continued. "Anyway, we were camping out under this beautiful full moon, talking about nothing as usual, when up walks this stranger. Barefoot, no backpack, not even a jacket. Californian, I thought—one of those woo-woo types?"

"Um-hmm," she responded, wishing he'd hurry up. She decided the soaring wings overhead belonged not to an eagle but to *Cathartes aura*. What her Kansas relatives would call a turkey buzzard.

"But no, he wasn't Californian—he said he was from the old-growth forest in Oregon: he was emphatic about that. I'd guess he was in his twenties, early thirties at the outside. But he was certainly a woo-woo. Said he was living off the land. Likened it to the Garden of Eden."

Sam dropped her gaze to the surrounding rocky plateau. "Here?"

"We all thought it was pretty strange. But he rattled off all the wild edibles, right out of the book—piñon nuts, juniper berries, cholla fruit. Told us he ate ant larvae and partridge eggs and jackrabbits and trout from the river in the canyon. Said the ancient Anasazi, who knew how to live in harmony with nature, showed him how to live. Even said he was a reincarnated Anasazi warrior, if you can believe that.

"So I guess they got tutti frutties in Oregon, too. But, you know, he looked healthy. So maybe he knew what he was talking about, living off the land. Course, it was summer then. Not the one before last but the one before that.

"Two years ago." She took another sip from her water bottle, stood up, and stuffed it back into her pack.

"Or was it three? Anyhow, after he left, we were missing a sack of macaroni and a packet of freeze-dried stew. Not to mention most of our matches. So Charlie's concept of living off the land was probably a little broader than we supposed at first." Another slurping sound.

"But the weirdest thing was that when we'd more or less run out of conversation and were all sitting around just staring at the fire, the coyotes started to howl. They often do, up on the plateau like that, in the summer. And this guy, he just lifted up his head and howled along with them." McElroy cleared his throat. "Made my hair stand on end, the noises he made." He paused again for a sip. "But you know, I sort of wanted to howl along with him. So I did. We all did."

Sam knew the feeling. She was about ready to howl with impatience right now. "And his name was Charlie?"

"Charles, Carlos, something like that. So we started calling him Coyote Charlie. I'm glad to hear he's still up there. Nice to know that someone can still live so free. Maybe he *is* a reincarnated Anasazi."

Sam thought about Coyote Charlie's regular performances. Everyone got a little wild now and then. But the phantom had made howling with the coyotes a monthly habit, almost like a religious ritual. "Since he's been showing up every month for years, Mr. McElroy, do you think maybe he moved here, that he's a local?"

"Call me Scotty; Mr. McElroy sounds like a school principal. A local? Hmm. Coyote Charlie a local? Never really thought about that." Sip, slurp, swallow. "Well, he couldn't be really local, like from Floral or Las Rojas. I think I'd recognize him if I saw him again. Besides, I pretty much know everyone that lives around here, and there's nobody his age who's *that* nuts."

His comment made her wonder how many other nutcases lived around the park or just how crazy one would have to act to be considered *that nuts*. Had the Unabomber's neighbors thought he was nuts? The Green River Killer's? In her opinion, most people didn't really pay much attention to others around them. The evening news was filled with citizens swearing that their good neighbor couldn't possibly have committed the murder he'd just been arrested for.

Scotty McElroy was still pondering her question. He finally said, "Maybe Charlie just visits once a month or so. You think he drives all the way from Oregon? That would be interesting, if he was somebody's weird cousin who cruised in once a month to howl with the coyotes. Say, you looking for that poor little boy?"

"That's right," she told him. "We think that maybe Coyote Charlie might know something."

"Hot damn. I sure hope this thing has a happy ending. I hope those cougars didn't get him."

She started to protest his mention of the cougars, then decided to simply say, "Me, too."

"I'll ask around, see if anyone knows anything more about Charlie, and get back to you." He sounded happy to have a mission.

"Thanks." Sam ended the call. Old-growth Oregon forests. Anasazis. Scotty's story reminded her of an article she'd read in the past, something she couldn't quite remember, some vague connection between Native Americans and trees.

Perez was still enmeshed in his own conversation, so she dialed her home number. A hostile male voice answered.

"Blake," she said, "it's Sam. I need you to do something for me."

"What time is it?" he whined. Blake was a night owl and had been known to sleep until noon whenever he had the opportunity.

"Nine thirty your time. You should have been up for hours by now. Sit up and get something to write with."

"Did anyone ever tell you that you were a wee bit dictatorial in the mornings?"

"I'll pay you for your time. Got a pencil?"

"A little overbearing? A smidgeon strident?"

"I need you to look through my clippings of environmental stories. They're in the lower right drawer of the file cabinet."

"You mean those mountains of paper that slither out onto the floor every time you open the drawer?"

"You don't have to read them," she said. "This could be really important, Blake. Just look for a newspaper clipping about activists trying to protect old-growth forests in Oregon. I think it was a couple of years ago, and I think the group had some weird name."

"Don't they all?"

"Maybe something to do with Anasazis."

"I'm writing this down. Anna who?"

"Anasazis." She spelled it for him. "Native Americans. Call me back tonight between nine and ten."

"Between nine and ten?"

"I'm in the middle of nowhere with no electricity; I can't leave this phone turned on all the time. But I'll turn it on between nine and ten P.M., your time." She ended the call and stuffed the phone back into her vest pocket.

Perez had his phone jammed against his ear, so she couldn't hear the other speaker. His end of the conversation wasn't very informative, just a couple of "uh-huhs," one "That's interesting. So who's keeping an eye on the Fischers?" A pause. "Oh, that's great. Well, I guess you get what you pay for."

The next thing out of his mouth was, "Really? Me? Today?" He cast a sideways glance in her direction.

That had to be about the website. A hot blush crept up from her collar and spread over her cheeks. She made a wrap-it-up motion with her hands, then jerked a thumb over her shoulder to indicate that they needed to hit the road.

"The birth parents?" he asked, ignoring her.

As he listened to the answer, he rubbed his fingers over the back of his neck. The park service backpacks rode high, tended to force the hiker's head forward; his neck probably ached. She wondered how Special Agent Chase Perez would react if she offered to massage *his* neck. His muscles, she imagined, would be firm, well defined, his olive skin smooth and warm under her fingers.

She brought that thought up short. What was the matter with her? How could things like that creep into her head now? She should be completely focused on finding Zack, which could save the cougars, as well as her assignment with SWF and her reputation.

Perez turned and caught her looking at him. She quickly shifted her gaze to the laces on her boots. Surprisingly, they were different colors. Then she remembered that she'd broken one just before leaving home. Surely the new one came from a matched set. What had she done with its mate? Jeez, she was a mess. Little wonder that Perez would conclude that her thought processes were as careless as her grooming, especially when he was accustomed to immaculate Agent Boudreaux. This morning Sam hadn't even glanced in the pocket-sized rectangle of polished metal that she used as a mirror. She quickly checked the fly of her canvas pants to make sure that it was zipped, then brushed a hand over her lips, checking for any remains of breakfast.

Perez concluded his phone call with a promise to check in at seven that evening, then stuffed the phone and notepad back into his pockets. They strapped on their packs, and finally started hiking again.

"What's interesting?" she asked.

He regarded her coolly. "You eavesdrop on everything?"

"I have extra-sensitive hearing."

His steady gaze made her feel foolish. She blabbered on. "I hear wasps chewing wood to make their nests. Fluorescent bulbs drive me crazy."

His eyebrows lifted. "I'll bear that in mind."

"It's no blessing, believe me." She bent to check a small shadowy area beneath a boulder. Nothing. She straightened and pushed a wisp of hair out of her eyes. "People treat you like you're crazy when you hear things they don't."

Perez studied a cleft in a nearby rock face as he said, "That's a symptom of schizophrenia. Hearing things that others don't."

The man could be damned annoying. Catching his gaze, she said, "Information, Perez, spit it out. I share mine, you share yours."

"I was talking to my partner."

Obviously. She gestured, a circular "continue" motion.

"Preliminary tests on Zachary's shoe have come back. No decent prints. But there were traces of animal saliva."

Not the cougar business again. She said, "There were dogs in the search crew. Or maybe the Fischers have one at home."

"Maybe. They haven't yet determined the type of animal saliva." He made a detour of a few seconds to inspect the backside of a boulder. When he returned, he said, "You were right about Fred Fischer and Buck Ferguson knowing each other. Ferguson was Fischer's Scoutmaster for nearly five years up in Orem, when Fischer was a teenager. As a matter of fact, Fischer's family credits Ferguson with straightening out Fred: saved him from the reformatory, they said."

Either Special Agent Boudreaux was spending all her time with her ear to the phone or she and Perez had a whole network of aides out there. Sam was jealous of the FBI resources. "What was Fischer up to that he needed straightening out?"

He shrugged and walked on. "Juvie records take a little time to get into. We're working on it."

"You think maybe Fred and Buck met up here on purpose?"

"Jenny Fischer says she never heard of Buck Ferguson. More likely Fred's just coming back to his old stomping grounds, like he says."

They rounded a bend into a new area and stopped to look around for minute. "The license check of vehicles in the campgrounds is complete," Perez said. "Counting back two days before Zack's disappearance, there've been three cars registered to felons. A Buick belonging to a child molester; Airstream camper registered to a guy in the habit of holding up convenience stores; and a Pontiac owned by a murderer."

"Good God!"

"We didn't count lesser offenses." ·

He had mentioned a convicted child molester. "Was the pedophile Wilson? The guy with the LEGOs and the animal crackers?"

He shook his head. "I told you he checked out. Ranger Castillo got his driver's license; we ran it through the system. Orrin R. Wilson, no criminal history whatsoever; not even a parking ticket. Lives in Rock Creek."

Rock Creek was a hamlet southeast of the park. Damn. She'd have bet Wilson had a sordid background. But he'd been in a camper, not a Buick, anyway. So much for her intuition.

"You and Castillo are fixated on this Wilson," Perez accused.

"That's because Castillo and I have actually talked to him. Wilson's creepy." She walked forward.

Perez stayed in step with her. "The pedophile is one Wallace Russell of Flagstaff. His car was registered at the campground two days before Zachary disappeared. No way to know for sure if he was driving it, though; the campground forms only ask for vehicle information."

Child molesters, murderers, armed robbers. She'd keep an eye on her neighbors in campgrounds from now on and keep the pepper spray close at hand.

He told her, "The rangers and sheriff's department are checking those three licenses against hotel records, backcountry permits, and parking tickets now."

They continued downhill, toward the ruins. Bluffs rose to both sides again, enclosing them in a shallow canyon. White stripes of minerals streaked the sandstone floor. Sam remembered how easy it had been to get lost here before she was familiar with the park. They separated briefly and walked the perimeter.

She saw nothing that might lead to Zack. And none of the details Perez had told her led anywhere. Then she remembered something he hadn't elaborated on, so when they met again down the path, she asked, "You mentioned Zack's birth parents?"

"Zack's birth mother lives in Colorado Springs. Agent Boudreaux called her. She was quite upset to have been identified and even more upset when she found out the reason."

"And the birth father?" she prompted.

"She couldn't, or wouldn't, identify him. Just said she couldn't afford to keep the child. Looks like a dead end." He aimed an index finger in her direction. "Your turn."

"Coyote Charlie is a Charles or Carlos or similar name, midtwenties to midthirties, from Oregon. Has a fascination with Anasazis and living off the land, was first reported here three years ago."

His eyebrows shot up.

She smiled and tapped the vest pocket that held her cell phone. "I have my resources."

He whipped out his phone and told his partner to run a match for Charlie through NCIC, whatever that was.

Sam was glad she could provide some information, however vague it might be. Could Charlie provide the key to unlock the mystery of Zack's disappearance? She shook her head.

"What?" He stuffed his phone back into a pocket.

"All this information zooms off in all directions like a spiderweb. How do you know which strand to follow? Is any of it relevant?"

"Welcome to the world of crime investigation, Summer. Try to think of it like constructing a puzzle. You've got to lay out all the pieces and sort through them before you can see how they fit together."

Sam wasn't sure she had the patience or the analytical ability to hold all the pieces of an intellectual puzzle in her head, let alone play around with them. Right now, it was a challenge just to keep up with all the events unfolding around her and to keep putting one foot in front of the

other. And the deadline for the cougar hunt drew nearer
with every moment they lingered, so she started hiking
again, heading for the ruins.

Ten minutes down the trail, a gust of air wafted a terrible stench around them. Sam's ruminations on the growing
list of suspects dissipated as the scent of rotting meat filled
her sinuses. *Rotting meat.* Her heart skipped a beat even as
she pinched her nostrils closed. "God. What *is* that?"

13

GUNSHOTS had been reported at Mirror Lake picnic grounds. Rafael Castillo caught two young men taking turns shooting at a post with a rifle. One was sighting down the barrel as he approached from behind, one hand on his service revolver.

"What the heck do you guys think you're doing?"

The fellow took his shot. The post shattered, sending bits of paper and wood flying through the air. They turned to face Rafael. They took in the park service shield, the service revolver in his holster. The one in back crumpled the beer can in his hand and shoved it into a jeans pocket.

The shooter either didn't recognize Rafael's uniform or was too drunk to care. "Shootin' cougars, man," he said, waving in the general direction of the post. Rafael now recognized the tattered remains nailed to the post as one of the park service's cougar posters. "Doin' a public service."

"You know, guys," Rafael said in a mild tone, "we've got professional hunters coming tomorrow. We've got it covered."

"Government hunters, I heard," the can crusher snarled. "Probably couldn't hit the side of a barn with an M16."

"Waste of time waiting for them," the shooter said. "We're here to nail that cat."

Rafael held out his hands. "Look, fellas, we don't—"

"No fuckin' cougar's gonna get away with eatin' a kid," the shooter interrupted. He thumped the butt of the rifle on the ground. Rafael flinched, anticipating a blast that would take off the guy's head. He was a little sorry when it didn't happen.

So much for Mr. Nice Guy. Rafael put his hands on his hips, unsnapped the strap over his revolver. "It's illegal to discharge weapons in the park. And it's illegal to even carry one when you've been drinking."

The shooter wiped his hand over his mouth. "Sorry about the beer, man." But when Rafael reached for the rifle, the drunk pulled it out of his reach. "I got the right to bear arms."

The other man nodded. "Constitutional right. It's the First Amendment."

The shooter took a step closer. "Government pig."

Rafael retreated to his truck, pulled the radio from his belt, and called for assistance from any other ranger in the vicinity. He wondered where Taylor, the other law enforcement ranger, was right now. None of the general rangers carried guns, but the sight of any other uniform would be welcome. He wondered if the park service would spring for a bulletproof vest. Or pay for his funeral.

SAM and Perez scanned the canyon. They both knew the sickly sweet stench was the smell of death.

"There." Perez pointed to a pile of brush twenty yards away.

Oh please, God, don't let it be Zack. Sam took shallow breaths though her mouth as Perez lifted away the topmost branches. Her heart lurched at the sight of a moist brown eye. Dull now, the light gone from behind the pupil.

Flies rose and buzzed around Sam's head. She clenched her teeth to keep from inhaling the insects. Perez brushed away a layer of dried leaves. The head, neck, and legs of a mule deer lay flattened against the sandstone, the stomach and back haunches chewed away.

"Cougar kill?" Perez's words were pronounced through the collar of his shirt, which he had pulled across his nose and mouth.

"I think so," she confirmed. "Cougars hide their kills if they can't eat the whole thing. They usually stick close by."

She brushed flies away from her forehead with the back of her wrist and shaded her eyes. Turning slowly in place, she surveyed the ground around them. A mottled lizard rested in the sparse shade of a mesquite bush. She lifted her gaze to the bluff nearby.

A sudden link with piercing yellow eyes jolted her. An adult cougar stood in a shadowy niche in the cliff just above them. A sharp intake of breath informed her that Perez had seen the animal, too.

The cat glared, flicking its long tail, its gaze locked with hers. She couldn't inhale. Her lungs burned. The black and white markings on its muzzle were striking. So beautiful, so fierce.

Then the cat snarled, revealing daggerlike teeth. The low-pitched sound echoed faintly against the opposing cliffside, as if another angry cat stood across the canyon behind them. Sam's scalp tingled. Her skin prickled into goose bumps as if a blast of cold air had just passed over her.

The sensation released her from her catatonic state, and she sucked in a breath of warm air laden with the taste of rotting flesh. "Back away slowly," she murmured. "Keep your eyes on him. Don't turn your back on him, no matter what happens."

They walked backward, feeling for the uneven ground with hesitant footsteps. The cat snarled once more, then leapt down from its shallow cave. In her peripheral vision, Sam saw Perez grab for his pistol. After one last nervous glance at them, the cougar bounded away down the canyon, its tail outstretched behind its body, its padded feet making no sound at all on the hard rock.

"Wow." Perez lowered his pistol.

"Yeah, wow," Sam agreed. "That was a close one."

"Wilderness Westin was scared?"

She batted a fly away from her temple with a shaking hand. "You'd be crazy not to be scared. Cougars are big predators, and we're intruding on this one's territory, right next to its kill. That cat weighs over a hundred pounds, and although he's still young, he's a hell of a lot better equipped for close combat than we are."

"He? Have you seen this cat before?"

She nodded. "If I'm not mistaken, that was Apollo."

"Apollo?"

She made a dismissive gesture. "We named them. Apollo is twenty-two months old; just taking off on his own, staking out his territory. His mother, Leto, and sister, Artemis, are probably close by."

Perez rapidly surveyed the rock walls around them.

Sam folded her arms across her chest and took a deep breath. "Now that Apollo's gone, you don't need to worry, although I wouldn't hang around these remains too long. Cougars care about three things: territory, prey, and self-preservation. Usually, all you need to do is stand tall and slowly back away. They don't kill for revenge or for pleasure. Unlike people."

Perez relaxed slightly and turned his attention to the long dark brown stripes that trailed away from the carcass. "Looks like that lion dragged this deer a long way. I thought you said they didn't do that."

"I said they didn't carry their prey far unless they were worried about other predators or scavengers. Remember all those coyotes last night?"

"So they *can* drag a large animal quite a distance."

She shrugged. "If they feel they have to." She knew he was hinting about Zack again.

His gaze explored the cliff the cougar had leapt down from. "There's something up there." He gestured toward the niche with his pistol.

"Would you please put that thing away?" She backed up

so she could match his line of sight from her shorter perspective.

A mound of red plaster filled one end of the niche. "Looks like an Anasazi storage bin. There are hundreds of those all over the park."

She walked to the wall and pointed to small indentations in the rock below the shallow cave. "These are finger- and toeholds, the Anasazi version of a ladder."

Perez tested a small depression with curved fingers, then hefted himself up toward the niche.

"Hey!" she protested. "All Native American ruins are protected, off limits. It's the law."

He continued to climb, dislodging a shower of loose sand and pebbles from a toehold in the rock wall. The mottled lizard dashed from its resting place across the canyon floor to wedge its thin body into the dark safety of the nearest crack. One of Perez's larger pebbles came to rest only inches from the lizard's new position.

Sam threw her arms up in exasperation. "Oh, I forgot, FBI agents are above the law. They go wherever they want to." She skirted the corpse of the deer and scrambled up the cliff after Perez.

He had pulled himself into the shallow cave and stood bent over, crouched beneath the sandstone ceiling. "We're not above the law—we *are* the law. You're damn right we go wherever we want to," he reminded her. "And this bin is big enough to conceal a two-year-old."

She crawled into the shallow cave and stood up, the ceiling a few inches above her head. There were a few advantages to being petite.

The grain bin was nestled into the corner of the sandstone pocket, protected from rain. Perez knelt to examine it. She crowded in beside him and peered through a break in the wattle-and-daub covering, holding her breath. The dust in that bin was God knew how many centuries old. Mouse droppings were scattered like pepper over lumps of dirt and sand and bits of broken pottery. She wondered how long hantavirus remained active in rodent scat.

She picked up a triangular shard of pottery. The outside of the reddish clay had been painted white, overlaid with a black design of zigzags and triangles. "That's typical Anasazi design," she told him. "Geometric patterns and stripes."

He rose to his feet, but had to stay hunched over because of the low ceiling. The heel of his boot crunched on a pile of wind-driven sand in the back of the shallow cave. As he stepped away, the sliding sand revealed a white object beneath the red grit.

"More pottery?" he asked.

Sand jammed up under Sam's fingernails as she dug into the pile. The object felt large and rounded, like a bowl or a pitcher. An unbroken bowl was unlikely, especially outside the protective cover of the storage bin, but it would be an exciting find. Aiding the FBI was probably a legal justification for violating park service regulations. And Perez was half Lakota. Maybe a member from one Native American tribe had the right to handle artifacts from others.

The object finally broke free of the packed sand.

"Got it." She blinked dust out of her eyes. The object was definitely not a bowl. It was strangely shaped, round on top, squarish at the bottom. A pitcher? She brushed at the clinging dirt, turned the white object around.

Two eye sockets stared blankly up at her.

14

THEY both stared at the skull that Sam held. On one side of the thick bone, a scrap of dried skin was plastered, with a few light brown hairs straggling out.

"Damn it!" Perez growled. "Why'd you touch that thing?"

"You asked if it was a ceramic pot, remember?"

"Well, try to remember exactly how it was positioned, and for God's sake, don't move your fingers. Don't get any more prints on it than you already have."

He pulled out his pocket camera and snapped two photos of the skull in her hands. She waited while he made notes. It felt wrong to hold the skull up in front of her, as if it were a prize to be awarded or a main course on its way to the table.

Her stomach churned. This was someone's head. The skull had once belonged to a person who felt and breathed. Her own head felt too light for her own body, and she hoped she wasn't going to pass out. Or throw up. "Is it—"

He read her thoughts. "Not Zack, no. Unless the flesh was all peeled off immediately." He bit his lip, considering. "I suppose that's possible—"

She stared at him in horror.

"Possible, but not likely," he concluded. He bent his knees, lowered himself beside her to peer closely at it. "But the skull is small, so it could be a kid's. Put it down exactly how you found it."

His condescending tone grated on her. "You want me to cover it up with sand again?"

"No, just position it as closely as you can remember to the way it was when you first touched it."

Sam knelt and placed the skull on its side in the dirt. She noticed a sharp ivory point jutting out of the pile a few inches from the skull. The spike of a vertebra bone? Feeling suddenly chilled and a little dizzy again, she wrapped her arms around her chest. "At least it's not Zack."

Perez ran a dirt-rimmed fingernail across the stubble on his chin, making a scratching sound. "I'd be happier if it were."

"Jeez, Perez." Could he get any more callous? She frowned, wiped her fingers on her pants legs.

"We still don't know what happened to Zack," he explained. "And now we have another victim."

Dear God. What a horrible thought. As she followed him down from the shallow cave, she was conscious that every touch of a finger, every scrape of a boot might contaminate valuable evidence.

"I'll have to get a Crime Scene team up here ASAP," he informed her as they walked away. "I don't know if an ID can be made—but you never know. Maybe we've stumbled on someone who's been on the missing list for a couple of years. Maybe someone who was camping and"—he snapped his fingers—"Coyote Charlie got pissed about an invasion of his territory. Or this might be the work of that cougar we saw. There may be teeth marks on the bones."

"You think a cougar dragged a kid up here and then buried the skeleton?"

"The cat was standing right here, wasn't it? I think it's possible that a cougar dragged the body up here, and then wind buried the bones."

"No!" She shook her head. "There's no rogue man-eating cougar. A cougar didn't kill whoever that is"—she pointed at the niche above—"and even if a cougar killed Zachary Fischer—"

His head snapped up.

"All right, I said it!" she admitted angrily. "It's possible that a cougar got him but not likely: we've found no remains. And what about the shoe, found miles away from where he disappeared? Trust me on this, at least: it's completely impossible that a cougar would drag anything up here from the valley. We are more than eight miles away from the campground where Zack disappeared. These aren't six-hundred-pound man-eating tigers, Perez. I refuse to believe that we have some killer cat preying on little kids!"

His face was grim. "Summer, if it's not a cougar, then it's going to be something worse."

KENT Bergstrom sat cross-legged on the warm rock, chewing a bite from a granola bar. His binoculars were fixed on a hawk perched on a gnarled piñon that jutted out of the cliffside. The raptor kept one wary eye on him as it ripped a gobbet of flesh from the dead rabbit it held under its talons. The bird raised its beak and downed the morsel with a single gulp.

Suddenly, the hawk raised its wings as if to take flight, called out a shrill alarm. Kent scanned the area. A few mesquite bushes, nearly devoid of leaves at this time of year. A prickly pear, ripe with reddish purple fruit and a nest hole that had been carved out by an enterprising owl. No movement. The hawk settled down and was eating again. He lowered his binoculars.

The mosquito buzz of a helicopter vibrated over near the escarpment. The rhythm didn't sound right, but that was probably just the sound bouncing off the dozens of hoodoos between here and there. He hadn't heard any news from HQ, and he hadn't bothered to request any. This was the third day of the search, and without evidence that Zack was still alive, Thompson would end the official effort at sunset. It was the regs.

If only they'd find Zack today, alive. Or, if the poor kid had to be dead, at least killed by something other than a cougar. He had never been as scared as he was yesterday, facing down those three armed men with nothing more than his citation book and pepper spray. One had sported a black Eagle Tours cap, no doubt a disciple of Buck Ferguson. Thank God it hadn't been Ferguson himself, who had a way of inciting the guys around him to violence.

But there'd be others. Earlier that morning, he'd heard Rafael's call for assistance. His gut twisted with guilt at the memory. He'd been so relieved when Rangers Leeson and Taylor responded, so glad that he wasn't within range to respond. Unbelievable how people worried about wild animals lurking in the bushes when their neighbors two doors down kept loaded semiautomatics under their beds.

He remembered the terrible words buried deep in his job description, something about "dispatching problem wildlife." He'd been so thrilled to land the ranger job, a job where he actually got to work outdoors with wild animals, that he'd skipped over the more onerous tasks on the list.

He could put in a few days collecting garbage, writing reports, giving lectures to tourists who would never venture beyond the visitor center. But could he kill a cougar to keep his job? Was it his job to decide which animals qualified as "problem wildlife"? He doubted it. Thompson and Tanner treated him like a drone most of the time. He suspected that was why they'd sent him on backcountry patrol: they were leaning toward "dispatching" a cougar or two and they didn't want their wildlife biologist around to muck up the works.

The buzz of the chopper was nearing now. The pilot was flying exceptionally close to the ground. The hawk leapt into the air and flapped over his head as the helicopter thundered by, invisible beyond the far wall of the canyon.

A cloud of dust rolled over the canyon rim. Then, amazingly, a mountain lion burst from the red haze, leaping down the nearly vertical cliff in twenty-foot bounds. A shower of pebbles shadowed the panicked cat, the noise of the rockslide growing louder as the roar of the chopper faded. If the cougar didn't veer from its current course, it would pass right beside Kent. He waited, holding his breath.

A deep-throated bark rang out behind him, the unmistakable bay of a hunting hound. "There!" someone shouted.

Kent scrambled to his feet. "No!"

The two hounds strained at their leashes, frothy strings of saliva flying from their mouths. Three rifles glinted in the sunlight. Kent's brain barely had time to register the fact that he was positioned between the men and the mountain lion before the rifles went off.

TWO faint cracks reverberated across the mesa. *Damn well better not be gunshots,* Sam thought. Did helicopters backfire? The rumbling whop-whop-whop of a distant chopper faded away, leaving only the wind moaning through the rock formations.

"Did you hear that?" she asked Perez.

He sprawled behind her on a rock, fiddling with his cell phone, a USGS map outstretched in front of him. "Hear what?"

She checked the sky overhead. Thunder? Clouds were building against the escarpment twenty miles away, but only wisps of vapor drifted above their position. No rain nearby for a long while yet.

She sat perched on the lip of the cliff, feet dangling over the valley below. "What now?" she asked. "Is Jeeves waiting with the helicopter just around the corner? Are you off to park headquarters to meet the Crime Scene team?"

He shook his head. "I need to stay here and search the area. There might be more."

More. She clenched her jaw, envisioning caves strewn with bones. Would Zack be among the dead?

"At least now you can call off the hunters," she said.

His gaze met hers. "Not my job. We've found no evidence of Zack. This could turn out to all be coincidence."

"Oh yeah. Cougars have been eating campers for years," she said sarcastically. "Maybe this is a special spot where they bring the bones, kind of like an elephant graveyard—"

"Okay, okay. This probably has nothing to do with cougars. But maybe Coyote Charlie's been making a collection up here."

Oh God. The human howler had always been a joke, a source of entertainment, of even a certain type of envy. Could the entire park staff have remained completely oblivious while a serial murderer dumped his victims here? She pulled her legs up and hugged them to her chest.

Perez flipped his cell closed with a sigh. "Dead battery."

She took him hers, punching in the satellite code as she walked. "Be my guest."

His fingers touched hers as he took the phone from her. "Your country thanks you."

"Now *that* would be a first."

He punched in some numbers. After a hesitation, he said, "Nicole—"

A loud burst of static from the radio in Sam's pack drowned out the rest of Perez's words. She pulled out the instrument, trotted beyond the rock walls to the edge of the plateau again. Radio communications from the valley couldn't reach this area. She hadn't expected to intercept anything but maybe a message or two from a passing helicopter.

"Three-one-one, three-three-nine." Kent. The radio emitted a screech like chalk scraping across a blackboard, a rasping sound, and then the faint voice again. "Three-one-one. Oh please, three-one-one."

Three-one-one was the dispatcher at headquarters. Something was wrong: Kent knew better than she that radio communication was impossible between much of the high country and the valley below. She pressed Talk. "Kent, this is Sam."

She released. Nothing but static and what sounded like a gasp. She tried again. "Kent, do you read?"

More static. Did he have his finger on the damn Talk button? "Kent? Kent?"

"Sam?" His voice was thin, scratchy—it sounded like they were connected by tin cans and string. "Sam, I can't raise HQ. I need HQ."

"I can barely hear you, and I'm a lot closer than park headquarters. Where are you? Over."

Heavy breathing. "Milagro Canyon . . . near Ghost Stack."

"Monument Ridge is between you and HQ. They can't read you. You'll have to climb up to the mesa."

A brief pause and a crackle of static. "Can't climb. I need help. Need HQ." He sounded disoriented.

Her knuckles whitened on the radio. "Talk to me, Kent. Explain your situation. Now!"

An intake of breath. "There's been a shooting."

"Who's been shot, Kent? Over."

A burst of static. Or was it coughing? "Mountain lion . . . here in front of me . . . still alive."

"Someone shot a lion?" So the cracks had been rifle shots, not distant thunder.

A loud exhalation. "Me, too."

Her chest tightened. "Say again, Kent?"

"Hunters . . . three guys. Shot a cougar." A ragged cough. "And me."

A surge of adrenaline shot through her bloodstream. "Are the hunters there with you?"

A gurgle. "Just the cat and me."

"Hang on—I'm on my way, Kent. I'll be there as fast as I can. Clear."

She tried to raise headquarters from her radio. As she expected, the signal was blocked. She sprinted to Perez and jerked the phone from his hand.

"Hey!"

She punched the End button and then speed-dialed the number for park headquarters.

"Heritage National Monument Ranger Station."

"We need a medical rescue helicopter at Milagro Canyon—a ranger's been shot." She grabbed her knapsack and threw it over a shoulder.

"What? Who is this?"

She was already running down the trail. Breathlessly, she identified herself, then yelled, "Kent Bergstrom's been shot! Get that helicopter up there. Milagro Canyon! Now!"

15

THE muscles in Sam's legs were screaming. Would this nightmare never end?

She had the phone pressed to her ear, listening to Tanner, who was telling her that the Civil Air Patrol choppers assisting in the search carried only rudimentary first aid and weren't insured to treat patients.

"I don't give a damn if they're insured or not!" she huffed. "They can land, they can pick him up, they can take him to the nearest hos—"

Tanner interrupted. "We have liability issues."

Kent had been shot and his boss was worried about liability issues? Tanner told her that the St. George Fire Department agreed to send their helicopter, but they'd have to stop at park headquarters to pick up a ranger to guide them to the exact position.

How long would that take? If she ran all the way, she could reach Kent in forty-five minutes. As a ranger, her friend had been trained in first aid. She prayed he was in condition to minister to himself.

Perez's footsteps pounded steadily behind her. They

reached the turnoff point to Temple Canyon, skidded down a cliff-hugging series of switchbacks, and flew past the Anasazi ruins. Did Perez notice the stone buildings crowded under the dark overhang? Probably not. No doubt his eyes were focused on the rocky trail, as were hers.

Her breath was coming hard; that was the altitude. Behind her, Perez was huffing, too. As they neared Milagro Canyon, they passed two MISSING posters, hung by Kent as he had made his rounds.

After what felt like days of lung-bursting effort, she and Perez pounded across a shallow creek on an ancient log bridge, climbed a small rise, and finally reached the narrow walled-in area known as Milagro Canyon. The cross-country sprint had taken them forty minutes.

She stumbled to a stop, holding her side, trying to catch her breath. Sweat ran down her backbone and trickled from her scalp over her cheeks. Beside her, Perez hunched over, still wearing his backpack, his shirt and face similarly soaked, his hands on his knees, gasping. Then she saw it. Amid the shadows and cracks in the stone surface, a wide swath of crimson gleamed wetly across the canyon floor.

The trail of blood led them to the shade of a rock overhang where Kent lay. She fell to her knees beside him. The front of his shirt and right sleeve were soaked with blood. Her heart pounded in her throat. They'd arrived too late. All that blood—

She squeezed her eyes shut, took a deep breath. *Get a grip, Westin. Now.* Opening her eyes, she focused on her friend. Kent's face was pale and shiny with sweat. He blinked. Thank God. Still alive.

Kent's backpack rested against a nearby rock. While Perez checked Kent, Sam dug out her friend's first-aid supplies—a ranger would have more than the basic Band-Aids and pills she carried. She burst the plastic encasing a metallic rescue blanket, shook it out, and covered Kent from the waist down, tucking it around his legs and feet. After two tries with shaking fingers, she used her teeth to rip open a package of sterile pads.

"Went right through the arm," Perez reported, "but there's no exit wound from the chest. Probably the same bullet."

The injury to Kent's right forearm had almost quit bleeding, but his chest wound was a red well of blood. She pressed two of the gauze squares to the ragged hole beneath the right collarbone. Blood soaked through the cloth, welled up between her fingers. She added two more pads, pressed harder, using both hands now.

"Hey," Kent wheezed. "How'm I s'posed to breathe with you squeezin' the life outta me?"

She was leaning on his chest to keep the life *in* him. She forced a smile. At least she hoped her expression looked like a smile. Her face felt paralyzed and tears blurred her vision.

"Guess . . . should've escorted those hunters out," Kent choked out. "Never should've trusted 'em to leave—" His blue eyes had the glaze of someone in shock.

"What happened?" Perez asked.

"I was . . . watching him come down . . . from up there." Kent directed them with his eyes. About fifty yards away and twenty feet above them in elevation, Sam spotted a splash of blood on a narrow rock ledge that cut diagonally across the cliff face.

"Oh Sam, he was . . . so . . . beautiful." His shaky smile slid into a grimace. "Then . . . dogs . . . behind me." He coughed, his forehead creasing in pain. "I stood up . . . blam! Next one got him."

Sam followed Kent's gaze. A hundred yards across the canyon, a cougar crouched in the patchy shadow of a ponderosa. The big cat glared at them, panting heavily as though the air was too thick to breathe. The sinews in its neck stood out as it strained to lick the blood leaking from a ragged hole high in its hindquarters.

She scanned the area, envisioning the whole episode. The hunters, low on the trail, training their sights on the cat on the hillside. They hadn't realized that Kent was sitting just over the next rise. He had stood up at the crucial moment.

Kent's eyes were on her. "Bad timing, huh?"

"What happened to the hunters?" Perez asked.

"Took off." Kent closed his eyes. "Bastards . . . Eagle Tours."

"What? What about Eagle Tours, Kent?" she asked. "Was it Buck Ferguson?"

"Don't think so," he mumbled between rasping breaths. He opened his eyes again. "Just saw . . . Eagle Tours . . . black cap."

Nodding, Sam glanced at Perez. "Sounds like it might be Buck Ferguson. He's been caught here with a rifle more than once."

Kent lay his head back against the stone. A bubble of blood formed at the corner of his mouth.

"Sam." He grasped her sleeve. "Save the cougar."

"I will if I can. Right now I'm more worried about you."

Kent coughed. "Save the cat."

Perez knelt beside her, placing his hand over hers on Kent's chest. "I'll take over if you want to check the cat."

Her eyes met Kent's. His chin dipped in a single nod. "Please." Then his eyelids closed.

She slid her hand out from under Perez's. Her palm and wrist were slick with blood. She wiped the wetness away on her pants and then pushed herself to her feet.

Perez said, "Hang in there, Kent. There's a helicopter on the way. It'll be here any minute now."

She walked toward the cat's position. Its yellow eyes widened. As she neared, the cougar spat and tightened its muscles to stand, but it wasn't able to lift its hindquarters from the rock. A growing pool of blood stained the stone beneath the animal. Each agitated stroke of the cougar's tail painted a fresh stripe of red in the dust.

"Take it easy, boy," she murmured, standing still. The cat was a large male. Leto's mate? His fur had the same gray tinge as Apollo's.

He raised a massive paw, claws extended, and snarled, his eyes wild now. Sam backed away slowly and returned to the men.

"He's been shot in the hindquarters," she reported. "I can't tell how bad it is. He can't walk, but he's still pretty feisty. That's a good sign, Kent."

Her friend's eyes were closed. She couldn't tell if he'd heard or not. Perez had rolled up his windbreaker and placed it beneath the ranger's head. Even with the roughness of two days' worth of whiskers lining his cheeks, Kent looked so young.

The faint sound of a distant helicopter drifted up the canyon. Thank God! It had made the trip sooner than she'd expected.

Perez placed a gentle hand on Kent's good shoulder. "The copter's arrived. We'll have you out of here in a few minutes."

Surprising them both, Kent opened his eyes and said distinctly, "I'm not going without the cat."

The helicopter neared, the thunder of the blades echoing in the narrow canyon. They'd have to land on the plateau above and bring the stretcher down.

"I mean it," gasped Kent. "I'm still pretty feisty, too." He raised his left arm, his fingers curled into claws, and wheezed out a weak imitation of a snarl.

"Knock off that crap," Sam ordered. "I'll see what I can do about the cat, but you're going regardless."

"Dart him. Tranq pistol . . . my pack."

"I'll dart you, too, if I have to, to get you on that copter."

The slapping of helicopter blades gave way to a low whine, then blessed silence. Sam ran to meet the two men who were struggling down the steep slope from the plateau above, bearing a stretcher with an emergency pack and oxygen tank lashed between the poles. Both men wore the navy uniforms of the St. George Fire Department. One sported a baseball cap with SUPER FLY embroidered on the front.

"How many people can your chopper carry?" she demanded.

"Six adults, tops. That includes the three of us."

"Do you have more than one emergency?" The other

fellow touched her pants leg where she had wiped Kent's blood off her hands.

Park Superintendent Thompson, his face beet red from exertion, skidded down the slope in a shower of gravel to join them. He studied her bloody clothing with concern. "You okay, Westin?"

"I'm fine," she snapped, swatting the medic's hand away from her leg. "It's Ranger Bergstrom who's been shot." She pointed toward Perez and Kent. Then she gestured across the canyon. "And a cougar."

"You've got to be kidding," said the pilot, staring at the animal. The cat had managed to pull itself up into a crouch. It snarled at the new intruders.

Kent's face now had a blue tinge she'd seen in her nightmares, but as the rescue workers knelt down beside him he opened his eyes. Sam took comfort in knowing that Kent was a fighter.

Thompson stood by Sam's side, shifting anxiously from foot to foot. He mopped his forehead with a handkerchief, staring doubtfully at the wounded cougar. "We should probably just shoot him." He glanced toward Perez, who already had a hand on his pistol.

"No way," Sam warned.

Thompson's head swiveled back, his expression showing surprise at her tone.

"Kent has darts. I'm a wildlife biologist, too, remember? I know how to use them." Sam unzipped the lower compartment on Kent's pack, found the tranquilizer pistol, darts, and a vial of clear liquid.

"I'm estimating the cat at about a hundred and thirty pounds," Sam said, praying she remembered the right proportions for the tranquilizer.

"Looks about right," Thompson agreed.

After measuring the dose and loading the dart syringe into the pistol, she walked to within twenty feet of the cougar. The cat sat up, its whole body shaking now. It growled. She raised the pistol. The cougar spat, its muscles rippling with tension. Its ears were folded back against its sleek head, its amber eyes on fire. How could anyone aim a bullet at such an incredible creature for sport? Not for self-defense, not to save livestock, but just to put out the light in those eyes.

She aimed at the cougar's hindquarters where the needle could lodge in thick muscle, and squeezed the trigger. The gun fired with a loud pop. The cat lunged to its feet with an outraged snarl.

Startled, she tripped over her own feet, came down hard on her backside and had to scramble backward like a crab. The cat's teeth snapped together a few inches shy of her calf. "Shit!"

Five pairs of male eyes were watching her. She pushed herself to her feet, thankful that she hadn't wet her pants. "Well," she said, "I guess it's a good sign that he can stand up."

"You didn't get him." Thompson pointed to the ground behind the cat.

He was right. The dart was embedded in the base of the tree. Even worse, she'd dropped the gun when she fell. The pistol now lay three feet from the cougar's new position.

"We're ready," the fire department medic shouted. "We've got to get going—this guy's lost a lot of blood."

"We're out of time," Thompson growled. "Agent Perez, can I borrow your pistol?"

"I'll do it." Perez reached for his gun.

The fire department team picked up the stretcher. "Put me down," Kent wheezed angrily. "I'm not going without the cat!"

Sam studied the cougar. The animal tried to touch his injured leg to the ground, wobbled for a moment, then sat down. His tongue slid in and out of his mouth as he panted. The effort of lunging at her had cost him severely.

"He's coming, Kent." She lowered herself to her hands and knees and crawled toward the pistol.

"Don't—" Thompson hissed.

She sprawled full length on the rocks, stretched her hand out as far as she could toward the pistol. The cougar snarled and raised a paw. The cat reached out at the same time she did but missed her arm by inches. Her fingers curled around the handle. She rolled back over the rocks, the pistol clutched in her fist.

Her hands were shaking so hard that she had difficulty loading the second dart. Thompson shook his head and reached for the gun.

Sam grabbed the tranquilizer pistol away. "No, I'm going to do it right this time." She clutched the weapon in both hands and strode toward the cat.

"She's a little hardheaded," Perez grumbled.

The superintendent nodded. "I know that."

The cougar stood, wobbling on its feet. Sam stopped her advance ten feet away and braced herself, her legs spread, clutching the pistol with both hands. One more chance. She aimed at the middle of its right rear haunch and fired. The cat snarled and lunged, stretching out a muscular paw with razor-sharp claws extended. She jumped back.

Perez ran to steady her as she staggered backward. "Did he get you?"

She pulled aside the ripped flap of her canvas trousers. Three red stripes gleamed against the skin, beads of blood beginning to ooze out. "Barely. Just a scratch."

The cougar stumbled, fell back onto his haunches, then collapsed on its side. The dart extended from its flank, the cylinder moving in rhythm with the cat's harsh breathing.

"We're loaded," the pilot shouted from above.

"Wait!" she screamed. "We're coming."

She gingerly prodded the cougar with her foot. "Is anybody going to help me carry this mountain lion or do I have to drag him up by his tail?"

Her belt and Thompson's were used to secure the big cat's feet. It took Sam, Perez, and Thompson to carry the animal up the slope, slipping and sliding with the limp burden in the loose gravel.

They slid the cat onto the helicopter floor beside the stretcher. It was painful to see both Kent and the cougar reduced to such dependent states, broken bodies to be carted around like so much baggage.

"Call Dr. Stephanie Black in St. George about this cougar." In the past, the vet had donated her services to help injured wildlife: she'd been instrumental in healing Leto and her cubs.

The medic anxiously regarded the lolling head beside his foot. Saliva drooled out between the cat's jaws. The animal's eyes were open but glazed and unfocused.

She tugged on the medic's sleeve. "Dr. Black. Can you remember that?"

The man nodded, his eyes still fixed on the tranquilized cougar. "Black," he repeated. His eyes widened as a patch of skin on the cat's back shuddered as if a fly had landed there. "Are you sure he's completely out?"

"He's paralyzed but not unconscious. He'll start coming out of it in about forty minutes."

The medic shot a glance toward the pilot. "Dave, let's go."

The pilot started the engine. Thompson clambered into the passenger seat, puffing.

"Damn!" Perez interjected. "Wait!" He trotted down the hill toward the canyon, yelling, "FBI business!" back over his shoulder.

The pilot's hands clenched on the controls. "No more than two minutes," he warned.

The medic inserted an IV into Kent's arm. He coughed wetly, but his eyes were open. He clenched his free hand into a fist with his thumb-pointed upward. "I'm okay," he rasped.

"No talking," ordered the medic. "And no more moving."

Sam returned the thumbs-up sign. "Hang in there, Kent."

Perez galloped up, jerked open the passenger door, and thrust the USGS map and a page of notes into Thompson's lap. "Get this to Agent Boudreaux ASAP and tell her to get a Crime Scene team to this location on the double."

"Crime scene team?" Confusion warred with annoyance in the superintendent's expression.

A flicker of anger crossed Perez's face. "Just get the message to Boudreaux. And see what you can dig up on Coyote Charlie."

"Coyote Charlie? That nut? What for?"

The pilot interrupted. "We've got to go. *Now!*"

Sam tapped Perez on the shoulder, gestured toward the open door. "Room for one more. You need to handle this yourself."

"You get in first," he told her.

"Not with the cat," the pilot shouted over the whir of the prop. "Only one. If either of you is coming, get in! This bird is leaving now."

Perez looked at her. "I don't want to leave you up here alone," he said loudly.

She studied his face. "Why not?"

They stared at each other for a second. Then she pulled on Perez's sleeve and when he leaned close, she said into his ear, "I'm headed for the ruins."

Perez nodded, then swung through the open door and slid into the jump seat by the medic's side, his boots straddling the inert mountain lion on the floor.

"Catch the hunters that shot Kent," she yelled. The medic leaned forward and slid the door closed.

Just before it latched, Perez shouted, "Don't go near that skeleton. And I damn well better not see anything about it on the Internet!"

The helicopter rose from the ground. She ducked her head to protect her eyes. Swirling sand bit into her bare neck and arms.

16

AT four o'clock, Thompson dropped Perez at the Las Rojas Police Station. Nicole met him at the door.

She eyed his bloodstained shirt and dirt-streaked khaki trousers. "You're in violation of dress code."

"So report me."

Nicole's turquoise silk blouse and cream-colored slacks were, as usual, immaculate. Her chestnut hair was clipped at the back of her neck with a tortoiseshell barrette. She folded her arms. "Are you sure you're okay?"

He gestured at the rust-colored streaks on his ruined shirt and pants. "None of the red stuff belongs to me."

"I brought you some clean clothes. They're inside."

"You broke into my hotel room?"

She smiled. "The maid was happy to open the door. By the way, you're an incredible slob, Perez. Do you always leave your underwear on the closet floor?"

"Only when I know you'll be visiting," he said. "I suppose you hang yours up."

"How's the ranger?"

"Don't know yet. They took him to surgery right after I talked to you."

"The cougar?"

Perez snorted. "Oh, he was pretty feisty even before we landed. I sat on him the last ten minutes of the flight."

Her face lit up. "That must have been interesting."

"Fascinating. I kept envisioning those two-inch fangs sinking into my gluteus maximus. Fortunately, the vet was there when we touched down."

"What's with Crime Scene?" she asked.

"On their way from Salt Lake, according to Martino. He was really pissed that they'd just come back from here."

She nodded, familiar with the normal grumpy attitude of the Crime Scene team leader. "They finished doing the kids' truck yesterday around two. Flew back last night."

Perez glanced at his watch. "A park ranger is standing by to escort them as soon as they arrive. If there are no hitches, they should be in position by four. That'll give them almost three hours of daylight—it should be enough to do at least a preliminary check of the immediate dump site." He turned toward her. "So it's obvious that I've been doing my part. How's the cushy end of the investigation going down here?"

Nicole stared him in the eye. "Don't give me that crap. I can tell you've enjoyed your little escapade in the wilderness. And don't think that I didn't notice the blond reporter pixie you were chasing. I don't think she's your type." She walked toward the station entrance.

He followed. "I have a type?"

The Las Rojas Police Station was quiet, devoid of the hectic bustle and coded conversations that he associated with big-city police stations. Nicole's heels echoed on the scuffed tiles as they crossed the lobby to the tiny interview room. "I'm surprised the press isn't here," she said.

"Give 'em time. When we left the hospital, they were doing live reports in front of the helicopter. They kept asking Thompson if the cougar was the one that killed Zack."

"You didn't tell them about the skeleton?" Reaching into her leather briefcase, she pulled out a stack of clothing.

"It'll get around soon enough." He thumbed through the folded articles. "Even boxers—I'm impressed, partner."

"I couldn't stand the thought of you wearing none." She faked a shudder.

He fingered the tie on the top of the stack. "I usually wear this tie with my blue shirt."

"It goes better with the gray."

"No shoes? Hoover would be shocked at an agent wearing hiking boots during an interview."

Nicole placed a hand on the interview table and leaned close, her face inches away from Perez's. "They wouldn't fit in my briefcase," she said in a low voice. "Hoover's dead. Go get changed before I shoot you."

He drew back. "You haven't had a smoke today, have you, Boudreaux?"

She gazed at him coolly. "I'm quitting."

"Again?"

She pointed to the door. "Go."

Perez decided that if Nicole were an animal, she'd be a Siamese cat. Sleek, sophisticated, smart, but more than willing to use her claws when necessary. He tried two doors before he found the changing room used by the local officers. He rolled up his stained clothing and stuffed it into a trash can. It looked like evidence from a homicide.

He checked himself in the mirror. Nicole was right: the tie did look better with the gray shirt. Wetting a paper towel, he scrubbed a smear of dried blood from his cheek, ran his fingers through his hair. He badly needed a shave, but that would have to wait.

He found Nicole pacing the hallway outside of the interview room. "The sheriff's still out on lunch break. He should be back any time now, and we can interview the boys then. They haven't deviated an inch from the story they were telling night before last."

"Did we really arrest them the night before last?" It

seemed like he'd been galloping around up on the plateau for at least a week.

Nicole gave him a curious look. "They're still claiming a shaggy-haired stranger hired them to pick up the money."

The heavy glass door at the front of the station opened and a party of three walked in. The two women argued loudly while the girl with them sobbed into her hands. One woman wore curlers; a canvas handbag dangled from one hand. The deputy at the desk straightened when he saw the shotgun clutched in her other hand.

"I love small towns," Nicole said, her tone implying exactly the opposite.

The unarmed woman's green blouse was blotched with damp red streaks. She stomped across the lobby to the desk and threw down a leather dog collar in front of the deputy. "That woman," she intoned, transforming the word into an epithet, "shot my dog."

The curlered matron waved the shotgun in the air. "I thought a mountain lion was hiding in the bushes, sneaking up on my little girl." She gestured at the crying girl. "See how upset she is?"

"She's freaked out because her mother shot an innocent Labrador retriever right in front of her eyes!"

The girl turned her face into her mother's ample bosom and sobbed more loudly.

Two news vans screeched to a stop outside the station door. A pair of female reporters dressed in white blouses and dark blazers raced for the door handle. The deputy looked hopefully down the hallway at the two FBI agents.

Nicole closed the door to the lobby, abandoning the deputy to his fate. Perez helped himself to a drink from the fountain. The chilled liquid tasted deliciously fresh in comparison to the tepid water he'd consumed from plastic bottles for the last twenty-four hours. His knees were going to ache for days—not to mention his back. How did Summer Westin pack her heavy equipment around up there day in and day out?

She blended so naturally into the surroundings of rock

and cactus and pines, clearly at home with the cougars and deer and eagles. Her petite size and silver-blond hair made her appear delicate, but that woman was made of cast iron. A few cougar scratches probably wouldn't even slow her down.

Five hours ago he'd been hunched in a cave, staring at a skull; two and a half hours ago he'd been trying to staunch the flow of blood from Ranger Bergstrom's gunshot wound. He'd galloped for miles over rocks and down sheer cliffs, carried an unbelievably heavy tranquilized cougar not once but twice, and zipped from desert backcountry to air-conditioned town in a fire department helicopter. A strange day. And it wasn't even five o'clock.

He wiped a drip from his lower lip. "Anything from the APBs or news coverage?"

She shrugged. "Hundreds of little blond boys being abducted all over the place; the cops'll never forgive us for this one. They'll be checking reports for weeks."

"Oh crap." It gave him a headache just to think about the logistics. He hoped the locals weren't complaining to the Special Agent in Charge of their FBI office. "Can we get some support from Salt Lake?"

"You know the SAC. Without some real proof to the contrary, he's assuming that the kid just wandered off or was eaten by a cougar. It's better for the budget. But your skeleton will shake a few dollars loose. Serial murderers always get their attention."

"How about this Wildlife Services business? It doesn't make a lot of sense to proceed with a cougar hunt right now." Summer would be so happy if he could pull off canceling the hunt.

"When did politics ever make sense?" Nicole said. "Now the secretaries of agriculture and interior have gotten involved. They're vowing to make our national parks safe again." She rolled her eyes. "The SAC's not going to touch it unless we have proof that Zack Fischer's still alive. It doesn't matter how many old skeletons we find."

A heavy sigh escaped his lips. "Anything more on those three felons you called me about this morning?"

"Yeah." She let go of the earring she'd been fiddling with. "Come on." She pushed open the door to the interview room. He followed her inside.

From her briefcase, she pulled a plastic bag containing a tiny red sneaker, swung it back and forth in the air. "Forensics couldn't get a decent print. But I told you that, didn't I?" She tossed it back into her case and extracted a notepad, then plopped down in one of the wooden chairs that ringed the table. "So far there's nothing of interest on the boys' lowrider, either, nothing that could have come from Zack or from his parents."

Perez pulled out the chair across from her. He leaned it back on two legs. He folded his hands across his chest and inspected the yellowed acoustic tiles on the ceiling. The room smelled of stale cigarette smoke.

Nicole read from her notes. "The murderer's back home in Las Vegas, according to Vegas PD. Nothing suspicious when they cruised his house today. His wife accused them of harassment, so they backed off. But they'll follow up if we want."

"Do we want?"

"I don't see any connection between a guy that got drunk and blew away his business partner eight years ago and this week's disappearance of a two-year-old, do you?"

Perez considered for a few seconds, then shook his head.

"The stickup artist hasn't shown up back in Ohio, but his credit card has been used several times between here and Denver. He's probably on his way home." She turned the page of the notepad.

"I don't see a likely link between armed robbery and Zachary, either."

"No," she agreed. "But I'm having Highway Patrol catch up with him just to make sure he doesn't have a toddler in his camper." She tapped the lined page in front of her. "Of more interest is our child molester, Wallace Russell. Like I told you, his Buick Skylark entered the park five days ago, two days before Zack disappeared."

Perez put his feet on the floor and returned the chair to

all four legs. He felt dazed. This case had started only three days ago?

Nicole continued. "Wallace Russell, arrested and released three times for indecent exposure, arrested and convicted twice for child molestation."

"Consisting of?"

She consulted her notes. "According to the five-year-old girl involved in the latest incident, he asked her to 'pet his magic mushroom to make it grow.'"

Nicole's gaze met his above the notepad. Her mouth crinkled at the edges.

"This shouldn't be funny." He clasped his hands together on top of the table.

She nodded. "We both know these perverts can escalate, and there's nothing funny about that. He'd apparently put his fingers around the child's neck; there were bruises there. It's just the . . . magic . . . mushroom—"

They simultaneously lost it. Perez laughed until his nose ran. He pulled out a handkerchief and honked into it. Across the table, Nicole wiped her fingers across her cheeks, smudging the mascara that ran down from her eyes. He held out his handkerchief to her. Her resulting disgust made him burst into laughter again.

Nicole slapped both hands against the tabletop. "Enough. They'll be in any moment now."

She kept her eyes averted, mopped at streaks of mascara with a tissue, composed herself as she regarded her face in her compact mirror. Perez blew his nose again, stuffed the handkerchief back into his pocket. From mountain lions to skulls to gunshot wounds to magic mushrooms. This must be what it felt like to trip on LSD.

Nicole snapped the compact shut. "Let's get back to it. Our pervert got out on parole two years ago. His address is in Flagstaff, but he hasn't been home for the last two weeks."

So Wallace Russell had been in the park but was currently unaccounted for. "Nobody's keeping track of this guy? What the heck has his parole officer been doing?"

"Twiddling his thumbs and counting the days to retirement, apparently. He did condescend to provide us with a photo, even if it's two years old." She waved the black and white square of paper in the air.

The door opened. Sheriff Wolford stuck his head in. "Have you seen the lobby?"

They nodded.

"Goddamn vultures." He ran his fingers through his hair, standing it on end. "Ready for the boys?" The man glanced at Perez, then at Nicole. "Something up between you two?"

"Nope," Perez snapped. "Bring 'em in."

The chair squeaked as Perez slid it back. He took the bag containing Zack's shoe from Nicole's briefcase, removed the sneaker, and set it in the middle of the table.

"Good idea," she said. "Let's see if they sweat." She sighed heavily. "This case is a mess, isn't it?"

So she thought so, too. "I'm not even sure where to look next," he admitted. "Do you think we have a chance in hell of finding this poor kid?"

"Something better break soon. Miller's getting antsy, especially now that we've asked for Crime Scene two days in a row."

Perez nodded. Their SAC wasn't long on patience.

The two teenagers filed in. Stripped of their padded jackets and air-filled tennis shoes, both Billy Joseph and Patrick Wiley appeared to have shrunk during their incarceration. Orange jail uniforms added a jaundiced hue to their complexions. The sheriff motioned for them to sit, then positioned himself behind them, his arms folded over his substantial belly.

"No lawyer?" Nicole asked.

The sheriff shook his head. "Their parents didn't want to have to pay the hourly fee for this part, and they wouldn't accept a PD. Said they didn't take charity."

"The parents aren't coming, either?"

"Mrs. Wiley's in the ladies'," Wolford replied. "She'll be here any minute." Right on cue, a middle-aged woman walked in, nodded to the agents, sat down next to Patrick. She wore a flowered shirtwaist dress. Her graying hair was scraped back from her red cheeks, held in place with two yellow plastic barrettes. She kept her eyes on the table.

"The Josephs aren't coming," Wolford added. "It's a fifty-minute drive from Floral."

"I had to take time off work myself," Mrs. Wiley murmured in a soft voice.

Perez was appalled. Would the parents take more notice if their kids had murdered someone? Maybe they didn't understand the seriousness of the charge.

Nicole tapped the tabletop impatiently. "Okay, we're all here, then. Ready, boys?"

Billy placed his palms on the table. Patrick nodded, a grim expression on his face. A large pimple had blossomed in the crease of his right nostril. His gaze focused on the shoe; he reached for it.

"What a dinky sneak!" He balanced it on the palm of his hand and held it out to his friend.

Billy squirmed in his chair, his cheeks nearly as red as Mrs. Wiley's. Patrick stared at the miniature sneaker, stole a look at his friend again, gazed back at the shoe. Finally, his eyes met the agents'. "Is it his?"

Nicole narrowed her eyes. "What do you think?"

Patrick dropped the shoe as if it was suddenly too hot to handle. Perez exchanged a glance with Nicole. Inconclusive.

Nicole got serious. "How did you boys put the ransom note together?"

The teens shot nervous glances at each other.

Perez turned to Nicole. "Think we should separate them?"

"We didn't send it," Billy blurted out.

"Then who did?" Nicole asked.

Billy's gaze darted to Patrick's, then back down to the table in front of him. "Don't know."

"The copy shop clerk described a young woman." Perez placed a grainy picture of Jenny Fischer in front of the boys. A head shot had been cropped from the family photo and blown up. Jenny more or less matched the description provided by the attendant in the copy shop from which the message had been sent. "Did this woman fax the message?"

Both boys barely glanced at the picture. "We don't know nothing about the ransom note," Billy enunciated carefully, as if he were speaking to an idiot.

Mrs. Wiley picked up the photo. "Isn't this that poor baby's mama? She's so young. 'Cept for that big red blotch there, she looks a little like Suzanna."

Patrick flinched noticeably.

Nicole perked up. "Who is Suzanna?"

The woman touched her son's arm. "Suzanna Christensen. Pat's girlfriend. They go to school together. She wasn't involved in this foolishness, was she, son?"

Patrick stared at the ceiling.

Perez recovered the snapshot. "Thank you, Mrs. Wiley. We'll talk to Suzanna."

Nicole laid photos on the table, snapping them crisply like a card dealer. "Wait until they're all out before you say anything."

Twelve photos, in three rows of four, depicted men in their thirties and forties, some with earrings and beards or mustaches, all with longish hair.

"Did any of these guys hire you?" Nicole asked.

The youths scanned the pictures carefully. Billy picked one up. An old jail photo of a baby-faced man. Long dark hair combed over a balding crown, then rubber-banded into a limp ponytail. The magic mushroom's old parole photo.

"This guy seems kind of familiar," the youth said. "I think I seen him over at the Burger House."

Patrick glanced at the photo in his friend's hand. "Doesn't look familiar to me. You're losin' it, buddy."

The sheriff peered over the boys' shoulders, then raised his gaze to Perez's and shook his head. He resumed his position against the wall.

Billy slid the photo back into its position in the grid. Patrick tapped an index finger on the middle photo in the lowest row. The boys exchanged glances. Billy nodded.

Patrick held the photo out to Nicole. "This is the guy."

Billy agreed. "He hired us to pick up the money."

Perez and Nicole examined the photo the youths had chosen. Fred Fischer's face smiled up at them from the slick paper.

JENNY Fischer sat alone in a booth in the Appletree Café. She held a coffee cup in her hands, stared into the black liquid. It was blessedly quiet, except for the whoosh of the vacuum cleaner that the waitress was running over the threadbare carpet between the tables. She couldn't take any more phone calls from the press. There'd even been someone from a talk show on TV. They all wanted to know how she felt.

How did they think she felt? She'd lost everything. Her parents had never liked Fred. She raised her hand, cupped it over the birthmark on her cheek. Why couldn't they understand that an ugly girl like her didn't have options? Worse, they'd been right; marrying him was a mistake. He'd been good to her for almost three years, but now, at the first sign of trouble, he disappeared. What kind of a husband was that?

Zack's orange plastic truck, missing its wheel, was on the table in front of her. She stared at it, the last thing her baby had touched. Why, oh why, hadn't she been playing with Zack, holding him, instead of fussing with that damn camp stove?

The FBI agents seemed to think that Fred might have something to do with her baby's disappearance. And Fred had been gone all that time after she'd discovered Zack was missing. And this whole cougar business. Fred had really started it by bringing them here, by pointing out the posters; hadn't he? Could she really have been that blind? That stupid?

"Mrs. Fischer."

She raised her head. The two FBI agents stood next to her table.

The female agent slid into the booth beside her. "Where's your husband?"

When Jenny didn't respond instantly, the agent turned to her partner. "I can't believe the sheriff sent the deputy off to some hunting accident; I specifically told him a twenty-four-hour watch."

The man slid into the opposite seat. Even though his expression was solemn, his clear brown eyes looked kind. "Where's Fred, Mrs. Fischer?" he asked.

"He told me he was going out for a cinnamon roll," Jenny said.

They both just stared at her, waiting. She slammed the cup down, slopping coffee over the red and white checkered oilcloth. Tears flooded down her face. "He's gone!" she choked out. "He's been gone since nine o'clock this morning."

She flung an arm onto the table. The spilled coffee seeped into the sleeve of her pink blouse, but she didn't care. Her fingers curled convulsively around the tiny truck. "I don't have Zack; I don't have Fred; now I don't even have a goddamn car!"

17

THE trail slanted uphill another mile to the mesa. Sam made herself keep looking in every crevice and under every bush. She tried hard to keep her focus on finding any hint of Zack, but it was hard to think of anything other than Kent and the cougar and how much her feet hurt. Her thigh throbbed with each step, and soon her head joined in. Each jolt was accompanied by a slosh from her water bottle and a metallic ting from objects clanging together inside her knapsack. A symphony of aches and pains.

Above her position, over the crest, helicopter blades reverberated. The racket grew louder, the noise hanging in the air. Sounded like the machine had touched down near ZigZag Passage. After five minutes, the low roar changed to a high whine, and the copter buzzed by overhead. A quick peek at her watch confirmed that more than four hours had passed since the rescue helicopter had left Milagro Canyon. Enough time to bring in Crime Scene investigators from Salt Lake City?

She envisioned Perez directing a team of thick-lensed forensic experts to the location of the skull. Or would

Agent Boudreaux take charge of the investigation? She hoped Apollo hadn't come back to his kill; she didn't trust either FBI agent not to shoot the lion on sight.

She stopped to check a shadow under a low bush. Nothing but dust. She straightened and went on.

"Zack!" she yelled, for good measure. "Zachary!"

She stopped for a minute to listen and heard the only response she expected, another shrill cry from the red-tailed hawk circling overhead. It sounded like one of this year's fledglings. They were always noisy when they were learning to hunt. Maybe they just couldn't contain their excitement at seeing the world spread out beneath them.

"Zack! Hey, little buddy, where are you? Answer me." *If you can,* she silently added in her thoughts. After finding the skull and seeing Kent and the cougar bleeding into the dust, it was hard to keep up the hope that Zack would be found alive and well.

The hawk screeched again. If only she shared that raptor's view now. Could the hawk see the investigators uncovering more bones? Coyote Charlie skulking through the canyons nearby? Could the hawk see Zack?

A dark crevice in the cliff wall nearby caught her attention, and she walked over to peer into it. It went back only about four feet, and no little boy huddled in the shadows there. She trudged back to the trail and resumed her uphill march.

She'd passed the two MISSING notices on her hike back from Milagro Canyon. She was beginning to despise those posters. If Zack had stayed with his parents, she would be earning her pay by writing about wildlife, ecology, the beauty of nature. Kent would be happy and healthy, and so would the cougar. There'd be no MISSING posters fluttering from rocks. There'd be no helicopters drowning out the birdsong. There'd be no teams of sharpshooters on their way to murder the cats. This was all Fred and Jenny Fischer's fault.

Then she remembered the young mother's anguished face. And she recalled the moment when she'd freed herself from the brambles and found the dark path empty in front of her. If she had just taken the time to talk to Zack's parents that night . . .

If that little boy was dead or in the clutches of some pervert, how was she going to live with that?

"Zack! Zachary!" No response except a faint echo from the surrounding cliffs. Even the hawk had gone now.

She checked her watch; she had a couple more hours of daylight. Temple Arch loomed to the east of the path, a blind arch where centuries ago, a half-moon of rock had fallen away from the overhanging curve of the cliff overhead. Tucked into the snug indent were the Anasazi ruins she and Perez had headed for this morning.

This was the canyon into which Coyote Charlie had disappeared. She shaded her eyes and peered at the steep cliff down which he'd vanished. There was no obvious path, but a closer inspection might reveal a line of ancient Anasazi footholds linking the protruding rocks that zigzagged up the vertical slope.

Coyote Charlie might be making a collection up here, Perez had said. It gave her the creeps to think he could be nearby, watching her right now.

"Zack! Answer me, Zachary!" Please.

She stood at the junction of Goodman Trail and Milagro Trail. Below her, three hundred feet down, Village Falls fell in a long horsetail from the cliff. The noise of the waterfall was barely audible, like the white noise of distant traffic. She licked her chapped lips, thinking of that clear cold water. But the round-trip to the falls would take at least thirty minutes out of the remaining two hours of sunlight: she couldn't afford it.

The stale liquid from her water bottle left a metallic taste in her mouth. She poured the last few drops into her palm and rubbed her face and neck. Her hand came away streaked with brick red smears. Kent's blood.

She pulled out her phone and called park headquarters. Jerry Thompson told her that Kent had come through surgery and was in intensive care; that he'd dropped Perez off at Las Rojas Police Station; that yes, an FBI Crime Scene team was working up above; and that no, he didn't know about the cougar.

Didn't give a damn about the cougar, she thought bitterly as she hung up. He'd been more than ready to shoot the wounded cat on sight. The superintendent struck her as more politician than conservationist; he'd no doubt cooperate fully with the "wildlife control officers" dispatched from USDAWS, even if he believed that killing the lions was pointless.

She called Lauren at SWF. Her voice mail answered. Was Lauren avoiding her now? She punched in Max Garay's number.

"Yo."

"Max? It's Sam. How's it going up there?"

"It was nice while it lasted," he said in his lazy fashion. "Easy come, easy go."

"Harding hasn't fired us, has he?"

"Us? Speak for yourself, WildWest. I'm a permanent employee; I'm the only one who can show Harding how to work his computer. And I've got about eleven thousand more photos to digitize here. But the answer you're looking for is, no, not quite yet."

"There's been a development since this morning."

"Found the kid?"

She hated to squash that hope in his voice. "No. But illegal hunters shot a ranger and a cougar this afternoon."

"Send it in," he said wearily. "Are the photos any good?"

Oh God. She was supposed to remember to take a picture of her friend bleeding to death in the dust? "I didn't get any."

"Uh-huh. I see. Get thee to the unemployment line, girl."

She hastily described the bloody events of that afternoon. She wanted to give him the skull, too, but remembered Perez's warning, so she stuck with Kent and the wounded cougar. "You could come up with something, couldn't you?"

"Yeah, I can see it. Maybe a bloody cougar—we've got enough archive shots of those—or maybe a long-distance shot of rescue guys packing someone out on a stretcher."

"Just don't lie—make sure it's legal."

"Always." He sounded annoyed. "I can handle the visuals. But what about the story?"

"I just told it to you. You or Lauren have to write it."

"You know I can't write."

"Max! This is an emergency."

"Oh, all right. Hang on." Something rustled in the background. "Okay, I'm ready. Just sum it up for me again, okay? Say it the best you can, like dictation."

She sighed with impatience, took a deep breath, and enunciated carefully, "This morning, three armed men invaded Heritage National Monument with the intention of illegally shooting cougars. These vigilante hunters wounded not only a mountain lion but a park ranger who attempted to stop the shooting."

"And that's Wilderness Westin, reporting live from Heritage National Monument," Max intoned. "Got it. On tape, loud and clear. Audio has much more impact than just words on the screen. I'll have it up in half an hour."

Wow. "I'm truly honored to be working with you, Mad Max."

"Likewise, WildWest. We could have been great."

She scuffed her boots in the dust. "It's not over yet."

An object at her feet caught her eye. She picked up the small piece, turned it over in her fingers. Black plastic, flat, with a hole in the center. Some kind of button? No, the size was right, but a button would have two holes. A wheel. The missing wheel! The round bit of plastic looked suspiciously like the toy wheel Zack had shown her, right down to the tiny tread impressions.

How many toy wheels looked like that? And how many would be way up here on a hiking trail? It had to be Zack's.

"You still there? Sam?"

"Max, you won't believe what I just found! Turn on that mike again." She stated, for the record, that she had just discovered a toy wheel, identical to one missing from Zachary Fischer's truck, near Temple Rock ruins in Heritage National Monument.

"We're back!" Max shouted into the phone.

"Stay tuned," she told him.

"Me and the whole world. Adam Steele keeps calling to find out what's new."

"Let him get it from the website just like everyone else." She pressed End. Energized now, she dialed park headquarters again.

As a busy signal beeped in her ear, her gaze traveled over the town house structures under the arch. Aside from the subterranean chambers of the Curtain, this was the only truly sheltered location in the park. The crumbling rooms and underground kivas would be perfect places to hold a child hostage. She redialed. Still busy. Damn it. She chewed her lip.

She pressed the End button and stared at the phone in exasperation. Why hadn't Perez given her his number before he'd left? Why hadn't she asked for it? Disgusted with herself, she turned off the phone and stuffed it into her vest pocket.

Seven o'clock. She was running out of daylight. She stashed the knapsack with all of her rattling equipment out of sight in a V of tree branches, hopefully out of reach of rodents. With her fingers curled around the tiny canister of pepper spray in her vest pocket, she stalked toward the dwellings, past the NO TRESPASSING notice.

The walls of the ruins were stacked sandstone, some still chinked with red mud mortar. A two-story town house stretched up to meet the limestone ceiling of the overhang. Tiger stripes of black desert varnish cascaded down from the arch above onto the buildings, furthering the illusion that the ruins were an outgrowth of the cliff.

The five one-story rooms that bordered the taller section had once had wattle-and-daub roofs. Now their crumbling walls stood exposed to the elements. Two kivas, the round cellarlike structures used for Anasazi men's ceremonies, had likewise originally been covered by thick roof beams and plaster, extending the plaza's flat surface. Now the kiva pits yawned open in front of the buildings.

Sam skirted the kivas and crossed what remained of the plaza floor. She stood for a moment in front of the two-story structure. A gust of wind whistled through the keyhole-shaped doorways and puffed across the plaza, dislodging a tumbleweed. The sphere of dry brush rolled several feet across the plaza, then fell into one of the kiva openings. It came to rest on the bench that lined the walls and sat there as if waiting for the ceremony to begin.

God, what she wouldn't give to have Special Agent Chase J. Perez and his gun by her side right now. Taking a deep breath, she stepped through the town house doorway, waited for her eyes to adjust to the gloom. Dust motes danced in a shaft of light that spilled from a tiny window near the ceiling. A rough ladder made of tree branches lashed together with rope extended from the floor through a rectangular opening in the ceiling. She anxiously studied it. She really did not want to poke her unprotected head through that dark hole. But her search had to be thorough. She climbed slowly, testing each step before placing her full weight on it.

The upper story was snug and dark. And, thankfully, empty. Two tiny windows faced outward, one above the other. The view from the lower window was panoramic, taking in the plaza, the trail along the cliff, and the valley floor below. The Anasazi who lived here must have felt smug, possessing such a prime location where weather, game animals, and enemies could be observed from the safety of the high cliffs.

The cottonwoods in the river valley below were molten gold among the green-gray of the willows and piñon pines. She wondered what the heck was going on down there. TV news crews trolling for stories of hysteria in the campgrounds? Armed vigilantes storming the park gates?

Here, seventeen hundred feet above the valley, it was eerily silent. The blue-green of junipers dominated the scenery. Topping the bluff across the valley, another thousand feet in elevation, a grove of aspens shimmered in brilliant autumn colors.

She crawled down the ladder and listened for movement outside before she tiptoed onto the plaza. As she entered the next structure, a mouse scampered across the floor, skirting the remains of a fire in the center hearth. She stretched out her fingers above the charred lumps of wood. No hint of warmth. Whoever had lit it was long gone. It was not surprising that someone would picnic here, or even camp—the ruins were a natural lure for hikers, despite the NO TRESPASSING signs. One corner of the floor appeared more dust-free than the rest, as if a rug had recently lain there. Or a sleeping bag. Graffiti scratched into the wall— *BJB + KJD*—was encircled with a crude heart. *Why is it,* she thought with disgust, *that some people can't resist leaving their imprint wherever they go? They're worse than dogs marking their territory.*

No ladder led up to the second-floor opening. She went back for the one in the town house next door. As she passed from one structure to the other, her skin prickled. An eerie feeling. Someone out there? She stopped and inspected the area, listening carefully. Nothing.

After positioning the borrowed ladder in the rectangular opening, she hesitated. Could someone have climbed to the second story and then pulled up the ladder? Or stashed Zack up here and then taken the ladder so he couldn't escape? She rubbed her fingers over the pocket that held the pepper spray just to make sure it was still there. Then she sucked in a breath and started up.

IN his hotel room, Perez thumbed through Fred Fischer's file, squinting wearily at the fine print that covered each page. There had to be a clue about where the man had gone. Raised in Orem. Member of a Boy Scout troop that hiked and climbed all over the state. Resident of California. Truck driver.

The phone rang. Ranger Rafael Castillo was at the other end of the line. Perez wasn't surprised; male law enforcement officers always reported to him, assuming that he was the leader of the FBI team. No wonder Nicole was pissed off so much of the time.

"The Fischers' Suzuki is in the park, in the Goodman Trail lot. The vehicle's empty."

"Where does that trail go?" Perez asked.

"It intersects the Milagro Canyon Trail just past Village Falls. If you don't turn off to Milagro, Goodman Trail goes up past the Temple Rock ruins. Just beyond that, there's a Y. You know ZigZag Passage?"

Perez groaned. "Intimately."

"Well, if you take a right on the Y, Goodman Trail comes out of the valley near ZigZag. If you take a left on the Y, you veer off through Sunset Canyon on the Mesa Trail, which you could follow all the way across the park to the north entrance."

After hanging up, Perez checked the map. When they'd parted at the helicopter, Summer Westin said she was going to the ruins. From there she might take either Mesa Trail or follow Goodman to return to her camp. What were the odds that her path and Fischer's would intersect? He hoped she wouldn't try to cross that damn rock bridge again on her own.

Why hadn't he gotten her cell phone number? Now he'd have to track it down. Even with the number, he didn't hold out much hope of contacting her; he'd seen her turn the power off each time after she'd used her phone.

He made several calls. The park superintendent told him there was already a watch on all entrances and exits from the park: they were doing their best to make sure all visitors were out before starting the cougar hunt tomorrow. But he reminded Perez that anyone traveling cross-country on foot could come out along the park borders almost any-where.

This was a nightmare. How the hell were they supposed to track down anyone with only two agents on the case?

The local charter flying outfit reminded him that nobody flew over the park after dark. They'd take him up to the pla-teau at dawn. The fire department told him the same thing.

He briefly considered hiking up in the dark. No. Ridiculous. The trail was steep, rocky, and bordered by sheer drop-offs: he didn't know where he was going, and he probably wouldn't arrive before dawn, anyway.

Summer Westin was tough. He thought about her leaping down from that boulder last night, scaring the hell out of him, about how she'd handled Kent's wounds and faced the injured cougar. Still, he wished she had a gun. He drummed his fingers on the small table in his room. A bottle of beer and a speckled water glass tinkled to the beat.

He pushed himself up from the chair, moving like a ninety-year-old. The stiffness was getting worse by the minute. And he'd thought he was in shape. He pulled a T-shirt out of the pile on the bed, pulled it over his bare chest, and went to tell Nicole about Fischer's car.

She'd switched to black jeans and a gold sweatshirt. On her the combination was elegant. Her room looked as if the maid had just squared it away. His partner always made him feel like an unmade bed.

She motioned him in, her cell phone pressed to her ear. *Weismann*, she mouthed at him. The forensic specialist of the mobile Crime Scene team. She put the phone down on top of a computer printout from NCIC and punched the Speaker button.

"I've identified your skeleton," Weismann's voice blared into the room.

Nicole was incredulous. "Already?"

"The miracle of digitized dental charts." A squeak followed.

"Where are you?" Perez asked.

Another squeak. "Las Rojas Police Station." The voice slid into a whisper. "What a dump! Still in the Dark Ages—"

"The skeleton, Weismann," Perez prompted.

"They do have computers here, at least. And a broadband net connection. I scanned all the specifics on your skeleton's teeth to Martino in Salt Lake. He faxed me back a couple of likely charts. Then I—"

"Cut to the chase," Nicole suggested.

"The winner is Barbara Jean Bronwin. Salt Lake verified the match. She disappeared a little over three years ago from Portland, Oregon."

AT the top of the ladder, faint squeaking greeted Sam's ears. She nervously pushed through the opening, half expecting to feel the whack of a board across her crown. The floor was covered with droppings. A flutter of movement above her head made her heart lurch into her throat. She raised her eyes. Black wings stretched and rewrapped themselves around silver-gray cocoons. The ceiling was alive with pipistrelle bats.

One of the three-inch-long mammals hooked its wing claws into the ceiling, flipped to a tail-down position, and defecated a stream of guano onto the floor. A baby bat the size of a hummingbird clung to the white fur of its breast; the pup squeaked in annoyance at its parent's gymnastics. The mother pipistrelle curled its feet and returned to the upside-down position, releasing its wing claws to wrap leathery wings securely around the baby.

Sam sighed with relief. She'd take bats over murderers any day. She crawled back down the ladder, exited from the town house onto the plaza. The sunlight had withdrawn from the ruins and from the trail beyond. It was nearly seven forty-five. Time was running out.

She quickened her pace, trotting from one room to the next, intent on checking all the ruins. The cougar scratches on her thigh throbbed with each step. Nothing but dust in the next room; no sign of a hidden doorway to back stairs. Rodents as well as dust in the next; a kangaroo rat leapt to a hole between the sandstone bricks and scurried away. A clump of tumbleweeds loomed menacingly in a corner, but when she kicked them apart there was nothing hidden behind them.

She couldn't shed her goose bumps, the feeling of hidden eyes on her. Her stomach growled. She pressed a hand over it, but it didn't do much to muffle the sound.

A branch cracked somewhere in the brush beyond the ruins. She froze. Juniper limbs moving in the breeze? Coyote Charlie? Fingering the toy wheel in her pocket, she crept toward the edge of the plaza.

"Mummmeeeeyyy!"

Her heart skipped a beat. The blood inside her head continued its rush, a deafening river of sound in her ears. Had she actually heard a feeble cry?

"Zack?" she said tentatively to the growing darkness.

The wind blew dry leaves across the plaza, making a shushing noise. Then a distant muffled bleat. A toddler? Or just the whine of the breeze through the ruins?

She shouted louder. "Zack!" Nothing.

She raced toward the last two rooms, the ones she hadn't yet searched. Dust and darkness in the first. Was that rustling? She approached the final room, slowing her pace until she was tiptoeing. Holding her breath, she placed her fingers on the keyhole-shaped door frame and leaned to peer inside. Masses of unidentified debris—at least she hoped it was debris—lay on the floor; it was way too dark to see what any of it could be. Damned if she was going to go in there and poke around without a flashlight in her hand.

Why was she the only one up here, anyway? Crouching in the shadows, her back against a wall, she dialed park headquarters.

"Visitors are not allowed in the ruins," the dispatcher told her. "And you especially can't be up there now. We're asking all visitors to leave for their own safety by tomorrow noon."

"I know all about the big cougar-killing spree you've got planned," Sam growled. "Listen to me! I want to talk to a law enforcement officer. Now!"

Rafael Castillo came on the line. "Sam, you need to vacate the area immediately." He told her about Fred Fischer. "There's a chance that he's armed," he warned.

She told about the toy truck wheel, mentioned the possibility that she'd heard a little boy's cry. She described the awful feeling that someone was in the ruins with her.

Rafael swore in Spanish. Then he said, "I'll get some-one up there as soon as I can. But it won't be before dawn. You get out of those ruins. Now."

She assured him that she would, that she'd call in when she got back to her camp. She turned off the phone and wrapped her arms around herself, trying to stop shivering.

Yeah, right. As if her conscience would let her just trot back to camp. Zack might be crying for help; Fischer might be on the way to move him or, worse yet, to kill him. She could be the little boy's last chance.

She took a deep breath and tried to chafe some warmth back into her arms by rubbing them with her hands. Her gut was still twisted into knots. There was a good possibil-ity that she was fantasizing the whole thing. Her father had always said that she had an overactive imagination. *Sum-mer, you're letting your imagination get the best of you again. There's nothing to get worked up about.*

He'd said those same words when she'd been frightened of her mother's hands, gnarled into claws, when she'd been terrified by the horrible gurgling gasps the ventilator made. *I have plenty to get worked up about! Kent, the cougar, the skeletons, the crying.*

The two remaining rooms beckoned. She had a flash-light in her knapsack. An energy bar, too: she'd eat it to soak up the acid in her stomach and come back with the flashlight to finish the search.

Walking hesitantly now, listening for any threatening sound, she exited the ruins and stumbled over the uneven ground through the dark brush. The flashlight would be welcome company.

The knapsack was in the tree where she'd left it, but it now dangled upside down, hanging from one shoulder strap. The pockets were unzipped.

18

SAM stared at the knapsack, her heart pounding. The leaves of a nearby Mormon tea bush fluttered in the wind, dislodging a small white moth sheltering there. No other sign of life.

She pulled the knapsack down and quickly inventoried the contents, more through feel than sight. Her flashlight was missing, and so was the radio. Damn! The camera, batteries, and storage cards were safe. Her credit cards and car keys were right where she'd left them. What kind of a thief leaves the valuables? In addition to the flashlight and the two-way radio, her crackers, her energy bar, her jacket, water bottle, and pocketknife were gone. Shit.

Shouldering the now much lighter pack, she turned to survey the ruins, rubbing the goose bumps on her arms. The top of the sandstone walls burned red in the last rays of sunset. The dark rows of windows staring out to the west reminded her of the multiple eyes of a lurking spider. Was someone watching from those spider eyes?

The sun had completely disappeared behind the escarpment to the west. The temperature was dropping by the minute. She checked her watch. It would be pitch black in less than fifteen minutes. Only an occasional glimpse of sky peeked through patchy clouds: there'd be little moonlight tonight.

She rummaged through her vest pockets, came up with a stub of a candle and a book of waterproof matches, her emergency supplies for starting campfires. No way would the candle throw enough light to hike for three miles to her camp. Then, aha! Her fingers wrapped around her penlight. Tiny, but it had a fairly powerful beam. She switched it on, grateful for the small spark of light.

Something whined above her head. She stopped, every tendon in her body tense. *Uuummmmmmeeeeeeee.* She pointed the penlight upward. A shower of pale leaves spiraled down toward her. The plaintive screech of two limbs rubbing against each other. Was this what she had heard? Her mind played back the faint cry in the ruins: *Mummmeeeyyyyy!* The whine of the wind mimicked the mournful sound: *Uuummmmmmeeeeeeee.*

Just the wind in the trees? She hadn't heard a child's cry? And maybe her pack had been rifled by a hiker, just passing by and in need of a radio and food. Right.

But no matter who—Coyote Charlie or Fred Fischer or the bogey man at the end of the path—was skulking around up here, he wasn't going to get away with scaring her off. She would check that last room. Detouring from the path through brush and boulders, she approached the far side of the ruins, where the plaza met the cliff. If someone was lying in wait for her, she wouldn't accommodate him by taking the most predictable route.

Her booted toes struck the first inch-high unseen step and she pitched forward in the dark. Her wrists took the brunt of the fall, but the shock radiated up to her sore neck muscles and down her aching back. She clenched her jaws to keep from yelping in pain. On impact, the penlight winked out, rolled away from her. She retrieved it, banged it against the palm of her hand. Nothing.

Tears of frustration stung her eyes. She forced them

away, swallowing hard, and zipped the now-useless metal cylinder into a pocket of her vest. She crawled up five more steps on her hands and knees, trying not to think of snakes and scorpions, before the surface flattened out and it was safe to stand.

The rising breeze gusted flurries of fallen leaves through the ruins. Not much chance of detecting another person by sound alone. The susurration of the dry foliage would easily mask the shuffle of footsteps. Every few seconds she threw a hurried glance over her shoulder to make sure someone wasn't sneaking up behind her.

At the rim of a yawning hole in the plaza, she paused. She hadn't inspected the kivas, either. The wind blew out the first match. Shielding the flame with her body, she struck a second, touching the match to the candle wick as soon as it flared up. The illumination provided by the small candle was minimal; only vague clay-colored shapes flickered below. A circular stone bench with a circular shadow beneath it. One little splash of red. Zack's sneakers had been red. So had his pants. She stepped carefully down the short pole ladder into the ceremonial chamber, brought the flame nearer to the object she'd spotted. A wrapper from a stick of cinnamon gum. She turned to climb out.

Something rustled behind her. Pivoting slowly, she held the candle out at arm's length. At the base of the stone bench across the room, among a drift of fallen leaves and tumbleweeds, something was moving.

"Zack?" She took a step closer. Mottled brown and black scales gleamed in the flickering light. A glassy eye regarded her with hostility. Snake? The creature suddenly lurched toward her.

Stifling a curse, she stepped back, smashing her knapsack with a clunk into the ladder and sloshing a spatter of melted wax over her fingers. She winced in pain. Damned lizard.

Filled with the dry autumn debris and then covered with a canopy of snow, the kivas would make good winter burrows for reptiles. It looked as though this one had decided to immerse itself in Native American archaeology for this year's hibernation.

Out of the kiva, she took a deep breath and exhaled slowly, staring into the darkness that surrounded her. A few weeks from now, this would seem like a bad dream. Maybe she'd write about this whole exhausting escapade later in a novel. Providing she survived.

THE living room was empty, with only the corner lamp on. No TV tonight. His two older girls were spending the night at a friend's house, Rafael Castillo remembered. Good, maybe he could finally get some sleep tonight, at least a few hours. And he didn't care if he was still on call, he had to have a beer: his nerves were shot. If the Daniel Boones this morning hadn't been falling-down drunk, if Leeson and Taylor hadn't shown up when they did, he'd probably be in the hospital with Kent Bergstrom right now, if not in the morgue.

According to the FBI agents, it looked like Fischer had sent the ransom note. What did that mean? Was he trying to cover up whatever he'd done to that poor little boy? And now he'd disappeared into the park, and might be skulking around the ruins where Sam Westin had found the wheel to a kid's toy. And if it really was from Zachary Fischer's toy, what did that mean—that the poor baby was up there somewhere? Alive? Not likely.

The FBI Crime Scene team was doing God knows what up on the plateau; the feebs wouldn't share that with lowly rangers. And to top it off, Thompson had the USDAWS hunters showing up tomorrow. The world had gone crazy. But there was nothing more he could do about any of it tonight. Maybe he'd have a shot of tequila along with a beer, then hit the sack.

From the bathroom came a splash, a low voice, a giggle. Anita must be bathing their two little ones, Enrique and Katie. Some time with his sweet babies would be welcome right now. His hand was on the bathroom doorknob when he heard a deep voice say, "Now, Enrique, Katie, we're going to play a secret game."

What in the—? The door snagged on the throw rug. He pulled the scrap of apricot shag flat with the toe of his shoe and shoved the door forward again.

"Papi!" Katie and Rique faced each other, their dark curls wet from splashing in the tub. Russ Wilson sat on the floor, tiny shirts and underpants strewn around him, a towel over his lap. One hand was on Katie's bare back; the other clutched the side of the tub. He turned a startled face toward Rafael.

"Your wife is—" he started. "Miranda will be back any minute. She's taking some pans down to—"

"Watch, Papi." Enrique pulled himself up on the tub side and held out a plastic measuring cup. He poured a cupful of water into the tub with a big splash.

Did Wilson's gaze stray to the boy's privates for a fraction of a second? He tried to analyze the expression on the man's face. Surprise, certainly. Had there been a certain slyness in Wilson's eyes before he'd recognized the ranger at the door, a certain sick pleasure?

Rafael put his hand on the butt of his pistol. "You'd better leave," he said. "Now."

STICKING to the shadows, Sam groped her way toward the last unexplored room. At the doorway, she pulled the pepper spray out of her pocket. She stepped quickly into the room, holding the cylinder in front of her with both hands. The wind gusted through the doorway behind her, creating a whirlwind of leaves that spiraled around a dark heap in the center of the room. She willed her pupils to adjust quickly. Her head pounded with tension, accompanying the banging of her heart.

She heard a hissing sound. An inhaled breath? Her skin prickled in anticipation. She waited to feel the grip of icy fingers around her throat, the barrel of a gun pressed against her temple. Another puff of wind blew in. Scratchy fabric suddenly raked across her left cheek. She gasped and stumbled back, collided with the wall, jerked her head sideways, raised a hand to fend off the attack. Her fingers rasped across serrated edges as she batted the object away.

She dropped into a crouch, her back against the wall, her arms out in front of her for protection. Her body shook with the pounding of her pulse. The gust of wind faded away. Her lungs burned with the effort of holding her breath.

She strained to hear the slightest whisper of noise and was finally rewarded by a puff of air propelling a few leaves across the dirt floor. She was alone. The wind had blown dried leaves against her neck, her shoulder. The breath she'd heard must have been her own. She brushed leaves from her shoulder, feeling again their serrated edges. With shaking fingers, she pushed the pepper spray back into her vest pocket.

Idiot. If someone were planning to kill her, he could have done it by now. She could have been easily trapped in any of the rooms. She'd lit the candle at the top of the kiva, spotlighting her location. She'd been noisy while she was shouting for Zack. If someone was observing her, he wasn't in any hurry to do her in. Maybe the thief *had* been Coyote Charlie. Scotty McElroy told her that items were missing after Charlie had left. Was this was how he spent his time: spying on hikers, pilfering supplies?

So Coyote Charlie was a thief. But was he a murderer? She'd always envisioned him as a blithe spirit, sort of like the fruit-toting hiker she'd met close to her camp yesterday afternoon.

The oddball's words replayed in her mind. He'd mentioned the Creator, just as Perez had when explaining his Starchaser name. Was that how Native Americans referred to God? The man had carried no backpack or water bottle, said he was "out for the rest of his life."

Had she been talking to Coyote Charlie?

She compared her memory of the hiker to the vision of Coyote Charlie in the moonlight last night. Different clothes. But they'd shared the same slender build. She felt a little safer thinking of that hiker. He hadn't seemed threatening or violent. He wasn't slimy like Weird Wilson. Maybe a little woo-woo, as McElroy had said, but not psychotic.

Had she imagined a little boy's cries? She fingered the wheel in her pocket. That, at least, was real.

"Zack?" she said loudly to the darkness. Then, "Charlie?" No response.

She extracted the lump of candle from another pocket and lit it once more. In the flickering light, the dark pile at the center of the room resolved itself into a heap of dirt and small rocks. Gnarled roots dangled from a hole in the ceiling like an avant-garde chandelier. The break in the roof accounted for the green slime that covered the floor of the room. She knelt and inspected the damp patches of lichen.

Several imprints were visible on the floor. Blurred outlines of toes as well as the marks of waffled soles, pointing in all directions. She walked around the pile of rubble. Patches of lichen had been scraped from the fallen rocks. One velvety lump of moss held an impression the shape of a big toe.

Could she stand on the fallen rocks and pull herself up through the opening? Maybe. It would be a stretch. Not only that, it would probably be a dumb thing to do; the roof had already proved to be unstable. But this could very well be Charlie's secret passage; he was tall enough and skinny enough to easily slip through the hole in the ceiling. Maybe she'd find a hidden staircase or tunnel that led to the mesa above. And, if Fred Fischer had used the ruins, too, then maybe, just maybe, she'd find Zack, tucked away in a secret chamber.

Leaving her candle on the floor, she retrieved a ladder from the adjacent town house. She struggled with the roots for a moment before she was able to slide the ladder into position. She tentatively placed a foot on the bottom rung, half expecting the roof to crumble at the weight of the leaning ladder. Nothing. Putting both feet on the rung, she bounced. Drips of water splashed from the dangling roots onto her head and shoulders and a shower of dirt dusted her hair, but no rocks or mortar fell. She picked up her candle and climbed, careful not to spill the molten wax over her fingers again.

The wattle and daub around the hole felt solid, strengthened by the network of juniper roots that spiderwebbed over the original plasterwork. She grasped the slender tree trunk and pulled herself up. Kneeling on the adobe roof, she set the candle down beside her and surveyed her surroundings.

The candle flickered madly now, down to the last few millimeters of wick and wax. Its intermittent light revealed the stonework of the adjoining structure to her left, a solid wall of rock in back of her. The curve of the limestone arch began somewhere in the darkness above her head and descended down to her left, where the cliffside was furry with moss. She crawled to it and pressed a finger to the lumpy growth, feeling the velvety dampness. The ruins backed up to the underground chambers of the Curtain. The wall here must have cracked in the last earthquake, allowing the continual dampness inside the cavern to seep out into the ruins. Was that the sound of trickling water? She was probably listening to the creek inside the Curtain.

With a last waft of smoke, the candle flickered out, leaving her in the dark, literally now as well as figuratively. The breeze was dying down. Between gusts, the nightly chorus of tree frogs drifted up from the canyon below. This was the end of the road, at least for tonight. No hidden stairways. No Coyote Charlie. No Fred Fischer. And no Zack.

Clouds blotted out most of the light from moon and stars, but the puffy billows were on the move, rolling quickly across the sky. A faint scent floated on the air: Camembert cheese? *Sure, Summer.* Her empty stomach had translated the acrid odor of the burnt candle wick into the smell of food. Damn thief—at least he could have left her something to munch on.

She checked her watch. Ten twenty. An hour earlier in Washington State. She suddenly remembered her request to Blake, switched on her phone, and dialed home.

"Deep Throat here," he answered. "Meet me in the southwest corner of the parking garage in two hours."

"Knock it off, Blake. I've got limited battery power."

"Did anyone ever tell you that you're no fun?"

"Did you find anything in the files?"

"Maybe." She heard the rustle of paper from the other end. "There's an article about sustainable logging on Indian reservations."

"In Oregon?" she asked.

More rustling. "No, it says Montana."

"Then that's not it. Next?"

"Native Americans claiming rights to shellfish harvesting along the Oregon Coast?"

She sighed. "Didn't I say that I was looking for something about old-growth forests?"

"It has the words 'old growth,'" Blake argued. He quoted, "The tribe once lived on these beaches, where the old-growth forests grow right down to the surf line."

The line was growing staticky. The Low Power icon was blinking; pretty soon it would glow constantly in warning. "Anything else?"

"One more. I found a clipping about these tree-sitters. They called themselves Earth Spirits, and lived in the old growth to—quote—'save the trees from the demons with chainsaws who worship money more than Mother Nature.' Unquote."

She straightened. "Read on."

"There's nothing specific that says anything about Native Americans, but they gave themselves kind of tribal-sounding nicknames: Eagle Kovich, Wolf Davinski, Fawn Bronwin, Panther Pederson, Kokopetti Dane."

"Kokopetti? Sounds more Italian than Indian."

"Uh, just a minute, let me turn on the lamp. Koko . . . it's Kokopelli, not Kokopetti. Kokopelli's that Navajo hunchback god, isn't he?"

"I don't know if he's Navajo or if he's a god, but yeah, he's some kind of southwestern Indian figure. No Charlies or Carloses?"

"Just animals and Kokopelli."

"All men?"

"It's kind of hard to tell for sure from this photo. Looks cold; they're all wearing stocking caps or hoods. But I'd guess three guys, two girls. Does it mean anything to you?"

"I'm not sure yet. Thanks."

"You'll be back in a couple of days?"

Assuming I survive the night, she thought. But she said, "Yeah, a couple of days. Pet Simon for me." She turned off the phone.

Could Coyote Charlie be an Earth Spirit? It sounded possible, even probable.

Avoiding the damp patches of moss and lichen, she positioned herself with her back against the vertical cliff wall, her knapsack at her side, and her legs straight out in front of her. One foot rested on the top rung of the ladder. She'd feel the vibrations if anyone started up, dowse him with the pepper spray she held in her lap, kick him in the head if need be. Was that a decent plan? She was so punchy with fatigue and hunger that it was hard to judge.

The surroundings were colorless in the patchy moonlight. The ruins, cliffs, boulders, and rock floor were all flat, dark gray; the trees and bushes black skeletons whose shadows lent the only depth to the monochromatic landscape.

Stars and wispy clouds mingled in a patchwork sky out over the valley. The heavens looked cold, but she felt warm enough in her sheltered location. The cougar scratches on her thigh were red hot and swollen, bulging through the rip in her pants. Damn. Why hadn't she grabbed the antibiotic ointment from Kent's first-aid kit? The fingers of her left hand throbbed where the wax had dripped over them. The muscles in her neck felt like wire rope that might break under the strain at any moment.

She'd thought that yesterday had been horrible, but today definitely took the prize. *Might be more skeletons up here,* Perez had said. Maybe a serial murderer had been operating in the park for years. Maybe nobody had noticed before because he'd picked off homeless people, like the

Mexican family she'd seen by the river, like the pregnant teenager Kent had mentioned. Maybe Zack was the first that anyone had missed.

Fred Fischer was on the run. The man had a history of violence and a convenient job, truck driving. Did he return to his favorite area periodically to hide his latest grisly trophy? The connection between him and Ferguson was troubling. What had Fischer been up to in his youth that Ferguson had "saved" him from? And how had Ferguson saved him?

And how was she going to keep the hunters from the cougars tomorrow? The questions were endless. Her answers, nonexistent.

HE inhaled slowly, analyzing the air for her scent. She was so tiny, so tired, so sad. He thought about going to her, stroking her hair while she was sleeping. Hair the color of moonlight. He would not have taken her things if he'd known who they belonged to. Then he'd heard her voice. Good thing the boy had been asleep, then. He looked over at the still form next to him, was startled to see the blue eyes looking back now.

"It's okay, son." He smiled at the boy. "Everything's going to be okay. I'll never let them get you."

He wished he felt as sure as he sounded. The helicopters, the hunters. They'd violated the Canyon of Souls, handling his beloved like she was garbage. He fingered the pistol that lay in his lap. He'd never shot one before; he didn't even know if this one worked.

The boy was sitting up now. The dim lantern light revealed the swallows returning from their sundown hunt and settling into their nests with high-pitched chirps. Then the child's wide blue eyes turned toward the water burbling below them. He held out a chubby arm in the direction of the shining liquid and raised himself onto his knees.

The man grabbed the boy's sweatshirt. "Don't you even

think of going near that water!" the man growled. "How many times do I have to tell you? You could die there."

A wave of dizziness swept over Sam. She pulled her legs up, wrapped her arms around them, lowered her forehead onto her knees. The fabric of her pants was scratchy, stiff with dried blood. Kent's blood. Cougar blood. What she wouldn't give to have Perez's magic fingers massaging her neck right now.

She wanted to hate Adam, but she felt only numbness toward him. He'd challenged her to prove that a cougar hadn't killed Zack, and so far she'd failed.

What a horrible world. She'd come to Heritage National Monument to write happy stories and take pretty pictures to show that nature was a precious jewel, that wildlife deserved to be protected. She felt as if a tornado had touched down and sucked her up into a vortex of missing children, skulls, pedophiles, self-serving TV reporters, and trigger-happy hunters.

A trio of twinkling lights moved slowly across the sky in a steady line, passing in and out of the clouds. Strange to think of people flying at hundreds of miles per hour while she had labored all day to hike a dozen on earth.

The chorus of tree frogs rose in volume. It was a comforting sound, a nonhuman sound, the true music of earth. She shouldn't sleep, she really shouldn't. Zack was still missing. Fred and Charlie were out there somewhere, their secrets still intact.

Kent and the cougar had been shot, and the USDAWS hunters were coming at noon tomorrow. And she'd accomplished nothing. How could she sleep?

Her head was spinning, her ears humming with tiny fever voices. Her leg throbbed. The deep rhythmic croaking enveloped her. She dreamed of trying to catch packages falling from helicopters overhead. On close inspection, the fallen objects turned out to be corpses of babies and cats.

* * *

A gentle percussion woke her. Tap. Tap-tap. Distant gunfire? Had the slaughter begun before sunrise? Raising her
head sent a sharp pain through her neck and shoulders. She
shook out her hands and lowered her legs, gritting her teeth
as she straightened her injured leg. The thigh was swollen
with infection, but bearable; she could make it back to
camp and doctor herself there. She was glad to be alive;
grateful that the rain of bodies was only a nightmare. The
helicopter, though, was real; she could hear the rumble of
its engine fading away down the valley.

The sky was a dark mauve. Dawn would be brightening
the eastern edge of the mesa above, but the sun had not yet
pierced the shadows of the Temple Rock overhang. She
leaned toward the edge of the roof on which she sat. Her
hand brushed something metallic. She picked it up. Her
energy bar, intact in its foil wrapper. How strange. Had she
had it with her all the time? A pile of cashews was heaped
beside it. A chill ran down her spine. She hadn't been carrying any nuts. She glanced around, her eyes wide.

A movement in the brush beyond the ruins caught her
attention: a fawn, its hooves echoing a hesitant trail across
the rocks. Tap-tap, tap-tap. Ready to bolt at any moment,
probably spooked by the helicopter. It sniffed the air deli-
cately. Had the racket scared off the doe, leaving the white-
rumped baby alone? The dark nostrils flared. Sam wondered
if the fawn smelled her; she was certainly fragrant enough.

The fawn tensed and pricked its ears, its liquid eyes
focused on the plaza below her. Probably waiting for a signal from its mother. Sam shoved the nuts and energy bar
into her vest pockets, rolled onto her hands and knees, and
crawled carefully to the edge of the roof to get a look.
Instead of another deer on the plaza, a man slunk toward
the ruins.

19

WITH the rising sun still behind the cliff, the man was in deep shadow; she couldn't make out his features. Fred Fischer? Coyote Charlie? She had to get a look at his face.

After leaping down the ladder, she hugged the wall as she crept to the doorway. There. Only a few yards away. He would cross in front of her in a matter of seconds. Crap! Was he coming *inside*? Coming for her?

She leapt out of the doorway, landed with her feet spread shoulder width apart, the pepper spray clutched in both hands and trained on him. "Freeze!"

The figure stopped, his arms dropping to his sides, a shapeless hulk in the dim light. Clothing rustled. Was he pulling a gun? The blood roared in her head.

Her finger pressed against the trigger of the pepper spray. "I said freeze!" Thank God her voice sounded stronger than she felt.

"This is as frozen as I get."

Chase Perez.

She ran to him, threw her arms around his waist. His nylon jacket parted and she laid her cheek against his chest.

The flannel shirt he wore underneath was soft as velvet. Her fingers slid beneath his daypack, identified the holster at the back of his belt. She breathed him in. Soap, deodorant, shaving lotion. Then her thoughts flashed to her own strong scent, to her filthy hair and bloody clothes. What the heck was she was doing?

Abruptly, she broke away, stepped back. The dawn air was frigid on her neck and hands. Only her cheeks were hot. "Sorry," she said.

"Don't be sorry." He grinned. "I can't remember when a woman was so glad to see me."

His cheeks and chin were freshly shaven, his dark hair barely tousled from the breeze. She must look a wreck. Her braid had slithered down inside her vest during the night. She pulled it out, patted down the wisps at her temples, and clasped her hands in front of her. Her fingernails were filthy, she noted with disgust. She tried to make her voice casual. "I've had a rough night."

"So I gathered. I tried to call you, but your phone was turned off."

She told him about the phantom in the ruins last night, about the energy bar and nuts she'd found this morning. She apologized again for grabbing him. "I think hunger made me a little hysterical." Not to mention a teensy fear of death. She leaned toward his pack and sniffed. "Is that turkey I smell?"

"Are you part bloodhound or something?" Perez reached into his daypack, pulled out a plastic-wrapped sandwich.

Her mouth immediately filled with saliva. "Is that your lunch?" Not that she really cared. "I'll trade you an energy bar and some nuts of questionable origin."

He dismissed the trade with a flick of his hand. "It's okay, I had a big breakfast. Pancakes, eggs, sausage."

"*You* probably had dinner last night, too." She tore the plastic wrap from the sandwich. "How's Kent?" she said through a mouthful.

"He's in intensive care."

Still? That didn't sound hopeful.

Perez noted her expression. "He took a bullet through the lung; that's never easy. But he's young. He's tough."

All that blood. Puddles and streams of it. Sam wasn't as certain of Kent's chances as Perez sounded.

"The cat's in great shape. But you might want to try a little higher dosage next time. I had to hold him down while we were landing."

She smiled at the image, took another bite.

"You'll have to get someone else to sit on him when you bring him back," he continued. "FBI agents are allowed to wrestle cougars only once a year. It's in the rule book."

"I'll try to keep that in mind."

"You look flushed." He held the back of his hand up to her brow.

She shied away from his long cool fingers. If he caressed her right now, she'd start blubbering or something equally humiliating. "Did you find Fred Fischer? Or the hunters? Or—please, God—Zack?"

"No Fischer, no hunters. The gate guards didn't spot any of 'em. No sign of Zack. But you'll be happy to know that the police in Floral showed up at Buck Ferguson's house with a search warrant last night."

She was surprised. "But Kent said it probably wasn't Ferguson."

Perez shrugged. "I neglected to pass on that tidbit. One hunter was wearing an Eagle Tours cap, and for all we know, one or more of Ferguson's rifles had been used. Besides, we wanted to see his reaction."

"What was his reaction?"

"Apoplectic."

Sam grinned. "I suppose it's too much to hope a television news crew was there?"

"No coverage. Sorry. We confiscated his weapons to check them against the bullet we recovered."

The scene in Sam's mind made her feel so good that for a fleeting moment she wondered if Perez had orchestrated the raid to please her.

"We can't let anyone believe that violating federal laws

will go unpunished," he said, dispelling her crazy notion. "Maybe Ferguson will think twice next time about inciting his followers to bring loaded weapons into the park."

She choked down the last mouthful of sandwich. "Have you checked Ferguson's whereabouts at the time of Zack's disappearance?"

Perez handed her a water bottle. "At home, eating dinner, or so he says. No witnesses; the wife was off visiting relatives in Idaho."

So Ferguson had no alibi. He and Fischer knew each other. Sam's thoughts tumbled wildly. Ferguson wanted to hunt cougars again; Fischer wanted . . . to kill people? In the bright light of day, that notion seemed bizarre beyond reason.

"Fred Fischer really tried to ransom his own son?" she asked.

"Looks like it. He was sure that Jenny's parents would come up with the dough. He just didn't count on us showing up to manage the process." Perez shook his head. "What a rank amateur. He didn't even get his hands on the money. His connection with Ferguson is troubling, though."

"Maybe Ferguson and Fischer are collaborating to sell Zack on the adoption market. Someone brought Zack up here."

"Oh yeah, Castillo told me. Let's see it."

She pulled the small wheel from her pants pocket.

Perez stared at it blankly.

"It's the wheel from Zack's truck."

He slipped a plastic bag from his pants pocket, held it out in a familiar gesture. She dropped the wheel inside. He examined it through the plastic. "Might be from the kid's toy. And Fischer was probably your thief," he added. "The timing's right."

She shook her head. "No, Fischer would have taken my money. All that was missing from my knapsack was survival gear. Which sounds more like Coyote Charlie; McElroy said he stole food from them at the fire circle. I've been doing more research, too. I think Charlie may be an environmental activist from Oregon, a member of a group called Earth Spirits."

"Speaking of Oregon . . ." Perez pulled a rolled-up tube of fax paper from his jacket pocket.

She studied the crumpled photo he gave her. Slender face, fine straight hair, thin, slightly parted lips. Pale eyes fringed with long dark lashes stared back defiantly, as if the teenager resented having her picture taken. "Am I supposed to know this girl?"

"Dental records matched our skeleton to her. Barbara Jean Bronwin, reported missing from Portland, Oregon, three years ago."

Bronwin . . . something about the name seemed familiar. "How'd she end up here all the way from Portland, Oregon?"

Perez shrugged. "According to her parents, at sixteen Barbara Jean joined a radical environmental group and spent her days chained to trees. The Bronwins own Portland Plywood, so you can guess how well Barbara's new political passion went over. Then she got pregnant."

In the photo, Barbara Jean Bronwin's huge dark eyes gazed earnestly into the camera. Like a curious deer. "Fawn Bronwin!" Sam blurted.

Perez raised an eyebrow. She told him about the Earth Spirits and their "Native American" names.

"Sounds like a match," he agreed.

Sam stared at the photo of the girl. So young, so righteous. *Pregnant*. She grabbed his arm. "Perez, remember the homeless girl Kent described? The one with the beautiful brown eyes, the one that was 'out to here'?" She held her arm out in the same gesture Kent had used. "It could have been Barbara. Kent said she was with a man back then. Maybe it was one of the Earth Spirits."

"Her parents couldn't supply any names," Perez said, "and we haven't located any of her friends yet. Apparently Barbara didn't live at home much; she'd been reported as a runaway several times. According to the report, a girlfriend said Barbara Jean was going to meet her boyfriend in Arizona. She was last seen hitching a ride in a semi."

Sam raised her head. "A semi? Fischer—"

He finished for her. "Has been a truck driver for years. And he drives all over the West."

Had Fred Fischer been the man in the park with Barbara? Sam's head was spinning. She'd found Barbara Jean "Fawn" Bronwin among the Earth Spirits while searching for Coyote Charlie. But Barbara Jean had a link to Fred Fischer? Fischer, Ferguson, Barbara, Coyote Charlie? Could they *all* know each other? The six degrees of separation theory was starting to feel very real. "How'd Barbara Jean die?"

"Her skeleton showed no signs of foul play. But that doesn't mean much. She could have been strangled or stabbed or suffocated."

Sam rubbed a hand across her brow. He raised his hands. "Who knows?" So many causes of death, so easily enumerated. Perez went on. "She could have died somewhere else and been dumped here. We have only bones to go on; and they've been exposed to the elements for six to twelve months."

"What happened to Barbara Jean's baby? Have they found more skeletons?"

He shook his head. "They're still looking. You may be right that Coyote Charlie's probably involved in this somehow—the fact that both he and Barbara are from Oregon is a heck of a coincidence. If he knew Barbara, maybe he came looking for her. But Fred Fischer's our current priority, and our first victim is still unaccounted for. Fred Fischer had means and motive, and Zack would go with him without a fight. We've got to find both of them."

A helicopter roared by overhead, flying low over the ruins. It rose higher and drifted out over the valley. She prayed it wasn't full of hunters.

Sam held her hands to her ears as she watched the chopper grow smaller, thinking about Fred Fischer. "Yesterday, you said Ferguson saved Fischer from reform school. Did you find anything more about that?"

"Ferguson got Fred into a 'tough love' sort of school. Woodland Challenge? Something like that."

Her heart skipped a beat. "Wilderness Challenge?"

"That sounds right."

A small flare of real hope ignited in Sam. She hefted Perez's daypack, shoved it at him. "We've got to go to the Curtain."

He nodded. "From what you've told me, it sounds like a good place to cache a body. Or multiple bodies."

"It could hold half the bodies in Arlington National Cemetery. But that's not the main reason we need to go there. Wilderness Challenge was the precursor to Outward Bound. They developed the climbing course."

"So Fischer knows the Curtain." Perez's brown eyes gleamed. "Is your leg up to the hike?"

She lifted the torn flap of her trousers to reveal the red weals, now puffy and edged with yellow ooze. "It smarts, but I'll live. We'd better hustle. It's five miles away and straight up most of the way."

His gaze rose to the cliffs above. "That's the only way in?"

"There's an opening in the cliffside about three hundred feet below here, where Curtain Creek empties out of the last chamber. We'll come out there, beside the waterfall."

"Can't we go in that way?"

"We'd have to climb up through the chambers instead of down. It'd take us just as long, and it'd be harder going— the walls are straight up in the uppermost room. We wouldn't be able to climb out that way without equipment. Let's get going. It'll take us at least two hours to get there."

"Not if I have anything to say about it." He stalked away toward the open area near the trail, his cell phone in hand.

She shouldered her knapsack. A helicopter roared close again. Damn machine. Pulling out the camera, she snapped a photo as the helicopter hovered low, ripping leaves from the aspens in a golden tornado. Then Perez was by her side again, his hand on her arm.

"C'mon," he yelled in her ear. "I got us a ride."

20

CRAWLING onto the helicopter felt like joining the enemy. Sam had signed dozens of petitions against aerial tours in wild areas.

Perez jumped in. Squeezing through the door, she dropped into the seat beside him, wincing at a sudden sharp pain from her leg wound. She was surprised to find Meg Tanner riding shotgun beside the pilot. The woman interrupted her conversation with the pilot only briefly to acknowledge them. "Agent Perez, Westin."

"Top of the Curtain, where Outward Bound goes in," Perez instructed. Tanner pointed to the map she held stretched over the instrument panel. The pilot nodded, and the helicopter rose from the ground.

"The Curtain's off limits to most visitors. What do you hope to find there?" Tanner asked. She scowled in Sam's direction. "And why is Westin with you?"

Perez leaned toward her. "FBI business."

Tanner glared at him for a few seconds, then turned and continued her previous conversation in a loud voice. "The press won't leave Jenny Fischer alone. I took her home with me last night so the poor woman could get some rest. The damn media! Even the locals have gone berserk—did you hear Mrs. Mendez shot the Carellis' dog?"

The pilot responded, "Not that golden Lab?"

Tanner nodded. "Thought it was a cougar sneaking up on Molly. And then last night, old Jack Kinley blew away one of his new calves. His own calf, in his own pasture! I hope he's ashamed of himself."

Sam's head ached. She tugged Tanner's sleeve. "Is the Wildlife Services hunt still scheduled for today?"

The assistant superintendent twisted in her seat. "They're at HQ now, assigning areas and gearing up. The plan is to start in from the perimeters at noon. With luck, they'll kill one lion and then this whole mess will be over and done with." Tanner turned back and resumed her chat with the pilot.

Over and done with? What about Zack? Had everyone already written him off? Sam watched the ground below, unwilling to entertain the idea of never knowing what happened to Zack and a cougar being killed for no good reason. They passed over Curtain Wash, where the skeletons had been found. The area was overlaid with crisscrossed ropes. Search grid. She counted three people in park service uniforms, two in blue windbreakers with FBI printed on the back.

"You got that NCIC stuff okay?" Tanner yelled at Perez. "That list of Charlies?"

The FBI agent nodded, patted his jacket pocket.

Sam leaned close to him. "Charlies?"

"A list of missing Charlies and a list of young Charlie types with criminal records from Oregon dating back three to ten years."

"And?"

He handed several folded pages to her. "Fifty-six. Too many to sort through."

She glanced down the first page of names, each accompanied by a brief physical description and the reason the person was sought. Perez had circled two: *Charles Richard Allen, thirty-four, reported missing four years ago. Carlos*

Jose Matera, twenty-eight, reported missing fourteen months ago.

Perez nodded. "Neither seems very likely. Allen was into drugs and pimping; Matera's only five eight. Our Charlie looked more like six feet to me." He shrugged. "He's probably not on the missing list. Lots of adults are never reported—especially if nobody wants them back."

How sad. At least she had a housemate who would notice if she didn't come home. Her mind flashed to Adam—would he miss her? She didn't know what she meant to Adam anymore. And now that she really thought about it, she wasn't sure they'd ever really meant anything to each other.

She flipped to the second page of names. Now out of the missing category and into the criminals. Here again, Perez had circled a few: *Carl Benson Lagos, twenty-eight, armed robbery; Jason Charles Dane, twenty-nine, trespassing; Karl Jacob Davinski, thirty-two, destruction of construction equipment.*

"Wolf Davinski!" She pointed to the name on the list. "He was one of the Earth Spirits, along with Fawn Bronwin. It's got to be Coyote Charlie."

Perez's eyes lit up. He held up his right hand. She smacked it with hers in a high five.

Barbara Jean Bronwin and Karl Jacob Davinski. *BJB + KJD.* At some point, Barbara and Charlie—Karl—had been a couple, at least in someone's mind.

They made the Curtain in less than ten minutes and descended into a noisy maelstrom of blowing grit. "Want us to stand by?" the pilot yelled.

Perez shook his head, signaled for the helicopter to lift. *Yes, get the infernal machine out of here,* Sam thought, hunched into a protective huddle.

As the helicopter faded away, she heard a flutter of feathers and a chirrup. A curious magpie swooped to a perch above them, hoping for a handout. The birds were already learning that helicopters meant people, who usually carried food. A trace of sage floated in the air. The poor plant had probably been ripped to shreds by the rotor whirlwind.

Curtain Creek trickled across the mesa floor, shimmering in the morning sun, then disappeared into a long gash in the earth. The slot canyon zigzagged away from them, rending the mesa floor as if a lightning bolt had broken the mountain in two.

"This is the famous Curtain?" Perez peered down into the crevice. "Doesn't look like much."

"The beauty is all inside."

"And how are we going to get down there?"

She moved to a stack of smaller rocks wedged between two giant boulders. After she had lifted away several of the smaller rocks, the edge of a metal footlocker was revealed. "The park service keeps climbing gear here for emergencies."

Perez watched her turn over several more rocks until she located the key to the brass padlock. She rummaged through the locker, extracted two tangles of nylon webbing and steel rings. She handed one to him. "Your harness."

She showed him how to strap on the webbing. When he'd buckled the last shoulder strap into place, he spoke in a low voice tinged with a British accent. "Ready, Q. Bring on the parachute."

"No chute, Bond. You'll want to remember that on your way down." She fastened her own shoulder strap. She pulled out two figure eight–shaped devices and two long coils of nylon rope.

He whistled a low note. "You must have at least two hundred feet of rope there."

"Three hundred and fifty, actually." She handed him a coil. "This is yours. Pick an anchor." A few yards away, a heavy steel ring had been set in concrete that filled a natural crack in the rock surface. Three more rings appeared at irregular intervals.

"Hardly in keeping with the natural surroundings," he commented.

"It's better than having people chisel into the rock or tie off to trees. And, as Kent would say"—she felt a sharp jab of pain at the thought of her wounded friend, but pushed it aside to continue—"it saves scraping up climbers from the bottom of the Curtain. It would be virtually impossible to get a stretcher down there."

He grimaced. "Let's not talk about scraping up climbers or stretchers right now."

She threaded the rope through one of the figure-eight descenders, clipped it to the D ring at Perez's waist, and pressed the rope into his right palm. "Hold this, and grab the other rope with your left."

She rigged up her own figure eight. "Hold the rope loosely in your left hand, just below your hip. Keep hold of the rope above the descender with your right hand."

"The friction of the rope pulling through the descender slows you down, so there's no need to grab the rope unless you want to stop completely. Lean against it, and walk backward. Keep your fingers loose."

He did as she instructed, staggering back on his heels with jerky steps as the rope slid through the device.

"You've got it." She straightened, letting her rope slacken to the ground. "That's as much practice as you're going to get. The only way to learn rappelling is to do it." She stuffed some ascenders into a pocket, then pulled the shoulder straps of her pack over her harness. Perez did the same with his.

They backed up to the crevice. Perez peered over his shoulder at the drop below, his face grim. Sam stifled a smile, remembering how nervous she'd been the first time she'd rappelled. "Balance on your heels and let out enough rope to hang your rear end out into space."

They let their ropes out and sank into sitting positions in the harnesses, their boots poised on the brink of the crevice. At least the man knew how to follow instructions.

"Now, keep your legs in front of you and just walk down the rock face."

With his legs straightened, the opposing rock wall was only inches from the back of Perez's head. He glanced nervously over his shoulder. "We're not going to get wedged in here, are we?"

"Don't worry—the space opens up down below. Let's go."

She took two steps down into the crevice, the rope sliding

through the descender with a whir. Perez didn't move. His
fingers were clenched around the rope. She grabbed her rope,
stopped. "You're not going anywhere until you release that
death grip, FBI. The rope doesn't move, you don't move."

"Just resting." He relaxed his fingers. The rope whirred,
dropping him about a foot. Panic shot across his face. He
grabbed the rope again and came to an abrupt stop.

"You'll get it. Just keep going. The friction will control
your speed."

Perez passed her with several long strides.

"And the friction also . . ."

He jerked his hand up with a yelp.

"I was about to say that the friction heats up the metal,
so don't touch it."

"No kidding."

She kept her own voice low. "Instead of just walking
down the wall, you can also push off—gently—and release
the rope at the same time. Then swing back in." She dem-
onstrated, gliding past him like a spider sliding down its
thread of silk. Her wounded thigh sent a jolt of fire through
her body as her boots slapped against the rock.

"Try it. Easy now, no he-man stuff, or you'll bounce off
the walls."

She pushed off, let a section of rope pull through, then
swung back into the rock face about ten feet below her previous position, wincing a little as she hit. Perez followed
suit, ended up slightly above her.

"Good. Keep your feet straight out in front."

He peered down between his braced legs. "How far is
the drop?"

"It's about a hundred and sixty feet right here."

"Great. Far enough to become a paraplegic."

"Quadriplegic is probably more likely. Or just plain
dead." Unfortunately, she said the last word too loudly, and
it echoed in the confined space. *Dead . . . dead . . . dead.*

Perez held a finger to his lips. "Someone might be down
there," he whispered. Then he made his hand into the shape
of a gun.

* * *

JUST after reporting for work, Rafael Castillo finally called
the Utah DMV to check up on Orrin R. Wilson. He'd been
awake half the night thinking about the guy. Was Wilson
really slimy, or had this whole Zack Fischer thing made him
crazy? God knows he'd hardly slept in the last few days.

"No problem, Ranger," the clerk said, back on the phone
after only a couple of minutes. "Here it is—Orrin R. Wilson, Rock Creek, no outstanding tickets. There's no jacket
whatsoever. Amazing. How many people reach the age of
seventy-nine without even a speeding ticket?"

"Seventy-nine?" The Wilson he knew was in his early
fifties at the latest. Who was this slimeball using Orrin
Wilson's name? The slimeball that had his smarmy hands
all over his kids last night?

"Give me his address," he ordered.

The newly laminated license! He was an idiot! He didn't
deserve to be a law enforcement officer. It wasn't a replacement license; it was a fake, a newly laminated composite of
information and photo. It was no comfort to know that Taylor had fallen for it, too. He kept his foot on the accelerator
all the way to Rock Creek.

Now, through the screen door, the elderly Ruth Wilson
blinked in confusion. She was still in her bathrobe, her
white hair in disarray, reminding Rafael that it was only
eight thirty on a Saturday morning.

"Orrin's in the nursing home, right where he's been
since Memorial Day," she told him. "He's not dead, is he?"
Tears filled her pale eyes.

He calmed the woman down, then asked about Russ
Wilson.

"Russ?" Her dried-apple countenance puckered even
more. Then a look of understanding dropped into place as
if the proverbial lightbulb had come on. "Oh, you must
mean Wally."

"Wally?"

"My son, Wally. He's not here right now, though. He's

borrowing our camper for a few days; his old Buick's in the shop." Her thin fingers clutched at her worn nylon robe. "I don't know why he keeps telling everyone to call him Russ, and I certainly don't know why he'd be using *my* last name now. I gave him a perfectly good name—Wallace. Wallace Russell."

"The child molester?" Rafael screamed at the old lady. He'd been keeping an eye out for Wallace's Buick for days, ever since his name had come up in the FBI check.

Ruth double-checked the lock on the screen door between them. "I don't know why people have to say nasty things like that about Wally," she said with a sniff. "Why, he's got himself a lady friend and everything now."

21

BANDS of pastel-colored rock rippled down like flowing curtains. They were gliding through millions of years. They'd already passed through the yellow schist that marked the period when prehistoric man first emerged, were fast approaching the lavender rock at the bottom, the color of the earth when the first mammals wandered this area.

The rhythm of rappelling and the colors and shapes of the rock always soothed Sam. In her current state of fatigue, the sounds and motions were almost hypnotic. Normally it would be easy to forget about life outside of the Curtain, about Zack, about Fred Fischer and Buck Ferguson, Coyote Charlie and Kent and the cougars and SWF and Adam and the whole sordid business. Except that now Perez's warning about someone waiting below with a gun had her itching all over, eager to reach solid ground where she could run instead of being an easy target dangling overhead.

A muffled thump from the bottom of the crevice told her that Perez had not landed well. He rolled to his hands and knees, the seat of his pants covered with damp sand. She pushed off hard and released her rope, landed on both feet on the packed sand floor and was immediately sorry as a stab of pain flashed up from her wounded thigh.

"Nine-point-five," Perez said. "You'd have to do it without the rope to get a perfect ten."

Perfect ten, echoed the walls.

"What happened to being quiet?"

He held out his hands. "Nobody here but us."

They stood in a large antechamber, approximately seventy feet long by thirty feet wide. At the bottom of the crevice, the undulating striped walls of the slot canyon met a floor of damp, fine sand. Sunlight streamed in from above in a narrow shaft, highlighting diamonds of water vapor. At one end of the crevice, Curtain Creek shimmered down the wall, a delicate bridal veil. The cascade became a shining ribbon across the floor and then disappeared into the darkness at the far end of the chamber.

"So this is the Curtain," he said. "It looks almost organic. Like we slid down the throat of a gigantic beast and now we're seeing it from the inside."

Holding her fingers well away from the hot aluminum, she unclipped her descender from the D ring on her harness. "Most climbers only know this chamber: it's called the Cascade Room. Outward Bound climbs right back up."

He looked skyward. "Good God. How?"

"Ascenders." She pulled one that was already threaded with a loop of rope from her pack. "They clamp onto the rope. You put your weight in one, slide the other up the rope, then move to it and slide the other one up."

"Sounds like work."

"It is. I brought them just in case. But it looks like we don't need them."

They stripped off their climbing harnesses and attached them and the ascenders to the dangling ropes. She made a mental note to tell park HQ that they'd left the park service climbing gear out. HQ would be annoyed, but she could blame it on the FBI. Perez explored the chamber, examining the rippled walls and the sandy floor.

"There are hundreds of different footprints in here," he

observed. "If there was any clue about Zack or Barbara Jean, we'd never notice."

"Maybe we'll have better luck below." She tucked an errant strand of hair into her braid. "From here on, it's strictly a rock scramble, with a few tight squeezes and wet crossings."

"Squeezes? Wet crossings?"

"The Curtain feels like a cavern because of its size, but it's really a slot canyon like ZigZag. The creek slithered down through a crack eons ago, carved out five chambers that descend through the rock layers. Get out your flashlight." She led the way to the far end of the chamber.

Barely visible in dim light, Curtain Creek spilled noisily down over a moss-covered rockfall into a smaller chamber some twenty feet below.

"Watch your step," she said in a low voice. "The algae's slippery."

They scrambled down the pile, clutching at rocks to steady themselves as they maneuvered over the uneven footing. At the bottom, Sam studied the chamber anxiously for a moment to be sure they were alone, then limped onto the wet sand and looked back. Perez's hair and eyebrows were frosted with mist, making him look as if he'd suddenly turned gray.

He stepped down beside her. Only the light from a narrow crack above illuminated the small room; the sun was a spotlight reflected in the glistening water. Two stout pillars of rock held up layers of stone overhead. Generations of swallows had glued mud nests onto the pillars, making the rock formations look as if they had sprouted warts. Several of the elegant long-tailed birds swooped and twittered overhead.

"This is the Drawing Room. In the springtime the birds are so loud, you can't even hear the water in here." She gestured at the floor of flat sand and rock. "Hardly anyone comes this way," she murmured, "So footprints might be preserved in this chamber."

Perez, now in the lead, inspected every inch of floor and walls with the flashlight he'd taken from his pack. At one point, the beam illuminated a rough wall drawing of two deer etched in ochre, and next to the crude animals were three handprints, two adult-sized and one tiny, with the fat palm and stubby fingers of a baby's hand.

"The Drawing Room—I get it," Perez whispered. "Anasazi?"

She shook her head. "The archaeologists say these are recent fakes."

The light in the chamber dimmed as if a bulb had just winked out. The narrow crack in the chamber ceiling revealed thunderheads gathering outside.

"Oh no," Sam groaned softly. "Looks like rain." A rumble overhead echoed her prediction.

"We'll be dry enough in here."

"You don't understand. When it rains, the runoff on the high mesa dumps into Curtain Creek. And remember, Curtain Creek runs through ZigZag Passage and then dumps into—"

"Here," he finished, his tone suddenly grim. His eyes focused on the placid stream of water trickling slowly across the chamber floor. "How long does it take the creek to rise?"

She sucked in a nervous breath. "It depends on how hard it rains, and how long. If it really pours, it can reach flood stage in a half hour."

A few drops spattered through the natural skylight to the chamber floor. Damn the weather forecast! It wasn't supposed to rain until tonight or tomorrow. She grabbed his sleeve. "Let's move along, Perez. We've got three more chambers to go."

He had to hunch to clear a bulge of rock over their heads. No threatening figures lurked in the shadows. She didn't encourage him to look for subtle clues. Time could be critical.

Splashing through water and clinging to the walls, they climbed over a DANGER! NO TRESPASSING! sign on sawhorse barriers and shuffled down a water-smoothed incline into the next chamber. Lightning flashed above, illuminating a large pile of tumbled rocks below a natural skylight.

"Wreck Room. Careful," Sam warned. "This is the one I told you about earlier. The ceiling's unstable here."

"Obviously." He played his flashlight beam over the island of rubble. The rain fell harder now, splashing against the large chunks of limestone. Flecks of mica glinted in the circle of light.

"It's been off limits for years now. Every time there's a little quake or a lot of rain, more of the overhang falls in. But it looks like we can still get through. Stay off to the side." Bats squeaked and swallows chirped high overhead. Sam wished she were wearing her rock helmet, as much to deflect guano as for protection from cascading rocks.

Perez moved his beam onto the chamber floor. In just the short time they had been here, the water had deepened and spread into a larger stream.

"Wait!" She grabbed his hand. "The rocks—I think I saw something."

Placing her hand over his, she directed the flashlight beam to the pile of debris in the center of the chamber. Rain-slickened rocks, spotted with emerald moss and rust-colored lichen, surrounded by swirling water. Lightning flashed, stabbing her pupils.

She took her hand away from his. "Never mind. It was probably just the lightning." The bright light slowly faded from her sight like the flash from a camera bulb.

"No," he said grimly. He held the beam steady. "There."

Wedged in between chunks of dark rock, a tiny white hand gleamed in the light. Stubby fingers curled skyward as if trying to catch the drops of rain that fell from above.

22

"OH God." A sudden rush of blood in Sam's head drowned out all other sounds. She stared in horror at the motionless fingers extending from beneath the rocks. Her heartbeat moved into her throat. Her chest hurt as though she'd been struck. *Breathe*. She inhaled painfully. *Get a grip on yourself, Summer*.

"There's no time to call your Crime Scene team." Her voice sounded surprisingly normal.

Perez moved the light to the water lapping at the sides of the rubble pile. Fat drops of rain splashed into the stream, a steady pattern of radiating circles overlaying the undulating ripples of the creek. "How high will the water get?"

She could barely hear the words through the roar in her ears. Her fingers trembled against her lips. She lowered her hand. *Breathe*. Focus on the surroundings, not on the body. The water was rising. How high, how fast? The curled fingers looked to be about a foot above the stream. Two patches of bright yellow lichen, like the eyes of some nocturnal creature, lurked at the edge of the water. "If it keeps raining like this, the creek will fill this chamber two to three feet deep."

"Then let's hope that the rain keeps up." His brown eyes were placid.

What the hell was he talking about?

"Otherwise, what I'm about to do could get me canned," he explained, wading across to the rock pile. "I forgot my camera. Let me see yours."

Moving as if in a slow-motion dream, she twisted her pack around to one shoulder, fished out the digital camera. Her pulse was slowing now, leaving her shaking. The constriction had receded from her throat. She waded across the chamber to join Perez. The water reached up to her calves; its coldness seeped through her pants legs and snaked into her hiking boots. Good. She needed that sharp cold right now. Rain drizzled from her eyebrows onto her lashes. She took up a position beside Perez and handed him the camera.

A raindrop fell from the tip of her nose as she bent over the little body. Bile rose into her throat at the sight as well as the stench; she swallowed hard. A huge chunk of sandstone obscured the toddler's chest and neck; Sam estimated the rock weighed over a hundred pounds. A smaller piece pinioned the lower torso and most of the left leg. The child's head looked like one of those marble nymphs' that adorned fountains in formal gardens, except for the deep indentation in his forehead where it rested against another rock. Golden hair, flattened by the falling rain, lay in commalike curls against a gray-pink scalp. The smooth roundness of the still, white cheeks contrasted with the jagged edges of the surrounding stones.

The flash went off. Standing ankle deep in the water, Perez took several shots of the body from various positions. Then he climbed out of the rising tide onto the rubble. He shrugged off his daypack and set it down a yard away from the body.

"Now we know what happened to Zachary Fischer," he said.

This hadn't been the ending she'd expected. She'd dreamed of photographing the scene as a warm, breathing toddler was placed in Jenny Fischer's arms. The gleaming eyes, the smile of gratitude. She remembered the feel of Zack's tiny damp hand in her own. Yes, her heart definitely hurt. *You'll find him, won't you? You know what my baby looks like,* Jenny had pleaded.

He'll be fine. That's what she'd told Zack's mother.

Perez studied the body, then focused on the gaping hole above and pressed the shutter button. "It looks like he was crushed by falling rock."

"Poor baby," Sam moaned.

"He might have been dead before the ceiling gave way."

A flash of lightning lit up the chamber. Sam grabbed for Perez's sleeve. "Oh dear God, look at his eyes."

He peered at the dark jelly that filled the sockets. "His eyes are filled with blood. Probably from the impact."

"He's so . . . colorless." A white marble child.

Perez placed his fingers on a rock next to the child's head and bent to examine the cold little face. "He's been dead for a while now. Gravity pulls the blood to the lowest points, you know."

"No, I don't know." She took a gulp of the chilly air, poisoned by a faint aftertaste of rotting flesh. "I'm a wild-life biologist."

That's all she'd ever wanted to be. She wanted trees and birds and cougars and deer. Not this. "You may be used to looking at bodies, but I'm not. This is the first time I've seen anyone who's been dead for days."

He handed her the camera, then straddled the corpse and curled his fingers around the largest rock that rested on the toddler. With a guttural growl, he straightened his arms and heaved off the largest rock, tossing it away from the rock pile into the stream.

Ker-plunk. Just like tossing rocks off the old bridge close to her grandmother's house. A universe removed from this horrible place and time. She forced herself to look again at the body, at the mess of broken flesh and smashed bone that the sandstone had hidden. The shorts and shirt the child wore were mashed into his flesh. Gagging, she turned away, focused her eyes on the water swirling around them.

Perez explained, "It doesn't smell too bad because it's so cool in here."

"Please," she said. *Please stop. This is a person. Was a person,* she corrected herself. The skull they'd found on the plateau had been more like an archaeological study. But cold flesh and battered limbs . . .

How was she going to live with this for the rest of her life? *Zack, I'm so sorry. I should have taken your hand and not let go until I put your fingers into your mommy's. Zack, Jenny, somebody, anybody—forgive me.*

Grunting, Perez lifted the second rock, flung it away. Water splashed over her from the impact. She leaned forward, searching for the yellow lichen patches that had marked the waterline. They had disappeared.

She turned toward Perez, keeping her gaze from the white marble flesh. Rain dripped down her neck, trickled down her spine.

"We've got to go," she urged. "This water is rising fast. We can wade it here in the Wreck Room, but down below—"

"Give me your pack."

She shrugged it off. He opened it and started tossing everything from her knapsack into his daypack: radio, keys, wallet, and cell phone tumbled in with a clatter. "Hey!" she yelped, clutching the digital camera to her chest.

"Your pack's bigger than mine."

"So?"

He spied one of the folded garbage bags she carried, grabbed it from the top of the heap. "We've got to take him with us. Otherwise the body may never be found." He spread the garbage bag on the rocks. "Hold this open."

She pushed the camera into his daypack with her other gear, then knelt and held the thin sheets of plastic apart. When he reached for the corpse, she turned her face to the ceiling, watched the curtain of rain shimmering down from the skylight. A couple of small pebbles, loosened from the overhang, bounced off the rock pile a foot away. "We've got to get moving, Perez. The whole overhang could collapse any second."

The putrid odor of decay increased in intensity, and Sam tried to inhale as little as possible. Wet clothing brushed against the skin of her wrists. The cold kiss of clammy flesh. Oh, Zack. Why didn't real life have happy endings?

"Okay," Perez murmured. She released her hold and backed away, then stole a look. The tips of two tiny white fingers protruded from the opening of the sack.

Perez pulled up the plastic. The fingers slid out of sight. He tied the attached handles together, then lifted the black mass into the knapsack, pressing down a little to get it in. He stretched the top flap over and tied it down. Not much to pack away, really. Sad, sad thought.

"I'll carry this," he told her.

This, not *him*. She shuddered and reached for Perez's daypack. She'd never use her knapsack again. She adjusted the straps of his pack to fit her smaller frame.

Another pebble pinged down beside them. A shower of red dirt fell into Perez's raven hair. "Let's go," he said, raking out chunks with his fingers.

Stepping off the rock pile, she gasped at the chill. The water now swirled above her knees. The current threatened to sweep her feet out from under her. She had to focus on the present. Zack's fate had already been decided; now she had to look out for herself and Perez. "Wade over to the right side—it's shallower there."

They felt their way cautiously around the edge of the room, bracing themselves against the rock wall. As they neared the stream's outlet to the next chamber, the water deepened. The roar ahead was ominous.

"How many more levels?" Perez shouted.

She turned her head toward him so he could hear. "Two. The Play Room—the next chamber—is wider, so maybe the water won't be as deep. There's a pretty big drop down to the last chamber. Then we have to get out onto the cliffside." *Making sure that we don't plunge the last seventy feet over Village Falls,* she added mentally. She'd warn him about that when the time came.

The creek, now more a river, roared through the ten-

foot-wide opening in the rock wall and dropped six feet
into the next chamber. The swiftness of the water was
frightening. She'd never been in a slot canyon during a
flash flood, but she'd seen the wreckage left behind—
debris that included the bloated, broken bodies of rabbits,
lizards, even deer trapped by the rising water.

Mist from the roiling stream filled the chamber beyond,
creating an otherworldly atmosphere.

"Dungeons and dragons," Perez bellowed in her ear.
"Through the porthole to the next dimension!"

Dead children didn't faze Perez. Threats of drowning or
dying in a rockslide didn't even slow him down. She
grabbed his jacket sleeve. "This is real, Perez. We could
die in here."

She had to make him understand. "Hold on to this wall
as you step through the opening," she shouted into his face.
"There's a ledge to the right—try to end up there."

He nodded. A drop of water fell from the tip of his nose
into her eye. Blinking, she turned back toward the surging
stream. She took a ragged breath, plunged a foot into the
torrent, and ducked through the opening.

The water was nearly waist deep at the top of the drop.
The current was tremendous. It took all her strength just to
keep her feet beneath her. She wedged her boot between two
rocks. A mistake. As she tried to pull herself around the
rock wall, she couldn't get her foot free. Wonderful; her
ankle was going to break. As momentum carried her forward, she waited for the pop of breaking bone.

Suddenly her foot slid free. Her shins banged against
underwater rocks. Pain ricocheted through her body. She
nearly fell to her knees. It would be suicide to go down like
that. Barely managing to stay on her feet, she groped for a
rough knob of rock jutting out from the wall. A lifesaving
handle.

Panting from exertion, she was able to pull herself up
onto the rock shelf that lay only a few inches under the
water. Concentrating on keeping both feet on the ledge and

both hands behind her on the wall, she sidestepped away from the opening and stopped to wait for Perez.

He faced her as he stepped through, trying to hug the wall as he swung around into the chamber. The water came up only to his thighs, but he had the disadvantage of a higher center of gravity. Arms stretched out, he searched for something to grab hold of.

Suddenly, he slipped, crash-landing on his hands and knees. The water rushed around his shoulders and chest. The torrent tipped him sideways. Sam's heart thumped like a freight train. His pack, now filling with water, would surely pull him under.

"Chase!" She stretched out a hand. At least a yard separated them. He wasn't looking at her. The muscles corded in his neck as he strained to hang on to something underwater. His lips moved. She couldn't hear his words above the roar of the falls. He was probably cursing. She certainly would be.

He reached for a rock that spiked up from the water near the wall. His fingers, white at the tips, curled around the jagged stone. The water geysered up in front of his chest, splashed into his face. His hand slipped from the rock and he fell back. His head went under.

Oh hell. She plunged one foot into the current and stretched to grab his upper arm. Her fingers didn't quite encircle the hard bicep under the slick nylon. The water surged coldly around her crotch and buttocks. She leaned back and pulled with all her might, sat down hard against the underwater ledge. She'd have a bruise the size of Seattle on the back of her thighs. Something in her pack thunked against rock: she prayed it was not her phone or camera, then wondered how she could possibly be worrying about equipment at a time like this.

Perez slid less than a foot in her direction, but it was enough. He got a firm grip on the rock spike and crawled back to his feet again. She let go of his arm and pulled herself erect on the ledge.

Water gushed out of his backpack and streamed down

the backs of his legs. He raised a hand toward her, knuckles bloody from scraping rocks.

"Thank you, Wilderness!" he gasped.

She heaved a sigh of relief. "Welcome to the Play Room, Starchaser. I thought you were a goner there for a moment."

"I'd never hear the end of it if I drowned in some back-country canyon in Utah. The FBI gets gunned down by vicious criminals or we don't die at all." He squeegeed water from his hair with dripping fingers.

She smiled weakly, the muscles in her face stiff. The cold and wet was getting to her. The temperature inside the Curtain was never more than sixty; the water was colder. Before much longer, hypothermia would claim them both. They had to keep moving; keep the blood circulating. The exit wasn't far now.

Her wristwatch, amazingly enough, was still working. It was nearly ninety minutes since they'd begun their descent, more than an hour since it had begun to rain. She took a deep breath, clutched at his arm again. "Look, Chase, I've got to tell you about the waterfall at the end. I didn't want to scare you, but after that last stunt—"

"Mommmyyy!" A thin little cry floated in the mist.

She gasped and turned her head in the direction of the sound.

"After that last stunt?" he prompted.

She turned back to him. "Did you hear that?"

"Hear what?"

"Mommmmyyyyyy."

"There! I just heard it again. A child calling for Mommy."

"I don't hear anything but water." He gently tipped up her chin with a cold finger and gazed into her eyes. "Neither do you, Summer. Remember, I've got the kid. In my pack."

The words hit her, a hard blow to the heart. He was right. The search was over; Zack was dead. Like the echo she'd created while rappelling into the first chamber: *dead, dead, dead.*

Were auditory hallucinations a symptom of hypother-

mia? She couldn't remember. Hypothermia muddled thinking, and hers was getting muddled fast. She had to focus.
She'd gotten them into the Curtain; she had to get them out.

"Summer?" He stared at the center of the chamber.
"How do we get out of here?"

The creek had completely flooded the chamber. Water
lapped at the walls that rose around them in a waffled pat-
tern up to a slash of sky at the top of the crevice. The pock-
marks in the rock walls, she now realized, were erosion
scars from floods like this over the centuries. The water
swirled around the chamber in a sluggish spiral, a dirty
whirlwind at its center.

"Good Lord. The Slide's underwater."

He waited for her explanation, a grim set to his mouth.

"This chamber tilts downward about fifteen feet or so.
The bottom is smooth; it dips abruptly toward that side."
She pointed to the far wall. "To get to the next level, you
pass through a hole about four feet in diameter. Normally
you can sit down in the water and glide over the smooth
rock, like a water slide. Sort of an Alice in Wonderland
experience, going though the rabbit hole." She stared at the
swirling gray water where the hole should have been. The
corpse of a small furry animal—a rat?—was sucked into
the vortex as she watched.

"Can we go back?"

She shook her head. "The drop from the Wreck Room
will be impassable now."

Perez studied the waffled rock walls. "I don't suppose
we could go up."

Sam took note of how the water-slick walls slanted
inward over their heads. Impossible.

"Wilderness Westin could climb out of here, couldn't
she?" Perez asked. "I've heard she's superhuman."

She gave him an exasperated look. How could the man
even think of joking now? "Don't believe everything you
read."

Lightning flashed overhead, its brilliance mirrored for a

second in the pool's surface. Thunder rumbled loudly over the roar of the water.

Perez had been right when he'd described the Curtain as a gigantic beast. It had swallowed them alive, and now it was going to digest them.

23

PEREZ placed a hand on her shoulder. "No worries. I swim like a fish." He gave her a reassuring smile, then pressed his lips together as something crossed his mind. "Correction," he amended. "I do need to breathe. I swim like a dolphin."

Then go for help, Flipper, she wanted to say. She swallowed, then told him, "The next chamber opens up like a cathedral. There'll be plenty of air there."

He leaned out toward the water. "Let's do it."

"Wait!" She grabbed his sleeve. Beneath the wet cloth she could feel him shivering. "Remember the waterfall down the side of the cliff? The one I told you about this morning?" It seemed so long ago. "Just below the ruins?"

He raised an eyebrow. "Are you telling me that's the exit from the next chamber?"

"Bingo." His eyes narrowed, making her wonder what was going on inside his head. "The waterfall comes out of a slit there, only a couple feet wide. We should be able to hang on to the rock there and climb out." *Please, God, make it so.*

"Sounds easy enough." He faced the whirlpool again.

Did he really grasp the danger? He'd never seen the next

chamber, didn't know what he was getting into. She clutched a larger handful of sleeve, pulled him toward her. "Once we're through the Slide—the hole at the bottom of this whirlpool—get to your feet, Chase. Village Falls is a seventy-foot drop. You've got to hang on to something or you'll go over it."

He gently detached her fingers from his jacket, bent down to bring his eyes level with hers. "Summer, I hear you," he said earnestly, still holding her hand. "Believe me when I say that I'll be doing my best. I trust you'll be doing likewise. Ready?"

"Mommmmyyyyy."

That ghostly cry—was it louder now? Sam squinted, peering through the mist, her eyes searching the pock-marked walls for the source of the sound. She clutched at Perez again, this time grabbing the front of his jacket.

"Now what?"

Raising a shaky finger, she pointed to a pocket in the chamber wall ahead. "Chase, tell me that's a hallucination."

Through the mist, a pair of round blue eyes peered out at them.

HIS hands gripped the wheel and his eyes searched the campgrounds, but Rafael Castillo's mind was on his nine-year-old daughter beside him. With her ivory skin, curly black hair, and warm caramel eyes, Rosa was going to be a knockout, just like her mother. They grew up so fast.

"Did Grandma's friend, Mr. Wilson, ever . . . touch you or the other kids?" There. He'd finally gotten the words out.

One of those strange plastic clamps gripped her hair at the crown. Didn't little girls wear ribbons anymore?

"He shook my hand once," she told him. "He didn't really pay much attention to me or to Christy. He wanted to play with Rique and Katie. He was always hugging and kissing on them." She thrust her chin out. "But Christy and me . . . we don't like him, anyway. His neck waggles like a turkey."

"Christy and I," he corrected automatically. Damn that man! And damn his mother-in-law for dragging the miserable excuse for a human being into their house. Wilson's camper and Wallace Russell had disappeared from the campground. He'd asked the local cops and Highway Patrol to keep an eye out for both vehicle and man.

The rain drumming on the windshield was mesmerizing. *Dios mío*, he was exhausted. Good thing he hadn't been sent up to the plateau: he could barely stand up. He prayed that Zack would still be found safe, but it didn't sound good—if Fischer would use his little boy to get money, what else might he do to that child?

Although all clues pointed to Fred Fischer, apparently Thompson was going to let the cougars be killed, anyway. Did his boss have any sense of justice whatsoever?

He pulled his hat on, then wearily pushed open the door of the truck. "Stay here," he told Rosa. "I've got to collect the camping fees. Then we'll get you to your dentist appointment."

He'd only gone a few steps when Rosa called him back. "They're calling you on the radio, Dad." She held it out the window to him. So grown up, so Anglo now. She rarely called him Papi anymore like the other kids did.

He pressed the Talk button. "Three-eight-six."

Leeson was at the other end. "Castillo, you lookin' for a big beige Wanderer?" He rattled off the license number.

Rafael's pulse quickened. Wallace Russell/Orrin Wilson's camper!

"It's stuck in the mud here on West Side Road. Driver says the tow truck's on the way."

"Keep it there until I arrive. Don't let the driver know I'm coming. I'll be there in fifteen. Over."

Rafael jumped in the truck, tossed the radio onto the seat. "Buckle up, Rosa," he told his daughter. It'd be rough, but he'd take the gravel-road shortcut just in case Russell got antsy.

He fingered his holster, unsnapped the restraining strap over his pistol. As he neared the West Side Road, he imagined what it would feel like to rid the world of a worm like Wallace Russell.

* * *

THE mist was thick in the Play Room. Sam could barely make out the apparition through the fog.

"Mommyyyy!" the little boy screamed.

Perez's mouth fell open. "I'll be goddamned—"

Sam stumbled toward the child, pushing a wave of water in front of her like the bow of a boat. As she neared, she could see that he knelt on the floor of a large water-smoothed pocket in the chamber wall. There had to be a way to climb the few feet up to the toddler's position. She put a foot up on a protrusion, lifted herself a foot, reached her hand up to him.

He spread his stubby fingers out to meet hers. For a second she felt his touch—feather-light, warm, a butterfly kiss—and then she slipped back down with a splash. A live little boy. He stood up and put a thumb in his mouth, looking down on her with a puzzled expression.

She forced warmth into her voice. "Zack?"

His face crumpled. "Coug-kittyyyy," he whimpered.

"That's right," she told him. "Come to me, Zack, and we'll go look for another picture of a kitty."

He remained a yard beyond her reach. "I want Mommy!"

She tried again, finding inch-wide grips for her boots, clinging to the wall, stretching hard. The yellow-haired child wore the sodden Pooh Bear sweatshirt, the same torn red sweatpants he'd had on at the trailhead, one tiny red tennis shoe. Pushing her pack onto the ledge, she tried again to climb up, gaining a few inches. It still wasn't enough.

"Come here, Zack," she coaxed, patting the lip of the pocket. "Sit down. Scoot out where I can reach you. I'll take you to your mommy."

The child regarded her uncertainly for a second, then took a hesitant step toward her. *Yes, Zack, yes!* She impatiently patted the rough stone.

A dark shape leapt from the shadows behind the child. A large hand clamped down over Zack's chubby wrist and jerked the toddler back. Zack shrieked.

The man was thin, his ribs prominent above the worn

leather belt that held up his ragged jean shorts. His cheeks were darkened with stubble, not clean-shaven as she'd seen him before.

"Charlie?" she gasped.

His eyes darted in her direction, then quickly flitted away. As he dragged the boy backward, Zack screamed, his shrieks of terror pitched high above the low rumble of the water.

"He's not yours!" the man yelled.

"Coyote Charlie?" Perez's voice came from behind her.

Charlie hesitated, his glistening eyes shifting quickly back and forth between Sam and the FBI agent. His expression was not tranquil now. He looked panicked, disoriented. He growled, an animal sound, and then hauled Zack up from the ground. Charlie clutched the struggling child to his chest, his pale eyes fixed on the FBI agent's face.

"Charlie!" Perez tried again. "Stop where you are!" Sam knew that the soft hiss she heard behind her was Perez's elbow sliding down the side of the nylon pack. He'd be reaching for his pistol.

"No, you're not Charlie," Sam said, remembering. "You're Davinski." Wolf Davinski, member of Earth Spirits; Karl Jacob Davinski, thirty-two, wanted in Oregon for destruction of construction equipment; *BJB + KJD* carved on the wall in the ruins. "Karl Davinski."

Davinski took a step closer. His eyes were wild, flitting first to her, then to Perez, back to her. He'd seemed so gentle that day on the trail. Was he schizophrenic?

"How are you, Karl?" Perez said it as if he'd known the man all along. "Let Zachary go. Put him down. It's not too late to make things right. Karl, put Zachary down."

"Karl, I want to thank you for the energy bar," she said. "And the nuts."

"Cashews," he spat. He pressed the squirming child against his chest, barely able to keep hold of him.

"That's right, cashews. And the grapes you gave me that day on the trail." How could she keep his attention, distract him from Perez? She pulled her camera from her pack and framed Davinski in the viewfinder.

Zack turned his head and bit the skin of the man's bare chest. Davinski held the toddler out in front of him with both hands, shook the child up and down. "Stop that, David!"

"He's not David, Karl. He's Zack." She tried to keep her voice calm. "He wants to go home to his mommy, don't you, Zack?"

Zack's arms and legs flew up and down violently. "David!" the man shrieked. "This is David!"

"Mommyyyy!" the boy screeched.

Sam snapped the photo. The flash startled Davinski; he staggered forward a step and nearly dropped Zack. The child's feet swung only a short distance above Sam's head. She slapped the camera down on the ledge, leapt forward, caught a handful of the red sweatpants above the boy's ankle. Davinski pulled back, and the child's pants slid down one side of his hips, revealing training pants beneath.

Zack screamed again. "Mommmyyyy!"

"He's mine!" the man roared above the din. "You took Barbie, but you won't get David! I saved him!"

Sam hung on. Davinski clutched the waistband of the boy's pants in his right hand; the fabric stretched tight between them.

The man's eyes widened, and Sam knew that Perez had drawn his gun.

"Davinski, let go of Zachary. I'm from the FBI."

Karl Davinski remained frozen in place, his wild eyes fixed on Perez's face.

"Davinski, this is not David. This is Zachary Fischer. Put him down, or I will shoot. I will shoot you after a count of three. One."

"He's mine!"

"Two."

"I saved him from the blue demon. I saved him! I won't let you have him!" He raised Zack up into the air, nearly jerking Sam off her feet.

The little boy's shrieks were deafening. She felt Perez step to the side to remove the child from the line of fire. In her peripheral vision, she saw the sleek semiautomatic

pointed at Davinski's head. She didn't want Karl Davinski
to die. There'd been too much blood spilled already.

"Three."

Perez's finger tightened on the trigger. Then lightning
cracked in several blinding flashes. Davinski jerked Zack
upward. The sweatpants slid from the chubby legs. He raised
the boy above his head. Sam fell back, clutching a handful of
limp fabric.

"No!" Her voice was lost in the rumble of thunder. The
click of Perez's gun barely registered. Zack kicked wildly.
The heel of his tiny foot caught Davinski squarely in the eye,
and he dropped the child. Zack's feet barely touched the
ground before the little boy launched himself toward Sam.

She grabbed for him. His sneaker hit her cheek. The
bare foot slipped through her fingers as he sailed over her
shoulder into the water.

No! She plunged in after him. In the middle of the pool
the water was chest deep, but she couldn't stay on her feet.
The spiraling current was fierce. Her knee banged against
an underwater obstacle. Where was Zack? The water was
murky; she was trying to see through mud. The current
dragged her toward the center; toward the drop through the
submerged hole to the next level.

She struggled to raise her head above the water. A pale
shiny object bobbed up next to her shoulder. She grabbed
for it, came up clutching an aluminum pan. Her elbow
cracked against an unseen rock. Where was Zack? He was
drowning!

Something smooth glanced off her rib cage. Her fingers
slid across a cool slick surface. Then she felt only water. A
punch landed squarely in the center of her abdomen. She
reached out with both hands. Her fingertips were brushed
by feathery strands. She knotted her fingers into them and
pulled. A yellow and pink head emerged from the water.
The lips parted and a gasp came out, followed by a wail.

Thank God. Zack, still breathing. She clutched him to
her chest and leaned back, trying to keep both of their heads
above the torrent. Her braid caught in an underwater snag,

snapping her head back with a jolt of pain. The swirling water pulled her legs under the surface. The Slide, the opening to the lower chamber! With an excruciating jerk, her hair came free. She felt for Zack's mouth, covered it with her hand a fraction of a second before they were sucked under the surface.

The rough sandstone scoured the skin from her backbone as she and Zack slid through the underwater hole. It was like being swallowed alive.

Against her better judgment, she opened her eyes to gray water. Dark blobs of stone. As she surfaced, a flash of lightning blinded her. She removed her fingers from Zack's mouth, pulled him higher on her chest. He coughed against her throat; she could feel the warmth of his breath. Good boy, Zachary.

They were in the last chamber now. The water surged beneath her, carrying them effortlessly toward the final drop. She pedaled her legs furiously, trying to find a purchase against the stone floor. Anything. She flailed with her free arm. A rock bit into her fingers. She closed them over the pinnacle, but the water dragged her past the handhold. Another flash of lightning streaked across the sky above.

Zack struggled on her chest. She'd been searching for him for days. Damn it, she wasn't going to let him go without a fight! She spread her legs wide in the hopes of stopping their progress through the surging water. Something sharp pierced the skin of her calf. A scrape started at her thigh, dug a trench up her back and threatened to tear her ear off as she passed over it. Stick or rock, it didn't matter. It hurt just the same.

She tried desperately to pull herself up into a sitting position, but Zack's weight was centered on her upper chest. He sobbed into her neck, his wailing distant compared to the roar of the stream surrounding them. They dipped and bobbed through the water. She kicked her legs again, trying to feel the rock floor that had to be only inches beneath her.

With a bone-jarring thud, her right foot slammed up

against rock, sending a shock wave of pain up her leg. A second later, her left foot thudded against a vertical wall of stone. Zack slid down her chest, coming to rest on her stomach. She clutched him tighter. They stopped. But the water didn't. It surged over her cheeks and splashed into her mouth. Zack struggled against her. She fought to maintain her hold on the boy, praying she wasn't holding his head underwater.

She contracted her stomach muscles, inched her chin out of the water. Over the huge lump that was Zack, she saw gray sky between her knees. And the tops of trees.

They called this chamber the Observatory, because of the view. Her legs straddled the narrow opening in the rock wall. She was at the top of Village Falls.

24

WALLACE Russell was chatting with Ranger Leeson beside the bogged-down camper when he arrived. Rafael leapt out of the truck into the muddy road, barking "Stay in the car!" at his daughter before slamming the door behind him.

Russell registered the murderous look on Rafael's face. "Excuse me," he said to Leeson, and took a step toward the camper. "I need—"

Before Russell could retreat to the safety of the camper, Leeson caught him by the arm and held him in place as Rafael approached, one hand on his service pistol. "You're under arrest, Wallace Russell—"

Russell jerked away from Leeson, thrust both arms into the air. "I didn't do anything to him! I never even had him, really."

With his free hand, Rafael pulled a plastic zip tie from his pocket. "Hands behind your back."

Wallace Russell kept his hands in the air. "I was going to take that kid back to his mother, honest. I didn't hurt him. Look!" He ripped off his toupee and bent over so the law enforcement rangers could see the purple bruise on the crown of his head. "I'm the one who got hurt!"

Leeson grabbed Russell's arms, forced them behind the man's back. Damn, he wasn't going to need the gun, after all. Somewhat reluctantly, Rafael snapped his holster closed and handcuffed Russell with the zip tie.

"Look," Russell cajoled, "maybe I can save you guys some time here. He doesn't need to tell about me and Zack, and I don't sue him for battery, okay? So everyone gets to go home."

Dan Leeson shot a look at Rafael and jerked a thumb at Wallace Russell. "*He* had Zack Fischer?"

"No!" Russell protested. "I never had him! I barely even touched him! He was running around in the dark all alone. I was helping him!"

"I checked the camper. There's nobody inside." Leeson said. "What the heck is going on?"

"Damned if I know," Rafael answered. "I was just nabbing this scumbag for parole violations. He's a child molester from Flagstaff."

Leeson held Russell's toupee out to Rafael. Wallace Russell bent over obligingly so that the shorter Rafael could place it on his head.

The toupee fell in the mud.

Rafael stepped on it. "Damn," he said dramatically. "Sorry about that." Squished into the muddy car tracks, the hairpiece looked like roadkill.

"What'd you want to do that for?" Russell whined. From his hunched position, he had a perfect view inside Rafael's truck. His face perked up. "Hey, that's Rosa, right? You're a lucky man, Ranger Castillo. She's such a pretty little girl. Look at those lips."

Rafael slugged Wallace Russell.

DURING her short stint as a seasonal ranger, Sam had taken photos of the falls from the outside—ragged red rocks framing an elongated diamond window through which the water cascaded in a shimmering curtain from the cliffside. From inside the chamber, the diamond frame enclosed billowing clouds punctuated by the green spikes of junipers. A lone aspen flashed its few remaining leaves, brilliant gold against the ashen sky. If she could sit up, she'd see the river valley below through the mist, like a mirage.

She was so tired, so cold. She struggled to hold her head up, to keep a grip on Zack, gasping for breath between surges of water.

Her mind flooded with the memory of the last time she had kissed her mother good night. Even with the ventilator, the poor woman had been gasping for oxygen like a fish out of water. She—nine-year-old Summer—had gone to bed at the usual time, wondering what kind of a God would make someone suffer so.

At dawn, it had been so quiet. No ventilator, no gasping. Her father sat in the same chair as he had the night before, hugging her mother's pillow to his chest. And her mother lay peacefully, her face serene at last. "Let's give thanks to God, Summer," her father had said. "We were so lucky to have her with us for so long."

She thought about Kent and the cougar bleeding in the dust and then the self-righteous hunters that shot them. Adam. Barbara Jean. That poor dead child crushed by the rocks. And now, Zachary Fischer—he hadn't moved for minutes now. Was he unconscious? The water bucked beneath her like a wild bronco.

A rock ground into her left kidney. It hurt like hell. Anger rushed through her at the unfairness of it all. *I proved myself, Adam, no thanks to you. And I've got news for you, Dad. I'm not thankful for suffering and death. And I'm not ready to die!*

She focused on her physical pain, zeroed in on the spasming muscles in her neck, the throbbing cougar scratches, the stinging scrapes along her backbone. She needed to collect all that sharpness and use it to cut through the fogginess that filled her brain.

She was right-handed; her grip on that side was stronger. She wrapped her left arm around Zack, made sure the fingers of her left hand were rolled into his sweatshirt. Pushing her right arm sideways into the current, she stretched her fingers out into the surging water. A rock, a branch, anything she could hold on to!

Zack kicked her hard, in the abdomen. Good, he was still alive. She could no longer feel her fingers, but she clenched the muscles in her left arm to keep him firmly against her. She paddled her right hand in the rushing stream. Where the hell was Perez? He'd said he could swim like a dolphin: why hadn't he come after her and Zack?

Her knuckles rasped over a stone. She twisted her wrist and curled her fingers around the protrusion. Did she have it? Her fingers were thick, lifeless. She made an effort to pull herself toward the rock. Her body moved sideways a couple of inches, causing her shoulder to sink beneath the surface. Water surged over her neck and chest. Zack kicked and shrieked, a high treble note over the background bass of the flood. But the rock held. She'd found an anchor.

Dare she move her left foot? She pulled herself to the right. The water shoved more forcefully against her. Broadside to the current, the surge would be more powerful. But she couldn't stay where she was. She'd be completely numb in another minute. Her muscles would gradually give way and she and Zack would slip over the edge and fall to their deaths on the rocks below. Wouldn't Adam love to get *that* on videotape. What a scoop.

The creek roared in her ears. Water kept spattering into her eyes. Maddening. Perez wasn't coming. Nobody was coming.

She clenched the muscles in her right arm and pulled. The water surged against her back, propelling her toward the opening. She straightened her right knee to keep her body away from the wall; she didn't want to smash Zack against the rock. The current threatened to rip her clothes from her body. She could feel water running between her toes and the insoles of her hiking boots.

Pushing off from the wall, she thrust her left foot into the current. It was immediately sucked into the surge of water leaping over the falls. The current was dragging her through the opening.

Her head struck a rock, but instead of stars, she suddenly saw clouds overhead. Her fingers scrabbled at the rocks beneath the water. Both her feet dangled over the precipice. She heard the thunder of water striking the pool far below.

Zack was slipping from her grasp. His legs dangled in the water between her thighs. She contracted her muscles and brought her legs up around him. She felt a tug between her breasts. Through the surging water she saw tiny fingers clutching her bra.

"Hang on, Zack!"

Her right hand had a tentative hold on a slippery rock at the edge of the waterfall. Another rock, blessedly dry, stood next to the one she held on to. She straightened the fingers of her left hand and withdrew it from Zack's sweatshirt. The little body slipped an inch. She tightened her legs around him. Was his head underwater? *Oh God, don't let him drown. Don't let me drop him.*

Now or never. She rolled onto her right side and reached for the rock. Yes, yes, she had it; through a blur of water she saw her fingers around the block of sandstone, even if she could no longer feel them. She dragged her body toward her handholds, conscious that she was dragging the toddler over the rocks with her. *Sorry, Zack, sorry.*

She wedged an elbow between the rocks, used it as a lever to pull her shoulders out of the water. If she hadn't been so numb, it would have hurt like hell. Flopping over onto her back, she shoved both hands against the rocks to drag her hips out of the torrent. Two small arms and a head covered with wet yellow hair emerged as well.

Grabbing the back of Zack's sweatshirt, she hauled his small body up onto dry land beside her. She collapsed across the lichen-spotted rock, her cheek in the dirt, panting with exhaustion.

Zack's lips were blue. His eyes were closed; delicate

purple veins visible in the pale lids. A long red scratch ran down from scalp to chin. Was he breathing? A trickle of water spilled out over his lower lip.

She didn't have the strength to do CPR. *Breathe, Zachary, breathe! Come on, boy.* A bubble of mucus formed at his nostril. Good sign; he had air in his lungs. But his chest was not moving. She tried to push herself up with a numb arm. Then he choked, spraying water into her face. Never had she been more willing to have a child spit up on her. He gasped, sucking in a big gulp of air.

Thank God. She clasped his little body close. At least they were out of the wind. They were even somewhat out of the rain. Were those tree limbs above? The rocks beneath her were definitely warmer than the water had been. Her feet were icy, though. She tried to wiggle her toes, heard squishing sounds. She bent her knees, pulled her boots out of the water onto dry land.

That was it; her last ounce of adrenaline had burned out in the water, and she was left with only uncontrollable shivering. She rolled onto her back, keeping Zack against her, his head snuggled into her armpit. Her eyes closed, shutting out the rolling clouds overhead. "Hang in there, little guy. Just a ten-minute break, and then I'll get you to Mommy." Although it would be a hell of a lot easier if Mommy came to them.

A little later—she couldn't have said whether it had been half an hour or five minutes—she came to with the unpleasant sensation of heavy raindrops pelting her face. She squeezed an arm around Zack's little body. He made a puppylike snuffling noise and curled into a smaller ball, shivering.

Teeth clenched to keep them from chattering, she dragged her body away from his and pushed herself up against the tree. Across her lower back, something ripped. She wasn't certain whether it was clothing or skin.

She studied her body as if it belonged to someone else. The front of her T-shirt had been ripped open. No wonder her bra had been so handy a lifeline. Her boots were cleaner than they'd been for months. The wet leather positively gleamed; not a speck of dirt on them. The gash ripped into her canvas pants by the cougar's claws now stretched from seam to seam. Her thigh gaped through, the paleness of the skin accentuated by the three red slashes. A similar tear adorned the other leg at calf level. What was this style called? Punk? No, grunge, that was it.

It was raining again, pouring down sheets of water over the valley. Or had it been doing that all along? She'd better get moving; she and Zack were both hypothermic. And the hunters would be shooting any minute now. Why the heck didn't angels or handsome heroes ever magically appear like they did in novels? Real life was just so damned much effort.

She pulled her knees up under her chin and braced her back against the tree. So far, so good. Shoving against the ground with her hands, she pushed herself up. The bark of the trunk raked against her skin. On her feet, she braced one palm against the tree and explored her lower back with the other. Not much left of either vest or shirt; she could feel the knobs of her backbone above her belt. Her fingers came away bloody. It was surprising that it didn't hurt more. That would probably change.

The boy still lay curled in a fetal position on the rock. Sam stiffly crouched over him, rolled Zack onto his back and ran her fingers over his small body. No unusual lumps or gushing blood. The boy whimpered and curled back into his former position.

"C'mon, buddy," Sam said. She scooped him up, apparently none too gently because he stiffened, wailed angrily, and smacked a small fist against her neck.

"You're welcome." She hefted him onto a hip and folded her arms around his small body. "I don't suppose you want to carry me?"

He glared at her for a minute, rain dripping from his hair and eyelashes, then bent his head and buried his face on her chest.

"That's what I figured." Her legs felt wooden. It was

amazingly difficult to lift her feet up the steep slope; each step felt as if it were yards above the previous one. She counted. She'd rest after fifty steps.

When she reached fifty, she knew that if she stopped to rest, she wouldn't be able to start again. At 215, she finally reached the ruins, staggered under the cover of the overhang and sat down heavily on a ledge. At least her motion had generated some body heat. Her teeth had stopped chattering, and Zack seemed to have stopped shivering as well. He clung to her like a baby monkey. Under normal circumstances she would have shrugged him off, but he felt warm against her stomach and chest. She'd have to get moving again soon; warm and wet would soon return to cold and wet.

Where the hell were Perez and Coyote Charlie? If only she had some dry clothes. Her cell phone would come in handy right now, too. Assuming it had any juice left in the battery. She rested her chin on top of Zack's blond curls. How the hell was she supposed to get this kid and herself down a mountain in time to stop the cougar hunt?

Something rustled behind her. Her heart immediately sped up, and in one motion, she slid Zack off her lap, twisted around, and grabbed a chunk of rock in one fist.

Perez stood twenty feet away, arms out, a day pack in his left hand, a look of surprise on his face. Either she was imagining things or little wisps of steam were rising from his body.

"Summer!" He shoved his gun into his waistband and walked over. "You're alive!"

"Nothing gets past the FBI, does it?" she croaked.

His clothing looked damp but more sweat-damp than floodwater damp. His gaze traced a path down her body that would have made her blush under other conditions. "Are you okay?" he asked.

She tried to shrug. The movement hurt. "No bones broken," she mumbled. "Least I don't think so. Where's Charlie?"

"Lost him back there." He jerked his chin over his shoulder but kept his brown eyes fixed on her. "Hi, Zack," he said to the boy. "We're glad to find you."

Zack wriggled under her arm and leaned into her side. "Monkey," Sam groaned.

Perez gave her a concerned look. "Did you hit your head?" His warm fingers brushed her cheek. "You're slurring your words."

"Hy-po-therm-i-a," she enunciated for him. So many syllables. She tilted her head toward Zack. "Him, too. Call for help?"

Perez shook his head. "My phone went under when I did."

"Mine's on the ledge. Back there." The chamber inside the Curtain seemed miles away.

"I'LL be right back." Perez turned and vanished back through the ruins.

Sam briefly considered turning to see where he was going, but it seemed like too much effort. She rested her chin on Zack's blond curls. Just one more minute, she told herself, and then she'd stand up. *Right.*

Perez returned, a pile of clothing in his arms. He laid it down on the ledge beside her, and then pulled Zack from her arms. "Let's get some dry clothes on you, okay, bud?"

Dry clothes sounded good. Sam checked the pile beside her, pulled out a green jacket. With awkward fingers that seemed swollen, she shucked off her torn vest and then peeled away the shreds of the T-shirt and her bra. She couldn't work up the energy to be embarrassed even if she'd been totally naked. She pulled on the jacket and zipped it up. Flannel-lined. Nice.

Beside her, Chase had peeled off Zack's wet clothes and dressed him in an adult T-shirt and his own blue nylon jacket. Chase ran his hands quickly up and down the toddler's arms, chafing his skin. "Warmer now, Zack?"

Good idea. She pushed herself to her feet, although it felt like she was moving in a Frankenstein-like fashion. Rubbing her hands over her own arms felt like a lot of effort, but it seemed to be working.

Chase stood Zack up on the ledge. The adult clothes

dragged on the floor, obscuring the toddler's feet. Zack wrapped his arms around her leg and smiled up at her. "Warm!" he chirped.

Although she was still soaked from the waist down, she was getting warmer herself. It was nice that the green jacket fit her so well. Which was weird, because she always had a hard time finding clothes that— "Hey, this is my jacket," she observed.

"Nothing gets by you Internet reporters, does it?" Chase grinned.

"Hypothermia," she said by way of explanation for sounding like an idiot.

He nodded and jerked a thumb over his shoulder. "I found your jacket back there, along with more clothes and cans of food. Looks like Davinski has been ripping off the tourists around here for a long time."

"Did you shoot him?"

"I tried. The gun misfired. Wet, I guess." He stood and chafed his own bare arms.

She hadn't seen Perez in short sleeves before. His arms were lean and muscular. His stomach was flat under a plain white T-shirt. He looked . . . capable. Maybe after this whole damn nightmare was over, they'd—

A flare of panic suddenly ignited in her water-chilled brain. She didn't have time to admire the man's physique! "Chase, my phone! The hunters! We've got to call park headquarters."

"First things first." He pressed an energy bar into her hands. She stared at the metallic wrapper. Could it be the same one she'd lost last night and found beside her this morning? It was surreal, the way the dang thing kept reappearing. She peeled down the wrapper and took a tiny bite. Its sweetness flooded her mouth. She lowered the energy bar to Zack's lips. The child placed both hands around it and pushed the snack into his mouth eagerly.

Perez sat on his heels, regarding the two of them. "You'd make a good mother."

"No." Her reply was vehement. "No. I'm not taking care of anyone."

His gaze met hers. "Sometimes, Summer, we all need taking care of."

Right, she thought bitterly. *And where were you when Zack and I were dangling over a seventy-foot drop?*

Zack held the remainder of the energy bar up to her with both hands. She took a bite, then gave it back to him, wiping a crumb from his chin. The cold water had sogged up her emotions as well as her clothes; she stifled a sob. All the times she'd held food to her mother's lips; all the times she'd wiped the dribbles from the spasm-clenched jaws. She'd never forget the beseeching look in those gray-blue eyes. What had her mother been asking for? An involuntary shudder ran through her. After all these years, she still didn't know.

She swallowed painfully. "Where's Davinski now?" she asked.

"He got away. There's a hole in the back of that pocket cave. He had it blocked up with rocks. It comes out into the ruins, about six feet above the roof where you slept last night."

The caved-in ceiling, the footprints in the moss, the dampness. She had slept just below that gap for hours. Had Davinski watched her all night? Had she really heard Zack?

"He had a stash of cans and packets of freeze-dried food back there, too, and some other stuff: clothes, pocket-knives, matches, that sort of thing. It looked like they'd been there awhile; like Charlie—I mean Karl—had been raiding the campgrounds for food and clothes.

"And there was a book. *The Anasazi Way.* The forensics team should get a kick out of it: looked like a cross between the *Mother Earth News* and some New Age bible." Perez rubbed his hands over a scratch on the right side of his face. "I was so close at first. Right behind him. But the pack slowed me down. Davinski could be halfway down the mountain by now."

That's right, Perez had been carrying her knapsack. She surveyed the room and spotted the blue nylon tilted against the wall beyond the fire pit. Dirty water dripped from the fabric down onto the floor. She didn't want to think about what was inside.

"David—wasn't that what he called him? David Davinski," she murmured. Cold, gray, dead. She understood it all now. The blue demon. Her intuition about Weird Wilson. The grapes. Even the odor of Camembert she thought she'd imagined last night had been real. "David is—was—the baby Barbara Jean was carrying three years ago. BJB plus KJD."

Perez frowned. "You lost me."

"Initials—they're carved into the wall of the town house, a few doors down. BJB plus KJD. Barbara Jean and Karl. Those handprints in the Drawing Room." A family of handprints: father, mother, baby. The items pilfered from campgrounds. Food, clothing, cooking utensils. The repeated sightings of Coyote Charlie. "They've been living up here for nearly three years."

Perez considered. "Well, Davinski's been here for that long. Barbara Jean probably died around six months ago. And David, just days or, at most, a week ago."

"Poor David." She looked down at the boy by her side. His hair was dry now, golden blond. Blue eyes stared into hers.

"Zack!" he chirped.

"Yes, you're Zack," she agreed. "But you do look a lot like David." She turned toward Perez. "Did my camera and phone survive?"

"I'll get your pack." He disappeared again.

Out beyond the plaza, the rain poured off the overhang in a translucent curtain of water. She sat down again, closed her eyes and listened to the hum of falling water. Zack climbed into her lap, and she hugged his small warm body. It would be so nice to lie down and go to sleep for a few hours. Maybe for a few days.

Footsteps scuffled in front of her. She opened her eyes to a blinding flash. Perez stood there, the digital camera in front of his face. "Now that's your photo," he said, his dark eyes shining.

Ever since she'd met Chase Perez, she'd been trying to think of a description for the clear brown color of his eyes. Finally, she had it: they were the color of a stream she'd drunk from on Vancouver Island. The surrounding peat bog tinged the crystal-clear water dark brown. Peat brown, dark but transparent at the same time. A smoky flavor, earthy and delicious.

He set the camera down beside her. She didn't want to think about how she'd look in the picture he'd just snapped. A sewer rat, an old hag. In a minute she'd take a picture of Zachary by himself. She glanced at her watch. A deep scratch marred the crystal, but the hands were still moving. It was a few minutes after two o'clock.

Two o'clock. The USDAWS hunters were to start from the park perimeter at noon. "The hunters!" She clawed at Perez's arm. "We've got to let Thompson know we have Zack!"

"I'm trying." Perez held her cell phone up to his ear. After a second, he shook his head. "Just static."

"It was almost dead last night."

"The light's still blinking."

"Try the satellite."

She gave him the number and her access code. He walked outside, but returned only a couple of moments later. "Can't get a damn thing in this storm. But the hunters won't be out in it, either."

She wouldn't bet on that. The hunters she knew prided themselves on overcoming the elements.

"The sky's brighter to the west; the rain might lighten up. I'll try again in a minute."

Zack looked a lot healthier than he had a half hour ago, but Sam knew that the toddler needed decent food and probably medical attention as well. She could do with a few Band-Aids and a beer herself. Maybe several Band-Aids and several beers.

"We need to go," she told Perez. "They'll be shooting any minute. We can walk out of the rain."

"I'll get the pack." He turned toward the far wall.

She shouldered her borrowed pack, took Zack's hand, and led him out onto the plaza. On the little boy, Perez's shirt and jacket dragged the stone floor like a nightgown. Zack stumbled on the material. As she turned to pick him up, Karl Davinski emerged from the shadows of the town house. His chopped hair dripped muddy water onto his bare chest. His eyes, locked on Zachary, were coldly determined. In his outstretched hand he held what looked like an antique revolver.

"David," he hissed. "Come to Daddy."

25

CLUTCHING a fold of her soggy pants, Zack shrank back behind Sam's leg. The barrel of the pistol was pointed squarely at her chest. Davinski's finger was on the trigger.

"Give me my son!" he roared.

Was the gun loaded? Sam saw a movement behind the armed man. Perez. Davinski saw her eyes focus on the point beyond him; he began to turn in the other man's direction.

"Karl!" Sam yelled, pulling her gaze back to Davinski.

He swiveled back in her direction, his eyes shifting from side to side now.

"I know you don't want to do this, Karl." She had to keep his attention. "This is not David. This is not your son. David is dead." She emphasized the last word heavily. "Like Barbara Jean."

The wraith shook his head violently, dislodging a shower of droplets from his tangled locks. The gun barrel wavered. Behind him, Perez crept closer.

"No," Davinski moaned. His gaze trailed downward and locked on Zack. The little boy's fingers clenched more tightly around Sam's leg. "David was lost for a little while, but I found him. I saved him."

"You didn't save David. David died in that cave-in," she said softly. "He was crushed by the rocks. David's dead."

Karl Davinski's eyes flickered as if she'd just jolted him with a stun gun. He wasn't completely disoriented, then. Sam reached back, put her hand on Zack's head. "This is another little boy. A different boy, Zachary Fischer. You found him in the campground, didn't you? Just like you found those grapes."

He looked startled that she'd put it together. Then his pale eyes blazed with anger. "Liar!" he shrieked. "He's mine. I saved him."

"This is not your son. This is Zachary, and his mother wants him back." Still looking at him, she slowly slid the pack down over her shoulders and extracted an arm from the straps.

Davinski's washed-out gaze connected with hers. "I made a mistake, and then David was lost. But he didn't get hurt; look at him! He was stolen!"

"Karl," she said gently. "You know that's not true."

His eyes blurred with tears. "But the blue demon had him. I saved him."

"I know you did, Karl." Wilson's mud-covered outfit had been blue. He was the shadowy man at the end of the path. "You saved him. But Zack is not yours to keep."

Davinski's finger pressed against the trigger.

Sam hurled her pack at Davinski and dove for the floor, pulling Zack down with her. A bullet whined over her head like a rocket-powered bumblebee. At the same time, there was a loud crack as the pack connected with Davinski's knees, and he staggered forward and tripped over it. Then Perez was on him. She rolled to her knees. Zack was on all fours, crying. She pushed herself up, ran toward the struggling men. Perez gripped Davinski's wrist; he slammed the man's hand against the floor. Another shot rang out, ricocheted off the plaza stones in a puff of dust, only a foot beyond the sobbing toddler.

Perez was on top of Davinski. No way to kick or punch one without getting the other. She stomped on the hand that held the pistol, felt metal and bone hard beneath her boot.

Karl Davinski howled. She heard a pop as another bullet exploded from the gun under the sole of her boot. She raised her foot. The limp hand drew away, leaving the pistol on the floor. She grabbed the weapon.

Davinski kneed Perez in the groin. The agent's body buckled in pain. Davinski shoved him away, slithered like a lizard toward the nearby opening of the kiva. He was halfway down into the underground structure before Perez recovered and grabbed his ankle. As they both tumbled into the kiva, Perez's foot caught the ladder. It fell with a crash after them.

Sam galloped to the stone edging around the kiva. Perez sat on Davinski's abdomen, struggling to pin the other man's arms to the ground. Davinski's legs flailed behind Perez's back.

"Stop it, Karl!" She pointed the pistol at Davinski's head. Neither man gave any sign of hearing her. Davinski kneed Perez hard in the back. Sam felt the blow in her own kidneys. It didn't look as if Davinski would be down for long.

Sam shouted again. "Stop or I'll shoot!" Yeah, right. She'd never shot anything but tranquilizer guns. But how hard could it be? Thousands of people did it every year, and some of them were idiots. Warning shot first; she really didn't want to kill anyone. She aimed just above Davinski's head and pulled the trigger.

The bullet pinged exactly where she was aiming, releasing a little puff of dust, then smacked off the wall behind Davinski and then off the wall just inches away from Perez's ear. Davinski flinched, but Perez amazingly did not. He delivered a blow to the side of Davinski's head that gave Sam an instant headache. As the other man went limp beneath him, Perez rolled off him and whipped a zip tie from his jeans pocket. Then Davinski shot up, managing to get his hands on the edge of the kiva, pulling himself up to the rim.

"You have *got* to be kidding," Sam groaned. As his head

emerged from the rim of the kiva, she drew back her foot and kicked out hard, connecting with his temple. Davinski dropped from the rim, hitting his head hard on the packed earth floor; he stayed down this time. Flipping Davinski over, Perez quickly bound his wrists together and then moved down to Davinski's legs, tying his ankles together only a second before Davinski started thrashing again.

Perez pulled himself to his feet. His hair was wet with sweat; his face was covered with blood and dirt. "God, Summer," he said, "Haven't you ever heard of ricochet?"

"You're welcome."

He hefted the ladder into place, leaned on it panting for a minute, and then climbed up.

Davinski rolled over and lay looking up at them. Across his left temple and cheek was the deep red imprint of her hiking boot. Sam was glad to see she hadn't killed him.

"Are you going to leave him down there?" she asked.

"Hell yes." Blood dribbled from a cut on Perez's bottom lip onto the collar of his white T-shirt as he leaned over and pulled the ladder out of the kiva.

Zachary ran to Sam and threw his arms around her thigh. Glaring at Davinski down in the kiva, he spat, "Bad man! I hate you!"

"That's right, Zack. He's a bad man."

The little boy picked up a loose rock and threw it, hitting Davinski in the thigh. Then Zack turned and grinned. *Probably not a behavior that should be encouraged,* Sam thought, but she couldn't really blame the kid.

She pulled the camera from her pack and captured a shot of Zack standing above his kidnapper. Zack happily obliged her by tossing another pebble down onto Davinski.

Sam put her hand on the boy's shoulder. "That's enough, Zack." She stared down at Davinski, who lay quietly, his pale blue eyes staring up, focused on nothing. "How could you let it all go so wrong, Karl?" she murmured.

"It was perfect," he said in a hoarse whisper. "Then Barbie got sick and left me . . ." A tear rolled down his weathered cheek.

"I know you loved her, Karl. And David's death was an accident, wasn't it?" she said softly. "Maybe he was just playing on those rocks?"

"He won't stay put unless I leave him on the island."

The pile of rocks in the Wreck Room, surrounded by Curtain Creek, would look like an island.

"And I have to go out hunting. I have to be a good father." Davinski groaned. "David's afraid of the water. I tell him he'll go over the falls." His gaze shifted to meet hers. "We live off the land. This is the Anasazi Garden of Eden, you know." Davinski's cracked lips curved into an eerie smile. "I was reborn here. And now David is, too. He was lost but now is found."

Perez had one eyebrow raised. "Guess that about sums it up," he said. "I'll come back for him and for the . . . David . . . as soon as we can get a copter up here."

Outside, somewhere far away, she heard the crack of a rifle shot. Then another. "The phone, Perez! Give me the phone." Grabbing it from him, she galloped to the edge of the plaza and lowered herself painfully down the steps onto the mesa, punching in numbers as she went.

She dialed the wrong number, got a gas station in Las Rojas. "Shit!" she yelled in the unlucky attendant's ear. She punched End, made herself take a deep breath. Two more pops drifted up from somewhere below. Definitely gunfire. She carefully punched in the park headquarters' number.

"Heritage National Monument." A woman's voice. Didn't sound familiar. She could barely hear it at all. The battery was nearly dead.

"Stop the hunt!" she yelled.

"Madam," began the answerer, "I understand that you're upset—"

"This is Summer Westin, up on the plateau. I'm with an agent from the FBI—"

"And I'm Cinderella," the woman snapped. "Look, ma'am—"

Perez, holding Zack in one arm, plucked the phone from her grip. He identified himself, then said, "I'm holding Zachary Fischer in my arms right now." He listened for a minute, then held the phone to Zack's mouth. "Say hi, Zack."

"Hi!" the little boy screeched. "Mommy?"

Perez moved the phone to his ear again. "We need a helicopter up here immediately. We're on the path below the ruins, starting down toward . . ."

"Village Falls," Sam supplied. "A helicopter could land near the bottom."

"Village Falls," he repeated into the phone. He paused. "I'm ordering you to stop the cougar hunt immediately."

Sam chewed a fingernail to the quick in the long silence that ensued.

"Well, you'd better damn well figure it out," Perez finally snarled. He punched End.

The look on his face was not encouraging. "What did she say?"

He pushed Zack up onto his shoulders. "She's on loan from Canyonlands. She's not sure who to call about the helicopter. And she didn't know how to contact the hunters."

THEY hiked down the rocky trail through the rain, which was now a mere drizzle.

"Fischer's still unaccounted for," Perez told his partner through heavy static. "I'll tell you the details later. I need you to call off the federal guns. Now."

"Nicole promised that she would try to end it ASAP," he told Sam when he'd ended the call. "At least that's what I thought she was saying. The phone went dead before she finished the sentence."

It wasn't enough for Sam, who watched her boots descend the trail as if they belonged to someone else. She should be running, screaming, anything to stop the senseless slaughter. Zack was finally safe and sound, but the cougars were going to die, anyway. But even as her mind was on fire, her body was, too. Every muscle ached. She felt every scratch and gouge: the cougar stripes on her thigh, the wide scrapes along her backbone. Her shredded clothing chafed against the welts and glued itself to the bloody areas. Her scalp throbbed nearly as much outside as her head ached inside.

Zack, wearing one of her black garbage bags for a raincoat, rode on top of the agent's pack. Perez kept a protective hand clutched around one of the child's ankles. Zack's fingers formed a pale headband across the FBI agent's bronze forehead.

The storm had transformed the bone-dry park into a spectacular display of falling water. Village Falls was a thundering cascade, and Sam shivered, watching it. She and Zack had almost plunged over along with all that water. The rain dissolved into a light mist. As a helicopter rocketed toward them, they waited near the shimmering pool cradled by red rock. Their clothing steamed in the sunshine.

"Take us to the hunters," Sam ordered the pilot. Perez rode next to the man, and Sam strapped herself, with Zack on her lap, into the seat in back, crowding in with a pile of equipment.

"My orders are to deliver you to park headquarters," the pilot said. "Medics are standing by to give you and the boy aid. And the press is waiting, too."

"Has the hunt been called off?" she asked.

"Don't know." The pilot swiveled his head in her direction and she found herself staring at her own reflection in his mirrored sunglasses. "I'm not part of that."

"You're about to become part of that," Perez snapped.

There were three groups of hunters. They found one cluster near the top of Powell Trail, where it flattened out over the mesa. Their dogs were still on leashes and there was no wildlife in sight. The pilot contacted the leader on his radio, then handed it to Perez, who delivered the order to cease and return to base. Looking up, the man in fatigues waved in acknowledgment.

They flew over the plateau toward the northern border of the park. The helicopter, buzzing low over the mesa, scattered a group of mule deer, and Sam watched the does and fawns dart frantically in all directions. In its panic, one fawn, trying to make an impossible leap to the top of a boulder, crashed into the rock and collapsed in a heap below.

Sam pressed her hand to the window and leaned close as they passed over.

"Bambi!" Zack chirped from her lap. "Bambi hurt!" He flattened his nose against the glass.

They both breathed a sigh of relief as the fawn unfolded its long legs and staggered after its mother.

The second group of hunters, only a couple of miles from the northern border of the park, seemed relieved to turn around and head back to their vehicles. The pilot was on his radio, quizzing someone about the location of the final group. He pulled a lever and they swung in a circle back in the direction from which they'd come.

"They're on Horsehip Mesa," he said. "Near Rainbow Bridge."

A cold dread gripped Sam. Leto's territory. She watched the helicopter's shadow slide over the mesas and canyons below. Life seemed distant and passing way too fast from up here. In one treed valley, she spotted two black hulks crouched in the sparse underbrush between the aspens. Black bears? She'd seen droppings during her tenure in the park but never an actual bear.

ZigZag Passage appeared below, then the yellow markers and two blue-coated workers of the FBI forensics team, shoulder to shoulder, discussing something. They looked up and, spotting Perez in the front passenger seat, waved.

The canyon fell away beneath them, and the pilot hovered over the chasm briefly, searching. Perez was the first to spot the hunt. "There." He pointed to the ridgeline.

Just east of Rainbow Bridge, two tawny shapes hurtled over the rough terrain toward the canyon lip. Sam sucked in a breath. Leto, Artemis. From the maze of hoodoos farther back, a third cat appeared, running full out after the others, with a pair of spotted hounds fifty feet behind. Oh God, Apollo, too.

Zack wriggled in her lap, digging a hard little kneecap into her thigh as he pressed closer to window. "Cougie!" he chirped. "Cougie run!"

The mountain lions were only a hundred yards or so from the hoodoos when the men appeared, four of them in desert camouflage gear, galloping after their dogs. One of them paused to sight down his rifle barrel, gave up, continued the pursuit on foot. The baying of the dogs was audible even inside the helicopter.

Perez picked up the radio. "Hunters below, hunters below. This is the FBI. Stop the hunt. I repeat, stop the hunt! Lay down your weapons!"

The chase below continued without interruption. The female cats had reached the rock bridge now and streaked across, running low and close to the wet rock. Steam rising from the arch rendered the scene surreal, mountain lions speeding through desert fog. Sam hoped that the arch escape route would finish the chase, but Apollo stopped at the eastern end and turned to face the hounds on his tail. A hundred yards back, the hunters halted. Two dropped to one knee. They raised their rifles.

"Set this thing down!" Sam yelled. "We've got to land."

The pilot shook his head. Apollo and the dogs danced close together, the hounds rushing in to nip at the cat, then retreating from the bared teeth and razor-sharp claws. They were directly overhead now and the cacophony of barking was loud.

"You have a public address system on this thing?" Perez shouted to the pilot. The man flipped a switch and handed Perez a set of headphones with a tiny microphone attached.

"Federal hunters below!" Perez shouted. "FBI. Cease fire! This is the FBI. Cease fire!"

One hunter looked up briefly. But then a puff of dust erupted from the rock near Apollo's feet, and the hunter sighted down his own rifle barrel again.

"Max volume!" Perez ordered.

"That's it," the pilot told him. "Maybe it's not working right."

"Cease fire! Lay down your weapons!" Perez bellowed into the mike.

He might as well have been shouting out the window for all the impact it had. Sam watched in horror as a hunter shifted from his rifle's recoil. Another puff of dust exploded under Apollo's belly. "Damn it!" she yelled in frustration.

Zack shifted under their mutual seat belt and started to cry. Sam's gaze searched the interior of the chopper, landed on a bright yellow nylon sack just to the left of her feet. The word EMERGENCY was printed on it in large block letters. Well, this was an emergency. She leaned over, dug her fingers into the slick material. Zack, squeezed beneath the seat belt in her lap, screeched. She hauled the sack up onto the bench seat next to her. Heavy.

Two more shots sounded below. Zack sobbed and kicked her as she struggled to drag the yellow bag across them both.

The pilot turned in his seat to look at them.

"Perez!" she yelled. "Open your door!"

He stopped his litany into the microphone.

"Open your goddamn door!" she shouted over Zack's screams.

"No!" the pilot yelled.

"Chase! Just do it!" Sam screeched.

Perez's form shifted to the right. Something clicked, and the door swung out. The dogs' barking was louder now, but nothing in comparison to Zack's screaming. The bag stuck in the confined space between seat and door. She punched it into position with her feet, booted it out into space.

The yellow bag hurtled down, spinning as it fell. It landed between Apollo and one of the dogs with a loud whump. Dogs and mountain lion all leapt into the air as if propelled by the impact, the dogs turning away toward their owners and the cougar launching himself from the canyon rim. At the corner of her vision, Sam registered the upright hunter stumbling, startled by the bag's impact, but her gaze was centered on Apollo, who seemed to hang suspended in mid-air as he leapt for the bridge. For an instant, the distance seemed impossible, the fall to the sandstone canyon floor below a certainty. But then his forepaws impacted the rock arch. The cat swung his hindquarters around, skidding slightly to the side as he corrected his course, then bounded across the bridge to disappear between the boulders at the far side.

The wind buffeted her face. Zack screamed into her ear. The pilot was swearing, something about a life raft and thousands of dollars. In the midst of the cacophony, she heard Perez ask, "Are you done?"

"I think so." She patted him on the shoulder in case he couldn't hear.

He closed the door with a thump, cupped his hand over the microphone, and issued the cease and desist orders again. The hunters finally responded by shouldering their weapons.

"Return to base," Perez's voice said over the loudspeaker.

One of the hunters raised his arms in a questioning gesture.

"Zachary Fischer has been recovered." Perez answered. "Alive and well."

At the mention of his name, the little boy stopped screaming. "Me Zack," he said softly. "I want Mommy!"

Sam ruffled the silky hair on the top of his head. "Okay, Zack. Let's go find her."

Their arrival had obviously been announced; a crowd awaited them in the headquarters parking lot. Even from five hundred feet above the valley floor, Sam could make out Jerry Thompson's rotund shape. Tanner's grizzled head was bent close to Jenny Fischer's bedraggled figure. Carolyn Perry's crimson KUTV blazer stood out like a flame. And worse, a blond man in a navy windbreaker and handsome enough to be an actor stood close by, holding a microphone and talking earnestly at a camera in front of him. What was Adam doing here? Walking backward, he positioned himself between the camera and the helicopter as they touched down on the asphalt.

As soon as the rotor slowed, Thompson was at the door.

The little boy tugged on Sam's braid. "Mommy?" he whispered hopefully.

Turning Zack around, Sam pointed into the crowd. "Mommy's right there. Why don't you wave at her?" She grasped his tiny hand and waggled it back and forth.

Jenny Fischer staggered forward, her hands clutched to her chest. The young mother's face was rigid with the tension of hope too long suppressed. She trotted toward them, her eyes fixed on her son. When only a hundred feet remained between them, Sam set the toddler on the ground.

"Zack?" Jenny's voice cracked.

"Mommy!" The little boy ran toward Jenny, then tripped on the long shirt and fell to his knees on the rocky ground. But his mother was there before the first sob could come out, wrapping her arms around him, lifting him up.

"Oh Zachary, Zack, Zack!" she cried, fiercely kissing the blond curls as she rocked him back and forth. "Mommy missed you so much! So very, very much."

She raised her eyes to Sam. Tears streamed down her face. "Thank you," she said. "Thank you."

The press pushed in around them. Sam was conscious of the multiple TV cameras focused on the scene. A microphone was in her face now, so close it was only a silvery blur. "Summer Westin, you're the hero of the day. What can you tell us?" Adam's voice. She pushed it away and crawled out of the helicopter, staggering on stiff legs.

"Babe?" Adam said in a low tone. "Are you all right?" Then his arms were around her. "I am so damned lucky! I came down for the cougar kill, but you delivered the real story. Are we the dream team or what?"

Over Adam's arm she could see Perez observing them, his expression cool, inscrutable. Thompson came forward to escort Jenny and Zack through the crowd; the TV crew and onlookers followed the reunited family toward the parking lot. Adam turned his head in that direction. Sam roughly pushed him away. After a surprised glance at her, he followed the media hounds, gesturing for his cameraman to shadow him.

She walked back to Perez, wishing he'd throw open his arms so she could fall into them. Instead, he crossed them and leaned toward her. "They'll be back," he whispered into her ear. "Escape while you can."

"It's over. It's really over."

He turned his head toward the helicopter. "For you. I've got to go back up and get Davinski. And the other pack."

"Make *her* go instead." Sam thrust out her chin toward a familiar figure strolling through the crowd toward them: Nicole Boudreaux, clad in tweed pants and a rust-colored turtleneck, her chestnut hair gathered neatly with a brown velvet ribbon at the nape of her neck. The woman was completely exasperating.

Both FBI agents took off in the helicopter. Tanner wanted to drive Sam to the clinic but quickly gave in to her threats to write articles about cowardly park management if she didn't take her to the hotel.

"You never were a team player," Tanner muttered.

Then suddenly she was alone at the Wagon Wheel Motel, and her world was blessedly quiet. She even got the same room as before. A fruit-filled care package from the Las Rojas Women's League was on the bedside table.

From his wooden frame, the deer stared at her, wide-eyed, as if surprised to see her still alive.

26

BY the time Sam finally emerged from a hot bath, all her gear had magically arrived at her room. Her computer lay on her bed, her camping gear was stacked on a plastic bag in a corner, and a tray of covered dishes wafted tempting aromas from atop the little table.

Drat. She had no excuse now. Sighing, she sat down to compose her final article for SWF. The photo she'd taken of Zack tossing a rock onto Karl Davinski was definitely a keeper, along with the photo of Davinski holding the little boy in the air. Even the picture Perez had snapped of her and Zack wasn't half bad. She looked like a cat that had fallen in a drainage ditch, of course, but a very well-washed cat. The lighting had been dim enough to hide the crow's feet around her eyes. Zack, naturally, was adorable. They could always edit her out of the photo if they wanted. The image of a handcuffed Davinski lying below his small smiling victim was dramatic: she wouldn't be surprised if magazines picked up that one.

The last file name disappeared from the queue. Sam sat staring at the blank blue screen, knowing she should unplug the modem line and reconnect the phone, but she dreaded the calls that would inevitably come afterward. After a couple of minutes of superb silence, her cell phone bleated from its recharger on the bedside table. When had she plugged that in?

The caller ID read simply *Washington*. SWF. Resigned to her fate, she answered. "Westin."

"I understand you're mad, babe, but you'll get over it." Adam.

She'd been expecting his knock at her door. "Where are you?"

"Corporate jet," he chortled. "We'll be back in Seattle in a couple of hours. Tune in at eleven to see us both on the news."

She didn't respond.

"You can't hate me forever. I made you a hero."

"After you dragged me through the mud. Not to mention nearly getting the cougars killed."

"That wasn't me, Sam; that was what the public wanted. Welcome to the news business. So it was a trial by fire; now you're one of us. And are we a dynamite team, or what?"

"Good question." She pressed End.

The cell phone bleated again. She picked it up and pressed Talk without saying anything.

"You did it, you really found him?" Lauren.

"Just sent you the photos," Sam told her. "And the story." Phones were ringing in the background. She gazed wearily around the room before she realized that the sound was coming from SWF's offices.

Director Steve Harding came on the line. "And you were on the six o'clock news! Did you see it?" He laughed heartily. She heard other voices in the background. This conversation was obviously on speakerphone.

"Good job, Westin." That was Max. "What a rush!"

"Guess what, guys? They're going to show our website again on the eleven o'clock news!" Lauren said loudly for everyone to hear.

"Eeee-hah!" General clapping and hoots.

Sam's back hurt. Her hands hurt. Her cougar-scarred leg, curiously, was the only thing that didn't. "Guys?" she shouted to the din. "I'm shutting off the phone now. It's almost dead. And so am I. I'm going to bed." Her finger moved toward the End button.

"Wait! Westin?" Harding shouted into the phone.

She winced at his volume. "Yes?"

"It was a great idea to do the series."

"Uh, thanks," she said. "I'm hanging up now."

"WildWest!" Harding's voice. "Wait! Wilderness! What's her real name again?"

A click. The background noise dissolved. Lauren had picked up the receiver and spoke to her without benefit of the surrounding crowd. "Think you can do it again?" she asked.

It was Sam's turn to laugh.

Lauren backpedaled. "Well, I don't mean exactly the same thing, of course. And you kayak, too, don't you?"

"Where?" Over Victoria Falls, through shark-filled surf at the Great Barrier Reef?

"The committee hasn't decided yet. Hey, we're heroes now, and they want us to repeat the act." There was a brief pause, then Lauren whispered through growing static, "Please don't say no."

"Ask me again in six weeks." Sam turned off the cell phone and the computer, and crawled into bed.

27

A light dusting of snow frosted the sandstone of Milagro Canyon. It reminded Sam of her grandmother's red velvet cake with cream cheese frosting. But instead of crushed walnuts, this layer cake was adorned with boulders and evergreens.

"Are we ready?" The woman's voice echoed in the narrow wash. Her black trench coat and high-heeled boots were distinctly out of place among the wilderness scenery, her ears were pink with cold. Spidery veins across her cheeks spoke of too many whiskeys in smoke-filled rooms.

An assistant rushed forward with a makeup puff and patted it across the woman's brow. "Almost ready, Ms. Secretary. The cougar's not here yet."

She pushed the assistant away. "I can't wait for some animal to show up. I've got to be in D.C. by eight tonight." She eyed the knot of press standing a short distance away. "I'll do my part now; you can patch it together later, all right?"

At the nod of a cameraman, she began. "Today I'm pleased to announce that more than eighty thousand acres of national forest land have been added to Heritage National

Monument." The handful of reporters cheered and clapped loudly, making it sound as if a crowd were in attendance. The secretary acknowledged the applause with a dignified inclination of her chin. "This additional land will ensure that the wild creatures of this beautiful park, such as our treasured American mountain lion, will always roam free." More cheers.

After a brief handshake with Jerry Thompson and the television reporters, the secretary of the interior and her entourage were gone. The departing army helicopter stirred up a cloud of dry snow.

What a difference a few weeks could make. Only a trace of brown darkened the sandstone floor of the canyon, a faint reminder of the pools of blood that had stained the rock a short time ago.

The arrival of another helicopter prompted a new flurry on the mesa above. When the snow had again sifted to the ground and the reverberations of the rotor had faded, a new group of visitors descended from the mesa above, carrying a large aluminum cage. Sam's heart lurched at the sight of a lean blond figure in the group. But it was a ranger she didn't know. It couldn't be Kent Bergstrom, at least not yet. Nerve damage had rendered his right arm useless for now: odds were that it would remain that way. She swallowed around a lump in her throat, focused, and snapped the photo.

Supporting the other sides of the cage were Dr. Stephanie Black, the veterinarian, and the rescue pilot from St. George Fire Department. In the rear, both hands clutching the cage to keep it from descending too quickly, she was surprised to see Special Agent Starchaser J. Perez.

Sam hurried forward. At the vet's direction, she crawled into the cage and slipped behind the cat's head, sliding her hands under its muscular shoulders. Velvety fur. The mountain lion's head lolled over her upper arm; its breath was warm on her neck. Through the bars of the cage, her gaze met Perez's. He winked at her.

They stretched the tranquilized cat across the canyon floor. Sam was reluctant to let go. She smoothed the fur over the feline's thick neck and stroked her fingertips across its black and white muzzle, caressing the silky coat and the stiff whiskers. A bittersweet wave of déjà vu washed over her. Less than two years earlier, she'd petted another sleeping cougar recently healed of gunshot wounds. Leto.

She gently squeezed the rough black pads of the male's huge paw, felt the razor-sharp claws against the palm of her hand. *Good luck, Zeus. May the rest of your life be long and healthy; may your offspring be many and proud.*

Dr. Black readied a syringe. She held it up to the light and depressed the plunger to squeeze out the air. A drop of liquid gleamed at the sharp tip. She turned to the onlookers. "Now?" she asked. "It will only take a couple of minutes for him to wake up after I give him this."

She injected the sleeping cat. Sam stood up, pulled out her camera, and positioned herself for a clear shot.

Carolyn Perry walked toward the cougar, motioned for her cameraman to follow.

"No," warned Dr. Black.

The reporter abruptly cut her short. "Shhh." She knelt on one knee next to the cat, her microphone held in front of her. "This is the mountain lion that was shot a month ago by illegal hunters in Heritage National Monument." The cat raised its head and glared at the cameraman, who stepped back a couple of paces. Carolyn continued unfazed. "As you can see, he's alive and well and about to become a free cat once more."

Buck Ferguson was noticeably absent. According to the locals, he and his wife had spent most of the last month with their daughter in Boise. Sane World had, for now, switched its website's focus to Western ranchers' historic rights to graze their cattle on government lands.

The cougar lurched to his feet and stood blinking at the handful of onlookers. Carolyn straightened and backed away. The cat swished his long tail back and forth uncertainly.

Sam snapped another photo, then reached into the pack at her feet. She raised a pistol into the air, pressed the trigger.

The gun's report was loud in the narrow canyon. The

reporters ducked; the vet dropped the clipboard she'd been writing on. The mountain lion gathered his feet beneath him and leapt a good fifteen feet away from the crowd. He bounded up the steep slope toward the helicopter, and then, catching sight of the strange machine, veered off downhill to the south, racing toward the canyon's exit. The muscles of his shoulders and haunches rippled under the tawny coat as he streaked across the rock; his long sleek tail streamed out behind him.

Oh, to be able to run like that, all out and effortless at once. Sam dropped the pistol into the pack, sat down on a rock ledge. Mutters of disapproval erupted all around her. Jerry Thompson and the TV crew glared. She plastered a cheery smile on her lips and waved. The hell with them.

Perez sat down beside her. "I see you're packing heat now."

"Starter pistol," she explained. "I borrowed it from a friend. I never want another cougar to get the impression that people are friends."

The FBI agent wore a fleece-lined leather jacket over an Irish fisherman sweater and blue jeans. The crease was gone from between his brows.

"You look . . . relaxed," she said.

"You clean up pretty good yourself. Did Save the Wilderness Fund send you?"

She nodded. "Follow-up story."

"I saw you on the news the night we brought Zack back."

"Us. You were there, too."

He smiled. "I read your last story."

"Mmmmmm." She didn't really want to talk about that.

"How'd you get that underwater video?"

Mad Max the video wizard, of course. Total panic, roiling water, our heroine about to fall to her death.

"You've no doubt forgotten that I had Zack *and* the camera," she told Perez.

A familiar light sparked in the back of his eyes. "Of course. Wilderness Westin would never be without one, would she?"

She felt a blush rising to her cheeks. In the last four weeks, she had thought more than once about trying to locate Perez in Salt Lake City but had rejected the idea as unprofessional. Cowardly was a more accurate term.

"I assume you'll be able to spare a few hours if we need you to testify?" he asked.

So it was back to work. "Do you know when you'll need me? I'm off to Kansas for Thanksgiving. My dad just got engaged, and some of the folks are throwing a little party for him, so it'll be more than just the usual holiday get-together."

She was looking forward to the event and dreading it at the same time. Her relatives would press her for details about a man—any man—who could potentially be husband material. She could hear the clucking now. Adam had been promoted to an anchor position in San Diego; she doubted that their paths would cross in the future. Maybe she'd tell them that she lived with Blake: that would give them plenty to talk about.

She took a deep breath of the clean air. She'd take more photos after everyone had gone. Winter was a time of geologic pastels, bark and stone textures, gleaming water, crystalline snow.

Perez spoke her thoughts. "This is such a beautiful place."

She could feel the warmth of his hand beside hers. Only a fraction of an inch away.

"Strange location to choose as a Garden of Eden, though."

A hawk cried overhead. Such a lonely sound.

"I feel sorry for Karl Davinski," she said. She couldn't bear the thought of such a free spirit being locked inside a cell.

"Don't waste your pity on him. He stands a good chance of being judged mentally incompetent. He may never stand trial."

She was glad that Karl's crazy act was convincing to others. He'd probably end up in a mental institution, but he wasn't really violent and surely he'd be released before long. "He lost everything: Barbara Jean, David, his home."

"Barbara Jean and David are the ones who lost everything," he countered. "Can you imagine living your life in a cave?"

From the description she'd heard, Karl and Barbara Jean had their pocket of the Curtain fixed up pretty nice.

They used the ruins for their patio, and the high mesas and canyons for their playground. It didn't sound half bad to Sam. "You think it's crazy to want to live in the wilderness?" she asked Perez.

"I think it's crazy not to acknowledge reality. They weren't living off the land; they were robbing campers. And Barbara Jean was little more than his captive."

"She wanted to be with Karl, according to her friends. She told them that he'd saved her, that he was romantic, that he swept her off her feet." Coyote Charlie could be romantic, Sam knew. She remembered the grapes he'd given her, the way he'd stroked her hair. The vision of him howling in the moonlight, wild and free.

"He brainwashed Barbara Jean," Perez argued. "She was just a kid; she didn't know better. If Davinski can be believed, it sounds like she died of pneumonia."

"I still feel sorry for him. His dreams got smashed; his loved ones died." She sighed. "The blue demon that Davinski said he saved David from. It *was* Wilson, wasn't it?"

"Wallace Russell, you mean." Perez shrugged. "He probably was the man you saw at the end of the path. According to Ranger Castillo, Russell gave some confused story about how he planned to take the boy back to his mother but got whacked over the head instead. And now he's not talking at all. But then, it's difficult with your jaw wired shut."

"Yeah," she said with a chuckle. "Rafael told me about that."

Perez made a huffing noise at the back of his throat. "I'll never doubt your intuition again."

She blinked. Again? That implied there'd be other times together. "What's going to happen to Fred Fischer?" she asked.

"He won't get more than a slap on the wrist. After all, he didn't kidnap Zack and he didn't get the money. He just tried to take advantage of the situation to get his hands on some hard cash." He shook his head. "Stupid man. Jenny and Zack were worth holding on to. Now he's lost both of them for good."

"All those rangers on overtime, and Fischer had already hitchhiked out."

"Hazard of the business," Perez commented. He ran a finger lightly along her jawline. "What's this?"

Sam thought she'd concealed the bruise with makeup. But then Perez noticed everything. "SWF volunteers relocated a black bear up in the Cascades last weekend," she said. "He wasn't quite as tranquilized as I thought."

His eyes twinkled. "I should have guessed." His thigh edged next to hers, radiating warmth. After a minute, he asked, "If I were an animal, what would I be?"

"A hawk."

He drew his fingers down his long nose as if extending it into a sharp beak.

She laughed. "No, it's not that. It's your eyes and the way you watch and wait. Resourceful, intense, wary." She pressed her leg a fraction closer to his. "And which creature would you choose for me?"

"An ermine."

A weasel? She frowned.

"A small, quick, intelligent creature. Good at hiding."

Except for the intelligent part, that didn't sound too complimentary.

"Fierce. Independent. Changeable, with lovely snow-white fur in winter." He pushed aside a strand of her platinum hair, his finger leaving a trail of fire across her cheek. "A beautiful wild thing."

"Rocky start," she commented, "but a brilliant finish."

He leaned closer. "Going back to Bellingham tonight?"

She swallowed, nodded. "My flight leaves six hours from now." *Ask me to cancel it; there'll be another one tomorrow.*

The whine of helicopter blades cut into her thoughts.

Perez looked toward the source of the racket. "Want to hitch a ride?"

Sam shook her head. "I've had enough of helicopters to last a lifetime. I'm hiking down after I make sure Zeus is okay. Come with me. It's a beautiful day."

He looked uncomfortable. "I have to be in Salt Lake in two hours."

Damn.

"I have a meeting in Seattle the week after next," he said. "Mind if I look you up?" His raptor gaze locked onto hers.

She considered for a moment. What would he make of her in her home environment? The ermine in her den?

Her hesitation unsettled him. "You don't have a man in your life, do you?"

Perez sounded pretty certain that she didn't. She gave him a hard look.

In a softer tone, he said, "I know Steele's gone to California."

"Simon's in my bed every night," she told him. "And Blake's in the other bedroom."

"Simon's your cat, Summer. And I'm sure you've noticed by now that Blake is gay."

It was so unfair. "You know everything about me. And I don't know any of your secrets."

He grinned. "It'll be a voyage of discovery."

The helicopter was revving up. He threaded his fingers through hers and squeezed her hand gently. "So I can come?"

She squeezed back, increasing the pressure until he winced. Pressing her lips to his ear, she murmured, "You have to promise me, Chase. Raise your right hand."

He did.

"Solemnly swear that you will *not* arrive in a helicopter."

"You have my word on it."

Finally, his lips met hers. His kiss was sweet, burning, and breathtakingly brief. And then Special Agent Chase J. Perez was gone, along with the helicopters and all the other humans.

Sam took a deep breath of cool fresh air, listening to the breeze, savoring the solitude of a place healing into wilderness once more. She pulled on her pack and hiked up to the ridge. Turning in a slow circle, she scanned the rocky landscape. With winter coming on, there were no lizards or snakes out sunning themselves now and few birds flying about on the high plateau. The berries and insects were gone, and the greenery that punctuated the smooth rock formations was now gray from nighttime frosts.

She walked a few steps down the slope and stopped, waiting. At first, she sensed him more than saw him. She pulled out her binoculars. There. Across the canyon, where the rock ledge rose up to the west, the lean form of a mountain lion, sitting in the shadow of an overhang, his tawny fur nearly invisible against the rocks behind him.

"The guns and helicopters are gone," she whispered.

They watched each other for a few breaths, listening to the wind as it moaned and whistled through distant hoodoos. After a few moments, Zeus stood up, climbed to the top of the highest rock, and stood there in the sunlight, surveying his domain below. The big cat turned his head and looked back at Sam over his shoulder, his golden gaze fierce and questioning. Then, after one flick of his black-tipped tail, the cougar leapt from his perch and vanished.

Awesome.

Turn the page for an exciting preview of
Pamela Beason's next Summer Westin Mystery . . .

BEAR BAIT

Coming soon from Berkley Prime Crime!

"SO, Summer," Lili said, trying the name out with a shy smile, "for this school project, I have to write a report on two careers." She took a deep breath and plunged on. "And I figured, since you're a wildlife biologist *and* a writer, you could help me with two at once." She hesitated uncertainly. "I mean, if you want to."

Sam blinked at her, not knowing whether to be flattered or appalled. "Is it okay to interview the same person for two different careers?"

Lili shrugged. "Ms. Patterson didn't say we couldn't."

"Wouldn't it be good to get more than one person's point of view?"

The girl's face clouded. She looked down at her toes and mumbled, "You don't have to help. It's all right. I'll try to find someone else."

Oh, for heaven's sake. "Okay. I'll help you, Lili."

"Yes!" Lili pumped her toothbrush toward the star-spangled sky.

It was nice to be the source of someone's excitement, even a thirteen-year-old's. "When is this paper due?"

"August seventh?" Lili shot a quick glance at Sam, as if expecting an objection. "Dad told me I had to get started in plenty of time for once."

"It's due in two weeks?" Sam only had three weeks to finish her environmental survey and write up her recommended management plan. Now she'd agreed to help Lili, too? Deep breath, she told herself. It was a junior high project—how hard could it be? "What's the first step?"

"I'm s'posed to come up with questions about each career," Lili said. "I'll do those tomorrow." She sighed. "I thought I'd hate summer school. But it's sort of okay."

There was a possible segue back to Lili's social life. Sam jumped at it. "Are there any cool boys?"

A loud boom rocked the fire tower. Sam grabbed the railing, knocking the tube of toothpaste from the rough two-by-four.

"Aunt Summer?" Even in the dim light, Sam could see that Lili's eyes were wide.

"It's okay." At least she hoped it was. She dashed inside, grabbed the binoculars, and focused them on Marmot Lake.

Like an anxious cocker spaniel, Lili followed close on her heels. "What *was* that?"

"I don't have a clue." Sam lowered the binoculars to look at Lili. Then lights flashed through the forest near the lake, and she raised the binoculars again. A set of headlights. No, two. Two vehicles. The road to the lake was now closed to the public, barricaded with a steel gate and lock. Nobody should be in there.

Should she call in the violation? The trespassers were leaving; the odds against catching them were high. The explosion was most likely local teens setting off fireworks. M-80s could sound like cannons, especially on a quiet night like this. The Quileute and Quinault reservations were still hawking firecrackers, even though the Fourth of July had passed weeks ago.

A yellow light bloomed from the darkness near the lake. Then another. The brightness splashed and spread. She grabbed the radio on the desk and raised it to her lips. "Three-one-one, this is three-two-five. Come in, three-one-one." She raised her finger from the Talk button. Nothing. She looked longingly at her cell phone on the shelf, but knew that it didn't work in some areas of the park. She tried the radio again. "Three-one-one, this is three-two-five."

"Three-one-one." The voice of the night dispatcher was hoarse. "Did you say three-two-five? Cat Mountain Fire Lookout? Where's Jeff?"

"Jeff went home. His mother's sick. This is Sam Westin."

"Oh, yeah. What's up, Sam?"

"I've got a fire at Marmot Lake." In the distance, a dead tree caught with a sudden rush, a knife blade of orange light in the darkness. The headlights strobed through thick evergreens as they raced west toward the highway.

The dispatcher's reply was clipped, all business now. "Copy that, three-two-five. Fire at Marmot Lake."

"I see at least three sources. Roll everyone you can get. Send them in on"—she checked the map beneath her fingertips—"Road 5214. Over."

"Roger that. 5214. I'll wake everyone up. Over."

"I'm heading for the blaze now. Over."

"You're a temp. Stay at the lookout. Over."

"I'm fifteen minutes away. I'm a trained firefighter; I have equipment."

"You are? You do? But—"

Sam cut her off with a press of the Talk button. "It'll be at least an hour before you can get anyone to the lake. Over."

The dispatcher chose not to debate that point. "It's against the regs. Don't do anything stupid. Three-one-one, out."

Sam dumped the radio on the countertop and pulled on her boots. She heard the radio call to Paul Schuler, the law enforcement ranger who patrolled the west-side camp-grounds at night. The rest of the calls would be made via telephone; other staff members would be asleep at home. If all went smoothly, the west-side crew might reach the lake in forty-five minutes. Most of them lived in the small town of Forks, less than fifteen miles away. But in that time, a fire could consume acres of forest. With luck, she might be able to extinguish a couple of small blazes before the wild-fire dug its ugly claws too deeply into the forest.

Lili jammed her feet into her own hiking boots.

"No," Sam said. "You're staying here."

Lili's fountain of dark hair bounced as her chin jerked up. "You can't leave me here! What if the fire comes this way?"

Good point. If the fire turned in this direction, she might not make it back to get Lili. Damn! "Then I'll have to drop you—"

"Where?" Lili's voice was shrill. "There isn't anywhere."

Sam stared at her, trying to think of a safe place to de-posit the child. Her mind was filled with visions of flames licking through the forest, a small fire growing larger by the second. Panic growing as birds and deer and bears circled within the smoke, tree frogs frantically searching for twigs that wouldn't scorch their skin.

"The trees are burning right now," Lili said, as if read-ing her thoughts.

Sam didn't need to be reminded: her imagination was loud with screams of terrified animals.

"I'll do *exactly* what you say." Lili made the sign of the cross over her chest.

"You bet you will." Sam blew out the Coleman, stuffed her flashlight and first-aid kit into her daypack. Her fire-retardant suit, along with shovels and Pulaskis, was locked into a metal toolbox in the park's oldest pickup at the bot-tom of the tower.

Lili worked in silence, throwing gear and water bottles into her own pack as Sam picked up the radio again. When the dispatcher finally answered, Sam informed her that Lili Choi would be riding with her to Marmot Lake. She heard a sharp intake of breath on the other end.

"No choice," Sam said into the radio void. "Three-two-five, out."